Brides of the Kindred

Book 7: Exiled

Evangeline Anderson

D1527758

PUBLISHED BY:

Evangeline Anderson

Brides of the Kindred

Book 7: Exiled

Author's Note #1: To be the first to hear about new e-book releases, join my new newsletter by going to www.EvangelineAnderson.com. I promise no spam – you will only get email from me when a new book is out for either preorder or for sale.

Author's Note #2: I'm happy to let you all know that I am going into Audio in a big way. I put **Claimed** *,* **Hunted,** *and* **Sought** *into the audio format and I had such a great response from readers and listeners, that I have decided to put ALL the* **Kindred** *books, plus all my* **Born to Darkness** *books into audio as well as my standalone book,* **Purity.** *If you have a long commute or you'd like something new to listen at the gym or just around the house, give it a try. The Kindred books are performed by the very talented Anne Johnstonbrown whom I hand-picked to read the series and she really brings the characters to life.*

Author's Note #3: I'm trying to find out which of my readers are also listeners. For a chance to win a free audio book, sign up for my new **Audio book newsletter** *by going to www.EvangelineAnderson.com. It's the same as my e-book newsletter, but only for audio. And as always, I promise not to bother you unless I have a new audio book out or I'm running a contest with an audio book as one of the prizes.*

Author's Note #4: *This is the seventh book in the Brides of the Kindred series. I recommend that you read* **Claimed, Hunted, Sought,** *and* **Found, Revealed,** *and* **Pursued** *before diving into Exiled.*

Hugs and Happy Reading and Listening to you all,
Evangeline Anderson

Table of Contents

Brides of the Kindred

Book 7: Exiled

Evangeline Anderson

Chapter One

"I can't wear this! Not out in public where everyone can see me!" Lissa stared down at herself in horror. The gown her new friend Kat had squeezed her into was the complete opposite of the flowing white priestess robes she was used to wearing. It was a rich royal purple and the material was stiff and binding. But it wasn't the cut or color of the gown that Lissa objected to—it was the fact that it was completely obscene.

"Lissa—" Kat began in a reasonable tone of voice but Lissa shook her head.

"Just look at me, Kat! I...I'm *exposed*." She pointed down to the stiff molded bodice of the gown that cupped her breasts in a tight embrace. The problem was, the gown only cradled the *bottoms* of them, leaving her nipples bare except for the tiny pieces of pale gold lace that fanned out of the tops of the cups to act as flimsy shields. They covered her—barely—as long as she stood perfectly straight and didn't shift around too much. *But what if I need to move quickly? What if I drop something and need to pick it up?* Lissa was sure if that happened, she would fall out of the dress completely, baring herself to anyone watching.

"You're fine as long as you don't bend down," Kat said, obviously having the same thought. "Just stand up straight and don't wiggle."

"But...but what about the bottom part?" Lissa motioned to the lower half of the gown. The skin tight bodice hugged her waist and hips, then flowed out behind her in an elaborate, shimmering, crystal encrusted train. It was the place where the bodice split, a few inches below her bellybutton, that worried Lissa. The dress showed her crotch in a most provocative manner.

"I know it's kind of...revealing," Kat said, frowning. "But you *do* have decorative panties to go with it."

Decorative was a good word to describe them, Lissa thought, because they really weren't very practical at all. A tiny triangle of gold lace that matched her nipple shields barely covered the small thatch of blonde curls at the apex of her sex. The back of the panties was a string—just one little gold string that ran up the back of her behind. Lissa had never worn undergarments like this before—Kat had called it a "thong". Lissa called it perverted.

"Please, Kat," she begged. "I just can't. It's not only that I'm ashamed to be seen in public like this. It's...it's that *Saber* will see me too." She could barely force her kinsman's name from her dry throat but she made herself do it anyway. He was the real reason she didn't want to appear in this obscene getup. Lissa was naturally modest and shy but his was the only opinion she really cared about. And if he saw her looking like this...*What will he think of me?* Lissa asked herself and was too afraid to contemplate the answer.

She and Saber were of the same clan—the Sun Clan of the Touch Kindred—and she had been adopted into his family after her parents had died. There was no blood tie between them but according to the strict laws of her people, the two circumstances made Saber her older brother twice over and, as such, completely off limits.

Despite this taboo, Lissa had allowed an illicit love to grow between them—a love she had subsequently ended. But to her lasting shame, she still had feelings for the tall warrior with the hazel eyes. He had comforted her after the death of her family and defended her from the bullies at the school they both attended as children. He had also saved her life when she was wandering in the desert, dying of dehydration. With so much history between them, how could she not still feel something for him? How could she not care what he thought?

A look of compassion and understanding filled Kat's blue eyes. "I get it, doll, and I'm really sorry," she said softly, breaking into Lissa's ragged thoughts. "But this is how they dress on Yonnie Six. In fact, this is one of the more *modest* designs—believe me, I searched through all of them. Those Yonnie girls aren't afraid to show a little skin."

"A *little* skin?" Lissa looked down at herself again. "Are you telling me there are worse gowns than this in the cube you packed for me?"

Kat cleared her throat and looked uncomfortable. "Just a few. Mostly the ones for more formal occasions like court balls and banquets. It's a good thing the Mother Ship has a clothing pattern replicator—I never would have been able to sew them all myself."

"But I can't be seen like this," Lissa protested.

Kat frowned. "You *have* to be, Lissa. You have to fit in or your mission is going to flop the minute you step foot out of the shuttle. How do you expect to recover the ancient scrolls that tell how to defeat the Hoard if you don't blend in with the rest of the Yonnites?"

"But—"

"You look gorgeous," Kat said firmly. "And don't just take *my* word for it." She turned toward the door, smiling. "Hi Saber. How do you like your new outfit?"

Her heart in her throat, Lissa whirled around before she could stop herself. She found herself face to face with her kinsman.

"Hello, Lissa," he said quietly.

"Saber. I didn't know you were here. I...I didn't want you to see me like this." She crossed her arms over her nearly bare breasts protectively and took a step back.

"You're beautiful, as always," he replied, his deep voice husky with emotion. "But I won't look if you don't wish me to." Resolutely, he kept his changeable hazel eyes, flecked with gold and green, fixed firmly on her face.

"Thank you." Lissa dropped her own jade green eyes and found that she couldn't show him the same courtesy he had given her. Though she tried not to look, her gaze wandered up and down the length of his large, muscular body. He was tall—over six foot six as all Kindred were—and his skin was a deep, natural tan. She couldn't help noticing that his chest was bare, revealing shoulders twice as broad as her own and rippling abdominals. Tight black trousers made of some stiff, shiny material clung to his lean hips and long legs. Lissa tried not to look at the crotch where an impressive bulge pressed hard against the fastening of the skin-tight trousers. Instead, her eyes skipped upward to his throat and her breath caught in her chest.

"Saber," she whispered, forgetting about her own state of dress—or undress—in her worry. "What...what is that?" Her hand darted up to touch the thick black collar fastened around his corded neck. Dangling from it was a long leather strip with a loop at the end.

"It's a leash," Kat said matter-of-factly, stepping forward.

"A leash?" Lissa looked at her, horrified. "But...you can't expect Saber to wear something like that. He's not an animal or a *pet* for the Goddess's sake!"

"No, he's lower than that—he's your body-slave," Kat said. "And you'd better get used to treating him like one or you're going to blow your cover before you even get your foot in the door at Yonnie Six."

Lissa opened her mouth to protest but Saber cut her off.

"She's right, Lissa," he said quietly. "Males on Yonnie Six are considered little better than domestic beasts. They exist only to protect and serve their mistresses."

"And you're willing for me to treat you like that? Like a slave? Like a pet?" Lissa demanded. Saber was a Kindred warrior—a proud male who was next in line to be the leader of their people. And she...she was just an orphaned girl with no family who had been exiled from her home world for the sin of caring for him. How could he humble himself to act like her slave?

Saber frowned, as though guessing her thoughts. "I'm willing to do whatever it takes to keep you safe," he rumbled. "If that means wearing these clothes and calling you 'mistress', I'll do it without hesitation."

Kat nodded approvingly. "See? Saber gets it. This isn't some game you're playing here, Lissa—both your lives depend on it. So you have to act the part—to really *inhabit* it."

"Says the girl who spent all of *one* summer at acting camp." The new voice came from Olivia, who was moving ponderously because of her advanced state of pregnancy. Behind her was Sophia, her twin sister who Lissa knew was also pregnant. She wasn't nearly as far along in her pregnancy as her sister but she was still showing quite prominently—possibly because she was carrying twins.

"Sorry to sneak up on you," Sophia said apologetically. "But we're both out of peanut butter and I was hoping you might have some, Kat."

Kat sighed. "Ah, the things I give up for my pregnant friends. Sure, help yourselves, raid the kitchen. I have a couple of jars in the cupboard." She nodded at the food prep area of her suite but to Lissa's discomfort, the two sisters didn't immediately follow their friend's prompt.

"So, is this one of the gowns you're going to wear on Yonnie Six?" Olivia asked with obvious interest. "It's gaudy but gorgeous — looks great on you."

"Thank you." Lissa still had her arms clutched protectively over her breasts. "Kat had it made up for me from some sketches she found while researching the Yonnite culture."

"Yes, Kat's good about that. She'll plan your wedding, host your baby shower, even manage your undercover infiltration of an alien culture. *Anything* but plan her *own* joining ceremony." She raised an eyebrow at Kat. "Isn't that right, hon?"

Kat frowned. "Very funny. With everyone around here popping up pregnant and Lauren and Xairn getting married, I haven't had time to work on my own stuff. So don't say another word, Liv — I'm not doing anything else until I'm sure that Lissa here is ready to go."

"Well, she looks ready for anything in that gown," Sophia said, smiling. She looked at Lissa. "Do you like it?"

"It's...not exactly what I'm used to," Lissa said, not wanting to hurt Kat's feelings by telling the truth — that she was absolutely mortified to be wearing the revealing gown.

"Well, at least it's not alive." Sophia patted her arm consolingly. "The *tharp* I had to wear when I went to Tranq Prime gave me fits. Of course, we get along just fine now but I wanted to *strangle* the darn thing at the time."

"Oh." Lissa crossed her arms tighter over her partially bared breasts. Sophia had a point—things could be worse. "I guess I didn't think about that," she admitted.

"It's not something you usually *have* to think about," Olivia pointed out. "Unless you're determined to wear a creepy living fur blanket as a dress. In which case whatever problems you have are on you." She stroked the crystal encrusted material admiringly. "That really shows off your figure—wish I could fit into something like it. I'm beginning to feel like I'll never have a waist again."

"You will again once the baby comes," Kat told her friend consolingly.

"Well, until then at least I can eat as much peanut butter as I want." Olivia turned toward the food prep area and caught sight of Saber who had been standing silently in the corner of the room. "Wow—didn't see you there, sorry." She looked him up and down and gave a low whistle. "Is this from Yonnie Six too?"

"Of course. You think he dresses up as a sex slave for the fun of it?" Kat demanded.

Olivia shrugged. "He might—how do I know? Saber is the first Touch Kindred I've ever met." She smiled at him. "And you're a really nice guy too—despite all the weird rumors we heard."

Saber nodded gravely. "Thank you. I'm doing my best to represent my people without giving offense."

"Honey, you couldn't give offense to *anybody* in that getup." Olivia grinned at him and then looked at Kat. "I want something like that for Baird."

"I wouldn't mind getting Sylvan into something like it too." Sophia smiled. "And I thought the Tranq Prime traditional outfit was hot."

"No fur boots but the tight leather pants more than makes up for that," Olivia commented and laughed. "Sorry, Saber, we don't mean to be looking at you like you're a side of beef. We really only came for the peanut butter. C'mon, Sophie." She tugged at her sister's arm and they both disappeared into the food prep area.

"Those two..." Kat shook her head affectionately before turning back to Lissa. "Now listen, hon, the gown looks great on you but it's not going to do the whole job. If you want to carry this off, you have to act the part."

Lissa frowned. "You said that before but I really don't understand. What part do you want me to act?"

"God, I wish I had some time to show you around South Tampa where all the rich bitches live and give you some real life examples but it's too late for that now." Kat sighed. "Basically you have to ditch the shy and humble priestess routine and become a rich, tyrannical bitch mistress from hell."

Lissa put a hand to her cheek. "But...I can't do that. I can't be that person. And I don't want to go out in public wearing these clothes. And I can't treat Saber like a...like he's nothing more than an animal. Like a slave." Her voice almost broke on the last word and she could barely force it out. When she'd volunteered for this mission, she had never imagined it would involve such personal degradation, or worse, such abject humiliation for the male she cared for most in the universe.

Saber stepped forward. "Lissa," he said in a low voice. "Amalla – "

But hearing the sweet, forbidden term of endearment was more than Lissa could bear.

"Forgive me," she whispered. Turning, she ran past Kat into the sleeping chamber where she had left her clothing and buried her face in the pillows.

* * * * *

Saber watched her go and had to force himself not to follow. *She is nothing to you now,* he reminded himself for the hundredth time. *She's a kinswoman — a member of the same clan. She's off limits.*

Still, he ached to go and comfort her, as he used to back when they were attending the same school and the bullies came after her. He wanted to fight to defend her honor, to keep her safe and protect her at all costs. If wearing the ridiculous skintight trousers and the black leather leash was the only way he could stay by her side and guard her, he would gladly do it. Why did it bother Lissa so much?

He wished he could ask her but his hands were tied—he had promised her he would keep his distance emotionally during their mission and he had to keep that promise. He shouldn't even have called her *amalla,* but the endearment had just slipped out.

Even if he could have gone after her, it was awkward to try and comfort someone you couldn't actually touch. Any kind of touching—physical or mental—between male and female members of the same tribe of the Touch Kindred was forbidden. In the past, Saber had broken that taboo but he couldn't do it again—not now and not ever again. The thought made his chest tight.

"Oh dear." Kat sighed, breaking his train of thought. "I'm sorry," she said to Saber. "I was going to see if your outfit needed any alterations but I think I need to go check on Lissa."

He nodded silently and she bustled away, calling his kinswoman's name. He turned, intending to go back into the small guest bathroom and change back into his normal clothing, when the door to the suite opened again and two large males walked in. One had light brownish blond hair and brown eyes and the other had black hair and black eyes. Saber had never met them but he guessed from the holo-pics he saw scattered around the living area they must be the Twin Kindred Kat was mated to.

Saber was standing in the shadowed hallway that led to the bathroom and at first the two were too busy arguing to notice him.

"I told you, Lock," the dark twin said in an angry tone. "She's ashamed of us."

"She's not—she never would be," the light twin protested in a low, vehement voice. "She's just been distracted by everything else going on lately. You know she's become the unofficial coordinator of every special event in our immediate circle lately, Deep. It keeps her busy."

"Too busy to introduce us to her kin? Too busy to—" The dark twin stopped abruptly, appearing to notice Saber for the first time. "Hey—who are you and what the hell are you doing in our suite dressed like that?" His eyes narrowed. "Where's Kat? If you've hurt her—"

"I'm Saber," Saber said quickly, stepping forward and holding out both hands, palms up, in a gesture of friendship. "Forgive me for startling you—I'm not here to harm anyone. Your bride was simply helping me prepare for my mission."

The light twin snapped his fingers. "You're the Touch Kindred Baird has been telling us about. The one who's been addressing the Council and speaking on behalf of Rast about the Hoard problem."

"I have been charged with speaking with the Counselor's voice, that's true." Saber nodded his head in agreement.

The dark twin frowned. "Well, Rast may trust you but I *don't*. I don't like having a Touch Kindred on the ship—especially not around my female."

"Take it easy, Deep" his brother said soothingly. "Baird says he felt the same way at first but both Rast and Sylvan have spoken for Saber and he's promised not to use his Touch abilities on any female while he's on board."

"A promise I have scrupulously kept." Saber frowned at the glaring dark twin. "If you knew how intimate a mind Touch is, you'd realize I would no more use it on an unknown female than *you* would go around fondling females you didn't know at random."

Deep continued to frown. "That's exactly what I'm afraid of. The stories I've heard—"

"Don't apply to me," Saber finished for him. "Look, I know you're not thrilled to have me aboard—none of the other Kindred males are. But I'm here on a mission and I have no interest in molesting any of your females, either physically or mentally."

"You should give him some credit, Deep," Lock, the light twin told his brother reasonably. "He has behaved honorably so far. And besides, you're the last one I'd think would be predisposed to think the worse of our new brother. You and Xairn get along fine and he's Scourge."

"That's different," Deep growled. "Xairn doesn't have the ability to go around *Touching* every innocent female he sees with his mind."

Saber felt a surge of irritation. "Let me ask you something, *Brother*," he said, frowning at the dark twin. "Would you say you're physically stronger than any female on the Mother Ship?"

Deep nodded shortly. "Of course. We love our Earth brides and they have great strength of character but physically, they're no match for us."

"So you could, if you wanted, go around raping every female you saw," Saber pointed out. "I mean, you have the physical strength to do it, don't you?"

"You sick bastard," Deep snarled. "I would never—"

"I wouldn't either," Saber said quietly.

"I think what he's trying to say is that just because you have the ability to do something, doesn't mean you'll do it," Lock said.

"I know what he's saying." Deep shot him a mistrustful look. "I just don't like the way he's saying it. And I *don't* like him being alone with Kat."

"I'm not." Saber held out his hands again, still silently asking for peace. He could understand the dark twin's anger—after all, he wouldn't want Lissa to be alone with a strange male, especially not one dressed as he was right now. "Lissa my...my kinswoman is here as well."

"Kinswoman?" Lock frowned.

"Sister. My little sister." The words seemed to stick in Saber's throat but he forced himself to say them anyway. After all, by the laws of his people they were true, even if his heart told him otherwise. "She is to be part of the mission to recover the stolen scrolls which were sold to a collector on Yonnie Six."

"Yonnie Six, huh?" Deep looked him up and down again. "Well, that explains the way you're dressed, at least. You know what they do to males on that planet?"

"I'm aware, yes," Saber said stonily. "I could hardly put on a collar and leash and not have *some* idea of what I'm getting into."

"You're very brave," Lock said quietly. "The Yonnites have the correct physical characteristics to make a genetic trade with us but we've never even approached them because of the barbaric ways they treat their males. Yet you're going among them voluntarily."

"That *does* take courage," Deep said grudgingly. "I don't know if I could do it. Don't know if I could *submit* so completely."

Saber took a deep breath. "I don't expect it to be easy. But I have to keep Lissa safe. For her I would do anything—dare anything. *Submit* to anything."

Deep cocked an eyebrow at him. "You may have to keep that pledge before long. I hope you mean it."

"I do." Saber thought of Lissa, of her wide jade green eyes still so innocent, of her tender pink lips which had never been kissed. They were going to an ugly place—it was opulent and extravagantly wealthy to be sure. But from what he had learned, Yonnie Six was seething with depravity and corruption. He was determined to protect not only Lissa's life, but her virtue and innocence as well. *No matter what it takes,* he told himself.

"She's more than just a sister to you, isn't she?" Lock said quietly.

"Of course not." Saber shifted uneasily. "We would never...I mean, by the rules of my people..."

"Uh-huh," Deep rumbled sarcastically. "She's just your sister but you're willing to die for her even though you don't love her at all. Keep telling yourself that. It's so obviously *true.*"

Saber frowned. "There is no blood relation between myself and Lissa. But we are connected by more than blood—by the ties of clan and adoption I am her older brother. Nothing can ever happen between us. Nor do I want it to."

"Are you sure?" Lock looked at him earnestly. "No one will judge you here, brother. No offense but we find your people's laws both archaic and much too stringent."

"Our ways of thinking may seem outmoded to you but they are the ways I have to return to once this mission is completed," Saber said stiffly.

Lock raised both hands in a gesture of reconciliation. "Just trying to help."

Saber merely nodded, not trusting himself to speak. As if he needed help to feel more for Lissa than he should!

"We'd better go find Kat," Deep said, frowning slightly. He nodded shortly at Saber. "Good luck with your trip to Yonnie Six. I wish you success in your...submission."

"Deep..." Lock threw his twin a reproachful glance. "I'm sorry, Saber. Please forgive my brother's rudeness and accept our best wishes for your mission."

"Thank you," Saber said stiffly. "Excuse me, I need to change." He turned to go but Deep's voice followed him down the hallway.

"You might as well just leave the leash and collar on. You're going to have to get used to it on Yonnie Six."

Saber felt tension creep into his shoulders but he refused to rise to the bait. Clearly the dark twin was spoiling for a fight but Saber was not the one to give it to him. A lifetime of controlling his emotions and restraining his abilities helped him keep his cool. Still, Deep's sarcastic remark burned. Exactly how far would he have to go with this ruse in order to protect Lissa?

All the way, he told himself as he turned into the bathroom and looked at the black leash and collar encircling his throat. *I'll go all the way if I have to.*

Chapter Two

"It's okay, hon. Everything is going to be okay." Kat's soothing voice and the cool cloth she put over Lissa's eyes finally helped end the tears.

"I'm sorry." Lissa sat up and pressed the cloth to her hot face, glad for its calming chill. "I don't know what's wrong with me. I guess...I guess I just didn't realize exactly what I was getting myself into when I took this mission. But when I tried on this dress..." She gestured to the stiff purple fabric still encasing her.

"When you tried it on, it made everything real, didn't it?" Kat said gently. "Look, I can understand. Sometimes we're put into situations we don't think we can handle. But you're strong, Lissa—a lot stronger than you think. You're going to do fine when you get to Yonnie Six—I'm just trying to give you the tools to work with once you get there."

"I know that." Lissa sniffed. "And I thank you for it, Kat. You've spent a great deal of time on this—as much or more than I have—researching the culture and the dress patterns." She sighed and ran her hand over the stiff, shimmering train. "It really is beautiful. I'm just not used to showing so much of myself. And I can't believe we're leaving *tomorrow*."

"Well, if it's any consolation, you've definitely got the figure to carry it off." Kat smiled at her. "There was a time when I would have killed to be as thin as you."

"And now?" Lissa raised an eyebrow.

"Not so much." Kat smiled. "I wound up with Twin Kindred — they're into big beautiful women on Twin Moons. So it all worked out."

"Are you going to be joined with them soon?" She felt bad for taking up so much of Kat's time. She'd been living aboard the Kindred Mother Ship for the past few months and in that time her new friend had hosted several baby showers and a joining ceremony for her friends. *And* she had also taken it upon herself to get Lissa all ready for her undercover mission. Lissa had been so worried about what she and Saber were about to attempt that it hadn't even occurred to her that Kat had other pressing business of her own to attend to. She looked at Kat uncertainly. "What Olivia was saying about you putting off planning your own ceremony in order to get me ready for my mission..."

"Don't worry about that." Kat made a shooing gesture. "I wanted to help. Besides, when Nadiah called and asked if one of us would mind pitching in to get you ready for your trip, everyone else was pregnant. Well, with the exception of Elise and she's still too wrapped up in her man to do much more than make eyes at Merrick and have lots and lots of bonding sex."

Lissa felt her cheeks coloring at the offhand way Kat spoke of such a sacred rite. "You mean...the Deep Touch?"

"Is that what your people call it?" Kat asked. "Sure, I guess so. Sex seems to be different with every kind of Kindred. How is it with yours?"

"I don't...I've never..." Lissa looked down at her hands, blushing.

"A virgin, huh?" Kat sounded unsurprised. "Well, with you being shut away on First World with a bunch of other priestesses I can't say I'm shocked. But you're going to have to get over blushing every time somebody talks about sex. From what I've learned, the Yonnites are pretty open about satisfying their appetites."

"I know." Lissa nodded. "That's my understanding too. It's just...so different from the way I was raised and the beliefs I've been taught to espouse."

"I'm sure it is," Kat said firmly. "But you're going to have to put all your moral outrage and shocked sensibilities aside if you want to do this right. You're not just protecting yourself—you're protecting Saber too. Remember, *you* are the wealthy mistress—he's only your slave. You're the one they're going to be looking at, scrutinizing to see if you're legitimate or not. And I don't want to scare you but if they find out you're not..." She let the sentence trail off ominously.

Goddess, she's right. Our lives hang in the balance—I have to get over my fear and do whatever is necessary. Lissa swallowed hard and lifted her chin. "I know," she said. "And I *can* do this—I know I can. I just...have to wrap my mind around it."

"You're going to be fine." Kat smiled encouragingly. "When you get there, don't even try to be yourself. What you need to do is picture the most imposing female you've ever met and pretend you're her."

Lissa frowned. The most imposing female she'd ever met...that was easy. *Minverna,* she thought, recalling the high priestess whose place she had taken and who had subsequently committed suicide. She was *also* the one who had stolen and sold the records Lissa and Saber were going to recover, but that wasn't what Lissa concentrated on now. Could she really channel the ex-priestess and use what she had learned from her to fit in on Yonnie Six?

"Do you have someone in mind?" Kat asked. "Someone you can imitate?"

"I think so." Lissa nodded. "I'm thinking of my ex-high priestess—the one Councilor Rast deposed. She was, as you said earlier, 'a tyrannical bitch mistress from hell'."

Kat laughed and patted her on the back. "Good. So go on— pretend you're her. Say something to me in her voice."

Slowly, Lissa drew herself up and frowned at Kat in what she hoped was a threatening manner. "What are *you* doing here?" she demanded in the haughtiest voice she could manage. "I thought I ordered you to be gone half an hour ago, *slave.*"

"Perfect!" Kat exclaimed in delight. "See—you're a natural. You're going to be *fine.*"

"I have to be," Lissa said, in her own voice. "Both my life and the life of my kinsman depend on it." She sighed and looked down at the skimpy bodice which barely covered her breasts. "I guess I'll have to get over my modesty and my shyness and just…act the part, like you said."

"Exactly." Kat nodded approvingly. "Good girl—you're going to go out there to Yonnie Six and knock them dead."

Lissa felt ill. "I *hope* there won't be any killing involved. No matter what part I'm playing, I don't want to knock anyone until they're dead."

"No, no." Kat laughed. "It's an Earth expression. It means you're going to do such a good job everyone will be completely awed by you. And you're going to be back here in no time with the scrolls that tell how to defeat the Hoard."

Lissa sighed. "I hope and pray that you're right, Kat. I truly do."

But inside she wondered if she was really up to the task. *I have to be,* she told herself fiercely. *I have to protect Saber and this is the only way.* She had no idea that her kinsman was thinking the same thing—she only knew she would do anything to keep him from harm. Even put aside her modesty and pretend to be someone completely different—completely alien to her own nature.

Chapter Three

Far from the Kindred Mother Ship, someone else was also planning to infiltrate an alien culture—although by rights, it should not have been alien to her at all.

L looked at herself in the viewer, rearranging the long, spiral blue curls that grew in a narrow strip down the middle of her head. She was disguised as a *lili* from Zabith for the moment, but she could change at any time. That was the beauty of having such a unique genetic makeup and being trained by one of the best shadow casters in the known universe.

For a moment she shifted to her original form—the one with long black hair, amber eyes, and a white star shaped birthmark between her breasts. Though it was the outward appearance she had entered the cold, unfeeling universe with, she didn't consider it her true form. That was because this particular shape belonged to another—to a girl who'd had it first—long before L came into existence. Still, it came in handy at times—especially while she was infiltrating the dreams of a certain Scourge warrior aboard the Kindred Mother Ship.

L sighed. She wished she could go straight to the Mother Ship now but Draven had insisted that she come to see him first. He had some special weapons he wanted her to deploy—as if a knife in the dark wasn't weapon enough. It always had been for L before, but the Hoard Master was paying good credit to have things done exactly to his specifications so she had to go along.

She concentrated again and shed her original form like water. Her eyes went from amber to vivid blue and assumed an exotic tilt as her hair turned pale pink. The tops of her ears took on a graceful point and her face became more triangular. A tiny nose, full pink lips and a peaches and cream complexion dusted liberally with lavender freckles completed her new look.

Exotic dancing girl from Julo—it was one of the first forms her shadow master had taught her. It had certainly brought the customers running—although they didn't run for long after Yex sliced their throats. L had been the perfect bait—the lure to drive any male mad with lust. A lust she thankfully had not had to slake, not after she was bought by Yex, at least…

L pushed the thoughts away. The past was the past, there was no point in dwelling on it now. No point in remembering the miserable time she'd spent in the skin trade before Yex had found her and recognized her unique abilities. Before he'd taken her as an apprentice and trained her in the shadow caster's arts.

"I am what I am," she said aloud to the viewer. "I am what I was forced to be. And for that I will have my revenge."

Yes, but first she had to go see Draven.

With a sigh, she went to the front of her little ship and set a course for the nearest wormhole that came out by Hrakaz. She didn't relish the thought of going to the bleak, dangerous world filled with brutish trolls and dirty, scuttling imps but such were the beings the Hoard Master chose to surround himself with and she had no choice. Still, she thought as she entered the coordinates, there was no need to advertise her presence until she had to. Maybe her dancing girl form could wait.

Walking back to the viewer, she looked at herself again as once more, her features began to flow and melt…

* * * * *

"Where *is* she?" Draven paced his opulent sitting room, his black boots scuffing the rare *aza* fur carpets carelessly. He'd woken early, the dreams caused by the venomous *skrillix* plant still tormenting him. He didn't like the images the dreams brought with them—the memories they forced him to relive.

This last one had been particularly bad. The final charge against the armies of darkness that had threatened the Goddess's domain…watching his friend and fellow warrior, Glorin, fall helpless into the abyss, his wings singed to ash before he could even think to fly…the laughing, ghoulish face at the top of the great divide crying, *"Where is your strength now, oh warrior of light? How do you plan to defeat me with your host fallen and your weapons gone? What can one lone warrior do against my might?"*

"No!" Draven's shout made the imp attending him jump in fright.

"Master?" It squeaked fearfully. "Is everything all right? Might I fetch you some wine to calm your nerves?"

"My nerves do not need calming." Draven used the pain voice, watching in satisfaction as brutal gashes appeared on the imp's dirty gray hide. They gaped like lipless mouths and began to leak the black ichor that passed for blood among its kind.

"Forgive me, Master," the imp moaned in distress but held perfectly still, obviously knowing that to move was to incur a worse, possibly fatal punishment.

Draven nodded. "That's right—stay as you are. Next time you'll have the sense to keep your filthy maw shut."

Yet, the small cruelty did not appease him in the way it should have. He continued pacing, his irritation at being kept waiting growing by the minute. Where was the shadow caster? By the seven hells, she should have been here by now! He hated that he had to use her at all. If only he wasn't confined to this filthy planet, he could do the job himself. He grew stronger every day and soon he would be able to leave but he was not quite ready yet...

A rapping on the door interrupted his stride. "Come," he called impatiently. It couldn't be the shadow caster—her ship had not yet landed on the barren surface of Hrakaz. If it had, his sentries would have notified him. But it might be one of his soulless servants, bearing some news of her.

The broad double doors swung open revealing a pair of trolls from the *Xix* tribe. Their immense size and heavy musculature were impressive, but not enough to offset the dull expressions on their lumpish faces. Gods, sometimes he got so *tired* of being surrounded by idiots!

"What?" he snapped, looking at the troll on the right. "What have you to say?"

"The one you wait for, Lord. Shadow caster," it said. "She here."

"That's impossible, she hasn't landed yet."

The troll looked confused. "But...she here, my Lord."

"Where?" Draven demanded. "I see nothing but you two imbeciles standing there."

"Here," the troll repeated stupidly. It glanced at the other troll in obvious confusion. The second troll returned the look, an expression of dull incomprehension in its piggy eyes.

Draven's limited patience was completely gone. He turned his pain voice on both of them and shouted, **"Where is she, you fools?"**

Gashes opened in their wrinkled, dirty gray skin but while the first troll bled black, the second bled red. Draven frowned at the thin crimson rivulets that decorated its hide. As he watched, the hide began to shrink and change color. Before he knew it, a slender, well-formed woman with dark blue hair and pale eyes was standing before him.

"That's going to cost you extra," she said icily, wiping at the cut on her cheek. "I didn't come here to play your twisted pain games, Draven."

"Nor do I expect you to," he said smoothly. "Please, come in, my dear L." He saw her eyes widen and nodded. "Yes, I know your name — or what you call yourself anyway. Though that was almost the only thing I was able to find out about you."

What he really wanted to know was how she'd gotten past his security and managed to land on the planet without anyone the wiser. Heads would roll on that account, he promised himself. But for now, he was intent on enjoying her company. The shadow caster was almost as sly as he was. It was going to be a rare pleasure to have her as a guest.

A rare pleasure indeed.

Chapter Four

"Okay, looks like you're all packed up and ready to go." Kat pressed a small dark pink cube into Lissa's hand. "That's got everything you need. Dresses, accessories, equipment—all you have to do is pick the one you want and add a drop of the regrowth serum. It's the blue bottle on the inside of the case. Just remember that there's no way to minimize the items in the cube again so you may have to leave some of this stuff behind when you come back— unless you want to cram it all into the shuttle."

"Got it." Lissa said dryly. "And don't worry, Kat—I appreciate all the hard work you put into my outfits but I don't think I could wear any of them outside Yonnie Six. So I won't be too upset if I have to leave a few behind."

"Of course." Kat smiled. "And don't forget, you're Lissa R'awr from the colony on Zetta Prime and this is your first time on Yonnie Six. The Zettas are a faction that broke off from the main planet and went in search of greater wealth the next system over. But they still consider Yonnie Six their home world and acknowledge the Yonnite empress as their sovereign. So you're like a country cousin come to see the big city sights."

"That's perfect." Lissa smiled at her. She and Kat had been spending every spare minute together perfecting what Kat called her "back story" until she finally felt ready to go. Although she still had some qualms about her mission to Yonnie Six, she was feeling much better than she had been at the dress fitting the day before. Even the sight of Saber, already dressed in his slave outfit, couldn't rattle her.

"Hello, kinsman," she murmured, nodding her head as he entered the small Kindred shuttle they would be taking to the Ganda system. "Are...are you ready to go?"

"As ready as I'll ever be." He winced as he sat down in the pilot's chair. "These trousers are pretty Goddess damned tight."

"Believe me," Kat said dryly. "You two are going to be the most discreetly dressed mistress and slave there. That's why I decided it would be best to go with the country cousin story – to explain your modesty and any confusion you may have about the local customs."

"I really appreciate everything you've done, Kat." Impulsively, Lissa threw her arms around her friend and gave her a hug. "Nadiah told me I would love all of you when I got here and she was right. You're a wonderful friend."

"Oh, stop it. You're making me blush." Kat grinned and her cheeks were pink as she finally pulled out of the hug. "You just make sure you're careful and don't do anything to blow your cover. I don't want to think what would happen if the Yonnites found out who you two really are."

"Don't worry," Saber said, as he adjusted the controls. "We're both prepared to play our parts to the hilt."

"You'll have to be," Kat said grimly. She looked at Lissa. "Now, you're sure you've got everything you need?"

"I've got the list of collectors Minverna sold to," Lissa said. "One of them happens to be the Yonnite cultural ambassador – we've arranged an introduction so we can go talk to her first. And I've got the mirror-mere dagger." She shivered as she said it. She didn't want to wear the instrument of her old High Priestess's death around her waist but it had been decided that such an obvious display of wealth would gain her instant respect in the rapacious Yonnite high society.

The dagger was made of a solid piece of the most rare and precious substance in the known universe—mirror-mere. Lissa would be wearing the wealth of a world strapped to her side. It was also the bargaining tool she hoped to use when she found the ancient scrolls she and Saber were looking for. No matter how much the collector who had bought them might enjoy owning such a rare item, Lissa was hoping they would be willing to trade for the fabulously opulent dagger.

"Well, it looks like you're all set," Kat said. "Do you have the bracelet—oh, I see that you do."

"Of course." Lissa looked down at the delicate silver wire bracelet which was set with a single pure white stone. "If there's any trouble it will change color, right?"

"Red indicates there's danger and you need to contact the Mother Ship," Kat said. "Black means you have to come back immediately. Of course, that would only be in the event of an attack where we were unsure about opening the fold so you could get safely home. I wouldn't worry about it too much but the Council agrees that the Hoard's aggression indicates they want war. So…"

"We have to keep in communication. I understand." Lissa nodded.

"Exactly."

"We'll be careful and we'll be back soon," Lissa told her, hoping it was true.

"I'm sure you will, hon." Kat smiled at her. "And—"

"Forgive me, Kat, but we really need to get going. The fold should be waiting and my understanding is, it takes massive amounts of energy to hold it open for any length of time," Saber said, doing something to the instruments.

"Right. Of course." Kat gave Lissa one last hug and then stepped back out of the small shuttle and went to stand by Sophia and Olivia who had come along to say goodbye. She gave a little wave and Lissa waved back.

"Closing the access door now," Saber warned her. "It's time to get strapped in for flight."

"Oh yes, of course." As the hatch closed, she went forward and sat beside him in the passenger seat. The viewscreen before them showed the shuttle bay doors already opening and beyond that, in the blackness of space, was the red gash of the fold. Lissa had already been through it once, when they had first come to the Mother Ship, so she wasn't afraid of going into the gaping wound in space. What frightened her was what they would find on the other side.

Saber gave her a sidelong glance. "Are you ready?"

"As ready as I can be." Lissa took a deep breath. "Let's go."

* * * * *

Kat watched them take off, her heart in her throat as the small shuttle lifted soundlessly and flew toward the shuttle bay doors. As it passed through the invisible atmosphere bubble that allowed the doors to open into space without sucking all the oxygen out of the ship, she felt like she might cry. Lissa had become very dear to her over the past few months and Kat couldn't help wondering if the timid, humble little priestess would really be able to pull off the part she had to play.

Please, Goddess, help her, she thought as she watched the shuttle slip through the massive doors and out into the darkness of space. *Help her and bring her back safely. Her and Saber both.*

"Hey, Kat woman." Liv's voice in her ear startled Kat out of her prayerful concentration. "You okay?"

Kat sniffed and nodded. "Yeah. Just worried about her. She's such a shy little thing—I did everything I could to get her ready but I still feel like I just threw a kitten into a shark tank and told it to swim."

"Oh come on now, you must be exaggerating," Sophia protested. "How bad can Yonnie Six really be?"

"They're pretty brutal." Kat sighed. "But Lissa knows that—she did the research right along with me. I just have a feeling that knowing it and actually *experiencing* it are going to be two totally different things for her."

"She'll be fine," Olivia said firmly, patting her on the arm. "You did everything you could to help her prepare. *Now* you can concentrate on your own business—like a certain joining ceremony slash wedding for you and your guys."

Kat frowned. "Don't start that again, Liv. I'll get to it when I can."

"I think you should try to make an effort to get to it sooner rather than later," her friend said seriously. "I don't mean to butt into your business but Baird says Deep has been grumbling lately about everyone having a joining ceremony but you three."

"That's not true," Kat said defensively. "Elise and Merrick haven't gotten joined yet."

"Yes, but they have plans to, very soon. You know that—you're helping Elise plan their ceremony," Sophia pointed out.

"Exactly. And I'll get to my own as soon as hers is out of the way."

Liv put a hand on her hip. "That's what you said after Lauren and Xairn's ceremony. Look, Kat, I don't know who made you the unofficial party planner of the entire Mother Ship but you can't keep putting your own business behind someone else's. At the rate people are hooking up and getting preggers around here, you'll *never* get joined to Deep and Lock."

"Yes, I will," Kat protested. "I mean, *eventually...*"

Olivia gave a sigh that echoed in the cavernous shuttle bay. "I know you love them, so what's the problem?"

"I don't *have* a problem, okay?" Kat snapped. "Geeze, guys, I'm a little stressed out right now, what with possibly sending my new friend off to her death. Do you think we could save the moralizing until later?"

"Fine." Liv looked hurt and Sophie looked shocked, which made Kat feel wretched.

"I'm sorry," she said as gently as she could. "I just...don't want to talk about it right now. Okay?"

"Sure, Kat, we understand." Sophia nodded and put an arm around Olivia's shoulders. "I should probably get Liv back to her suite and get her some breakfast anyway."

"Right." Liv gave her a grin that looked a little forced. "It's been at least an hour since I had any seaweed or spinach waffles. I need to feed."

"And I'm hungry too." Sophia smiled. "Now that I'm eating for three. C'mon, womb mate."

Feeling guilty, Kat watched the two of them walk off. Sophie and Liv were her two oldest friends—she knew she ought to be able to talk to them about what was bothering her. It was just that she'd spent so much time denying, even to herself, that there was a problem, she found it really hard to share.

I'll think about it later, she promised herself. *Maybe after I help Elise and Merrick with their ceremony.* She felt a twinge of guilt for putting off her own joining again but she placed it to the back of her mind resolutely. There would be plenty of time to plan a wedding for herself and Deep and Lock later.

Chapter Five

"Are you almost ready?" Saber called, adjusting the shuttle's controls minutely as the purple-gray sphere of Yonnie Six grew larger in the viewscreen. "We've been given clearance to land."

"Almost...done." Lissa's words were punctuated by the swish of fabric. She was changing in the back of the shuttle — taking off her modest white priestess robes and putting on one of the dresses Kat had prepared for her to wear on Yonnie Six. Saber wondered if what she was changing into looked anything like the purple dress she'd been wearing the other day. He could still recall how revealing it had been — the way her rosy pink nipples had peeked out from behind the pale gold lace and the tiny panties of the same material, which barely covered her sex...

The mental image made him instantly hard and he winced as his rigid cock strangled in the too-tight pants. There was another rustle of fabric behind him and he had an almost overwhelming urge to turn and look, to see what she was wearing and how much it showed. *Goddess, have to stop thinking like this! Have to stop imagining her sexually.* He kept his eyes forward instead, looking at the viewscreen as though he could stare a hole through it.

At last, Lissa came forward and sat beside him. Out of the corner of his eye, Saber could see she was wearing a dark blue gown cut low in front. When she twisted in her seat to buckle herself in, he saw it was cut even lower in back. Low enough to see the softly rounded tops of her buttocks. His cock surged against the tight black pants again and he cursed himself for a lecherous fool but somehow he couldn't drag his eyes away from the enticing sight.

Lissa turned and caught him watching. Her face went pink. "I…it was the most modest one I could find," she stammered. "I…I…"

"Forgive me for looking." Saber averted his eyes, staring at the viewscreen again. "I shouldn't have."

"It's all right," Lissa mumbled, clearly embarrassed. "I mean, I guess you can't help…" She shook her head and settled back in her seat, her arms crossed tightly over her breasts.

"I'll try to help it from now on," Saber vowed in a low voice. He was filled with shame for the embarrassment he had caused her. *If only you weren't so damn beautiful. If only I didn't dream of taking you in my arms every night. Of Touching you…*

He felt his other sense—his Touch sense—wanting to reach out to her. He ached to caress her with his *whisper-fingers.* To stroke the strands of blonde and jade green hair away from her flushed cheek and kiss her warm skin. To touch her physically as he was Touching her with his mind…but that was wrong. So wrong. And honestly, he didn't even know if it would be possible.

They had both been injected with the kinship compound as infants—a kind of inoculation to make physical contact with a member of the same tribe utterly repellent. Though Saber had touched her skin before and even kissed her forehead when they were younger, he had never dared to touch her in a sexual way. If he did, would he feel a surge of revulsion and see the same disgust mirrored in Lissa's jade green eyes?

He hoped not but he couldn't be sure. Not unless he tried and he knew that he would never do that, never dare to lay a hand on her in such a brazen, forbidden fashion. Lissa could barely stand his eyes on her—how would she bear his hands? No matter how much he might wish it, the experiment to see if they were able to have physical, sexual contact was completely out of the question. And without being able to have skin-to-skin sexual touching, there was no way they could ever experience the Deep Touch together.

Just the thought of that—the mental image of holding Lissa naked in his arms as he penetrated both her mind and body at the same time—made Saber feel like he was going to burst out of the damn too-tight trousers he had been forced to wear as part of his slave outfit. But he had to put the idea out of his mind. It was forbidden and wrong. Depraved. It was—

Lissa cleared her throat, pulling him out of his illicit thoughts. "Um..."

"Yes?" Saber turned to her slightly, trying not to notice how revealing her dress was.

"I...um..." Clearly she was searching for a new topic of conversation. "When will we land in Opulex?" she asked, pointing at the growing point of light that served as a beacon to the capital city of Yonnie Six.

Saber shook his head. "We can't land directly in the city—only on the fringes of it," he said, banking the ship and heading for the designated landing area. "We have to stay to one side of the trench until we're cleared to go through to Opulex."

"The trench?" She frowned. "I don't think I read about that."

"Well, you were busy studying the culture, not the cartography." Saber gave her a small smile. "It's the mining trench around the city. They have enormous deposits of rare and precious minerals on Yonnie Six. It's where most of their wealth comes from."

"Oh. Of course." She nodded.

"And the trench also serves as a natural barrier around the city," he went on. "Although it limits the expansion of the city—which is why most of their growth is vertical." As he spoke, the towering buildings of Opulex came into view. Their needle-like points rose high into the murky Yonnite atmosphere, piercing the clouds of smog that veiled the lower portions of the bustling city.

"I see," Lissa murmured, her eyes glued to the ominous sight. "It's...not very pretty, is it?"

"No." Saber thought of the verdant fields and sprawling, lush farmlands of his own home world. "It's not." And if what he'd read was true, Opulex was even uglier on the inside. But he didn't say that out loud. It was clear that Lissa was upset enough already—he didn't want to add to her unease about their mission. Carefully, he set them down in the designated landing area. "We're here," he said, not looking at her.

"Well." Lissa took a deep breath. Rising, she shook out her dress and threw back her hair. With hands that trembled only a little, she buckled the shining mirror-mere dagger to her slender waist and then threw Saber a glance. "Let's go."

She made her way to the hatch of the ship and Saber followed, trying to keep his eyes on the ground instead of her luscious ass—a losing battle. He gave an inward sigh. This mission was going to be even more difficult than he'd imagined.

* * * * *

Lissa hooked the small purple cube that contained all her supplies and wardrobe over her arm and slapped the button to open the ship's hatch. The sight of the barren landscape of rocks and raw, churned earth that greeted her was daunting but she didn't let it stop her from marching down the steps and setting her feet firmly on the ground — ground which she promptly sank into up to her ankles.

"Oh!" she gasped and took a step back, out of the sucking mud. Unfortunately, it pulled the small, elegant satin slipper she'd been wearing right off her foot, putting her off balance. She pinwheeled her arms and would have fallen backward if Saber hadn't caught her.

"Easy!" His strong hands on her bare shoulders felt warm and certain. The forbidden skin-to-skin contact made Lissa's heart race.

"Thank you." She straightened up hurriedly. Was it her imagination or did Saber's hands linger on her skin before he finally released her? *Just my imagination, surely,* she told herself, her heart still pounding. *He promised he wouldn't touch me. He only steadied me to keep me from falling – that's all.* Carefully she pulled her other foot out of the sucking mud as well. She lost her other slipper but not her balance. Then she stood there, barefoot on the last step, and looked around.

"Well this is a Goddess damned mess," Saber muttered behind her. "Now what?"

As if in answer to his question, a large male with a bald head and broad, bare shoulders came slogging around the side of the ship to stand in front of them.

"Oh, hello," Lissa said uncertainly, taken aback.

"Little mistress," he muttered, bowing deeply. "I am Llewelyn, body-slave to Lady Sha'rak the cultural ambassador of Yonnie Six."

"Well, it's very nice to meet you. I—" Lissa began but the slave ignored her and unrolled a long, thin metal parchment, which he held it out in front of him. Just as Lissa was wondering what in the universe he could be doing, the shiny surface of the metal flickered and an image of a beautiful woman who looked to be in her early forties appeared on it. She had silvery blonde hair with blue streaks in every shade from the palest powder blue to deep indigo running through it. The shimmering mass was swept up into an impossible swirl atop her head that looked like it must have taken hours to achieve.

"Lady R'awr? Can you hear me?" the woman on the parchment asked.

"I can." Lissa leaned forward, being careful not to fall in the mud. "Um, thank you for coming to greet us," she said.

"Think nothing of it, my dear. I greet all the new arrivals of distinction and rank." Lady Sha'rak smiled in a friendly way. "So you've come all the way from Zetta Prime, have you? Is the purpose of your visit for business or pleasure?"

"Oh, pleasure of course," Lissa answered quickly. "We, uh, I mean, I, simply wanted to see the sights of Opulex with my own eyes. I've heard how, um, how very beautiful it is all my life." She hoped her lie wouldn't be too apparent—honestly, as far as she could tell this was one of the ugliest places in the universe. But maybe the city itself was nicer once you got inside it—she hoped anyway.

"You have? Really?" The ambassador laughed. "Oh my poor, innocent dear. I'm afraid you have much to learn. But what we lack in beauty in Opulex, we certainly make up for in *sensation*. I'm sure you know what I mean." She winked at Lissa who smiled weakly back.

"Um, of course," she said uncertainly.

"I can see you have *no* idea. But that's all right—you'll soon find out." Lady Sha'rak laughed again and then looked at Lissa more closely. "You know, I had some R'awrs in my own family tree—

way back several generations ago. Do you think we might be related?"

"It's possible, I suppose," Lissa said cautiously. "I would certainly be honored if we were."

"How sweet." Lady Sha'rak nodded. "Well then, why don't you come across the trench so I can greet you in person?"

"I'd love to," Lissa said. "But, well...how? I just took a single step in the mud and it sucked off both my shoes. I'm not sure I'll be fit to be seen if I have to go much farther."

"Have your body-slave carry you, of course." The ambassador sounded a touch impatient. "My man, Llewelyn can provide him with mud-waders. He'll lead you to the trench crossing and bring you safely to my home. Don't worry," she added, perhaps seeing the uncertain look on Lissa's face. "He's trustworthy, even without a leash—I've had him since I was sixteen."

"Oh...of course." Lissa nodded. "I, uh, wasn't worried about that." What she'd been worried about was being carried in Saber's arms. But there didn't seem to be much she could do about it at the moment.

"Well, you *should* be." Lady Sha'rak's indigo eyes widened. "After all, we all know what filthy beasts males can be if not properly trained and controlled." Her eyes flicked to Saber, standing protectively behind Lissa. "Speaking of which, that brute of yours is positively *huge*. I assume he's thoroughly broken?"

"Of course." Reaching behind her, Lissa grabbed the black leather leash attached to Saber's collar. "He's um, completely in control. I mean," she went on hastily. "*I* am in complete control of *him*. He's not a threat."

"Well..." Ambassador Sha'rak frowned hesitantly. "All right. If you *say* so. I just can't have any unbroken males in my house."

Behind her, Lissa could hear a faint, barely noticeable growl coming from her kinsman's throat. She hoped the Yonnite Ambassador couldn't hear it. "Saber is completely trained, I assure you," she said, giving a tiny tug on the leash. Abruptly, the growling stopped.

"Very well." Lady Sha'rak nodded regally. "You may come. I'll see you in my house at ten past the hour *exactly*. Oh, and don't worry about your shoes, my dear. We can always get you another pair."

She nodded once more and the metal parchment went suddenly blank. Lady Sha'rak's body-slave, Llewelyn, stowed the parchment in the pack on his back and pulled out a pair of oversized, high black boots which he thrust at Saber.

"Put them on. Next transport leaves in ten," he grunted.

Saber took the boots stiffly and pulled them on over his own. When he was finished, he stood up and stepped down into the mud. "Now where?" he asked the body-slave.

"This way." Llewelyn jerked his bald, gleaming head. "Bring your mistress and keep up. If we're late, my lady will give me the pain-taste. I don't fucking like that."

"Of course." Saber turned to her and held out his arms. "Mistress?" he murmured, gazing up at her.

Lissa looked at him uncertainly but the taciturn Llewelyn was already slogging through the mud, yards ahead of them. There was no time to be squeamish or embarrassed. Not if they wanted to get to the ambassador's house on time. Mutely, she leaned forward, allowing Saber to scoop her into his arms.

He held her carefully, like a baby, as he made his way through the squelching mud. For her part, Lissa tried to stay stiff in his arms and to keep their contact to a minimum. It was exhausting to be so rigid—it would have been much easier to just let herself melt against him and relax but Lissa was afraid to do that. Afraid of what Saber might think of her and afraid of the feelings that might rise and drown her if she allowed herself even the tiniest bit of flexibility. So she did her best impression of a stiff, inflexible stick as he carried her until they reached the side of an enormous trench.

"Oh," Lissa murmured in awe. The trench was more like a canyon—its crumbling, lipless mouth gaping hungrily in a vast yawn that threatened to swallow them whole with one misstep.

"This way," Llewelyn muttered, jerking his head. "In here."

Lissa looked where he was pointing and her stomach dropped down to her toes. "In here," appeared to refer to a small cart with two long seats—one in front and one in the back. They were separated by a narrow metal tongue which divided the topless cart into two compartments—neither of which looked safe.

Even more dangerous appearing, however, was the track the cart ran on. It was a thin, spindly bridge that looked no more substantial than a spider web as it crossed the cavernous trench.

"In here," Llewelyn repeated impatiently. "My lady is expecting you, mistress."

"Oh. Of course." Lissa nodded. "But...are you quite certain it's safe?"

"'Course it is. Travelers to the city always come this way. We don't lose more than two or three a cycle."

"Really?" Lissa felt her throat get tighter. She had never much minded heights on First World—there, near the holy mountain which was the center of the Goddess's power, she was able to manipulate the sand to bear her up so she didn't need to fear falling. Here, however, she was far from her power source. She doubted she could lift a single grain of dirt from the ground, let alone summon enough to provide a cushion if they fell into the ominous trench.

"Nah, not really." Llewelyn's grim face broke into a smile. "That was a joke."

"Not a very funny one." Saber, who had clearly picked up on her fear, scowled at the other male. "If you frighten my mistress with your talk, you'll have *me* to answer to. Is the cart safe or not?"

"Perfectly safe," the body-slave muttered sullenly. "There's a force field all around it to cushion any blows and keep it from collapsing. They just make it *seem* dangerous to discourage anyone who isn't serious about coming into the city."

"Well, we're serious. *Very* serious." Lissa took a deep breath. "So let's get in."

"Very well." Saber was still frowning but he settled her carefully in the front of the cart. Then, after stripping off the muddy boots and giving them back to Llewelyn, he climbed in the compartment behind her.

"Hey, that's where *I* ride," the body-slave complained. "There's only one cart. Unless you want me to sit with your mistress?" He raised his eyebrows at Saber who shook his head quickly.

"Of course not." He moved up to sit behind Lissa who was forced to get as close to the front edge of the metal cart as she could. It wasn't very comfortable because the cart was small and Saber was large. She could feel the heat of his big body branding her mostly-bare back. With a flash of embarrassment, she hoped he wasn't looking at the nonexistent back of her dress.

"All right now." Llewelyn climbed in behind them and did something to a set of recessed buttons on the side of the cart. "Hang on," he muttered. "It's a bumpy ride."

Lissa gripped the metal edge of the cart, feeling it bite into her hands roughly. The metal was chipped and peeling, sharp enough to cut flesh in some places, but she didn't care. She wanted something to hold on to if she had to cross this vast divide. *You could hold on to Saber,* whispered a little voice in her head. *Even though he promised not to touch you, I'm sure he wouldn't mind.*

Yes, but *Lissa* would mind. Sternly, she told herself to keep her grip on the cart and not be a coward. *I'll just look straight ahead and it will be over in no t –*

Suddenly, with a squealing of rusty hinges, the cart jolted forward over the thin, spindly bridge and she had to bite back a gasp. Oh Goddess, they were actually going to do this! They were actually going to roll across the yawning void with nothing between them and death but a cobweb-thin bridge and a rickety cart.

"Close your eyes if you want," Llewelyn said from behind them. "The view doesn't get any better."

Lissa wanted to close her eyes but somehow she just couldn't. They were rolling out across the trench now and her eyes were glued to its steep sides. *Don't look down,* she commanded herself as she tried to measure the distance between the cart and the far end of the trench. *Whatever you do, just don't look down.*

To distract herself from the awful temptation of staring into the abyss, she tried to concentrate on other things. There wasn't much to see in the murky half-light of Yonnie Six and there was nothing to listen to but the squeal of the cart's wheels and the soft, even sound of Saber's breathing behind her. But there was something else – something Lissa hadn't expected. A smell – a warm, delicious scent seemed to be rising up out of the cavernous trench. It was almost indescribable – like a mixture of fresh baked bread, exotic spices, and an undertone of warm, animal musk. The closer they got to the middle of the great divide, the stronger it grew until it was almost overpowering.

The scent made Lissa feel strangely dizzy and it seemed to form pictures in her mind. She began daydreaming about what it would be like to lean back and rest against Saber just as she had wanted to earlier. The image was so real, so incredibly vivid, she could almost feel the skin of his broad, bare chest against her back and his strong arms surrounding her. He would kiss the side of her neck, nuzzling her just under the ear while his hands found the front of her dress and pulled it apart to cup her breasts...

No, what's wrong with me? Lissa shook her head, trying to clear it of the forbidden vision. But it was strangely vivid and hard to get rid of. What was going on?

"Mind the Dream Gas," Llewelyn said, as if in answer to her question. "It's particularly strong here near the middle of the trench."

"Dream gas?" Lissa asked, shaking her head again. "What's that?"

"That, my lady, is the byproduct of the strip mining we do here on Yonnie Six. It's harmless in small doses and it brings fantasies to life—at least in your mind."

"What kind of fantasies?" Saber sounded as uncomfortable as Lissa felt.

"*All* kinds of fantasizes." Llewelyn sounded like he might be laughing at them. "Why, friend, are you having images of your mistress?"

"Of course not!" Saber's voice was sharp. "She is my mistress, I would never—"

"There's no shame in it. A slave that doesn't love his mistress enough to have visions of her is no slave at all," Llewelyn said. "I've been with my lady since her sixteenth birthday and I still want her. When she lets me service her…or when she takes the rod to my ass and punishes me—" He broke off abruptly, as though realizing he was saying too much. "Forgive me. The gas makes you talkative. It's one of the side effects."

"*One* of the side effects?" Lissa asked in a trembling voice. "What are the others?"

"Well, there's—"

The cart lurched suddenly, tilting dangerously to one side. Lissa felt herself tilting right along with it and suddenly she found herself staring into the abyss. The distant ground was so far below she couldn't make out any details but it was horrible just the same. *Where's the force field he talked about?* she thought, gripping the sides of the cart so hard she felt the jagged metal gouge the soft skin of her palms. Panic rose in her throat to choke her. *Where is it? Why isn't it stopping me from falling? Why —*

"Goddess!" Saber grated behind her. One muscular arm reached around her waist and drew her close to him while the other shot out to brace against the side of the cart. The next minute, the cart had righted itself and was speeding along the narrow bridge again but he didn't let her go.

"Sorry." Llewelyn didn't sound the least bit repentant or worried. "Must have hit a pebble on the track. It happens sometimes."

"It had better not happen again or you'll pay for it." Saber's growling voice seemed to thrum through Lissa's entire body. "By the Goddess, you'll pay until you can't pay anymore."

"Touchy, aren't you?" The body-slave still sounded completely unperturbed. "Don't worry, your precious mistress will reach the other side all right. Only the ones my lady doesn't care for get dumped and I think she's taken a little shine to yours."

Lissa felt her heart go cold despite the warmth of Saber's encircling arm. Dumped? Did they actually use this horrible cart contraption to get rid of unwanted visitors? Or was it another one of Llewelyn's morbid jokes?

Before she could come to a conclusion, the cart reached the other side of the trench. Mercifully, their ride was over. But as they turned away from the cart and followed Llewelyn to a hovercar parked on the other side, all Lissa could think was that they would have to go back this way as well. It was, after all, the only way back to their ship and off planet.

She had better take care to stay on the ambassador's good side, she decided with a shiver. Very good care indeed.

Chapter Six

The hovercar ride was uneventful, much to Saber's relief. He was still in a rage about what had happened—or almost happened—during their ride across the trench. He wanted to pound the ambassador's body-slave to bloody sludge for daring to frighten Lissa so but he knew he couldn't.

It was clear how important it was to Lady Sha'rak that a male be properly "trained and broken". If he decided to beat up her body-slave, it would only make her think he was wild and unmanageable—a danger that had to be removed. And if he was taken from Lissa's side, how could he possibly defend her? No, he would have to bear it. But he promised himself it would be the last insult he allowed anyone to pay Lissa. She was his to protect and defend and he intended to do that no matter what obstacles stood in his way.

Even more disturbing than the near accident and Lleweyln's implied insult, however, were the effects of the Dream Gas. The body-slave had been right about the visions that rose before Saber's eyes as they traveled over the trench. He had seen himself holding Lissa in his arms, touching her, kissing her...and it had been so *real.* So real he could almost see himself doing it—could feel the silky touch of Lissa's body, taste her salty-sweet skin, smell her warm, feminine scent as she moaned in his arms and gave herself to him. The vision had been so strong it was more like a hallucination—no, more even than that. It was like an out-of-the-body experience in which he could see himself doing things but couldn't stop.

It was strange and troubling to feel so out of control of his actions, to be unable to suppress his hidden desires. Saber shook his head. He hoped fervently that their ride over the trench would be their first and last encounter with the strange Dream Gas.

"We're almost there." Llewelyn's dry voice interrupted his inner musings. "We're late, though. My mistress will be most displeased with me." He indicated the chronometer at the front of the hovercar, which stood at fifteen past. His rough voice sounded angry, as though the lateness was their fault.

"Oh, I'm sorry," Lissa said at once. "We should have hurried more, Llewelyn. I hope you won't get into too much trouble."

The ambassador's body-slave cast a surprised glance over his shoulder. "Oh no, little mistress—the fault is mine. And even if it wasn't, a female never begs the pardon of a male. At least, not here on Yonnie Six." He raised an eyebrow at her. "But perhaps you do things differently on Zetta Prime?"

"Of course not." Lissa's pale face went red. "I, uh, I just mean I don't want to upset the ambassador."

"Never fear about that," Llewelyn said darkly, facing front again. "It's not *you* Lady Sha'rak will be upset with."

"I see," Lissa mumbled and sat back in her seat. She shot Saber a quick, uncertain glance and then looked down at her hands. But though she had barely looked at him, he had read the fear and self-doubt in her lovely eyes. She was worried about betraying their true identities—what Kat had called "blowing their cover"—by her unconventional actions and words. He wished fiercely that he dared to hold her hand. He wanted to entwine his fingers with hers and give her a reassuring squeeze. Wanted to send her some signal that everything would be all right. But of course, that was impossible. He had to keep his distance.

With a sigh, he stared out the window at the busy streets of Opulex whizzing by. They appeared to be moving through an incredibly crowded urban area. Tall buildings stood shoulder to shoulder with scarcely any space between them, their long shadows casting the city into gloom. Or they would have, if every available surface wasn't covered in glowing signs. Saber saw every imaginable service and product being offered for sale, including several that were considered illegal, immoral, and impossible on his home world. *Body Modification,* read one glowing sign. *Make your mistress proud.* Another proclaimed, *Need more to satisfy her? We can give you three extra inches and girth to match. Low cost, minimal pain.*

Other, similar signs sped past in a blur of light until Saber stopped trying to read them. Instead, he concentrated on the pedestrians he saw on the broad sidewalks. There were many richly dressed females, always accompanied by at least one and often several body-slaves. The males were dressed as he was, with tight black pants and bare chests. Most of them wore collars and leashes around their necks although a few had some other device that resembled a spiked necklace with glowing purple lights instead.

For some reason the body-slaves wearing these odd necklaces followed even closer to their mistresses and appeared even more abjectly humble than the ones wearing leashes. Saber didn't know why but the sight made the pit of his stomach cold. What in the seven hells was going on in this Goddess forsaken city?

Before he could get an answer to his question, Llewelyn turned the hovercar sharply and aimed right for the side of one of the huge buildings. Saber threw a protective arm across Lissa, a shout rising in his throat. But just at the last moment, part of the mirrored side of the building rose, creating a gap just big enough for the car to pass through.

"Thought I was going to ram it, didn't you?" The body-slave threw a sardonic glance over his shoulder as they drove in and the building shut behind them. "Not a chance. My lady will punish me for getting you here late but that's nothing to what she'd do if I wrecked her precious hovercar."

Saber frowned, a growl rising in his throat. He liked the ambassador's body-slave less and less and his urge to pound the insolent male was growing by the minute. It was an urge he reined in with effort—he hadn't spent years perfecting his self-control to lose it with this imbecile.

"Um…Saber?" Lissa's voice was slightly breathless and he became aware that his arm was still thrown protectively across her, pressing against the soft mounds of her breasts. In fact, one side of her dress had slipped open and the creamy curve of her right breast and the pink point of her nipple had popped into view.

Goddess! The sight made Saber instantly hard.

"Forgive me." He pulled his arm back as though he'd been stung. "I was just trying…I mean, I thought we were going to crash."

"Of course." Her face was red as she adjusted her dress and Saber thought his own must be as well.

Llewelyn turned his head and gave them both a curious gaze. "Are the both of you well?" He frowned at Saber. "You act like you've never touched your mistress before. Don't you service her on a regular basis?"

Saber cleared his throat. "Of course I do. I mean—"

"We're here," the body-slave interrupted, pulling the long black hovercar into an empty spot by a bank of elevators. "Come on, we need to get you up to my mistress's floor at once. We're late enough as it is."

He jumped out of the car and held the door for Saber and Lissa. Saber climbed out first and held out a hand to Lissa. After a long moment of hesitation, which caused Llewelyn to look at them oddly, she took it and allowed him to help her out.

"Should I carry you, mistress?" Saber asked stiffly. "Your feet are bare and the pavement may be rough." He indicated the gray tarmac beneath his feet.

Lissa went red again. "I, uh, no thank you, Saber. It's not far to the elevators." She glanced at Llewelyn. "Um, if that's where we're going?"

He nodded proudly. "Of course. My lady owns the entire top floor of this building—which isn't something many can say." He frowned. "But you really should let your body-slave carry you, little mistress. It isn't proper for a lady of your rank and distinction to let her bare feet touch the floor."

"Oh, is that the custom here?" Lissa asked nervously. "It's, uh, different on Zetta Prime. We go barefoot there all the time."

Llewelyn's eyebrows shot up. "Really? That's not what I've heard." He frowned. "Do you not enjoy your slave's touch? If he isn't to your liking, I'm sure my mistress can assign one of her own lesser body-slaves to you while you're here. She won't mind—she has dozens."

"No!" Lissa went pale. "I mean, no thank you. Please don't mention any such idea to her. I…I want no other male to touch me but Saber."

"Really? You could have fooled me—you jump a mile every time he lays a hand on you." He bowed. "If you'll forgive me for saying so, little mistress."

"I…um…" It was clear Lissa was at a loss for what to say. Saber wanted to help her but he couldn't think of any plausible explanation to give for why he and Lissa jumped like they'd been burned the moment they touched either.

We're not doing a very good job of this so far, he thought grimly. *If we can't even fool a body-slave, how are we going to fool the ambassador herself or any of the other important collectors we have to approach to find the missing scrolls? We have to start acting our parts much better than we have been if we want to escape detection and get what we came for.*

Wordlessly, he scooped Lissa into his arms and, to her credit, she didn't protest. But she didn't give any indication of enjoying his touch either. Instead, she went completely rigid, just as she had when he carried her through the mud. It hurt Saber's heart to see the frozen expression on her face and feel the tension in her slender body as he held her. Just once he wished he could feel her relax in his arms, just once he wished to see pleasure in her face when he touched her, not fear.

Forget it, he told himself roughly. *It's not going to happen.* Still, she needed to loosen up a little if they were going to get through this ruse intact. Saber resolved to talk to her about it later when they had some privacy — whenever that might be.

* * * * *

Lissa held herself stiff as Saber carried her toward the bank of elevators. She knew what they were, from talking to her Earth friends, though the idea of a small box that took one from floor to floor had been a foreign one back when she lived on First World. This would be her first ride in one, however, and she was anxious to see what it was like. Maybe the sensation of being magically lifted into the air would take her mind off the feeling of Saber's warm arms around her. It was hard to be so close to him and not let herself react but she forced herself to stay rigid.

The golden doors slid open, revealing a plush, pink lined box that reminded Lissa of the inside of a box of fancy chocolates. Kat had shared some of the Earth treats with her—just the memory made her mouth water.

Llewelyn went in first and held the doors open so that Saber could carry her in. He entered silently, being careful not to bump her head, and then stood stolidly as the ambassador's body-slave pressed one of the buttons.

The elevator rose quickly with a soft humming sound and, almost before Lissa knew it, the shiny gold doors were sliding open again to reveal a richly appointed entry hall.

"This way," Llewelyn led the way down the hallway, which was lined with holo-portraits of formidable looking females. Each of the females were wearing elegant but revealing outfits and their eyes seemed to follow Lissa down the hall, staring in mute accusation.

We see through you, they seemed to whisper. *We know what you truly are...a fake. A fraud. An imposter. You don't belong here. Leave while you still can...*

Stop it! Lissa shivered and turned away.

"Are you all right, *amalla?*" Saber murmured under his breath. "You seem upset."

"I'm fine." Lissa risked a glance up at him but seeing his changeable hazel eyes, so filled with concern, was too much for her and she had to look away again. "Fine," she repeated, wishing it was true.

At last they reached the end of the hallway and Llewelyn threw open a pair of tall wooden doors, carved with strange alien faces. Beyond the doors was a room filled with billowing silk curtains in every shade of blue.

Just like the streaks in the ambassador's hair, Lissa thought. And just as she did, the curtains parted enough for her to see Ambassador Sha'rak herself standing at the center of the room.

"My Lady Sha'rak, ambassador of Yonnie Six, owner of the top floor of the Barad building and favorite of the Empress Kallis," Llewelyn intoned gravely, making a sweeping gesture toward her.

"Welcome." The ambassador smiled sweetly and waited while Saber made his way through the billowing silk panels to stand in front of her, still holding Lissa. "It's lovely to have you here in my home," she added, smiling at Lissa and ignoring Saber completely.

"Oh, uh, thank you." Lissa struggled a little. "Put me down," she whispered to Saber.

He frowned. "I should hold you. Your feet will get cold."

"No, put me *down,*" Lissa insisted in an undertone.

"Very well." Reluctantly, she thought, he sat her on her feet. "My lady." Lissa made a deep obeisance. "It's very kind of you to receive me into your home. I am eternally grateful for your benevolence."

"What lovely manners." The ambassador beamed at her, her sharp eyes flicking over Lissa, taking her in from her bare feet to the shining mirror-mere dagger strapped to her waist. "I'm delighted to meet you in person, my dear. Tell me, where are you staying while you're here in Opulex?"

"Oh, I hadn't really thought..." Lissa was caught off guard. "I suppose we thought we'd just find a lodging house."

"We?" The ambassador raised one elegant blue eyebrow. "Do you have another person with you?"

"Oh, well yes." Lissa felt her cheeks get hot as she nodded at her kinsman. "I just meant, you know, Saber and I."

Lady Sha'rak frowned. "You consider your body-slave a *person*? How very singular."

"Well, I mean..." Lissa grasped hastily for an explanation. "I've had him since my...my twelfth birthday, you know," she said at last. "So he's...almost part of the family."

The ambassador shook her head and made a disapproving *tsking* sound. "I can see you're much too kindhearted with your slaves, my dear. You ought to remember that no matter how fond we get of them, males are still just animals. Animals that need to be trained and kept in check. Speaking of which, will you excuse me just for a moment?"

"Oh, um, of course." Lissa backed up a step uncertainly, wondering what the ambassador was going to do.

The welcoming smile on Lady Sha'rak's face faded into a disapproving frown and she pointed at Llewelyn, who had been standing silently behind Saber. "You. Llewelyn."

"Yes, Mistress?" The body-slave came forward at once. To Lissa's surprise, Lady Sha'rak drew back and slapped him hard across the face with no warning.

Smack The flat sound of her dainty hand connecting with his hard jaw made Lissa jump. From the corner of her eye, she saw Saber's hazel eyes widen—obviously he was surprised as well. She half expected the body-slave to retaliate in some way—if not with actions then at least with angry words. Instead, he fell to his knees at his mistress's feet.

Lady Sha'rak put one dainty slipper out from under her stiff skirts and Llewelyn leaned humbly down to kiss it. "Mistress," he murmured, sitting up and rubbing his red cheek against her thigh.

"Never mind your groveling." The ambassador sounded impatient. "What time did I say I wanted to see Lady R'awr here in my dwelling?"

"At exactly ten past the hour, my lady." The body-slave spoke impassively, as though he expected to be punished and was prepared to endure his sentence without comment or complaint.

"And what time was it when you actually entered my greeting salon?" she continued.

"Twenty past the hour, Mistress."

"Making you late—as always." The ambassador glared down at him. Though her body-slave was huge compared to her petite form, it was clear she had no fear of him. "You know what follows, Llewelyn. I must give you the pain-taste. Are you prepared to take your punishment?"

"I am." He nodded stolidly.

"Very well." Stepping back, Ambassador Sha'rak pulled apart the top of the deep blue dress she was wearing. It parted easily, baring her breasts which were full and thrusting.

Lissa gasped and immediately averted her eyes but not before she noticed something very peculiar—one of the ambassador's nipples was bright ruby red and the other was a cool sapphire blue.

"It's all right, Lady R'awr," the ambassador said, forcing Lissa to glance up again. "Llewelyn needs others to witness his shame. Please *do* watch as I punish him."

"Oh, right. Thank you," Lissa said faintly. "I, uh, that's very kind of you."

"Think nothing of it." Lady Sha'rak nodded magnanimously and then beckoned to her body-slave again. "Come, Llewelyn, take your punishment."

The big slave sat up straight and silent, still on his knees before his mistress. She leaned forward slightly, allowing him to take the nipple which was painted bright red between his lips.

At once, Llewelyn's eyes began to water and his face went dark with obvious pain. But he didn't pull away. Instead, he continued to suck his mistress's nipple, slowly caressing it with his tongue and lapping gently at the tender bud as she purred in pleasure and stroked his bald head.

It seemed to go on forever and Lissa forced herself to watch though she felt like her face was on fire. She'd studied the Yonnite culture before coming here but nowhere in the literature had she read anything about this strange punishment. How long was this going to continue? Watching something so intimate, especially with Saber right behind her, also watching, made her feel squirmy and hot with embarrassment. Goddess, if only it would end…

"Well, well…enough, Llewelyn," the ambassador said at last, sounding rather breathless. "You may have the sweet-taste now, to ease your pain."

At once her body-slave released the red nipple—which was now a normal pale pink color, Lissa saw—and sucked his mistress's other nipple, the blue one, between his lips.

Immediately his face cleared and his eyes stopped streaming tears of pain. He took the second nipple in the same, unhurried fashion he had the first, lapping gently to begin with and then sucking deeply, to take as much as his mistress's breast into his mouth as he could at once.

Lady Sha'rak's breath was definitely coming faster now and she was pressing herself against her slave's mouth, clearly enjoying this part of the punishment as much as he was. To her mortification, Lissa saw that a thick bulge was growing inside Llewelyn's tight black pants. She couldn't help thinking how he'd admitted to wanting his mistress — to fantasizing about her and loving it when she let her service him. *I think I can guess exactly what kind of "service" he performs for her,* she thought uncomfortably and then tried to banish the thought as the performance went on and on.

Finally, just as Lissa felt she might sink through the floor in mortal embarrassment, the ambassador tapped Llewelyn's bald head and murmured, "Enough."

Reluctantly, the big slave released her second nipple, which was also now a pale pink in color, and sat back on his haunches. "Thank you, Mistress," he said, his deep voice husky with lust. "For correcting me."

"Yes, well..." The ambassador straightened up and pulled her dress closed. "You always *do* seem to need extra correction, Llewelyn. Just remember to be on time in the future. If you're late again, I'll have to use the rod on you instead of the pain-taste."

Llewelyn's dark eyes flashed but he only nodded impassively. "Yes, my lady."

"Very good." Ambassador Sha'rak cleared her throat and looked at Lissa. "Now where were we? Ah yes — I was asking where you were staying."

"Just at a lodging house — if you'd be so kind as to recommend one?" Lissa said hesitantly.

"Nonsense, my dear." The ambassador laughed. "I can't let you stay in some pokey little dump when you might be a distant relation! Besides, I can see how *innocent* you are, especially when it comes to our ways here on Yonnie Six. You must stay here with me."

"Oh, you're too kind!" Lissa exclaimed with real enthusiasm. "I accept your offer with all my heart, Lady Sha'rak." She could scarcely contain her excitement. Staying here with the ambassador would enable them to search her house — or floor — much more easily. And Lissa was sure that with such a distinguished person as their host, she and Saber would be invited to all the best parties. An introduction to the other collectors on her list was practically assured, and all because the ambassador liked her!

This is too easy, she thought exultantly. *Why, we'll find the scrolls and be back home before the solar week is out!*

But Ambassador Sha'rak's next words brought her crashing abruptly back down to reality.

"I'm so glad you've accepted," she said, smiling fondly at Lissa. "Because I really want to take you under my wing, so to speak. It's clear you don't know the first thing about disciplining a body-slave and *I* am the one to teach you."

"Oh, er, well…" Lissa swallowed hard, trying to think of a way to refuse without hurting her new hostess's feelings. "Actually, since I've had Saber for so long he's, uh, he's really no trouble at all," she said. "I mean, he's always so good and obedient I never have to do a thing to…to make him mind."

"Is that so?" Lady Sha'rak's elegant blue eyebrows shot up in surprise. "What about the way he refused to put you down earlier, as soon as you commanded him to? A slave should obey his mistress's every order *at once.* Also, when he finally *did* comply with your order, he just stood there. Not once did he bend to kiss your foot."

"Well, my feet are dirty right now from going barefoot," Lissa faltered. "And we don't really…do that so much on Zetta Prime anymore."

"Oh? You don't require your body-slaves to make a proper obeisance? How strange." Lady Sha'rak frowned. "Well, what about the way he stood there and met my eyes so boldly when you were first introduced? A proper body-slave doesn't make eye contact with a female—especially a high ranking one his mistress is meeting for the first time."

"Oh, I..." Lissa wasn't sure what to say. "I had no idea he was, uh, looking at you," she said, though she couldn't help feeling like the Yonnite ambassador was nit-picking. "Forgive me, my lady."

"I will forgive you with all my heart," Lady Sha'rak said magnanimously. "As long as you promise to let me guide you and teach you the proper way to train a male. After all, you can hardly go out in polite society until you've learned, and being the ambassador I have to attend *lots* of parties. I want to be able to take you with me."

"I see." It was exactly what Lissa had been hoping for—the party part where she got to meet lots of influential Yonnites who might have the missing scrolls, that was. The part where she had to pretend to let Ambassador Sha'rak teach her to train Saber *wasn't* so good. But she didn't know what else to do.

Forgive me, Saber, she thought, risking a glance behind her at her kinsman. He looked back at her, his face as impassive as Llewelyn's had been while receiving his punishment. But Lissa thought she saw a spark somewhere deep down in those green and gold flecked eyes. Feeling a deep sense of misgiving, she turned to the ambassador and tried to smile.

"I'd be honored to take instruction from you, my lady."

"Excellent!" The ambassador smiled. "Well then, first things first. I saw how confused my display of the pain-taste and the sweet-taste made you. Have you never seen such before?"

"No, never," Lissa answered truthfully. "It, uh, is not the fashion on Zetta Prime at the moment."

"So strange." The ambassador frowned. "They usually follow us so closely. But then, I suppose you have other things to keep you occupied." She smiled at Lissa. "Here, let me get you a starter kit."

As if on cue, Llewelyn held out a little brown leather case worked all over with golden embroidery. Lissa took it and looked at it uncertainly.

"Well, go on—open it!" Lady Sha'rak sounded excited, as though she'd just given Lissa a particularly nice present.

"All right." Lissa opened the case. Inside was a tiny red bottle, a tiny blue bottle, and a small pot of what appeared to be some kind of salve.

"Do be careful with that," the ambassador said anxiously when Lissa pulled out the red bottle to look at it. "It's extracted from the burning blossom—one of the hottest substances in the known universe. You put it on your right nipple—only and always your right, you know for that is the custom—and make your slave suck it off, as I did to Llewelyn, if he displeases you."

"And this one?" Lissa lifted the blue bottle.

"The antidote to the burning blossom extract, of course. It has numbing and cooling agents as well as a very pleasant, sweet taste. It can be used to cool your slave's mouth after a punishment, or as a reward for when he pleases you." Lady Sha'rak smiled. "I don't give rewards very often though—pain is a much more effective motivator, you know."

"Of course," Lissa said faintly. "But..." She looked apprehensively at the red bottle again. "If this is one of the hottest things in the universe and you expect me to put it on my..." She cleared her throat. "In such a sensitive area. I don't see..."

"Oh, that's what the pot of soothing salve is for." The ambassador nodded to the little pot. "You must coat your nipples with it thoroughly first and only then can you apply the two elixirs. Both of them *must* be licked directly off the skin to be effective. Be very careful when you're putting on the burning blossom extract though—if it gets on your bare skin it burns like fire and even the antidote won't help. It can only be dissolved by saliva."

"I see..." Lissa nodded. Inside she was thinking there was *no way* she was ever going to wear this stuff. Or even if she did, there was no possible way she'd use it. Just the idea of letting Saber suck the various "elixirs" from such an intimate part of her body made her feel like sinking through the floor in embarrassment.

"I'm glad you get the idea." Lady Sha'rak smiled. "And don't forget that you must wear it every day. You must not leave your rooms without a prompt and effective way to discipline your slave."

Lissa had a disturbing thought. "But what about when I retire to my rooms and I want to take it off? If it can only be dissolved by, uh, saliva..."

"Oh, that's only if it gets on your *bare skin*. I'll send a bottle of the solvent to your rooms so you can remove the extracts at the end of the night. Provided you put the soothing salve on first, you should have no trouble." The ambassador smiled and patted her shoulder. "Of course, that's assuming you haven't already had them removed by your slave. And we know how very unlikely *that* is. Males need *constant* discipline." She gave a light laugh as though correcting a slave through the use of painful chemical agents licked off an intimate part of one's anatomy was entirely normal.

Which it probably is here on Yonnie Six, Lissa thought unhappily. Aloud she only said, "Thank you, my Lady."

The ambassador nodded. "You're very welcome. Now then, it's almost time for dinner so I'll send you to your rooms to get ready."

"Oh…dinner?" Lissa had never felt less hungry in her life. She wondered if there was any way she could beg off and get their host to excuse them. But Lady Sha'rak's next words crushed her hopes.

"It's just a small gathering tonight, myself and Lady Pope'nose. I'll be so excited to introduce my long lost distant cousin from Zetta Prime to her."

"Oh, thank you. It's very kind of you to claim me as a relation," Lissa said tentatively. "But I was just wondering, well, we've had such a long journey…"

"Oh, you must be tired, you poor thing." Lady Sha'rak patted her shoulder again. "Of course, I didn't even consider that! How dreadfully rude of me." She sighed. "Ah, Lady Pope'nose will be so disappointed. Well, maybe you can meet her later. She's a dear friend and quite important in the cultural world—one of the foremost collectors of antiquities on the planet."

At this, Lissa's ears pricked up. "Um, antiquities did you say?"

"Why yes, that's how I met her, you know. I dabble in them myself just a bit. Of course my collection isn't as large and extensive as Lady Pope'nose's but I do all right for myself." Lady Sha'rak laughed modestly.

"Since you know so much about antiquities, I wonder if you might have anything from the Hoard Wars in your collection?" Lissa asked, deciding to take a chance.

"The Hoard Wars?" The ambassador frowned suspiciously. "Those are rare and valuable items indeed. Why do you ask?"

"Um, my family has some interest—it was my father's special area of expertise. In fact," Lissa added, with sudden inspiration. "This is one of the pieces he collected before he died." She patted the mirror-mere dagger at her side and smiled. "We think it dates from First World around a thousand years ago."

"Oh, indeed?" Lady Sha'rak's eyes flitted hungrily to the dagger and then away again. "Well, I'm afraid I don't have anything from that era but Lady Pope'nose might. Though she doesn't collect objects so much as written or recorded records. They're so much more useful in sensation play."

"Oh, of course," Lissa said blankly. She had no idea what sensation play was, but it was sounding more and more like Lady Pope'nose was the person to start with when searching for the missing scrolls.

The ambassador laughed. "I can see you have no idea what I'm talking about—how could you, though? I'm sure you don't have Dream Gas on Zetta Prime. It's only found here on Yonnie Six."

"Oh yes, Dream Gas." Lissa's heart was suddenly pounding as she recalled the extremely vivid hallucinations she'd had while crossing the trench. They had been positively indecent. "We... I mean *I* experienced that for the first time on the way here."

"Exciting, isn't it?" Lady Sha'rak's eyes gleamed. "And it's so much better when combined with the right medium. I'll show you but not tonight—we're having a big Dream Gas party tomorrow and I want my synapses to be fresh. Of course you'll be attending as well. Oh, it's so exciting!" She gave Lissa a quick hug. "I'm so glad you're here, my dear. I *do* love company."

"I'm glad to be here too." Lissa smiled, hoping she sounded sincere. "And, well, I think I'm feeling better now. Not so tired. I'd like to accept your invitation to dinner after all and meet Lady Pope'nose. She sounds like a wonderful person."

"Oh, she *is*." The ambassador beamed. "I'm so glad you're coming. Well, now..." She straightened up. "We have about an hour to prepare. Just enough time to get yourself serviced if you like and dressed." She put a hand on Lissa's arm. "Don't wear anything too fancy now. Remember, it's just a little informal get together."

"All right," Lissa said, wondering what she was going to wear. *All* the dresses Kat had packed her seemed formal to her. She supposed she'd just close her eyes and pick one.

"Very good then," Lady Sha'rak said. "Llewelyn," she said, motioning to her body-slave. "Take Lady R'awr to the red guest suite and then come to my chambers and service me. And *hurry* or I swear I'll take the rod to you!"

Llewelyn's dark eyes flashed. "Is that a promise, my lady?"

"Why you insolent...I ought to fit you for a collar right now, today!" the ambassador snapped.

"Yes, my lady." Llewelyn murmured. "You always say that. And yet I've no collar on yet."

Lissa looked at him, confused. He was wearing the same close fitting black collar that Saber had on. What was the ambassador talking about?

"That tears it!" Lady Sha'rak looked really angry now. "As soon as you show Lady R'awr to her room report to me and assume the position. I'm giving you the rod."

"Yes, my lady." Llewelyn bowed deeply but there was a look on his face that made Lissa think he was anticipating the punishment rather than dreading it.

The ambassador's eyes flashed as she looked at Lissa. "And *that's* how you deal with a defiant slave, my dear. Sometimes only the rod will do." Turning, she swept through the blue, billowing panels of cloth and disappeared from view.

"Um, yes of course." Lissa called after her. She supposed the ambassador intended to beat her slave with a rod in order to make him more obedient. *Please Goddess,* she prayed. *Don't let me have to do that to Saber. I couldn't bear to hurt or humiliate him.*

"This way," Llewelyn said, interrupting her private thoughts. "We must hurry. My mistress is waiting. No doubt she's strapping on the rod as we speak." There was a definite light of anticipation in his eyes as he spoke, which made Lissa wonder again what exactly Lady Sha'rak was planning to do to him. Maybe it wasn't a beating after all…

Llewelyn was already on the move and Lissa had to hurry to keep up with the body-slave. She and Saber would simply have to make sure that the kind of treatment Llewelyn was about to receive was never perceived as necessary by Lady Sha'rak. That should be possible, right?

Of course it will, she told herself firmly. But she couldn't help the uneasy feeling of dread that settled in the pit of her stomach as they left the room and followed Llewelyn down the opulent hallway to their suite.

Chapter Seven

"Lissa, we need to talk." Saber paced outside the bathroom door. She had been in there for nearly an hour doing the Goddess knew what and finally he couldn't wait any longer. They were about to miss their chance for a private conversation and there were some things that needed to be said before they went out in public in this sadistic, male-hating society again. "Lissa?" he called again. "Are you all right in there?"

"I'm fine," came her muffled reply. "Just fine, Saber. I just need a few more moments of privacy so I can find the right, uh, outfit to wear tonight."

Saber sighed. Knowing Lissa, she was probably trying to find the least revealing clothing possible in the small purple cube Kat had packed for her. Not that he blamed her—her natural modesty was one of the things he loved and admired in her. But modesty didn't look to be one of the characteristics that would get them very far on Yonnie Six.

Which was one of the things he needed to tell her—only he didn't quite know how to go about doing it. After all, how could he barge into the bathroom and tell her she was being too reserved? Or demand that she stop acting so shy about baring her body in the revealing dresses she was expected to wear here on Yonnie Six?

I'll sound like a bastard, Saber thought unhappily. *An unprincipled bastard who just wants to ogle her body.* What was the human word for that kind of male? Oh yes, he'd heard Kat and some of the other Earth girls say it—Jerk. He was going to come off like a real jerk.

And yet he felt he had to say *something* to Lissa. At the very least they needed to talk about their public behavior and plan their next move.

"We need a strategy," Saber muttered to himself, still pacing. "Some way to—"

Just then there was a breathless scream from behind the bathroom door.

Saber ran to the door at once and grabbed the ornately carved knob—it wouldn't budge. "Lissa?" he yelled. "Lissa, are you all right? What's happening in there?"

"N-nothing," she gasped but her voice was tight with pain and fear.

"Tell me," Saber insisted. But all he heard was the sound of running water and under it, a soft whimper of pain. "Lissa?" he shouted again but there was still no answer.

Grimly, he gripped the knob and threw his shoulder against the door as hard as he could. If she wouldn't open the door, he'd damn well *break* it in. There was no way he would stand idly by while the female he cared for was in pain or danger. No way in all the seven hells.

* * * * *

Lissa hadn't meant to get any of it on her. She'd just been looking...

It happened just after she'd finally settled on a dress for the night—a deep crimson sheath with a high neck that fell straight to her upper thighs before flowing out behind her in a stiff train. The dress would have been modest except for a wide diamond cut out in the chest which exposed most of her upper torso. However, it also had a panel of black lace that attached on either side and mostly obscured her bare breasts—which was what Lissa was most interested in. She didn't even mind the ridiculously high platform heels that went with the dress, though she felt like she was constantly being pushed forward by an invisible hand when she tried to walk in them.

The main thing was that the dress hid her breasts—well, mostly, anyway—and didn't show her crotch. That was enough for Lissa since so many of the dresses Kat had packed her failed to meet these two simple requirements. She still didn't know what she was going to wear to the "sensation party" Lady Sha'rak was so excited about but at least for tonight she felt somewhat covered.

After finally wiggling into the dress—which wasn't easy without help—she sat at the small, ornate dressing table at one end of the enormous gray and black marble bathroom and twisted her hair into a simply chignon at the nape of her neck.

Such ugly hair – she looks like a tzeeba with those green stripes!

The voices of her long ago tormentors from the school she and Saber had both attended when they were younger echoed in her head. Lissa's long blonde hair with its streaks of jade green was normal enough for a Kindred female, but completely alien on her home world where everyone had dark brown hair and eyes. Saber had defended her when the bullies taunted her and had stopped her from cutting her hair by telling her it was beautiful.

He also told me I was beautiful. He cared for me even though I was different. Lissa wrapped her arms around herself and sighed. If she closed her eyes, she could almost remember the way he had hugged her, feel the forbidden press of his lips against her forehead, which was the only place Saber had ever dared kiss her. But even those embraces, which would seem chaste and tame to an outsider, were forbidden on their home world of Tarsia. Forbidden but oh, so sweet.

And now here we are together again and we're on a planet where I have to treat him like a slave...like some kind of pet! Lissa felt ill when she remembered the way Llewelyn had groveled before the ambassador and kissed her offered foot even after she had slapped his face. Lissa knew she couldn't treat Saber like that. She just *couldn't.*

Not to mention the fact that she also couldn't let him suck pain and pleasure elixirs off her nipples.

The thought brought a hot blush to Lissa's face and she stopped fiddling with her hair and stared instead at the small leather case containing the two compounds and the soothing salve. Should she put them on tonight? Would Lady Sha'rak notice if she didn't? It seemed like a pointless gesture—after all, Lissa had absolutely *no* intention of using the elixirs for their intended purpose of punishing her "slave". But was the lace that covered her breasts thin enough to reveal if she skipped what the ambassador seemed to consider an all important step in her evening dress? After studying herself in the oval viewer attached to the dressing table for a long moment, Lissa reluctantly decided that it was.

Sighing, she opened the case and took out the little red bottle. She frowned at it, lying so innocently in the palm of her hand. She didn't want to offend their hostess, but she was still extremely reluctant to paint her nipples in what amounted to red hot chili pepper sauce. Maybe she ought to take a closer look before she started recklessly slathering herself in the stuff.

Very carefully, she unscrewed the tiny lid and pulled it off. Attached to it was a long thin wand with a tiny brush at the end. It reminded Lissa very much of the little bottles of polish she had seen Kat using from time to time to paint her fingernails different colors.

Only fingernail polish didn't have fumes that smelled like fire and pepper rising from it. Lissa took a careful sniff and winced. *Goddess that's strong! And she expects me to put it on my nipples?*

Just then there was a knocking at the door.

"Lissa, we need to talk," Saber's deep voice sounded a little muffled through the thick bathroom door. "Lissa? Are you all right in there?" he asked.

Lissa called back something about being fine and added that she needed a little more time to get dressed for dinner. There was no way she was going to tell him what was taking so long was that she was trying to decide whether to paint her nipples or not.

She took one more look at the little red vial and its crimson coated brush. She'd jumped when Saber first knocked and had nearly spilled the entire contents of the bottle all over herself—what a mess *that* would have been!

No, she told herself firmly. *I can't do this—I just can't. I'll have to think up some excuse to give the ambassador but I just can't.*

Delicately, she began to replace the lid...and that was when one single tiny ruby drop fell from the brush and landed directly between her breasts.

The pain was immediate and devastating—like someone had aimed a blowtorch at her chest. A breathless cry of agony was torn from her lips before she could stop it. *Goddess, it hurts...it burns!*

Outside the door, Lissa heard Saber demanding to know what was going on. Forcing herself to sound normal, she called back, "Nothing." He said something else but she couldn't answer again. All she could think about was the pain and how to stop it.

She had the presence of mind to set the red bottle down on the dressing table and then ripped off the band of black lace. Balling it in her hand, she scrubbed madly at the tiny red drop between her now bare breasts. But though she wiped away the ruby droplet easily with the lace, the pain continued. Indeed, it seemed to be increasing. It felt like someone had dripped acid on her sternum and it was eating a hole through her skin, trying to reach her heart.

Lissa whimpered in pain. What could she do? Then her eyes fell on the blue vial which had spilled out of the case when she jumped in pain. *The antidote! Of course!*

Hurriedly, she unscrewed the blue cap and pulled out the tiny brush. With trembling fingers, she painted a line of icy sapphire blue between her breasts, right where the droplet had fallen.

For a moment she thought she felt the pain ease just a little. But before she could breathe a sigh of relief, it blazed back to life, the fire between her breasts burning even hotter than before.

Oh my Goddess! What's wrong? Why didn't it work? Vaguely she remembered Lady Sha'rak saying something about how the antidote didn't work if the burning blossom elixir got onto bare skin.

But what else can I do? I'm on fire! Wait – fire, that's it! Lissa's eyes were drawn to the gold and silver taps that crowned the deep marble basin in the center of the room. She wasn't sure if it was some kind of shallow bathtub or maybe just a very deep sink but at this point she didn't care. *Water – I need water!*

She was in so much agony by now she could barely think but somehow she managed to stagger over to the basin and turn on one of the taps full force. Water blasted out and Lissa scooped up handfuls of the icy liquid to splash it on her chest. The stiff red fabric of her dress became saturated and drooped but Lissa didn't care. She didn't give a damn if her dress for the evening got ruined—she just wanted the fire between her breasts to be put out!

But the water wasn't helping either. In fact, Lissa was very much afraid that it might be spreading the fire around. It wasn't just the spot between her breasts that was burning now—the sides of her breasts were also hot and when she looked down, she could see what looked like a red, angry blush spreading across her skin from her throat almost to her navel. The red blush throbbed like a live thing—her inflamed skin screaming that she was *burning. Burning up...*

Goddess, what was she going to do?

Just then the bathroom door burst open and Saber came rushing in.

"What in the seven hells is going on in here?" he roared.

Lissa turned from the water basin, no longer able to hide her panic. "It was just a drop," she cried, rubbing futilely between her breasts where the burning was growing by the second. "Just a drop but it keeps spreading and burning and the antidote doesn't work and water just makes it worse—"

"A drop? A drop of what?" Saber's eyes followed hers to the dressing table where the little red bottle sat innocently, as though denying the pain and destruction it had unleashed. "Seven hells!" he growled. Rushing forward, he took Lissa by her upper arms and glared at her anxiously. "Where? Where did it get on you?"

"Here." Heedless of her bare breasts, she nodded down at the red patch growing between them.

Without hesitation, Saber leaned down and licked her exposed skin.

Lissa was so shocked at first she couldn't say or do anything. Then, as he licked her again, his warm tongue blazing a trail through the fiery pain, she suddenly came back to herself.

"Saber, no!" she gaped, trying to push him away. But there seemed to be no stopping him.

"Hold still." His deep voice was a growl, rumbling through her as he continued to lap her exposed skin. He ignored Lissa's efforts to get away and bent her over his arm, the better to expose her injured areas as he continued to lick and suck.

Lissa finally stopped struggling and went limp. There was clearly no stopping him and besides, what he was doing was actually working. The horrible burning between her breasts was easing at last. It was as though Saber was actually licking away the pain—erasing it with the broad, leisurely strokes of his warm, wet tongue.

But though he was easing one kind of burning, he was leaving another in its place. As her pain eased, Lissa found that her heart was beating faster and faster, her blood racing through her veins at the illicit act they were performing.

Here she was, half naked and completely drenched, draped over Saber's arm as he explored the sensitive area between her breasts with his mouth and tongue. It was a far cry from the chaste kisses he had once pressed to her forehead—a far cry indeed. And though she knew she ought to be shocked and shamed and hate every moment of it, Lissa couldn't. Instead, she felt herself melting, losing control as her legs turned to rubber. The tender V between her thighs grew first hot and then wet as the warm tongue bath went on and on.

"Goddess..." she moaned softly as Saber gently laved the slopes of her bare breasts. He wasn't just licking away the burning blossom elixir anymore, he was exploring her, tasting her in a way she'd never expected to let him. Lissa gasped as the warm tip of his tongue slid dangerously close to one rigid nipple. Part of her wanted him to lick her there—to take the tight pink bud in his mouth and suck as hard as he could, just as Llewelyn had done with Lady Sha'rak. But that would be wrong...wouldn't it? In her half delirious state, she couldn't exactly remember why but she was sure it would be for some reason.

"Am I getting it all?" he murmured and she realized he was talking to her.

"Oh...um..." Lissa tried to pull herself together enough to answer. "I...I think so."

"Are you sure? What about here—does it hurt here?" He kissed the slope of her right breast and brushed one gentle finger lightly around the broad pink ring of her areola.

Lissa gasped and moaned as her nipple tightened mercilessly at his gentle almost-touch. "I..." She couldn't answer. "I don't know," she gasped at last.

"Or here?" Saber's fingers finally found her aching nipple and he squeezed it lightly, sending a surge of pure pleasure down her spine. "Tell me, *amalla*," he murmured, his eyes blazing. "Do you need me to lick you here?"

Amalla, her mind whispered. Saber's pet name for her. It was a term of affection which meant "beloved one" or "cherished little sister."

Which is what I am, Lissa reminded herself as a sudden surge of horror swept over her. It didn't matter that they weren't related by blood—she and Saber were still of the same clan. Which meant everything they were doing was completely forbidden—completely unforgivable.

Why aren't the kinship compounds stopping us? she asked herself wildly. *I ought to be feeling nothing but disgust right now. Nothing but revulsion at letting him touch me so intimately. Instead...*

Instead, she never wanted him to stop. Which was exactly why they had to *right now.* Before things went even an inch farther.

"Saber, no!" she gasped, pushing at his broad chest. "I can't....we can't..."

"Forgive me." He let her go at once and took a step back.

"I'm so sorry," she said miserably, crossing her arms over her bare breasts. "But this...it isn't right. You know it's not. We're of the same clan."

"You're right. I shouldn't have...I'm sorry." His deep voice was hoarse with emotion and she couldn't help looking up at him.

As she took him in — his broad, bare shoulders slumped in dejection — Lissa became suddenly aware that his eyes were watering and his face was red.

Goddess! At once a different kind of guilt swamped her. He'd licked the horribly hot burning blossom elixir off her skin to save her and transferred the effects to himself. The inside of his mouth must be on fire!

Quickly, she reached for the antidote serum. She uncapped the bottle and started to offer it to Saber but he shook his head.

"Has to be licked off bare skin, remember?" he muttered hoarsely.

"Oh...of course." Lissa looked down at the tiny applicator brush coated in sapphire blue uncertainly. Where exactly on her body did Saber expect her to paint the antidote so he could lick it off? What should she do?

"Here." Apparently sensing her indecision, Saber took matters into his own hands. Taking the brush from her, he painted a long, blue streak down the top of her right index finger. Then, slowly, his eyes never leaving hers, he lifted her hand and sucked her finger deep into the warm, wet cavern of his mouth.

A soft moan fell from Lissa's lips as Saber searched her eyes with his own and continued to suck. He bathed her finger gently with his tongue, lapping and swirling in a way that seemed more about showing her exactly how he felt than getting the antidote. It seemed to go on forever, his eyes holding hers with a mute promise as he sucked and bathed her finger, never letting her go for an instant as he worked on her.

By the time he was done Lissa felt weak in the knees all over again. "Oh," she whispered softly as he finally released her wrist and slowly slid her finger from his mouth. "Saber that was…" She shook her head. There were no words to describe what she felt.

"Lissa," he said softly, his eyes meeting hers. "We need to talk."

Chapter Eight

Saber paced the floor in front of her, his arms crossed behind his back and tried to think how to begin. He thought of dozens of different ways but somehow none of them seemed right. There was just no good way to say what had to be said. Finally, he opened his mouth and simply spoke the truth.

"I've wanted to taste you like that for a long time," he said, looking at Lissa as he spoke. "And not just there. I've wanted to lick you everywhere, to explore your entire sweet, luscious body with my tongue. To make you moan my name while I licked you…tasted you…"

She turned red, then white. "You…you have?"

"You know I have," he said roughly. "It's wrong—we both know it is—but that hasn't stopped me from thinking how it would be. How your skin would taste, how you would feel pressed against me while I—"

"Saber, we can't!" she interjected. "We shouldn't even *talk* like this—you're my kinsman."

"Not here, I'm not." Saber rounded on her, his hands clenched into fists at his sides. "Here I'm just your devoted slave—and that's how you have to treat me, Lissa. The way I have to treat you as my beloved mistress."

Abruptly, he dropped to his knees in front of her and rubbed his cheek against her thigh.

Lissa jumped as though she'd been stung. "Saber, no! Get up," she implored but he remained on his knees before her, looking up.

"We have to forget about our kinship through the Sun Clan," he said stubbornly. "We have to stop jumping every time we touch each other and acting so Goddess damned awkward and careful around one another."

"I...I don't know if I can," Lissa whispered. "I...I don't even know how we're able to touch each other at all. What with the kinship compound..."

"The kinship compound doesn't seem to be working," Saber said dryly. "At least, it's not working on me. Is it on you?" He looked up at her, his chest tight. "Do you...does my touch repulse you?"

Lissa bit her lip. "You...you know it doesn't."

Saber felt the tightness in his chest ease. "Good. At least that makes playing our parts here easier."

"I guess..." Lissa shook her head. "But I just don't...I can't imagine treating you like Lady Sha'rak treats Llewelyn."

"You'll have to do a hell of a lot more than imagine it," Saber said grimly. "You'll have to *do* it."

"But I can't! I don't want to slap you or make you grovel and kiss my foot or—"

Saber cut her off by lifting one of her dainty feet, clad in a ridiculously high heel, and kissing her instep gently.

"Oh..." Lissa's breath fell out of her in a long sigh and her eyes widened with surprise.

"*I don't mind,*" Saber told her softly, rubbing his cheek against her slender ankle. "Whatever we have to do, however you have to treat me, I don't mind. After all, we're here for a reason—to find the lost scrolls. That has to supersede everything else."

He didn't add that he actually *wanted* to be more to Lissa, wanted to forget their kinship status forever and be allowed to touch her intimately. He'd already said that earlier and it had upset her terribly. Better she think that his eagerness to serve her was all in the name of their mission. Better by far.

"Well..." She sounded like she was wavering. "But...but what about other things? Like punishing you with those horrible elixirs." She glanced at the blue and red bottles still standing on the dressing table and shivered.

"At least now I know what to expect," Saber said stolidly. Though he really didn't crave another encounter with the burning blossom compound, he knew he could bear it if he had to. Especially if it meant he got to suck Lissa's ripe, pink nipples into his mouth and bathe them gently with his tongue. Just the thought made his cock rock hard inside the too-tight black trousers he was wearing.

His thoughts must have showed on his face because she blushed, her cheeks going deep red. "No, I mean...you can't...shouldn't, um, taste me there."

"No, but I will if I have to," Saber said matter-of-factly. "I'll take my punishment like any good, obedient slave would do and you'll punish me like a stern but loving mistress. It's the only way to get through this."

Lissa nibbled her lush bottom lip. "I suppose you're right."

"I know I am," Saber said, rising to his feet at last and crossing his arms over his chest. "We'll do whatever we have to do while we're here to recover the scrolls. Then, afterward, we'll go back to the way things were before."

"Oh...of course." Was it his imagination or was there a look of sadness in Lissa's lovely eyes as she nodded? Did she possibly still have feelings for him, after all these years? Saber forced himself to push the thought away. They had however long it took to find the scrolls to be together. It would have to be enough.

"Come on, Mistress," he said gently. "Let's get changed for dinner." He looked at her soaked and bedraggled outfit. "I'm afraid you need a new dress. Yours is a little, ah, damp."

Lissa made a choked sound which was half laugh/half sob. "Yes, I think you're right. All right, let's get changed."

* * * * *

Lissa sat numbly at the dinner table—which was a low platform near to the ground. It was in the center of a plush dining room bigger than most normal people's houses and was surrounded by plump, supportive white pillows decorated in gold and silver needlework. The idea appeared to be to recline against the pillows in a half sitting—half lying position Lissa found very strange and uncomfortable. Of course, it wasn't the only thing about Yonnie Six that was making her uneasy—nearly every single custom here seemed to be well outside her comfort zone.

Not that she could show it.

I have to act the part, have to treat Saber like my slave and let him treat me like his mistress. As a matter of fact, they had already started their new roles, even before they got into the opulent gold and white dining room.

Lissa looked down at herself. She was wearing the very same stiff purple and lace gown that had caused her so much embarrassment and consternation during her final fitting with Kat. But it wasn't the dress she was staring at—it was her red and blue painted nipples which peeked out from behind the little golden lace fans.

Lissa had not been the one who applied the elixirs.

Oh, she had tried to, but after the horrible experience with the single burning droplet between her breasts, her hands shook when she picked up the little red vial. Even though she had applied the soothing salve generously over her tender pink buds, she still couldn't bring herself to paint the horrid, burning stuff onto such a sensitive area of her anatomy.

Finally Saber, who had been standing there watching her because he insisted on helping her get dressed, stepped forward. Sinking to his knees before her, he took the red bottle gently from her trembling hands.

"Let me," he said in a low voice, looking into Lissa's eyes.

"I don't know if you should," Lissa whispered, her insides twisting with conflicting emotions. Doubt, fear, guilt, desire… To have him so close to her, looking at her while she was sitting there, her breasts completely bare…It was so wrong. And yet she couldn't help the way her body reacted. The way she felt drawn to him…

"Well, I don't think *you* can—not with your hands shaking like that," he said firmly. His voice dropped to a softer tone. "I'll be careful, Lissa, I swear. If it starts to burn even a little bit just tell me and I'll take care of it right away."

"You mean…" Lissa swallowed hard. "By sucking it off."

"Yes." Saber looked her in the eyes. "It's the only way. And I might have to do it before the night is out anyway."

"No, you won't," Lissa said quickly. "I swear I won't do that to you, Saber!"

"Don't make promises you might have to break," he said soberly. "And don't hesitate to do whatever you have to in order to make this look real." He nodded at her bare breasts. "Now hold still—I don't want to make a mess of this."

Lissa didn't want him to either so she sat perfectly still, her entire body tense as he painted her right nipple bright red with the burning blossom elixir. Saber went slowly, checking with her often to make certain she was feeling no pain. In fact, he was so gentle and soft-spoken that Lissa was almost able to forget the illicit nature of the act he was performing.

This is how he would make love to me, she couldn't help thinking and then blushed at the thought. She tried to push it away but the mental image persisted. She could just imagine Saber kneeling between her thighs, guiding himself inside her slowly and carefully, checking every moment to be certain she was feeling no pain, that she was able to take him…

Stop it, I have to stop thinking like this!

But despite her inner recrimination, the forbidden thoughts and images had continued and were still continuing now, as she reclined on her gold and silver embroidered pillow and waited for dinner to be served.

Across from her sat Ambassador Sha'rak with Llewelyn behind her, waiting attendance. To Lissa's right, was Lady Pope'nose, a tall, imposing woman about the same age as the ambassador. She had sharp, aquiline features and jet black hair with golden streaks, which was piled on top of her head. Behind her sat a body-slave who looked to be only a little older than Lissa.

Instead of a plain black leather collar and leash, Lady Pope'nose's slave had on a strange silver and black necklace with purple lights that blinked periodically. He had an air of frightened inexperience that made Lissa nervous just watching him. Lady Pope'nose had already explained that he was new and she was still "breaking him in", which Lissa supposed accounted for his almost palpable anxiety. She *did* wish, though, that the poor thing wouldn't jump every time his mistress so much as shifted her position. What was he so afraid of? Well, aside from the burning blossom elixir, which he might be forced to ingest at any moment. On second thought, Lissa didn't blame him for being so jumpy.

Saber, who was sitting just behind her own cushion, was the exact opposite of Lady Pope'nose's nervous slave. His presence at her back was like a rock—solid and comforting. Lissa felt stronger just having him near, even if her thoughts *did* keep returning to forbidden territory when she felt the heat of his big body behind her and caught a whiff of his warm, masculine scent.

"Oh, at *last!*" Lady Sha'rak said, breaking Lissa's train of thought. "Dinner is finally served. I'm so sorry it took so long, my dears," she continued, nodding at Lissa and Lady Pope'nose. "I'll have the cooks flogged the minute I get the chance."

"Oh, don't do that," Lissa said without thinking.

Lady Pope'nose stared at her in surprise. "Why ever not, my dear? We've been sitting here waiting for *ages.* Clearly the cooks need a little motivation to get dinner out on time. And what could be more motivating than a nice flogging?"

"I'm afraid Lady R'awr is rather too softhearted when it comes to slaves." Lady Sha'rak gave her a disapproving look as the male servers placed dishes and bowls of steaming food on the table. "I've been trying to give her some pointers but so far we aren't making much progress."

"That's not what I meant," Lissa protested. "I just meant...I meant..."

"Yes, dear?" Lady Sha'rak looked at her with raised eyebrows.

Lissa tried to get into her role. *Be tough. Act like Minverna would have acted!* "I meant that flogging is too good for them," she said.

"We have much stricter punishments when it comes to tardiness on Zetta Prime."

"Oh?" The ambassador looked surprised. "Do tell, my dear. Is it a collar offense on Zetta?"

"A collar offense indeed," Lady Pope'nose interjected. "If it's not, it should be! I keep telling you, Manda," she continued, addressing Lady Sha'rak. "That you need to get all your slaves fitted with collars. It really does do wonders for their attitude. Take Tobias here." She nodded at the nervous slave hovering just over her left shoulder. "He was positively *intractable* at first. But now that I've got the latest collar on him I have no problems at all."

"The latest, did you say?" Lady Sha'rak studied the silver and black necklace with its blinking purple lights around Tobias's neck with some interest. "What exactly does it do?"

"It feeds directly into the pain centers of the brain." Lady Pope'nose sounded proud, as though she'd invented the horrible contraption herself. "The moment I say the pain word, he's in instant agony—like every nerve in his body is burning."

"A pain word, you say? So it's voice activated?" Lady Sha'rak continued to stare at the collar avidly.

"Yes—no more irritating remotes. I was *always* losing mine." Lady Pope'nose fluttered her long white hands in a helpless gesture. "Now all I have to do is remember a single word. Well—two as it happens. One to activate the collar and one to cut it off. Here, watch..." She turned to her slave, who was visibly quivering behind her and said, "Tobias, *trab.*"

Immediately Tobias fell over and began writhing in agony. His eyes rolled up in his head and his body jerked, almost as though he was having a seizure. Hoarse, awful noises of pure pain came from his throat.

Lissa gave a strangled gasp. *No!* she wanted to shout. *You have no right to torture him like that. Stop right now, you horrible woman!*

But as the words rose instinctively to her throat, she felt Saber's large, warm hand squeezing her shoulder. She turned her head slightly to see him and he shook his head. Lissa widened her eyes in protest. She couldn't just sit here and let this awful torture go on right under her nose without saying something about it — could she? But Saber had a point. If she made too much of a fuss, she might blow their cover.

Still, it was terribly hard to just sit there and watch as the poor hapless slave writhed in pain. Foam was actually beginning to seep from between his clenched teeth and dribble down his cheeks. Looking across the table, Lissa saw that even Ambassador Sha'rak looked a bit disconcerted.

"That's enough, Nola," she said finally. "I'm afraid he'll break something, flopping about like that."

"Very well." Lady Pope'nose seemed completely unconcerned. "Zax," she said loudly.

At once, Tobias stopped thrashing. He lay in a panting heap on the floor, his whole body trembling and a soft, hoarse sob came from his lips. Lissa's heart clenched like a fist. It was the sound of a creature in agony, a hopeless sound that tore at her and brought tears prickling to her eyes. But no, she mustn't cry! She couldn't let the other two women at the table see how the brutal torture, which was obviously an everyday occurrence for them, had affected her.

Lissa lifted her head and cleared her throat. "That seems, er, most effective," she said at last, hoping her quavering voice didn't betray her true emotions.

"Indeed." Lady Sha'rak still looked discomforted. "Quite."

"Oh, it *is*." Lady Pope'nose nodded earnestly. "The only drawback is that prolonged use can cause permanent nerve damage. But I say it's a small price to pay for obedience."

Lissa had to look down to keep herself from glaring at Lady Pope'nose with pure loathing. What a repulsive woman! She wondered if Lady Pope'nose would count permanent nerve damage a "small price to pay" if *she* was the one wearing the collar?

"Well, now that your little demonstration is over, I think we ought to eat before everything gets cold," Lady Sha'rak said a bit too brightly.

"That sounds like a good idea." Automatically, Lissa reached for the steaming dish in front of her, which appeared to contain a mound of tiny blue and green grains with red berries mixed in. She had already lifted her utensil—a broad, flat scoop that looked more like a trowel than a spoon—when she realized that the other women at the table were staring at her.

"My dear Lady R'awr," Lady Sha'rak said a bit stiffly. "I'm not exactly sure how they do things on Zetta Prime but here on Yonnie Six it is considered *very* bad form to feed yourself."

"Oh, I'm so sorry!" Lissa put down the trowel-like implement at once with a flush of embarrassment. "I just thought, since we're having an informal dinner…"

Lady Pope'nose laughed, a very unpleasant *cawing* sound. "We're never *that* informal, Lady R'awr. I mean, where do you think you are—the jungles of Rageron?" She looked at the ambassador. "It appears you have a bit more than you thought to teach your little relative before you set her loose in polite society."

Lissa shot the unpleasant woman a look of irritation and wished that they were all back on First World. There she could have blasted the smug expression on Lady Pope'nose's narrow face with her Goddess given powers. Here she just had to sit and take it.

Not that I ought to be thinking of blasting anyone, she told herself firmly, trying to regain control. *But if I can't feed myself, how in the Goddess's name am I supposed to eat?*

Her question was answered when she looked across the table and saw Llewelyn spooning some kind of steaming soup into Lady Sha'rak's mouth. Oh, so *that* was how it was done.

She was about to turn to Saber and command him to start feeding her, but she found he was one step ahead of her. When she turned her head, he was already waiting with a scoop of the grain and berry mixture and a wry look on his face.

"Open up, Mistress," he murmured with the tiniest glint of humor in his hazel eyes. "Let's get you fed."

Feeling ridiculously like a baby bird, Lissa opened her mouth and he tipped the mixture in. The taste was rather strange—a kind of sweet meatiness she hadn't expected from a grain mixture. But then Lissa felt something odd—something was *moving* in her mouth!

Her first instinct was to spit the mouthful out but she had already embarrassed herself once and she didn't want to do a repeat performance. She forced herself to swallow and shook her head when Saber offered her another bite.

"Excuse me, Ambassador Sha'rak," she said. "But I was just wondering...I don't think I've ever had this dish before. Can you tell me what it is?"

"Really? You haven't?" Lady Sha'rak looked truly surprised. "But it's—" She stopped abruptly and frowned.

"It's what?" Lissa asked, wondering what she had done wrong now.

"It's *dosi* grubs and *shum* berries," Lady Pope'nose said, smiling at her. "Isn't it delicious. Tobias, more!" she snapped at her trembling slave who had recovered enough to feed her. "And no sniveling—you know how I abhor it."

"Yes, Mistress." He brought another mouthful of the bug and berry mixture to her mouth with a hand that trembled so much Lissa was surprised he didn't spill it all over her. But though she didn't want to see the hapless slave hurt again, most of her mind was still trying to process what his mistress had said.

"I'm sorry…" She cleared her throat. "But did you say *grubs?* As in *bugs?*"

"Why yes, of course," Lady Sha'rak said. "They're dormant until they feel the heat of your mouth. Then the little devils come to life and go crazy trying to get away while you chew them up." She smiled. "It makes for a most interesting dish, don't you find?"

"Ah, yes. Most interesting," Lissa croaked. She groped for the fluted silver glass a slave had filled earlier with some kind of fermented drink. At the time she'd thought that it smelled just awful but now she was willing to drink anything to get the dreadful sweet, meaty taste of the live grubs out of her mouth.

Once again, Saber was ahead of her. When she turned, he lifted the glass to her lips and Lissa drank deeply, wincing at she did. The stuff was incredibly thick and bitter and it burned her throat horribly going down, but there was no doubt it got rid of the taste of the grubs.

"Do be careful with that, my dear," Lady Sha'rak said mildly as Lissa gulped the bitter brew. "That's *Barish* honey wine and it's quite strong."

"Thank you," Lissa said, almost choking, when Saber took the glass from her lips. "I…it's kind of you to warn me."

"Just didn't want you getting too tipsy to go into the relaxation grotto after dinner." Her hostess smiled kindly. "Why don't you try some of the Kornithia eyeball soup? It might agree with you better."

Lissa had no intention of eating anything with eyeballs in it. She sent a mute appeal to Saber who nodded slightly and took her plate. He went unobtrusively around the table and came back to her with a cluster of small blue and green fruits that looked both juicy and mercifully bug-free.

"Mmm." Lissa smiled at him as he popped one of the small fruits between her lips. It burst on her tongue in a rush of sweet, refreshing juice that washed the taste of the bitter honey wine away completely. "These are wonderful."

"Oh, do you like bung clusters?" Lady Pope'nose wrinkled her long, skinny nose. "I find them terribly drab and prosaic myself."

"Well, *I* think they're delicious," Lissa said a touch defiantly. Really, she hated the arrogant woman more every minute she had to share a space at the table with her. *But I'm not here just to eat,* she reminded herself. *And it doesn't matter what I think of her as long as she has what we need.*

"Lady Pope'nose," she said, after chewing another bung cluster fruit. "Our lovely hostess, Ambassador Sha'rak, has told me that you're the leading collector of antiquities here on Yonnie Six."

"Oh, well, I wouldn't say *the* leading collector." Lady Pope'nose gave an affected little laugh. "After all, Snyra Hake'bean has a collection *almost* as big as my own and she's *nearly* as knowledgeable."

"Really?" Lissa widened her eyes, as though in wonder. The name sounded familiar — she was certain Hake'bean was also on her list of collectors to check out.

"Indeed, yes. And Lady Hake'bean is the one hosting the sensation party tomorrow night." Ambassador Sha'rak sounded excited.

"That's so *interesting*. My family collects antiquities too," Lissa said to Lady Pope'nose. "Tell me, have you ever run across anything from the Hoard Wars that took place on First World about a thousand years ago?"

"As a matter of fact, yes, I have. I made a recent acquisition I consider to be the pride of my collection." Lady Pope'nose looked at her proudly. "I really can't talk about it yet though—I'm still having it appraised."

"Oh, of course." Lissa felt her heart sink.

"But it will be back soon and I'll be unveiling it. I'm actually planning a little event around it. You're both invited, of course." Lady Pope'nose nodded magnanimously, as though she was conferring a great favor.

"Oh, thank you," Lissa said humbly. "That's very kind of you. My father was so interested in artifacts and records from that era."

"Well, it was a very thrilling time." Lady Sha'rak raised her eyebrows meaningfully. "There were so many exciting *sensations* to experience." She looked at Lady Pope'nose. "*Will* you be using your new acquisition for sensation play, Nola?"

"I haven't decided yet." Lady Pope'nose tossed her head. "I may allow it but only to a few of my very best and closest friends."

"Oh, how exciting!" Lady Sha'rak clapped her hands and smiled. "Nola, you are *such* a tease."

"I know." Lady Pope'nose smirked. "But enough talk of antiquities. Did I hear you mention the relaxation grotto, Manda? Have you finally gotten it finished to your liking?"

"Yes, and you two will be the first to experience it. Has everyone eaten enough?" Lady Sha'rak asked brightly.

"Um, I have but..." Lissa hesitated. "I was just wondering...what do you feed the slaves? Saber hasn't had anything and—"

"You're much too attached to that body-slave of yours, my dear." Lady Sha'rak frowned. "He can eat in the kitchen with Llewelyn later. For right now, the relaxation grotto awaits."

"Excellent. Let's go." Lady Pope'nose pushed aside the spadeful of food Tobias was offering her, which, unfortunately, caused it fall in her lap, directly onto her ornate silver and orange dress. "Tobias!" she shrieked, her eyes bulging. "Just *look* what you've done! This dress will be ruined! *Ruined!*"

She looked to be working herself up into a towering rage and Lissa was already cringing inside for the poor body-slave who would doubtless once more be suffering the tortures of the damned.

"Tobias?" Lady Pope'nose shouted. "Tra—" But before she could get the pain word out, Saber bumped against the table, causing Lissa's wine glass to topple over into her lap.

"Oh!" she gasped and stood at once. It was too late though, the wine was already soaking into the tiny gold lace panties which were visible at the opening of her dress.

"My goodness," Lady Sha'rak exclaimed. "What a lot of clumsy slaves we have tonight! Don't *you* spill anything, Llewelyn, or I'll think we're under some sort of a curse."

"No, Mistress," her body-slave murmured smoothly. "I wouldn't dream of it."

"Still," Lady Sha'rak continued thoughtfully. "This *is* a rather good teaching opportunity."

"What are you talking about?" Lady Pope'nose asked sullenly. Her own accident had been overshadowed and, as Tobias had carefully removed the small mess so that her dress looked as pristine as ever, she had nothing to complain about. Lissa thought she looked sulky, like a child robbed of the attention she thought was her due.

"I'm talking about teaching my tenderhearted little cousin here to discipline her slave," the ambassador said patiently.

Lissa's heart jumped into her throat. "Oh, no, Lady Sha'rak. I'm sure it was just a mistake! Saber would never—"

"It doesn't matter if he did it on purpose or not, my dear. Clumsiness in a slave *cannot* be tolerated. You must punish him." Lady Sha'rak looked at her sternly. "I see that you have on the pain-taste and the sweet-taste elixirs." She nodded at Lissa's nipples, which were peeking out from behind the gold lace. "Put them to good use."

Lissa felt like her insides were being twisted inside out. Despite the fact that she had known it might be necessary, she still felt horribly uncomfortable with the idea of letting Saber suck her nipples, especially in public. "I …I…but I *couldn't*," she stammered, feeling her cheeks get hot. "Saber's been with me for years and I've never had to…to use such measures on him before."

"All the more reason to put him in his place now," Lady Pope'nose said firmly. "In fact, forget about the elixirs—they're *so* outdated. You can borrow Tobias's pain collar instead. It responds to the pain word no matter who is wearing it. Tobias," she snapped, turning to her slave. "Come here and let me remove your collar at once."

"Yes, Mistress," he murmured meekly, kneeling before her and leaning over so she could reach the back of the pain collar.

"No!" Lissa gasped, horrified. "No, I won't use that...that *thing* on my...on Saber! I won't!" She put herself between Saber and Lady Pope'nose, determined to protect him at all costs. Just the *idea* of seeing him writhe on the floor in pain the way Tobias had was enough to make her sick. *Never. I'll never let that happen to him!* she told herself fiercely.

"Well, if you don't want to use Lady Pope'nose's collar then you *must* use the elixirs." Lady Sha'rak was beginning to look irritated. "May I remind you, my dear Lady R'awr, that you agreed to be guided by me in this matter?"

"Yes," Lissa said miserably. "Yes, I know, but—"

"Mistress." Suddenly Saber was on his knees before her. "Please," he murmured, looking up at her. "Please punish me."

"Saber?" She looked at him uncertainly.

"You've always been a kind and gentle mistress," he continued softly. "But Lady Sha'rak is right—I was inexcusably clumsy. There should be no exceptions made for me just because I've been your slave for a long time. I should receive pain as well as pleasure from your hand." And taking one of her hands, he kissed her palm gently, as though to illustrate his point.

Lissa felt her breath fall out of her in a long sigh. *Whisper-fingers* brushed lightly through her hair and a voice seemed to murmur, *all right. It's going to be all right.*

With a start, she realized he had just Touched her with his mind. It was another thing he had promised not to do on this mission, along with his promise not to touch her physically. But though both promises had been broken beyond repair, Lissa found that she couldn't be mad.

His caress was so intimate it made her melt, so sweet it filled her with longing. Under his Touch she felt herself calming. Her stomach, which had twisted itself into a knot, slowly relaxed and the tension headache building between her eyes was smoothed away.

To her right, she saw Lady Pope'nose frown and shiver. Across from them, Lady Sha'rak had a dreamy look in her eyes. "Did you feel that?" she murmured.

"Feel what?" Lady Pope'nose snapped. "I felt nothing but a chilly draft. Really, Manda, you should look into it. A guest could freeze to death in this place."

"It...felt quite warm to me." Lady Sha'rak sighed and Lissa realized with a start that both she and Lady Pope'nose had been affected by Saber's gentle mind Touch as well. It was as she had told Nadiah when confessing her feelings for him back on First World—any time a male of the Touch Kindred was caressing another with his mind, a Touch Field was formed that spread out and encompassed even disinterested outsiders.

He mustn't Touch me again, she thought, feeling worried. But Saber didn't. He just kept looking up at her, that quiet, waiting expression in his warm hazel eyes. *He's waiting for me to give in. He knows I have no choice.*

"Very...very well," Lissa whispered, hardly able to get the words out. "You're right, Saber. You *do* deserve a punishment." With trembling hands, she pulled down the top of her dress, baring her breasts completely. "Come," she said, beckoning to him. "I must...must give you the pain-taste."

"Yes, Mistress."

He was so tall she didn't have to lean down very far. Saber put his hands on her waist to hold her in place and sucked her right nipple into his mouth with no hesitation at all.

At once, his face began to go red and she could tell he was in pain, but he refused to be rushed. He lapped and sucked her nipple, obviously making sure to get every last trace of the burning blossom extract off, despite the fiery pain that had to be burning his mouth.

"That's enough," Lissa whispered breathlessly at last. "Now…now take the sweet-taste."

"Yes, Mistress." Obediently, Saber took her other nipple into his mouth at once.

Lissa was relieved to see the pain clear from his eyes and his skin return to its normal tone. But it was different this time. Before, she had been too concerned about the agony he must be feeling to really pay attention to how it felt to let him taste her in such an intimate spot. Now that she knew he was no longer in pain, she began to really feel the effects of his mouth on her.

Holding her eyes with his, Saber licked gently at first, swirling his tongue around her sensitive bud and sending flashes of heat and cold throughout her entire body. Then he sucked harder, taking as much of her breast into his mouth as he could, his hands tightening on her hips as he did so.

The deep pull of his hot mouth against her sensitive breast tightened Lissa's nipple and sent sparks of desire to the tender V between her legs. She could feel her pussy getting hot and wet though he hadn't even touched her below the waist.

"Goddess," she gasped and somehow found her hands were buried in his hair, pulling him closer. "Goddess….Saber, *please…*"

So good…feels so good! her mind was whispering. Somewhere inside she knew they needed to end this. Surely the effects of the burning blossom elixir had been neutralized by now and Saber must be considered adequately punished, even by Ambassador

Sha'rak's stringent standards. But somehow she couldn't make him stop.

It was as though she had been waiting for this moment for years — maybe from the very first time she had met him. She felt as she had when she was wandering lost in the desert — parched and dry — and Saber's touch was like the water she so desperately needed. Under his warm mouth she felt herself blossoming, unfurling like the petals of a delicate flower, which can only be coaxed open by the right hand. Her legs were like rubber and between them her sex was so hot and slick and swollen she felt she might explode.

"Well, well...I think I see why you're so reluctant to punish your body-slave in public."

Lady Pope'nose's sharp voice cut through the haze of desire that clouded Lissa's brain. She jerked and tore her eyes from Saber's, turning her head to see both Lady Pope'nose and Ambassador Sha'rak staring at the show they were putting on.

"Oh my Goddess," she gasped, pulling away from Saber abruptly and yanking the skimpy top of her gown up as high as she could. How had she managed to forget they had an audience? Her behavior had been so shameful! So absolutely *appalling*.

"Don't stop on our account." Lady Sha'rak sounded mildly amused. "I remember what it was to be young and have all your juices flowing. Go ahead and let him finish you off with his tongue if you like. We'll wait."

"Finish me with...with his..." Lissa couldn't even get the words out. The mental image of Saber pulling down her gold lace panties and getting between her thighs to lick her throbbing pussy was so vivid she could feel her entire body getting hot with embarrassment. Goddess, how could Lady Sha'rak even *think* of such a thing? It was wrong and unnatural, surely. Yet when she dared to glance at Saber, she saw something like hunger in his gold-flecked hazel eyes. Could it be that he didn't find the ambassador's suggestion as wrong and forbidden as Lissa did? Could he actually *want* to do such a thing? Just the thought made her blush even harder. Surely not! And yet...

"Actually, Manda, I'd just as soon *not* wait, if you don't mind," Lady Pope'nose sniffed, mercifully ending Lissa's internal debate. "I'd rather go to the relaxation grotto for a bit before I have to go home."

"Oh, of course. Right this way." Lady Sha'rak ushered her out of the opulent dining room. But as she left, she threw a wink over her shoulder at Lissa. "Go on then, my dear. Just come along to the grotto as soon as your slave makes you come."

Lissa cleared her throat. "Actually I...I'm not feeling quite well all of a sudden. I think...think maybe I drank too much of the honey wine earlier. It seems to have gone straight to my head."

"Oh dear." Lady Sha'rak looked concerned. "Well then, off to your rooms. I'll see you tomorrow, my dear. And pleasant dreams."

"Th-thank you," Lissa managed to stammer. She stood there, her entire body tense as a wire, until their hostess finally left the huge dining room. And then, without another glance at Saber, she gathered her skirts and ran, trying to put as much distance as possible between them and the act they had just committed. Trying to run away from the feelings it had caused inside her, feelings she couldn't smother or forget, no matter how hard she tried.

Chapter Nine

Saber started to go after her...but then he stopped himself. It was clear that Lissa needed to be alone. But Goddess, how he wished he could hold her in his arms and tell her how he really felt. Tell her what a pleasure it had been to give her pleasure, to see that warm, half-lidded look of desire on her face and feel her small hands in his hair, urging him on. His mouth still stung with the aftereffects of the burning blossom compound but to Saber it was worth it — a thousand times worth it — to be able to taste the female he loved in such an intimate way.

With a sigh, he decided to check the kitchen and see if he could get anything to eat. Maybe after he finished his meal, Lissa would have had time to calm down and they could talk.

It took him some time to find the massive food storage and prep area but, when he did, he was greeted with the sight of no less than seven different types of appliances for cooking and eight for cold storage. There were vast copper counters that seemed to stretch for miles with cutting implements hung from racks on the walls. The floor was made of firm but bouncy interlocking mats, clearly meant to mitigate the effects of standing on one's feet all day.

Saber frowned thoughtfully as he looked at the mats. For all her show of being a hard mistress, it was clear that Ambassador Sha'rak wasn't as heartless as she wanted to appear. Why else would she have such flooring for her kitchen staff? And there was also the matter of the pain collars — Saber hadn't seen any of her slaves or servants wearing one. A truly cruel mistress, like Lady Pope'nose, wouldn't hesitate to have her entire staff fitted with the horrible torture devises but Lady Sha'rak had done no such thing. Why?

His stomach growled and Saber decided he couldn't spend all night contemplating their hostess's true nature. Not if he wanted to eat. He looked around for someone—one of the cooks possibly—to ask for food. But despite the vast space, there was only a single surly-looking cook working on what looked like some kind of delicate pastry gilded with gold and silver frosting.

"Excuse me." Saber went up to him but the pastry chef paid no attention. "Excuse me!" Saber said, louder. Still no response.

He was about to repeat himself one more time, even louder, when a voice behind him said, "Don't bother with Enry there. He's deaf as dirt and to be honest, he wouldn't help you even if he *could* hear you."

"Is that right?" Saber turned to see Llewelyn standing behind him with an amused look on his face.

"Uh-huh." The body-slave nodded. "Enry's a surly old bastard—my lady only keeps him around because he makes the most gorgeous pastries. She's the envy of all her friends because of it." He gestured at the delicate confection iced in gold and silver. "That's going to the sensation party tomorrow. Better let him finish it or it'll be your hide."

"I wasn't trying to ruin his work," Saber said stiffly. "I was just looking for something to eat."

"Well you're in the wrong place. Slaves' larder is back here. Come on." Llewelyn led the way into a small back room with several cold food storage areas. He began opening cupboards and pulling out ingredients at once. "There's nothing as fancy as what our mistresses had for supper, of course," he said, as he placed various foods on a small table in one corner of the room. "Strictly simple fare for the likes of us."

"That's fine," Saber said shortly. "I don't mind simple food."

"Don't mind it—hell, I prefer it!" Llewelyn declared. "Better any day than a bowl of grubs or eyeball soup. But my lady always has to pull out all the stops when that bitch Lady P comes to supper—otherwise she'd gossip about what a dull meal she had and my lady would never live it down."

"I see," Saber said carefully. "And does Lady Pope'nose come to dinner often?"

"Too often if you ask me." Llewelyn's face was grim as he began rolling various ingredients into a large blue flat bread. "Manda is always in such a state after she leaves. It takes me forever to work the knots out of her shoulders and ease the tension in her lower back." He smiled fondly. "Not that I mind putting my hands on her, you understand."

"You seem to be on very familiar terms with your mistress," Saber said neutrally as he followed Llewelyn's example and put what appeared to be some kind of pink meat and leafy purple vegetation in the center of a blue bread wrap.

Llewelyn laughed and added an acidic smelling bright green condiment to his wrap. "And you're *not?* I saw the way she looked at you, friend—you've got her eating out of the palm of your hand. Why, I'll wager that punishment she gave you tonight is the first you've ever gotten from her."

"It is at that," Saber acknowledged truthfully enough. "She's never even raised a hand to me before."

"Of course not—she loves you." Llewelyn tucked the corners of the flat bread in and rolled the wrap and its ingredients tightly before taking a bite. "It's an enviable position for any slave to be in," he continued, once he had swallowed.

"And what would you call your own position?" Saber asked, taking a cautious bite of his own creation. To his relief, it tasted quite good—in fact, better than good—*delicious.*

"Oh, my lady cares deeply for me. More deeply than an outsider might think. She values my ability to *give* as well as to *receive* if you take my meaning."

"Of course." Saber nodded, though he really wasn't sure what the body-slave was referring too. "I see."

"I know you do—I can always tell."

"Tell what?" Saber was tired of playing guessing games.

"That you're a closet dominant, just like me." Llewelyn grinned and nudged Saber's arm. "So what does your lady like you to do? Order her around? Tie her down? Come on, you can tell me."

"I...can't speak of my mistress's private business so freely," Saber said, frowning.

Llewelyn snorted. "Private business. Right." He took another bite of his blue wrap. "Listen, I understand—really, I do. I mean, if it ever got out, our mistresses would be shunned—never received in polite society again. And you just met me so I don't blame you for being closed mouthed. I'm just trying to let you know you're not alone. I mean, you oughta see my lady's secret stash of male-dom porn—it's amazing."

"So you're saying Lady Sha'rak likes it when you boss her around?" Saber raised an eyebrow at him.

"I never said anything like that," Llewelyn said quickly. "All I'm saying is...I'm not always on the *receiving* end of the rod. That's all." He raised his eyebrows at Saber who nodded thoughtfully.

"I see."

"No, you don't." Llewelyn gave him a disgusted look. "Why, I bet your lady has never once used the rod on you, has she?"

"She doesn't beat me, if that's what you mean."

"You know damn well that's not what I mean." Llewelyn got a distant look in his eyes. "My lady first took the rod to me when I was eighteen and she was seventeen." He shrugged. "Well, she'd had me for a year by that time. I suppose she was ready and it didn't matter if *I* was or not. Not that any man is ever really ready for…" He trailed off, shaking his head.

"Where were you before you came to Lady Sha'rak?" Saber asked.

"In a training house in the heart of the city—Handor House, actually." Llewelyn sounded proud. "She picked me out herself—I was a birthday present to her from the Old Mistress, who was long since passed into the depths of the abyss."

"And were you glad to be picked?" Saber was genuinely interested. What would it be like to be raised to be a slave? To know your fate was entirely in the hands of another?

"I was when I saw her eyes," Llewelyn said thoughtfully. "I could tell she was no Lady Pope'nose, even back then." He smiled fondly. "Ah, that's twenty cycles ago now. And here we are, still playing the same games."

"Games like…secret domination," Saber said, raising an eyebrow. "You said she had a stash of male-dom porn. Does she happen to have anything else? Anything about the Hoard Wars that you know of?"

Llewelyn frowned. "You and your lady both seem very interested in that period of history. Why?"

Saber shrugged. "Lady R'awr is a collector. She was hoping to find some pieces to study while we're here. If I can point her in the right direction, she'll be very *happy* with me, if you know what I mean." He raised his eyebrows significantly.

"Of course, I get it." Llewelyn nudged his elbow and grinned. "It's always good to have your lady in your debt. Well, I don't know about the Hoard Wars, but I *do* know my lady has other Kindred documents she uses for sensation play sometimes. Those damn Kindred are so dominant and protective of their women—it's exactly what she likes."

"I see. Thank you, I'll tell my lady." Saber took a final bite of his wrap.

"Fine. Just don't tell her who you got the information from." Llewelyn finished his own wrap as well. "Better go—I'll need to give Manda her massage as soon as that bitch Lady P goes out the door."

"Of course." Saber nodded at him. "Good night and thank you."

"My pleasure." Llewelyn winked. "We closet Doms have to stick together, right?"

"Right," Saber murmured. But inside he was already considering everything the body-slave had said and wondering how exactly he could put it to good use...

* * * * *

The quiet rapping at her door made Lissa jump even though she knew it was probably just Saber. She had taken a quick bath in the marble basin and was already in bed, snuggled under the covers.

Actually, she'd been planning to pretend to sleep when he came in, but she called out, "Yes?" before she thought about it.

"It's just me." Saber's deep voice was muffled. "May I come in, Mistress?"

Hearing him call her that gave Lissa a strange feeling. She knew Saber was only keeping up their cover story but she couldn't help remembering how he had knelt before her and begged her to punish him. She could still feel his hot mouth sucking and lapping her tender nipples, making sure every trace of the elixirs that coated them was gone... Goddess! Her face felt hot just remembering it.

"Mistress Lissa?" Saber asked again and she realized she was taking too long to answer. Looking down, she took stock of herself. She had on a virginal white gown that covered her completely and the silky, royal blue comforter spread over the massive bed was pulled up to her neck. It should be safe enough to let him come in.

"You may enter," she said, trying to sound like an imperious mistress, although she thought it was more likely she sounded ridiculous.

"Thank you." The heavy door swung open silently and Saber entered. He gave her a quick look and then shut the door. He was holding a covered bowl in his hand but he stopped by the foot of the bed. "May I approach?"

"Oh, Saber..." Lissa didn't know whether to laugh or cry. It was all so bizarre. "Of course you can *approach*," she said. "And stop calling me Mistress now — we're alone in here and you checked the rooms earlier for listening devices."

"True." Saber came over and sat carefully on the side of the bed. "I brought you some more fruit." He indicated the bowl. "Thought you might still be hungry."

"Oh, thank you!" Lissa struggled out from under the heavy comforter and sat up eagerly. In fact, her stomach was growling since she'd barely had any dinner at all but she had been resigned to waiting until breakfast the next morning. Really, it was very thoughtful of him to remember how little she'd eaten and guess she might be hungry.

"Here you are, I'm not sure what it's called but I tasted some and it seems fine." The fruit Saber revealed was pale pink with dark blue spots and slightly larger than the bung clusters she'd had at dinner. It was juicy with a sweet-tart flavor that burst on her tongue when she took a bite. "Mmm, delicious!" she murmured, going for another bite.

"Careful, you're dripping." Saber cupped her cheek and wiped a tiny trickle of juice from her chin with his thumb.

Immediately, Lissa froze. His hand on her skin felt so warm, so right. Suddenly her heart was racing and she could barely swallow the bite of fruit. For a long moment Saber's eyes held hers and she was reminded of the way he had looked at her while he sucked her nipples.

"Um, thank you," she murmured at last, pulling away and looking down at the half eaten fruit in her hand. "I should…maybe I should go get a napkin."

"I'll get you one." But instead of going he just sat there, looking at her. Then he put his thumb in his mouth and sucked away the droplets of juice he had captured from her chin. "It *is* delicious," he murmured, his voice deep and soft. "Lissa, about what happened tonight…"

Lissa's heart was knocking against her ribs as though it was trying to get out. She couldn't get into this with him right now. She just *couldn't*. "I…um, don't worry about the napkin. I'll get it myself." She was about to hop out of bed and run for the bathroom when Saber put a hand on her arm.

"No, you stay. I'll be right back." He left and returned a moment later with a soft facecloth which he handed her silently.

"Thank you." She blotted her chin with it though she didn't really need to and then put it neatly on her lap. Her appetite had deserted her and she didn't want to eat any more of the fruit, no matter how delicious it was. But it seemed rude to let it go to waste after Saber had gone to the trouble to bring it to her.

"So I found out something interesting about our hostess tonight." Saber's voice was lighter and the smoldering light had gone from his hazel eyes. Lissa wasn't sure if she was glad or sorry about that.

"What—something about Lady Sha'rak?" She raised her eyebrows and nibbled more of the succulent fruit.

"Un-huh." Saber nodded. "Llewelyn told me."

"Well, what did he say?" Lissa demanded. Now that they were talking about something besides what had happened earlier, a little of the awkwardness between them had disappeared and she felt much more comfortable.

Saber raised his eyebrows and leaned forward confidentially. "Apparently, Ambassador Sha'rak is secretly submissive. Or at least, she's not as totally dominant as she's led us to believe."

"What?" Lissa shook her head, uncomprehending. "When you say submissive, you mean she likes to—"

"Submit sexually. To give up control of her body to someone else—in this case Llewelyn, if he's telling the truth."

"Oh my," Lissa murmured faintly. She had heard of such things before—mostly from the human girls on the Mother Ship. In fact Lauren, the girl who was joined to a Scourge, was apparently in some kind of long term relationship with him that centered around exactly that. Kat and the others were always teasing her about it, though Lissa had never found it very funny.

"Are you all right?" Saber had a worried frown on his face.

"I don't..." Lissa cleared her throat. "I guess I don't understand why anyone would want to do that. I mean, I know it's common here but the slaves...they don't have any choice but to, uh, submit. But why would someone who didn't have to give up control and let someone else, uh, do whatever it is they do, of their own free will?"

"Maybe for love," Saber said softly. "I got the distinct impression that the relationship between Llewelyn and Lady Sha'rak is much more complicated and considerably deeper than they want anyone to know."

"So she submits to him because she loves him?" The concept still seemed foreign to Lissa.

Saber nodded. "As far as I can tell. But apparently he submits to her too, on occasion."

"What a strange relationship." Lissa frowned. "But why would Llewelyn tell you all this?"

Saber looked slightly uncomfortable. "He seems to think you and I have the same kind of, ah, arrangement that he and his mistress do."

"What?" Lissa felt her cheeks get hot. "He thinks I let you, um, dominate me?" She didn't know whether to feel embarrassed or indignant. "But *I'm* the one who's supposed to be dominating *you*," she pointed out.

"I know." Saber looked like he was trying not to laugh. "You look upset. Do you *want* to dominate me?"

"You know I don't," Lissa said at once. "When you knelt at my feet tonight and begged me to punish you, I—" She stopped abruptly, biting her lip.

"You what?" Saber prompted gently.

"I..." Lissa took a deep breath. "It was hard," she whispered at last, putting the bowl of fruit on the large, ornately carved stand by the side of the bed. "I...I didn't want to hurt you."

"I know." He was looking into her eyes again and somehow she found she couldn't turn away. "But it was worth it, Lissa. Worth the pain to taste you that way."

"Oh..." Lissa didn't know what to say to that, how to react. "Saber —" she began.

"I know we're only doing what we have to do in order to complete our mission and get the lost scrolls," he continued, still looking at her. "But even though we have to go our separate ways when this is over, I intend to enjoy it while it lasts. And Lissa..." He raised her hand and pressed a gentle kiss into her palm. "I'd rather have pain from you than pleasure from anyone else," he murmured.

For a long moment, Lissa was speechless. "Saber," she began at last but he only shook his head.

"Anyway, the point of all this is that I think we ought to check Lady Sha'rak's house, er, *floor*, very carefully. It's possible she might have the scrolls." He put Lissa's hand down gently. "Llewelyn seems to think she's partial to Kindred documents because of the dynamic between Kindred males and their brides."

"I see." Lissa looked down at the hand he had been holding and tried not to wish he was still touching her. "Well then, we'll see if we can get some time away from her tomorrow to search. Maybe I can pretend to be sick and we can search around after she goes out for the day."

"A very good idea." Saber smiled and she couldn't help thinking how handsome he was, which made her want to blush again. "Well..." He stretched his arms over his head, giving her an excellent view of the muscles in his broad, bare chest flexing. "I guess we'd better get some sleep. Where's my place?"

"Oh, um...I'm not sure." Lissa bit her lip. Of course the bed was big enough to share but the idea of Saber lying so close beside her all night made her feel so nervous she felt sure she would never get to sleep.

"Look at this." Saber, who had been scrutinizing the room, suddenly reached down and pulled a large brass handle attached to the side of the bed. Lissa had seen it earlier and assumed it was some kind of decoration but to her surprise, when Saber pulled, a whole other, much smaller bed came out. It wasn't nearly as fancy as the vast sleeping platform she was lying on, being little more than a mattress nestled inside the drawer, but it was long enough for Saber's tall frame, though a little narrow for his shoulders.

"Are you sure you want to sleep there?" she asked uncertainly as he tried it out.

"Sure. It's obviously meant for a body-slave. He lies here, close to his mistress, so he can hear her if she needs anything in the night." Saber looked up at her. "I *could* use a pillow, though."

"Oh, of course—here." Lissa gave him several of the large, fluffy head bolsters that adorned the huge bed. "Better?"

"Much." He smiled up at her. "Just try not to step on me if you get up in the middle of the night."

"Of course I won't step on you," Lissa exclaimed indignantly.

"You'd better not!" Saber grinned and sat up. "I'll just go have a wash and get changed. Do you want anything before I go, Mistress?"

"Stop calling me that!" Lissa found herself smiling back, despite herself. "It still sounds so *strange*."

"But it feels so right, doesn't it?" Saber winked at her. "Admit it—you like bossing me around."

"I do not!" Lissa protested. She knew Saber was teasing her, as he used to when they were younger, but she couldn't help rising to the bait.

"All right then, whatever you say." Saber was still laughing as he walked into the bathroom.

Lissa stared at his broad back until the door shut between them. Then she took another long look at the small slave bed and sighed. Well, there was no point thinking of it now. Trust Saber to be a perfect gentleman and not complain about sleeping on the tiny, thin mattress instead of sleeping beside her on the vast, cushy bed.

Feeling guilty, she called softly for the lights to extinguish. Then she lay back down and tried to get comfortable. If only she could invite Saber to share the bed with her. But who knew what kind of trouble that would lead to...

"Lissa, are you awake?"

Saber's soft, deep voice came from beside and slightly below her. Lissa opened her eyes but found she couldn't see anything in the velvety darkness.

"Lights dim," she murmured and a very faint golden glow, like the light of a single candle, came from the corners of the room. "I'm awake." She rolled over and looked down at him. "Are you all right?"

"I'm fine. I was just worried about you." In the faint light, his eyes looked more gold than hazel.

"Worried about me? Why?" Lissa looked at him uncertainly.

"I've been thinking about those elixirs — the burning blossom one especially," Saber murmured. "I'm just wondering if I got it all off."

"Oh, you mean earlier when you, um, sucked me? My nipples, I mean?" Lissa's heart was suddenly racing but she tried to keep her voice steady.

"Mm-hmm." Saber nodded. "I just wouldn't want you to hurt yourself if I missed some — you know, if you touched yourself and then rubbed your eyes or something like that. It could be bad."

Lissa shuddered at the thought of getting the burning blossom elixir in her eyes. It would likely make her go blind. "That **would** be bad," she admitted. "Maybe…maybe you should come up here and check me. Just to be sure." The minute the words were out of her mouth she couldn't believe she had spoken them. But she had no wish to call them back. No wish at all.

"All right." Saber sat up and Lissa held the covers open for him, inviting him in. He climbed into bed beside her and took her in his arms at once.

"I guess I'd better take a look and make sure you're okay," he murmured, his deep voice thick with some emotion Lissa was afraid to name, even to herself.

"I guess so," she whispered, her pulse racing.

The virginal white gown she was wearing had a row of tiny round buttons almost up to her chin. Saber deftly unfastened them, flicking each one open until there was a narrow trail of bare skin from Lissa's throat all the way down to her navel.

He looked at her. "Can I?"

"Please." Lissa could barely get the word out. Her blood was thrumming in her veins and her body felt heavy and tense at the same time. Goddess, what was he going to do?

Saber peeled back the sides of her white gown, baring her breasts completely in the dim light. "Beautiful," he breathed and Lissa felt like a goddess, lying there almost naked before him. "So perfect," he whispered and cupped her right breast, the one that had been painted with the burning elixir.

"Is...is it all right?" Lissa asked breathlessly.

"I think so." Saber thumbed the small pink nub gently and she gasped, feeling her nipple harden at his touch. "Although maybe...maybe I should suck it again. Just to be sure."

"I think you should," Lissa heard herself saying. "Please, Saber, suck them...suck my nipples again and make me feel good."

"As my lady commands," he murmured. Leaning down, he sucked one ripe, pink point into his mouth and began to bathe it with his tongue.

Lissa writhed helplessly under his tender ministrations. She could feel her pussy getting hot and wet again as he sucked and licked her nipple. Could feel herself wanting him, wanting his mouth and hands in places she'd never dreamed she would want to be touched and tasted before.

"Oh!" she groaned aloud, unable to help herself. "Oh Goddess...Saber, please..."

"Lissa? Lissa, are you all right?" A large warm hand on her shoulder woke her and she gasped, sitting bolt upright in the darkness.

"Saber?" She reached for him and felt him by touch, standing by the side of the bed. "Lights, dim," she said, just as she had in her dream. For it had been a dream, hadn't it? Frantically she examined the front of her gown but the myriad of tiny round buttons were all still firmly in place. So then why did her nipples throb as though someone had been sucking them? Why was her pussy so wet and hot and swollen that she nearly cried out when she shifted her legs under the covers?

"Lissa?" He was peering at her anxiously now. "Are you all right?"

"Yes. Yes, I think so. I just had the strangest dream that you were...were..." She trailed off, feeling her cheeks heat.

"That I was what?" He sat on the edge of the bed and looked at her.

"That you were…were examining me to make sure you got all the, uh, all the elixir off my…off me," she stuttered, twisting her fingers in her lap.

"That's strange." Saber frowned. "I was having the exact same dream. Did I…had I unbuttoned your gown? And was I…" He cleared his throat. "Was I tasting you again?"

Heart pounding, Lissa nodded. "Yes. Yes, you were. I was…it felt so…" She shook her head. "But it was only a dream, right?"

"Right," Saber assured her but he looked troubled too. "I just wonder why we're having the same dream at the same time. It's so strange. I would almost say we were dream sharing but—"

"But that *can't* be," Lissa said quickly. "I mean, we're of the same clan. We couldn't form a bond like that—it isn't possible."

"It shouldn't be possible for us to touch each other without disgust and revulsion, either," Saber pointed out quietly. "But I feel nothing but pleasure when I touch your soft skin, when I taste you, *amalla.*"

"*Moch Daer…*" she whispered, giving him the old, cherished nickname before she thought about it. Then, somehow, she got hold of herself. If they weren't careful, the dream was going to turn into reality and Lissa knew she couldn't have that on her conscience. "I mean, Saber," she corrected herself. "That…anyway, that's not how dream sharing works, is it?"

"I don't know." He still looked troubled. "I didn't think so." With a sigh, he ran a hand through his hair. "Go back to sleep, Lissa. I'm sure it was just a dream and everything will seem better in the morning."

"All right." She allowed him to tuck her securely back under the covers. When he was done, Saber leaned down and gave her a soft, chaste kiss on the forehead.

"Sweet dreams, *amalla.*"

"You, too," Lissa whispered. But she wasn't sure if she meant it or not. After all, the dream they had somehow been sharing was the sweetest she had ever had but it was also forbidden. Forbidden and so very, very wrong…

Chapter Ten

"You're looking lovely, as always, L," Draven drawled, smiling up at her from the plush fur covered sofa he was sitting on.

"Thank you." L returned the smile with no warmth in her eyes. She'd been here only a day and already she was ready to leave. It wasn't just that Hrakaz was a bitter, barren world peopled almost entirely by idiot trolls and sniveling imps—it was Draven. He...bothered her.

Oh, he was handsome enough, she had to admit. With those broad shoulders and that lean, muscular body, he was enough to tempt any female. She even liked the neatly clipped goatee and mustache that matched his black hair. As far as she was concerned, not many men could get away with facial hair. But Draven wore his with style and élan—it made him look slightly sinister and emphasized his strong jaw.

But though his face was handsome and his body was mouthwatering, there was something missing in his eyes. And it wasn't just that they were pure silver disks with no pupil, it was something else. Some fundamental warmth that all living creatures possess—or should possess, anyway. It was lacking in Draven and the resulting emptiness behind those silver eyes made her nervous—she, who was never nervous around anyone!

I can always just kill him if he bothers me too much, she told herself. But after being here for a while, she wasn't so sure. When he looked at her with those empty eyes, she felt frozen inside. Frightened and yet also somehow...intrigued. Was that the right word? She wasn't sure. Why should a man who scared her also turn her on? *He doesn't,* she told herself fiercely. *I'm just reacting to his strength. His presence.* And she had to admit that Draven had more presence about him than any other male she'd ever met. There was something inside him...something she sensed but couldn't name. Some kind of past tragedy perhaps? But no, that couldn't be right. Well then, maybe—

"Who are you wearing tonight?" Draven asked, breaking her train of thought. L knew he was talking about the outward appearance of her body, not the clothing she had on.

"I'm an exotic dancing girl from Julo." L twirled slowly in front of him, showing off her pale pink hair, vivid blue eyes and lavender freckles. The shape of her body was slender but full in the breasts and hips, which was basically the same as her original form.

"I like it." Draven nodded thoughtfully. "But not as much as the form with black hair and light brown skin. You know the one I mean—with the amber eyes."

L couldn't keep the surprise from her face. He was speaking of her original form, the one she almost never wore. As far as she could remember, she'd only showed it to him once. Why would he pick that out from all her myriad of disguises as his favorite?

"I...don't wear that one much," she said, turning away and pouring herself a glass of some eye-wateringly strong alcohol. She wasn't sure what it was but it was blue and fermented—good enough for L.

"And why, may I ask? It suits you very well." Draven was suddenly right behind her, purring in her ear. L felt a shiver run up her back as the heat from his big body branded her spine.

"I don't like it," she said, moving pointedly away and taking a sip of her drink. It burned like fire going down and she had to fight not to choke.

"But *I* do." He moved up behind her again, refusing to take the hint, and brushed the long pale pink hair from the side of her neck. "You're beautiful," he breathed, nipping lightly at the side of her slender throat. "In all your forms, darling."

L tried not to shiver as his hot breath bathed her throat and his warm, spicy masculine scent enveloped her. Between her thighs, her pussy was getting hot and wet. Gods, for being such a bastard he certainly seemed to know what he was doing when it came to sex! Not that she would ever let him finish what he was trying to start.

She waited until he was sliding one large, capable hand down the inside of her thigh and then quickly morphed into one of his own trolls, complete with thick, wrinkled gray skin and appalling body odor. As an afterthought, she added a huge, erect penis, which jutted out from between her thighs and thrust into Draven's seeking hand.

With a low cry, he jumped away and L turned to face him, grinning from a face that had a wide, drooping mouth and six inch tusks. "Not so pretty now, am I?" She leered at him and made a few obscene thrusts with the immense phallus. Of course it was fake—a mere extension of her skin. L was fundamentally female and could only project the outward appearance of a male, but Draven didn't know that.

At first he looked disgusted but then, to L's surprise, he threw back his head and laughed. Against her will, she found herself liking the sound. It was a low, pleasant chuckle that sounded more real than anything she'd heard from him yet.

"No, you're not pretty in that form," he said at last, grinning at her. "But you *are* formidable. And smart. Which is extremely sexy, no matter how you may try to disguise it."

L frowned and let herself melt into her usual form—that of a curvy female with pale skin and dark blue hair. "I appreciate the compliment but what I most want is my orders to be gone from this rock."

"You want to leave me so soon?" Draven put a hand to his chest. "My darling, I'm *hurt*."

"I'm not here to keep you company, you said you had a job for me," L reminded him tightly. "A job we would both benefit from aboard the Kindred Mother Ship. You said we wanted the same thing—bloody revenge."

Draven frowned. "Well, as it happens, I've been rethinking the 'bloody' part."

"What?" L stared at him in disbelief. "You're supposed to be this ruthless killer. Your Hoard has wiped out entire planets and you don't blink an eye. But now you want to spare the bastards who—" She stopped short, biting her tongue.

"Who what?" Draven looked at her intently. "What did they do to you, L? Why do you hate the Kindred so much?"

"None of your business," L snapped, looking away. "I have my reasons to want them all dead—I thought you did to."

"I did—at first." Draven began to pace, his hands folded behind his back in an almost meditative way. "I've had my share of problems with them. Hell, one of their leaders put me out of commission for almost a thousand years. When I woke up, I wanted to kill them all. *Slowly*." The blank silver disks of his eyes turned on L, making her shiver.

"So what changed your mind?" she asked, trying to keep her voice steady.

He shrugged. "I guess over the last thousand years I've developed something new — let's call it a sense of humor. So I began to plan something a little more devastating."

L glared at him. "What could be more devastating than death?"

"*That*, my dear, is what you're going to find out." Draven rubbed his hands together. "Oh, I *do* envy you, getting to witness it all first hand. What I wouldn't give to see their pain and confusion..."

"Witness *what?*" L was running out of patience. "What am I going to be doing once I get aboard the Mother Ship?"

He frowned. "Not to change the subject but how *are* you going to manage that? The Kindred have tripled their security measures lately. I doubt they'll let a stray craft anywhere near their orbit, let alone invite the pretty lady who's flying it aboard. No matter how tempting your many disguises, I don't see how you're going to manage it."

"I managed to get onto Hrakaz without any of your people being the wiser, didn't I?" L raised an eyebrow at him. "Besides, why would I be fool enough to approach them from space?"

"Where else are you planning to approach them from?" Draven sounded irritated. "The fifth dimension?"

"Of course not. Think about it — where are they getting their brides from? Earth. That miserable little nothing of a planet is their only weakness. They're constantly importing new brides from its surface up to the Mother Ship."

"I see." Draven's eyes gleamed and he laughed again. "My dear, you're quite diabolical."

"I know." L smiled modestly, then glared at him. "And I *thought* once I got up there, aboard the ship, I was going to have something special to use—a weapon of mass destruction that would blow them out of the sky."

"Of course. But that's a very crude solution, don't you think?"

L gritted her teeth. "I don't care if it's crude—it's final. It's *satisfying*. Now are you going to give me something to blow the fuckers up or aren't you?"

Draven made a *tsking* noise. "Such language. Do you kiss your mother with that mouth?"

"I don't have a mother—or a father." L lifted her chin. "I make my own way. And I'm about to make my way *out* of here unless you give me a reason to stay."

"All right then. Here." Draven held out his hand. In his palm was a tiny silver device no bigger than the tip of L's thumb. "Don't lose it," he said as she picked it up carefully and examined it. "It's taken me ages to make. And it's tied to my will—I'm the only one who can reverse its effects."

L started to give it back. "Damn it, I don't want to use anything reversible on them. I want something *lethal*."

Draven sighed. "Yes, but when you blow your enemy up, they're gone and you can't toy with them anymore. You can't *laugh* at them."

L looked at him blankly. "I don't understand."

"Nor will you until you detonate the device. Just place it in the middle of the Kindred ship, in their sacred grove, and be certain you're alone at the very edge of the ship before you set it off with this detonator." He handed another, equally tiny silver device.

"But—"

"Then wait and see all the fun." Draven grinned. "After it goes off, you can go around killing them at will if that's what suits you. That is, if you can find the right people to kill. I guarantee there will be plenty of confusion to cover your tracks."

L frowned. "You're not making sense. Why can't you just tell me what this damn thing does?"

"Because that would take all the fun out of it, now wouldn't it?" Draven gave her a slow grin that sent another shiver down her spine. Gods, how could anyone be so sexy and so frightening at the same time?

"Fine." She sighed and pocketed the device. "But I want all my pay up front. If you're planning on blowing me up along with the entire Kindred ship, I want to be sure your money goes up with me."

Draven frowned but finally nodded. "Agreed. All I ask is that you wear a little recording device when you set it off. I really want to see the results."

"Me being wired will cost you more," L warned. "I don't like to work with surveillance on me."

"It won't be on you—it will be on whatever you see and hear." He produced something else from his pocket and held it out—a sparkling crystal stud. "Wear it in your ear, your eyebrow— wherever you're pierced. Just put it somewhere on or near your face so I can see what you see."

Reluctantly, L took the crystal stud. "All right but like I said, it's going to cost you extra."

"My darling, I would expect nothing less." Draven gave her a charming smile. "Now, I know you're anxious to be on your way but would you do me the honor of staying one more night?"

"I'm not sleeping with you, if that's what you're thinking," L said flatly. "I'd like to think I have better taste in males."

"Again, you wound me." He put a hand to his heart melodramatically. "But though it would be my very great pleasure to bed you, that wasn't what I had in mind. I just wanted a little company for my evening meal. And I thought you could use a good night's sleep before you started." He cleared his throat. "It's rather cramped quarters, sleeping in a space ship — don't you think?"

L frowned and shook her head. "Discomfort isn't a good enough reason to delay. I should be on my way to Earth — I'm going to be looking for a very specific situation to get aboard the Kindred Mother Ship."

A look of frustration passed over Draven's sharp features. "I have space folding technology, remember? I can have you there in a matter of minutes."

L spread her hands. "Then send me. Let's go."

Draven sighed and dragged a hand over his face. "Look, L, how can I put this...I'm *lonely.*"

L raised one dark blue eyebrow at him. "Excuse me?"

"That's the real reason I want you to stay one more night." Draven frowned. "You see how I live — my only companions are soulless idiots and sniveling sycophants. I am bound to this planet and the only company I get are people I have to torture." He sighed. "I can, of course, project my likeness across time and space but it's an exhausting effort that takes a lot out of me. All I want is one quiet, relaxing evening chatting with a beautiful, intelligent woman who's my intellectual equal."

L crossed her arms over her breasts. "You don't really think I'm your equal — you don't think *anyone* is. You're an arrogant bastard."

"Guilty as charged." Draven gave her a hint of a smile. "But that doesn't lessen my admiration for your intellect, my darling. Just grant me a single evening of stimulating conversation, please?"

"And how do I know that conversation is the only "stimulating" thing you have planned?" L demanded.

"I was out of line earlier, I admit it. But tonight I promise to be strictly hands off." Draven held up his hands, palm up as though to illustrate his point. "If you like, you can put on your troll identity again to make yourself feel safe." He wrinkled his nose. "Although if you do, I must insist on having my dinner upwind of you, I'm afraid."

L laughed and felt her determination to go wavering despite herself. "All right," she said at last. "I'll stay. But only for the conversation and the soft bed, which I will occupy *alone.*"

"Certainly. Come, let's go to the dining room and see what the chef has prepared tonight." Draven gave her a courtly nod and held out his arm for her.

After some consideration, L took it.

"All right. Let's go."

Chapter Eleven

"If you're not ashamed of us, why do you refuse to introduce us to your mother's mother?" Deep demanded.

"I...I..." Kat looked at Lock appealingly. This was the first really big argument she'd had with Deep since the three of them had fully consummated their relationship and sealed the three-way bond between them. Usually when they had minor tiffs, the light twin was right there to help her. But this time he simply stood there, leaning against the kitchen counter with his arms folded over his chest. When Kat shot him an appealing look, he simply shrugged.

"Don't look to my brother for help, Kat." Deep, who was the dark twin of the pair, looked genuinely angry. "He feels the same way I do. He's just too kindhearted to say it." He took a step toward Kat, his black eyes blazing. "Now I'll ask you again, why are you ashamed of us?"

"I'm *not*, all right? That isn't it at all!" Kat put her hands on her hips, fully prepared to give as well as she was getting.

"Then why haven't you introduced us to your relatives? Why haven't you planned our Joining Ceremony?" Deep thundered. "Lauren and Xairn had the most elaborate joining imaginable with both Scourge and Human customs planned by *you* and yet you won't even *talk* about a ceremony for the three of us."

"My lady Kat," Lock murmured, coming forward at last and taking her hand. "Forgive Deep for being so *loud*." He gave his brother a glare. "But it hurts us that you don't want to acknowledge our relationship."

"Lock's right. We want to—damn it, what's the Earth word?"

"Marry," Lock supplied quietly.

"Yes, we want to *marry* you in the presence of the Goddess and all our families. Our mother has been asking lately when the ceremony will be held."

"She's very excited to give us her blessing and it worries her that we haven't even set a date yet." Lock looked at her appealingly. "We never told her but I think she has an idea of how close we came to losing you and she *likes* you, Kat."

"She wants you for her daughter under-the-law, or whatever the hell you call it," Deep growled.

"It's daughter-*in*-law." Kat looked at the two of them and shook her head. "You know this is the opposite of how things are supposed to be, right? I mean, it's supposed to be the *girl* nagging about setting a date and the *guy* or *guys* in your case, are supposed to be trying to put her off and delay."

Deep frowned. "Is that the human way? How stupid."

"It's called fear of commitment," Kat snapped. "And right now I wish the two of you would have a little of it."

"But why should we fear to commit to you, my lady?" Lock looked genuinely confused and hurt. "We are bound together by ties stronger than death—why should we not wish to have a ceremony celebrating those ties?"

"No, the question is why doesn't *Kat* want to have a ceremony," Deep snarled. "And *I* say it's because she's ashamed of us."

"For the last time I am *not* ashamed of you!" Kat threw her hands in the air. "You want to meet my grandma? My *deeply religious, Southern Baptist* grandma and tell her we're about to be married—all *three* of us? You want to give an old lady a heart attack? Well then fine, we'll go. Hell, let's go right now." She turned to march out of the kitchen but Lock caught her by the arm.

"My lady," he murmured softly. "We do want to meet her but not like this. Not in anger."

"You said you wanted to see her. You s-said you wanted to g-go." To Kat's horror, she was beginning to tear up. "Crap," she muttered, rubbing her arm quickly over her eyes.

"Little Kat..." Deep's voice was oddly gentle, considering how angry he'd been earlier. "We don't want to hurt you, we just want to love you."

"And part of loving you is knowing your family," Lock said. "You can't keep your mother's mother in the dark forever. She knows you're living aboard the Mother Ship now and everyone on Earth knows there's only one reason an Earth female comes aboard and stays."

Kat knew it was true. In her heart, she was certain her grandmother already knew she was bound to a Kindred. She just wondered how Grandma would take it when she realized Kat was actually bound to *two* of them.

She let out a little sound that was half sob/half laugh. "I guess you're right. And I know my grandma will love both of you—I just don't know how she'll react to knowing you're both with me. I can see her now giving me that disapproving look of hers and saying, "Kat, sweetie, *two* of them? At the *same time?*"

Deep frowned. "After all this time, are you really still ashamed of what we do together when we love each other?"

"Well, no..." Kat bit her lip. "But you have to understand. On Earth there aren't many stable, long term Male/Female/Male relationships going on. Mostly when you hear about a girl who gets with two guys you're talking about the plot of a new porno. And when you add the fact that the two guys are brothers, well, then you're taking it to a whole new level of kinky."

"Lock and I don't touch each other that way." Deep sounded indignant. "The most we do is fuse our shafts together when we enter you as one."

"And what we do together isn't pornography—it's making love," Lock added.

Kat sighed. "I'm just telling you how most people on Earth see it—how my grandma is probably going to see it. She raised me pretty strict—this is going to be a blow for her."

Deep frowned. "If you're that worried about her, maybe only one of us should go. You should take Lock—he's less offensive than I am. You can pretend he's the only male you're with. That should make the mother of your mother happy."

"No!" Kat's heart was suddenly in her throat. This was how she had nearly lost Deep last time. He had been determined that he was no good for her or Lock and had tried to cut himself completely out of their three-way relationship. They had a bond now—one that she was fairly sure couldn't be broken. But it still made her nervous to see the dark twin trying to bow out.

"No," she repeated. "I love both of you. I want both of you to be there. Just…" She ran a hand through her hair. "Just let me call my grandma and be sure she'll be home. We can go tomorrow afternoon. That should give me time to think of how to explain."

She started to leave again, to go to the viewing room where she could place a call to Earth. Of course, she could have used the Think-me but she didn't like startling her elderly grandma by making her think she was hearing voices in her head. Besides, some things needed to be said face to face.

"Wait, Kat." This time it was Deep who caught and held her.

"Yes?" She looked up into his dark eyes, trying to see if he was still mad. But there was nothing but tenderness in his face as he spoke.

"Thank you," the dark twin said simply. "This means a lot to me—to both of us. Meeting your family, planning our ceremony."

"We haven't gotten to the ceremony part yet," Kat pointed out. "Let's be sure we can tell Grandma without putting her into ICU before we start hearing wedding bells."

"But I'm sure when we *do* have a ceremony, it will be spectacular." Lock came up from behind her and pressed close, sandwiching her between himself and his brother. "Weren't you planning on having a cake with bonding fruit cream in the center?"

Being caught between their two large, muscular male bodies was a position that used to make Kat feel helpless and frightened. Now it made her feel loved and secure. And hot...very, *very* hot. She could smell Lock's bonding scent—the warm, comforting aroma of the light twin's desire for her. But even stronger was Deep's scent—that delicious dark chocolate and sex smell that made her mouth water and her pussy wet at the same time.

"Yes," she murmured, wishing her voice didn't sound quite so breathless. "I...actually, I *was* planning on a cake with one special layer that had bonding fruit puree. Lauren was going to make it for me."

Bonding fruit—the sweet, triangular fruit that was native to Twin Moons—was the thing that made her relationship with Deep and Lock possible. Without its almost magical stretching properties, which allowed her to accommodate their larger-than-average Kindred sized shafts, she never could have managed to make love to even one of them, let alone both at the same time.

As she thought about it, Kat suddenly realized she'd had more than her fair share of the delicious fruit lately. She usually tried to limit herself to just one a day but there had been several that were on the verge of being too ripe to eat and she hated to let them go to waste. So she had eaten three or four of them earlier that day with hardly a thought as she read her way through the latest bodice ripper romance she'd gotten from Earth.

Kat had just been trying to escape her worries for a while by drowning them in fantasy, but now a few scenes from the racy book came back, making her shift from foot to foot uncomfortably. Deep down, she knew it wasn't just the book that was bothering her — bonding fruit had an aphrodisiac quality that she had never grown an immunity to, no matter how often she ate it. And it had been a long time since she and her men had made love — too long, really.

Kat had been putting them off because of her inner turmoil, not wanting to let them into her body while she was trying to keep them out of her mind. Now the bonding fruit built up in her system was beginning to really make itself known in the form of throbbing nipples and a pussy that was suddenly damp with desire.

"Little Kat…" Deep's voice rumbled through her, making her squirm some more. "It's been while since we took you, hasn't it?"

"Has it?" Kat tried to sound unaffected and knew that she failed. "We've all been so busy, I didn't even notice."

"*We* noticed." Lock kissed the back of her neck in a leisurely way that made her pulse jump. "We've been missing you, my lady. Missing your luscious curves."

"Not to mention your soft, wet pussy," Deep growled softly.

Kat shifted uncomfortably. She needed this but at the same time, she was reluctant to give in. She loved the three-way bond she shared with Deep and Lock but sometimes she just wanted to be alone in her own skin. Reluctantly, she decided to put off her need a little longer. She had to have time to get her head on straight before she let her two men into it again.

"Look guys, I really should make that call to my grandma," she said, sliding out from between them. "So now really isn't the best time for this."

"No, now is the *perfect* time." Deep's voice was suddenly hard again. He looked at Lock. "Hold her, Brother."

To Kat's absolute shock, Lock grabbed her as his twin directed. She tried to struggle but he held her arms gently but firmly behind her back. "Relax, my lady," he murmured in her ear. "Don't fight us."

"Don't fight you? What the hell do the two of you intend to do?" Kat demanded.

"Tell me, little Kat, have you heard of the Law of Conduct?" Deep asked, answering her question with a question.

"No, I…wait a minute." Kat's eyes widened. "Liv told me about that. Isn't that the one that says something about a Kindred being responsible for his female's conduct?"

"Exactly." Deep nodded. "And you haven't been behaving very well lately, have you, sweetheart?"

"I…I don't know what you mean," Kat stammered. She was still too much in shock to fully comprehend what was going on. Her men had never acted like this before—*never.*

"Yes, you damn well *do* know what I mean," Deep growled. "You've been shutting everyone out—even your closest friends. And you've closed your mind and your heart to Lock and me—the two people you should be able to trust with anything."

"Can I help it if I sometimes want a little mental privacy?" Kat snapped.

"We understand your need to keep some things to yourself, my lady," Lock said from behind her. "If you want us not to pry into a certain area, all you have to do is ask us."

"Put up a mental 'keep out' sign in your mind if you have to," Deep said, frowning. "But don't shut us out completely. That's wrong."

"And it hurts," Lock added quietly. "It reminds us of how things were between the three of us before we finally sealed our bond. That's...not a place we want to return to."

Kat slumped a little, relaxing in the light twin's grip. "All right, you've got me. I know I haven't been very, uh, open lately. I just...didn't want to worry the two of you."

Deep glared at her. "I'm glad to hear you admit your sins but it's too late for apologies, sweetheart. You've done wrong and now you have to be punished."

"Punished? *Punished?*" Kat stared at him in disbelief. "I can't believe you! Where do you get the nerve to *mmph!*"

Her last word ended abruptly because Deep leaned down and cut her off with a kiss. Not a soft, tender lover's kiss but a hard, demanding exploration of her mouth. A sign of possession—a mark of ownership.

At first Kat was so angry she wanted to bite him. But then, against her will, she found herself responding. The dark twin's bonding scent filled her senses and his mouth on hers, so hot and possessive, made her legs feel like rubber. By the time he finished his ruthless assault of her mouth, her lips felt bruised and her breath was coming fast and hard.

"Now, little Kat," he growled softly, looking into her eyes. "You're going to take your punishment like a good girl. Do you understand?"

"But what…what are you going to do to me?" Kat felt like she was drowning in the bottomless black pools of his eyes.

Deep gave her an evil grin. "Why, anything we want to, sweetheart. Anything at all."

"Don't worry," Lock added in her ear. "We won't hurt you, my lady—we would never do that. We're just going to give you what your body is craving."

"I'm not craving anything except for you two bastards to let me go," Kat said but her voice wavered alarmingly and her knees still felt like rubber.

"Is that right?" Deep cocked an eyebrow at her. "So you're saying you're not feeling any kind of sexual need right now? You're telling me your body isn't crying out to be touched…tasted…*fucked?*"

Kat's breath caught in her throat as his eyes blazed into hers. "No," she lied defiantly, lifting her chin. "I'm just fine."

"Is that right? Let's just see about that, shall we?"

Kat was wearing a dark green wrap dress that tied at the side. Before she could protest, Deep had loosened the tie so that the dress suddenly gaped wide. The open fabric panels framed her black lace bra and panties perfectly. In the past Kat would have felt self-conscious about her state of near undress—but that was before she learned that Twin Moons Kindred really did love full figured women with curves. Now the gesture just made her mad.

"What do you think you're doing?" she demanded, though she could hardly get the words out.

"Proving you wrong." Deep traced the edge of her bra, trailing one teasing finger across the lace. "So you don't want us right now… Don't need us…" he mused.

"N-no," Kat said but her voice was less certain now. The dark twin's touch was setting a fire across her skin. A fire she knew she couldn't put out alone.

"Then it wouldn't have any effect on you if I did this?" Deep found the fastening to her front hook bra and peeled the lacy black fabric away, leaving her breasts suddenly bare.

Behind her, Lock sucked in his breath. "Your breasts are so beautiful, my lady," he murmured in Kat's ears. "So full and luscious."

"Not to mention how hard your nipples are." Without warning, Deep pinched one of her tight buds between his thumb and finger.

Kat gasped and bucked back against Lock but the light twin still held her firmly. "Relax, my lady," he murmured in her ear. "Deep only wants to teach you a lesson."

"Why, you..." Kat was torn between anger at their arrogance and desire to feel more.

"Lock is right—you should just relax and take your punishment." Deep gave her a lazy smile. "If you don't behave, we'll be here all night. Not that I would mind." He pinched her other nipple, sending sparks of pleasure-pain from the tight little nub straight to Kat's pussy.

"You...you..." Kat couldn't find the words.

"Did I hurt you, sweetheart?" Deep murmured. "Want me to kiss it better?"

Without waiting for an answer, he leaned down and sucked one of the nipples he'd been tormenting into his mouth. Kat moaned at the hot suction and thrust her chest forward, wanting more— *needing* more—despite herself.

"That's right, my lady," Lock breathed in her ear as Deep turned his attention to her other nipple. "Give yourself to the pleasure. Deep and I love you so much. We just want to show you."

Deep pulled back at last, leaving her nipples aching and tender. "And teach you not to ignore your needs. Don't you know it's dangerous to let the bonding fruit essence build up in your system without some release?"

"It is?" Kat shook her head. "I...no one ever told me that."

"Well, it's true." Deep looked almost angry now. "It's another reason you deserve to be punished. Lock and I know you eat some every day and yet it's been days since you let us fill you."

"We waited for you, my lady," Lock told her, sounding sad. "We hoped you would come to us."

Kat raised her eyebrows. "Well, maybe you should have waited a little longer, *boys.*"

Deep frowned. "That doesn't sound like the words of a female who's learned her lesson."

Kat's heart started pounding even harder but now that he was no longer touching her, she felt more in control of herself. "And what lesson is that?"

"That you need us every bit as much as we need you, damn it." Deep's eyes flashed. He leaned closer and looked Kat in the eyes. "You feel empty inside—admit it, Kat. You need to be filled."

"I'm fine." Kat didn't know why she was being so stubborn, so defiant. She knew what Deep was saying was true—she felt a deep ache that went to her core. It was a hunger only her men could satiate. But though she loved him, there was still something in Deep that sparked her irritation and rebelliousness.

"If you're fine, why are your panties soaked?" Deep demanded.

"They're not," Kat insisted although she knew it wasn't true.

"Then you won't mind me sliding my hand inside to check and see if you're telling the truth, will you?" Deep raised an eyebrow at her.

Against her will, Kat felt a slow, hot tendril of desire uncurl inside her belly. This twisted little game they were playing was really beginning to get to her! And she still wasn't ready to admit defeat.

"Do your worst," she told Deep defiantly. "I'm not afraid."

"But you *should* be, sweetheart," Deep growled softly. "Because if I find out you're lying, your punishment will be that much worse."

"You still haven't even told me what this 'punishment' is supposed to be. You...*oh.*"

Her words ended in a groan as Deep's large, warm hand slid into the waistband of her black lace panties and cupped her pussy.

"Gods, you're wet." Deep's voice was hoarse. He looked at Lock. "I haven't even parted her pussy lips yet and already I can feel her honey coating my palm."

"Stroke her gently, Brother." Lock sounded anxious. "Show her how much we love her."

"Of course, I will." Deep's talented fingers teased her swollen pussy lips apart and one gentle fingertip began to circle the aching bud of her clit.

Kat gasped and would have collapsed if Lock hadn't been holding her up. God, she needed this *so badly.* She couldn't understand how she could have put it off so long. She was so close to the edge she thought she was going to explode at any time but somehow Deep was keeping her from it. Though he stroked and caressed her sensitive clit over and over, he somehow managed to keep from taking her all the way. It was maddening but Kat knew if she said anything he would win.

"What's the matter, little Kat?" Deep was watching her face avidly as he continued to tease her unbearably. "Feeling a little *frustrated?*"

"Damn you, Deep!" Kat bucked her hips, unable to keep up the pretense   anymore.
"Stop teasing me and make me come!"

"Oh, I don't think so." Slowly, Deep withdrew his hand from her panties and sucked the finger he'd been stroking her with, making sure to clean away her honey thoroughly. "Orgasms are for good girls, little Kat. Girls who admit they're bad and agree to accept their punishment."

"You bastard!" Kat groaned. Her need had grown to monstrous proportions. It was as though Deep had struck a match inside her and the small flame he'd started had become a blazing inferno of desire that threatened to consume her.

Deep laughed. "Yes, I am. And I'm going to continue being a complete bastard for a while longer, sweetheart."

Kat bit back a moan. "At least put your fingers inside me," she said, hoping she didn't sound like she was begging. "Please, Deep, I can't...can't take much more. Please...fill me."

A look of compassion flitted over the dark twin's face. "Don't worry, little Kat. We'll give you what you need." He nodded at his brother. "I think she's ready—let's bring her to the bedroom."

Lock lifted her into his arms and Kat didn't even try to fight him. As angry as she was at Deep, she realized that he was right. She'd been denying her desire for far too long and now she was weak with the need to be filled—to be fucked by her men.

"Please," she moaned softly as Lock laid her down in the middle of the huge bed built for three. "Please, I need you...both of you."

"It's all right, my lady." Lock kissed her cheek gently and curled his big body against her back. "We'll take good care of you."

"Like we always do." Deep lay down facing her and Kat noticed hazily that somewhere between the kitchen and the bedroom, he seemed to have shed his clothes. From the feel of Lock's bare skin against her back, he was naked as well.

And so am I, she thought, looking down at herself. God, how had they undressed her without her noticing it? She had a vague memory of hands pulling at her bra and panties but nothing else.

"Let me lick your pussy, my lady," Lock murmured, breaking into her jumbled train of thought. "Let me ease your pain."

"Yes..." Kat found herself rolled on her back, her hands buried in the light twin's hair as he parted her thighs.

"So sweet," he murmured as he spread her swollen outer lips. "So beautiful."

"Lick her deep, Brother," Deep commanded hoarsely as he cradled Kat's head in his lap. "Taste her sweet pussy—get her ready to take us."

Kat had never felt more ready in her life. The bonding fruit was really kicking in now, reminding her of the first time she'd tried it back on Twin Moons. There she had basically overdosed on the damn stuff and it had taken Deep and Lock all night and a very large dildo to ease her need. This time she was glad no sex toys would be needed—just Deep and Lock fused together deep inside her.

She cried out as Lock's hot tongue parted her folds and rasped gently over her swollen clit. "Oh, God...please...*please...*"

"That's right, Kat." Deep stroked her hair away from her face and leaned down to kiss her. "That's right, open yourself. Let Lock make you come."

"I thought...thought you said orgasms were only for g-good girls," Kat gasped.

Deep gave her a sardonic grin. "Maybe we can make an exception just this once." He kissed her again, thrusting his tongue between her lips just as Lock plunged his tongue deep into her pussy.

Kat moaned at the double penetration and arched up, wanting more, wanting both of them so badly. Gone was her anger at their "punishment", gone was her stubborn refusal to admit she needed them. Everything had been burned away in the heat of her desire—everything but the need to have them fill her.

She felt an orgasm coming as Lock licked her, like a wave washing over her at the beach, and she cried out and clutched at his hair. But though the wave of pleasure felt wonderful, it was too gentle to really help. Kat knew from past experience that she could come all day but until she was penetrated—deeply penetrated and taken—her need wouldn't ease.

"Please!" she whispered when Deep let her up for air. "Please, I need you inside me—both of you."

"And we need to be inside you, little Kat." Deep's voice was both tender and rough with desire. "How do you want us? One in front and one in back?"

"No." Kat shook her head almost frantically. "Both of you at once. In...in my pussy. *Please.*"

"Your wish is our desire. Come, Brother," he said to Lock who was still lapping and sucking Kat's slippery folds. "Our lady needs us."

"Of course." Lock was suddenly at her back again and Kat knew they were joining together—fusing their shafts to create a single thick cock—the only instrument capable of curing her raging need. She moaned with frustration until she felt the broad head brushing her aching pussy.

"Now," Deep murmured in her ear and then, suddenly, the deliciously thick shaft was breaching her entrance and driving deep into her hungry pussy.

Kat cried out and writhed between them, feeling herself stretch to accommodate the single massive shaft. She could never get over how good this felt, how incredibly complete it made her to be filled by both her men at once.

Deep, she sent through the mental link she had neglected much too long. *Lock, God, need you. Need you both so much!*

We need you too, little Kat. Deep held her hips and looked into her eyes as both brothers, moving as one, thrust into her.

It's been so long. I feel close...so close. Lock's mental voice sounded strained.

Me too. Deep didn't sound worried at all. *But that's all right because Kat is going to come with us. Aren't you, sweetheart?*

Kat couldn't deny the much deeper orgasm that was finally reaching a peak within her. She knew they had barely begun but Deep's teasing and the bonding fruit in her system ensured she was coming rapidly to the point of no return. She wished she could make it last but there was no way, she was coming...coming...

Don't worry, little Kat, Deep whispered through their link. *We'll have plenty of time for more leisurely lovemaking later. Right now, just come. Lock and I want to feel you squeezing us while we pump you full of our seed.*

Kat couldn't have stopped if she'd wanted to. With a low cry, she felt her orgasm overtake her completely. Compared to the one she'd had earlier, this was like a tidal wave, rushing over her, making every muscle in her body tense, every nerve ending tingle. It was so good...so incredibly good it was almost too much.

"God!" she cried aloud. "Lock...Deep...coming! Coming so hard."

"My lady!" Lock groaned at the same time Deep growled,

"Little Kat. Going to fill your sweet pussy with cum."

The wet heat and the pulsing between her legs proved he was telling the truth. With a moan, Kat closed her eyes and gave in to the intense sensation of being so completely owned, so thoroughly fucked and filled by her men. God, they drove her crazy sometimes but she loved them. Loved them so much...

We love you too.

Kat wasn't sure which of them whispered it or if they both sent it together.

I just hope you forgive us for punishing you. This voice clearly belonged to Lock.

Kat sighed as another warm wave of pleasure flowed through her. *You never even told me what the punishment was.*

This is the punishment, Deep murmured in her mind. *Lock and I proving you wrong – proving that you need us as much as we need you.*

Kat felt too good to be mad anymore. *I forgive you.* She sighed happily. *And here I thought you were going to spank me or something.*

Hmm. Deep's mental voice sounded thoughtful. *I suppose that can be arranged.*

"Don't you dare!" Kat glared at him until he laughed and shook his head.

"All right then, if you're not up for corporal punishment, how about some more of this kind?" He and Lock thrust simultaneously into her again, making Kat moan as the thick shaft pressed hard against the end of her channel.

"Yes," she managed to say. "Yes, I think that would be fine. Excellent, in fact. And...*oh.*"

She could say no more.

Chapter Twelve

The hazy sun of Yonnie Six didn't exactly shine brilliantly through the windows but it was still bright enough to wake Saber from his sleep. He yawned and stretched, promptly hitting both elbows on the sides of the damn drawer that housed his bed. Cursing under his breath, he sat up and tried to work the stiffness out of his neck. Goddess, he'd slept in some uncomfortable places but the damn slave bed was like sleeping in a coffin!

"Good morning."

The soft voice coming from above him made him start and look up. Seeing Lissa's sleepy eyes and the soft smile that curved her lips made his day instantly better.

"Morning, Mistress," he said, smiling. "Did you sleep well? Any more dreams?"

"No." She bit her lip in that unconsciously sensuous gesture she had. "You?"

"None," Saber admitted and it was true. "I slept like a baby," he continued, which was a lie—the slave bed was much too cramped. But he didn't want her to feel bad about not having him in the big bed with her. After everything that had happened between them, he could understand how nervous she was and why sleeping together would be a bad idea.

"About that dream. I've been thinking that maybe—" Lissa began but a loud rapping on their door interrupted her.

"First Meal in fifteen minutes." Llewelyn's voice came floating through the thick door. "My mistress is expecting you, Lady R'awr."

"Oh, of course." Lissa sat up at once. "Please tell her I'll be right down."

There was a general rush to get dressed and Saber never did get to hear what she thought of the erotic dream they had somehow shared. He resolved to ask her about it later—if they had time. But Lady Sha'rak's morning announcement made him think they were going to be very busy.

"The sensation party has been delayed," she said, as soon as Lissa sat down across from her. "I know it's *too* awful but I thought we could have some fun here today instead. Besides, my dear, you really need a bit more training in how to handle your slave before you go out in public."

Lissa got red in the face but only nodded. "I'm sure you're right, Lady Sha'rak."

Saber kept his own face blank and merely set about feeding his "mistress" breakfast, which seemed to be a much simpler meal than the elaborate dinner of the night before. There was a hot drink with an herbal, spicy smell, which Lissa seemed to find pleasant, and some thin, crispy wafers spread with a sweet paste that smelled slightly nutty.

Lissa seemed to find it awkward at first, to be fed by him, but they soon found a rhythm and it became easier. Saber hoped she wasn't too uncomfortable because he certainly wasn't. In fact, he genuinely enjoyed serving her.

It wasn't because he was submissive, though he didn't really mind that part of their current "cover story". No, the reason he enjoyed serving her was that a lot of what he was doing—fixing her food and making sure she was well nourished, taking care of her, protecting her—was something a Kindred warrior who was trying to win a mate would do during the first part of his Claiming Period.

Saber tried not to think about the other things he would be doing if he was actually trying to win Lissa as his bride. Bathing her…massaging her with scented oils…tasting her…*Gods!* He shook his head, trying to force the erotic images and thoughts out of his brain. Though he knew it was beyond wrong, the very idea of tasting Lissa—of spreading her creamy thighs and thrusting his tongue deep in her sweet pussy until she moaned and begged for more—had his cock rock hard inside the tight black slave trousers he wore.

He was concentrating so hard on pushing the thoughts out of his mind and keeping a blank expression on his face that he missed something the Lady Sha'rak said to him.

"Saber?" Suddenly he realized that all eyes at the table were upon him. Lissa was looking at him with concern, Lady Sha'rak with deep disapproval, and Llewelyn was smirking at him from across the table in a way Saber didn't like at all.

"Excuse me, my lady." He made a bow in the ambassador's direction. "Were you speaking to me?"

"I most certainly was," she snapped, her blue eyes sparking with indignation. "I asked that you pass Llewelyn here the *gak* butter to spread on my *tildo* wafers and you completely ignored me!"

Saber could feel Lissa tensing beside him and he was instantly sorry for his inattention to detail. She had painted her own nipples with the elixirs that morning and somehow wiggled into the tight pale green dress with a deep V front all by herself. Though Saber had offered to help, she had refused him and he had understood why — she was trying to put some distance between them after the events of last night. And here they were barely done with breakfast and it looked like she would have to "punish" him again.

Not that Saber counted it a true punishment. He didn't mind the fiery pain in his mouth if it meant he got to suck her sweet, ripe nipples and make her moan. But he knew how much shame and anxiety the act caused Lissa — for that reason alone he wished he could have refrained from offending their hostess.

"Please, my Lady," he said, bowing low, though it irritated him to show such abject submission to anyone but Lissa. "Please forgive my inattention to you. I have no excuse for my rudeness."

"Well." Lady Sha'rak looked somewhat mollified. "He's well-spoken for a slave, I *will* give him that, my dear," she said, speaking to Lissa and once again ignoring Saber. "That honeyed tongue is probably what's kept you from training him properly all these years. Am I right?"

"I...suppose so," Lissa said, sounding miserable.

"Well, that all stops *now*." Lady Sha'rak threw down the rich silken square she'd been using as a napkin and stood up. "Come, my dear Lady R'awr. If we are to get you ready to go to the sensation party, we need to start now. And I'm afraid we have a *lot* of ground to cover."

"Of course." As she stood, Lissa shot him a look of pure misery.

At that look on her face, Saber felt even worse about his gaff. He wanted to tell her it was all right — that whatever paces Lady Sha'rak made Lissa put him through, he wouldn't be upset. But he couldn't risk anyone else hearing their exchange and he could see Llewelyn watching avidly as they all left the table. All he could do was nod in what he hoped was a reassuring way and follow her obediently.

Lady Sha'rak led them to another part of the floor, in a separate wing they had yet to visit. As they walked through the high, arching doorway into a new room, Lissa gave a little gasp. And indeed, Saber found he had to bite the inside of his cheek sharply to keep from exclaiming.

The walls, flooring, and ceiling of the immense room were all covered in crimson padding. It was spongy and giving to walk on, making Saber think of a training room where warriors could spar together without anyone getting injured.

But non-injury didn't seem to be the point of this room. In fact, it appeared at first glance to be exactly the opposite.

On every wall hung implements of torture and subjugation. There were paddles and floggers, crops and canes. There were restraints of all kinds and several pieces of furniture that appeared to have straps where a slave's arms and legs would go to tie them down. In addition to all this, there were many, *many* devices Saber had no name for and no idea what their uses could be. Although he was certain none of them could be pleasant.

"This is my private training room." Lady Sha'rak turned to face them and threw out her arms, encompassing the strange array.

"Oh my," Lissa murmured faintly and Saber saw with concern that her face had gone pale. "I...don't know what to say."

Lady Sha'rak laughed. "Don't worry, my dear. Most of this is for advanced methods I'm sure you're not ready for yet. We're just going to work on a few simple discipline techniques and some public submission protocols. Just enough to get you through the party—all right?"

Lissa bit her lip. "I guess so."

"Good, then let's begin," Lady Sha'rak said briskly. Moving to the center of the room where there was a long, padded black bench, she settled herself upon it and crooked a finger toward Lissa. "Come here, my dear, and show me how you generally discipline your slave."

Lissa walked forward slowly and Saber trailed her. "I...I..." Lissa cleared her throat. "I mostly just reprimand him verbally, I suppose."

"Not nearly good enough." Lady Sha'rak frowned. "There are levels of discipline, my dear, just as there are levels of offenses a slave does to earn such discipline. Now what would you do, say, if your slave forgot to bring something you'd specifically told him to bring to a party?"

Lissa licked her lips nervously. "I'd...make him go back and fetch it?" she asked, obviously hazarding a guess.

Lady Sha'rak threw her hands in the air. "And leave yourself unattended at a party? Unthinkable! You'd call another slave from your home to fetch it to you and in the *mean*time, you'd punish the one who forgot in the first place. Very *publicly*, I might add, to be certain he learned his lesson." She sighed. "I'm sure I don't know what they're coming to on Zetta Prime when the young people don't even know how to do such a simple thing as discipline a slave."

"Forgive me," Lissa said humbly. "As I said before, Saber has just always been so well behaved."

"Not quite as well behaved as you think," snapped their hostess. "He still doesn't direct his eyes down where they belong. He still doesn't greet you properly. And until you give him a little taste of pain, he'll never learn. Now stand here, in the center of the room," she directed Lissa. "And have your slave stand across from you."

They arranged themselves as she demanded, standing in front of the black padded bench where their hostess was lounging as

Llewelyn stood behind her at attention. Saber's heart twisted in his chest as he looked down into Lissa's lovely green eyes. He could see the anxiety this "training" session was already costing her and he only hoped she wouldn't be too upset by whatever it was Lady Sha'rak insisted she do to him.

"There. Now look at the way you're standing," Lady Sha'rak said sharply. "Look at the way he's looking at you—as though he's your equal! He must keep his eyes down and never look you in the face unless you're speaking to him. Slave—look down!" she snapped.

At once, Saber dropped his eyes and studied Lissa's small feet instead of her face. She was wearing simple silk slippers a shade darker than her light green dress and they fit her tiny feet very well. But he couldn't help letting his eyes trail up. The green dress was split high, like most of the other Yonnie dresses Kat had packed her, and her long, slender legs were fully revealed.

Likewise visible were the lace panties she had on, which went with the dress. They were trimmed in green but the tiny V of white lace in the center was what held his attention. It was so skimpy and translucent Saber swore he could almost see the outline of her plump little pussy lips through the thin material. In fact, the green lace border skimmed just along the middle of her mound and when she shifted uncomfortably, they pulled lower, revealing a neatly trimmed patch of blonde curls and the start of her slit. Goddess, what he wouldn't give to kiss her there! To pull down her panties and plunge his tongue deep into her sweet, hot depths. To—

"There he goes again!" Lady Sha'rak exclaimed, breaking into his forbidden thoughts.

"What do you mean? He's looking *down*, just as you said," Lissa protested.

"Looking at *you*, more likely. And like a lover—not a slave. Why, he's practically eating you up with his eyes! It's *most* improper." Lady Sha'rak sounded scandalized. "Slap him, my dear."

"What?" Lissa looked at their hostess, plainly startled.

"You heard me. Do not tolerate such insolence—slap his face this instant!"

"I..." Lissa looked absolutely miserable. "Must I?" She gave their hostess a pleading glance but Lady Sha'rak was glaring at her.

"If you don't, *I* shall. It's clear your body-slave is well overdue for this. As he himself said last night, he needs to learn pain as well as pleasure from your hand."

Lissa looked up at him and Saber risked a quick look back. Then he leaned forward, lowering his head to make himself easier to reach. He didn't fear a slap from his lady's palm—he was a warrior and had suffered much harsher blows before. Indeed, the only thing that worried him was how bad Lissa was going to feel about hitting him. But there was no way around it—she was going to *have* to do it or risk offending their hostess and jeopardizing the mission.

A quick flick of her eyes showed him that Lissa must be realizing the same thing. She gave him a look full of apology and then reached up and slapped him.

Saber barely felt the blow—it was more like a pat than a slap and he was certain it wouldn't leave a mark. Unfortunately, Lady Sha'rak seemed to come to the same conclusion.

"No, no!" she stormed. "*Not* like that—you have to show him you're not to be trifled with. You must dominate him completely. Slap him, *hard*, Lady R'awr!"

Considering what Llewelyn had told him about secretly dominating his mistress, Saber considered her insistence that Lissa dominate *him* rather ridiculous. But he knew that if they didn't do this correctly, things were only going to get worse.

"Really, Mistress," he said softly, daring to look into Lissa's eyes again. "Is that the best you can do?"

"He's taunting you!" Lady Sha'rak was on the edge of her seat, her cheeks red with irritation. "This is too much, my dear—you *must* act!"

Lissa looked as though she was being pushed to the limit. Saber could see the determination building in her eyes and the tense set of her shoulders.

He leaned even closer and murmured, "Do it," in a voice so low he was certain no one but she could hear.

"Fine!" Setting her lush pink lips in a tight line, Lissa pulled back her arm, and slapped him as hard as she could.

It was a respectable blow and Saber did everything he could to make it look even worse than it was. He let his head rock back as her hand connected and even put his fingertips to his cheek as though in surprise and pain. The tingling in his skin let him know that this slap would probably leave a mark—good, maybe it would satisfy their hostess's lust for corporal discipline.

"Saber..." he heard Lissa whisper brokenly. "Your cheek..."

He didn't reply. Instead, he took her hand—the one she had slapped him with—and pressed a soft kiss into her small palm.

"Mistress," he murmured and let her hand drop as he stared down at her slippers, trying to look like a penitent slave. He ached fiercely inside—not from her slap but from the broken sound of her voice. A swell of hatred rose inside him—a deep antipathy toward their hostess, for making the female he loved so upset.

"Good, much more like it." Lady Sha'rak sounded encouraging. "Look at him, my dear—you've almost put him in his place."

"Almost?" Lissa asked in a quivering voice and Saber risked another glance at her troubled eyes. He wished again that he could comfort her but there was no way to do it without blowing their cover—not now, anyway.

"You cannot ignore the verbal taunts he made to you earlier," Lady Sha'rak was saying firmly. "You must punish him severely this time."

"So...you want me to slap him again?" Lissa sounded so upset at the idea that Saber felt his insides twist.

"Not necessarily." Lady Sha'rak sounded thoughtful. "I *would* say you should give him the rod—nothing puts a slave in his place as quickly or as effectively. But the more I study him the more I see that your body-slave is much like my own."

"How is that?" Lissa sounded uncertain.

"My Llewelyn isn't much fazed by pain." The ambassador cast a fond glance over her shoulder and she and her slave smiled at each other briefly. "I do punish him with it on occasion, of course, but I've found it much more effective to use pleasure to bring him into line."

"Pleasure?" Lissa sounded honestly confused. "But...how?"

"You shall see. But first, I think we need some touch-me-not manacles. Llewelyn, be a love and get me some from the small cabinet in the corner, will you?"

The body-slave moved swiftly to do her bidding and before Saber knew it, Lady Sha'rak was slipping inch wide copper bracelets around his wrists. She adjusted them until they were firm and snug, though not painfully so, and then pressed a small copper remote, which Llewelyn handed her. Saber heard a small but ominous clicking sound from both cuffs and then Lady Sha'rak nodded in apparent satisfaction.

"There now. That should do it," she said, settling herself on the padded black bench again.

"What are those things you've put on Sa—on my slave?" Lissa demanded, looking upset.

"Nothing but a small deterrent, my dear. They will do no long term or lasting damage to your slave, I assure you. They will simply keep him from self-pleasuring. Until you remove them, he will be unable to gain relief unless you grant it to him personally."

"I'm afraid I don't understand," Lissa said, frowning. "I thought the whole point of this…this exercise or whatever it is you have in mind, *was* pleasure. And how can you punish someone with pleasure, anyway?"

"It's very simple, my dear. And it's not pleasure so much as *delayed gratification.*"

"Delayed gratification?" Lissa repeated warily. "How does *that* work?"

The broken sound was gone from her voice, at least, which made Saber's heart feel lighter. But he had a bad feeling about the thick copper bands locked around his wrists. Still, he was glad they seemed to be moving on to something that didn't appear to involve slapping. Clearly Lissa felt the same—she would rather do anything than hurt him.

But Lady Sha'rak's next words made his lighter mood suddenly evaporate.

"Cup his cock," she said, looking at Lissa.

Lissa nearly choked. "I'm sorry…*what?*"

"You heard me." Their hostess sounded impatient. "Do as I say and take his cock in your hand."

Lissa's cheeks were bright red but it was clear she didn't dare disobey. Slowly she reached forward and placed her palm lightly against the bulge beneath Saber's tight black trousers.

Saber fought to remain impassive but though she was barely touching him, he felt the light brush of her fingers against his shaft like fire. Gods! How often had he wished to feel her stroking him there! And now all that was separating them was a thin panel of cloth.

But Lissa's timid gesture didn't seem to please their hostess.

"For the Goddess's sake, Lady R'awr," she snapped. "You act as though you've never touched a male before! Do it right—reach into his pants and grasp his shaft."

Saber knew for a fact that Lissa never *had* touched a male like she was being directed to touch him. She had spent the last several years living in a temple filled with women and before that, she'd been with only him. And despite their love, they had never gone this far, even though Saber had secretly wished they could.

Her lack of experience notwithstanding, she was going to have to learn quickly. And to her credit, she honestly tried.

Saber didn't know which way to look as Lissa, her face now aflame with embarrassment, fumbled to get her hand down the front of his trousers. But they were too damn tight—she couldn't manage. It seemed like she was about to give up when Lady Sha'rak spoke again.

"You, slave—why are you standing there like a lump? Open your trousers for your lady!" She gave him a glare. "And you'd better be very, *very* careful not to touch your equipment or I promise you'll regret it."

Saber obeyed at once, unfastening the magno-tabs that held the waist in place and unzipping slowly, being careful not to touch his own bare skin. To his embarrassment, his shaft was harder than ever—the minute his zipper came down it sprang free to stand at attention between his thighs like an exclamation point.

"Very nice." Lady Sha'rak's eyes raked over him and she nodded approvingly. "Now stand at attention, hands behind your back."

Saber did as she commanded, feeling like some kind of prized beast put on display.

"I can see why you put up with so much, my dear," Lady Sha'rak murmured to Lissa. "He's *very* well hung. A shaft that size must give you considerable pleasure."

"I...thank you. It...it does," Lissa murmured in a voice choked with embarrassment. She didn't seem to know which way to direct her gaze, but her eyes kept returning to Saber's shaft as though she couldn't look away.

Of course she can't look away—she's probably traumatized, he thought with a surge of irritation for their officious hostess. *She's never seen a male's equipment before and I'm on the large side even for a Kindred. No doubt she's scared to death right now!*

Unfortunately, his anger didn't make his shaft deflate in the least. Instead, it seemed to grow even harder, throbbing between his thighs as though begging to be touched...stroked...

"All right now that you can reach it, take it in your hand," Lady Sha'rak was directing Lissa.

Lissa didn't answer or protest this time. Instead she reached forward and rested her hand lightly on his bare shaft.

Saber bit the inside of his cheek fiercely to stifle a groan. Even this light touch was enough to make him crazy. *Her hand,* he couldn't help thinking to himself. *Her hand is on me! She's touching me!* And the Goddess knew he wanted her to touch him so much more…

But even this wasn't enough for the relentless Lady Sha'rak. "No, no—take him *firmly* in your hand," she told Lissa. "Wrap your fingers around his shaft."

Her cheeks burning red, Lissa complied. Or tried to, anyway— her slender fingers couldn't quite encircle Saber's aching cock.

"Now…now what?" she asked Lady Sha'rak in a strangled voice.

"No, my dear, you stroke him." Their hostess gave her a knowing smile. "Slowly but firmly—up and down. That's it," she continued as Lissa began a slow up and down caress as directed. "Excellent—now don't rush it. Let him feel your dominance."

But dominance wasn't exactly what Saber was feeling. Instead he felt a hot rush of pleasure every time Lissa's soft, slender fingers slid over his heated flesh. His cock throbbed in her little hand, his balls—still enclosed in the black trousers—ached and grew tight with the need to come.

Relax, he told himself sternly. *Just relax and think of something else.* But he couldn't—couldn't take his mind away when one of his deepest fantasies was becoming a reality. He stood with his legs braced apart, his hands clenched into fists behind his back, and his cock throbbing with each sweet stroke of her fingers, feeling like he was going to explode.

Goddess, it was shameful but her soft hand was too much for him. He was getting closer by the minute—what kind of punishment would their sadistic hostess make Lissa inflict on him if he came? And how traumatic would it be for Lissa if he suddenly shot his load all over her trembling fingers?

"Do you see the tension in his body? The way his jaw is clenched?" Lady Sha'rak demanded. "You've got him right on the edge—right where you want him, my dear."

"Yes... I guess I do." Lissa's voice sounded almost dreamy. In the beginning, there was no doubt she'd been horribly embarrassed by what she was forced to do. But now...could she be...enjoying it? Surely not.

Yet, when Saber risked a quick glance at her face, he saw an expression of eager curiosity in her eyes. *She likes it!* he thought. *She likes touching me—exploring me the way I want to explore her!*

The thought was a revelation—since she'd never seen or touched male equipment before, Saber had been afraid she would be repulsed or frightened by him. But the look on her face made it clear the opposite was true. Lissa was enjoying this—not as much as he was, perhaps—but she was far from repulsed.

Knowing that she didn't hate what she was doing—that she actually *liked* touching him—was almost too much for Saber. He could feel the hot cum building in his balls and his shaft grew even harder, threatening to erupt at any moment.

"My lady!" he gasped at last, in a strangled voice. "My lady, *please!*"

"Saber? Am I hurting you?" Lissa looked up at him at once, her eyes filled with uncertainty.

"No," he muttered through clenched teeth. "No, but I...I can't take much more. I'm about to—"

"Stop!" Lady Sha'rak interrupted commandingly. "Stop touching him this instant, my dear," she told Lissa.

Reluctantly, Saber thought, Lissa pulled her hand away. She looked at Lady Sha'rak. "Now what?"

"Now we wait for a moment." There was a look of cruel amusement in their hostess's blue eyes. "I think it's a good time to practice how your slave acknowledges you in public."

"It is?" Lissa looked troubled but their hostess nodded firmly. "I mean...now?"

"Absolutely." Lady Sha'rak nodded firmly. "Now, start at the beginning: how do you have him show reverence to you when you go out?" she asked.

"He should kiss my foot." Lissa looked relieved to know the answer.

"You heard her, slave." Lady Sha'rak snapped her fingers imperiously. "Get down and kiss your mistress's foot."

Saber nodded submissively though he was boiling inside. He began to stuff his aching cock back into his trousers but a sharp shock to his fingertips made him curse hoarsely and jerk his hands back.

"Uh-uh-uh, slave. Did you forget about the touch-me-not manacles you're wearing?" She gave him a stern frown. "You will be unable to touch your equipment without pain until such time as your mistress deems it time to remove them." She gestured at Lissa's small green slippers. "Now kneel at your lady's feet and make a proper obeisance."

Stiffly, feeling ridiculous with his throbbing member still exposed and his fingertips tingling, Saber got to his knees. He leaned low and pressed his lips to the top of Lissa's little foot.

Offering the token of submission burned but again, only because it was Lady Sha'rak giving the order for it. He knew he wouldn't mind doing this for Lissa — he wouldn't hesitate for an instant if she was the one asking. He *did* mind, however, putting on a show just to please their sadistic hostess. Had he really thought to himself just the night before that she wasn't as cruel as Lady Pope'nose? Clearly he had been wrong. She was a true bitch and it seemed his torture was far from over.

"Very good," she said to Lissa as Saber raised up again. "And now, how does he show reverence to you when you are announced at a formal party?"

"Um...he kisses my other foot?" Lissa sounded worried.

"Of *course* not, my dear. He kisses your *panties.*"

"He...he does?" Lissa swallowed audibly. "I mean, of course he does. Saber," she said, snapping her fingers. "Kiss me...kiss my panties, I mean. Show the proper respect."

This time Saber was more than glad to submit. Leaning forward, he pressed his cheek to the small triangle of green and white lace and inhaled deeply, filling his senses with her intoxicating female fragrance. Gods, if only he could kiss her without the panties in the way! But this was better than nothing.

Slowly, tenderly, he placed his lips at the very center of the white lace. Behind the thin barrier, he could feel her soft pussy lips parting for him as he pressed carefully forward. He knew if he could just slip the flimsy barrier to one side, he could have his tongue buried to the hilt in Lissa's sweet, wet cunt.

"Oh..." The soft exclamation fell out of Lissa like a sigh and Saber felt one soft little hand slip into his hair. Gods, he was *dying* here. Being so close to her and not being allowed to taste her was sheer torture. His exposed cock throbbed for release between his thighs but there was nothing he could do about it—nothing at all.

"Very nice." Lady Sha'rak said, breaking the moment. "Of course, if the company at the party is extremely posh and important, you can always direct your slave to tongue you in order to show extra reverence and submission. I recommend wearing split panties just in case. Do you have any? If not, I can loan you some."

"I...I...split panties?" Lissa seemed to be at a loss for words and Saber thought that even if he had been allowed to, he couldn't have spoken either. Was their hostess actually saying that he might get his wish after all? To taste Lissa, no matter how briefly, was what he wanted most in the universe. But how would she feel about it? Would she hate him for it if he had to do it? Or would she display the same eager curiosity she had when she was stroking his shaft? He risked a quick glance up and saw that she was looking down at him, her cheeks stained scarlet with mortification.

"Mistress," he murmured, and pressed another slow kiss to the white lace that was now becoming damp from her honey.

"Saber," she whispered and caressed his hair tentatively. The simple, hesitant gesture sent a shiver through Saber's entire body and he felt the fire within him re-ignite with a sudden blazing rush. He was just about to lean forward again and push the panties to one side when Lady Sha'rak's strident voice burst his fantasies of finally tasting Lissa.

"Enough obeisance! Order him to rise."

The sharp command made them jerk apart and Saber looked up at Lissa again.

"On your feet, slave," she commanded, obviously trying to copy Lady Sha'rak's demanding tone. "And...and keep your hands behind your back."

"Yes, Mistress." Saber got awkwardly to his feet. Rising, he stood as he had before with his legs spread and his arms behind his back, feeling both vulnerable and foolish.

But despite his negative emotions, he was also hotter than he had ever been in his entire life. Was he starting to enjoy his submission to Lissa? It seemed like a foreign concept but he honestly found he kind of liked taking orders from her—especially orders with a sexual overtone.

"Very good, though he could have been faster." Lady Sha'rak nodded.

"Thank you." Lissa looked at her. "Now what?"

"Now you're going to stroke him again. And again and again and again. But you will never—*never* let him come." Their hostess gave her a cruel smile. "*This,* my dear, is the true torture. Your slave will never dare to disobey again once you master the technique of delayed gratification."

Oh Goddess! Saber looked up at the padded ceiling. He already had the worst case of the blue balls he'd ever had in his life—how was he going to survive this torture? And yet, he had no choice. As Lissa's small, soft hand encircle his aching shaft once more, he set his jaw and forced himself to hold still and take it.

What else could he do?

* * * * *

Lissa looked at Saber from the corner of her eye as she pulled out yet another ancient document to look at. Lady Sha'rak was out in the town, running errands before dinner. After the lengthy training session she'd put Lissa and Saber through, she had declared there were some things she simply *must* get before the party. To Lissa's relief, she had taken Llewelyn with her, promising to be back in time for dinner. Now that they had the entire floor to themselves, it was the perfect opportunity to search the ambassador's private library for the missing scrolls.

And also, apparently, the perfect opportunity to ignore each other and pretend nothing had happened.

There had been silence between them since the ambassador had left and Lissa was upset and anxious—how did Saber feel about her now? Did he hate her for abusing his body so? For fondling him without his permission? They had been working for almost an hour and he'd been perfectly silent all that time. Though he said nothing, he still moved stiffly, as though he was hurting exactly where she had touched him. Oh Goddess, had she been too rough?

Lissa didn't *think* she had been—Saber had certainly seemed to enjoy her hand on him while she was stroking his shaft. And to tell the truth, she had rather enjoyed it herself. She'd never seen male equipment before but Saber's had been...nice. Well, more than nice, actually. He had been hot and throbbing in her hand and yet the skin of his shaft had been so soft—it was like stroking a heated iron bar with the texture of rose petals. To be completely honest, touching him so intimately had made her feel warm and tingly all over.

But Lady Sha'rak *had* forced them to continue the exercise over and over for a *long* time. Maybe Lissa had over done it. Had she done him some kind of lasting injury?

"Saber," she blurted, unable to keep her worried thoughts bottled up any longer. "I...I think you should let me examine you."

"What?" He turned to her, both eyebrows raised in evident surprise. "Examine me where? And why?"

"Where...where I touched you." Lissa could feel her cheeks getting hot but she refused to back down. She pointed to the large bulge in his crotch where his cock was barely contained by the tight black slave trousers. "I...I need to see if I've hurt you or done you any lasting harm."

"Hurt me? You think you *hurt* me?" His face held a mixture of laughter and irritation. "Why would you think that?"

"Because of the way you're moving—it's like you can barely *walk*. I need to see if I've bruised you or—"

"Lissa, I'm *fine*," he interrupted. "I'm not hurt."

Lissa frowned stubbornly. "I don't believe you."

"Too bad," Saber shot back, with a frown of his own. "You'll have to take my word for it because I'm *not* opening these damn trousers again. I barely got back into them last time."

"That's because you're all swollen and hurting," Lissa protested. "If you'd just let me see—"

"You think you can help me by touching me more, is that it?" His jaw clenched. "Sorry, but it's not going to happen. It would only make the problem worse."

"But—"

"*Amalla*." He caught both her hands in his and looked earnestly into her face. "Please believe me, your touch didn't harm me in any way. This is a problem I can..." He coughed. "I can take care of myself. As soon as I get these Goddess damned manacles off."

"I'll ask for the remote at dinner," Lissa promised. "I'm sorry I didn't think to before Ambassador Sha'rak left."

"We were both distracted," Saber said shortly. "Now, come on, we don't know how long she and Llewelyn are going to be gone. We need to get this whole library searched by the time they get back."

"We've been through hundreds of scrolls and documents, though," Lissa protested. "And none of them is even from First World."

"It's valuable property—she probably won't have it out in plain view." Saber went back to hunting through the triangular stacks of

books and scrolls and data disks. "It'll probably be hidden like—
hello, what's this?"

He took several thick leather bound volumes out of their
triangular shelf and stared with some interest at what was behind
them.

"What is it? Did you find something?" Lissa came up behind
him and tried to look over his broad shoulder. He was so much
taller than her she couldn't see much but she did manage to catch a
glimpse of a small opening that seemed to extend deep into the
bookshelf.

"I did." Saber pulled something out and then frowned. "There's
a false back to the bookshelf here and it has some documents. I
don't think they're the scrolls we're looking for, though."

"Oh..." Lissa took the small triangular paper book from him
carefully. There was a picture on the front of a large, muscular male
with no shirt on. He was holding a small, slender female to him
forcefully, bending her over one brawny forearm and staring deep
into her eyes.

"Very strange," Saber murmured, frowning at the picture.

"It looks like one of those books Kat and the other Earth girls
like to read back on the Mother Ship," Lissa said. "Kat calls them
'bodice rippers'." She opened the book and tried to concentrate on
the strange, squiggly writing. Luckily the shot of translation
bacteria she'd had before leaving the Mother Ship enabled her to
read what was written aloud.

*"He pulled her to him and Ka'tha had no choice but to come. She tried
to protest but then his mouth was locked over hers, devouring her, taking
what she had never intended to give. Ka'tha fought him, or tried to,
anyway, but she could feel her will weakening as the savage kiss went on.
Soon he had completely overpowered her and she was helpless in his arms.*

"Admit it," he growled. "Tell me I'm your master."

*"But you're not," Ka'tha protested. "I bought you. **I'm** supposed to be **your** mistress."*

"Not anymore," he growled and took her mouth again, proving who was really the master.

"Oh, my." Lissa looked up. "I think this is some of that, uh, male-dom pornography you said Llewelyn told you about."

"I think you're right." Saber took the triangular book from her and flipped through it thoughtfully, stopping here and there to peruse certain passages more closely. "There's no doubt the male is mastering the female – which is the exact opposite of how they do things here."

"Kat loves those kinds of books," Lissa murmured. "She says sometimes you just want a male to take charge." She looked at Saber who was staring at her with one eyebrow raised. "Oh, um, I mean...that's what she says, anyway," she stammered, blushing.

"I have to admit, this kind of thing..." He nodded at the book. "Doesn't seem nearly as strange as what we're uh, doing now."

"I guess..." Lissa looked down. "Do you hate me now?" she asked in a rush. "I mean, for what I did to you?"

Saber's answer was quick and reassuring. "Of course not! You're only doing what you have to."

"But..." Lissa lifted her eyes to his. "I slapped you. And I...I tortured you. I didn't want to but –"

"Of course you didn't want to. *Amalla...*" He took one of her hands and raised it to his lips. "Didn't I tell you I'd rather have pain from your hand than pleasure from anyone else's?"

"But Saber..."

"And you didn't really hurt me," he went on. "In fact, having you touch me...feeling your hand on me...it was..." He cleared his throat and his voice dropped lower. "It was one of the greatest pleasures I have ever felt," he murmured, massaging her palm gently with his thumb.

"It...it was?" Lissa looked at him, wide-eyed. His touch on her hand felt so right—it sent tingles through her entire body. She couldn't help remembering how good it had felt when he dropped to his knees and kissed her through her panties, couldn't help wondering if he'd wanted to do more...

Saber nodded. "I've dreamed of that, you know. Of feeling your hands on my body and knowing we were right for each other. Knowing that the kinship compounds they injected us with couldn't stop our feelings, couldn't halt our pleasure in touching one another..."

The kinship compounds. Of course, because we're of the same clan. For a moment she'd almost managed to forget it. His touch was so gentle and his warm, masculine scent was so intoxicating. She would almost swear it was his mating scent but of course his body wouldn't release pheromones like that for her—not for one of his own clan. Or at least it shouldn't...

"Saber, we *can't.*" Lissa drew her hand away from him and took a step back. "You know we can't."

"I know." He turned away and put the forbidden book back in its hiding place. "But I can't help wishing. I—"

"We're back. Did you miss us?" Suddenly Llewelyn came into the room, a sarcastic smirk on his face. He was followed by Lady Sha'rak.

"Hello, my dear—did you have a pleasant afternoon?" she asked Lissa.

"Oh yes. We were just…" Lissa cleared her throat, glad that they had moved away from the section where the forbidden book was hidden. "I mean, *I* was just catching up on some light reading. Your library has so many fascinating books and documents in it."

Lady Sha'rak gave her a pleased smile "I *am* proud of my little collection although it's not nearly as complete as Lady Pope'nose's. Still, it serves me well enough for sensation play and that's what's important, right?"

"Of course." Lissa wished she could ask exactly what sensation play was, but she'd been pretending to understand for so long it would look suspicious if she asked now. She supposed she'd have to find out at the upcoming party.

"So." Lady Sha'rak clapped her hands. "I'm *exhausted* from shopping all afternoon. What do you say we have a nice light supper in the relaxation grotto?"

"That sounds lovely." Lissa smiled. "I've been curious about your grotto ever since you first mentioned it. I'm so sorry I didn't get to see it with you and Lady Pope'nose."

"It is a *gorgeous* space. You'd swear you were actually in a cave out in the wilderness—a very nice one, of course." Lady Sha'rak smiled. "Come, let's get you into some relaxation robes and I'll have Llewelyn inform the chef that we're going to eat in the grotto."

Lissa followed their hostess, trying to keep a polite smile on her face. But inside she was torn. The things Saber had said to her, the way he had looked…could it be that he truly still felt for her as he always had? But no…

Stop it! she told herself fiercely. *I absolutely cannot fantasize about Saber like this. We're here on a mission and after that we'll go our separate ways. Saber will go back and succeed his father as the Over Chief of the Touch Clans and I'll go back to being the head priestess on First World.*

We'll never see each other again and that's good — it's right. The right thing to do.

But why did doing the right thing make her feel so desolate inside?

Chapter Thirteen

Relaxation robes appeared to consist of four sheer panels of silky, peach-colored fabric that hung from Lissa's shoulders and straight down to her ankles. The panels were joined at the shoulders and split in the front and also the back so that when she moved, Saber could see her naked flesh from all angles.

The hard bulge of his cock throbbed again and he wished for the hundredth time that he could make the damn thing go down. But though hours had passed since the tortuously pleasurable session of "delayed gratification" Lady Sha'rak had put them through, he was still hard enough to fuck a hole through a brick wall. And of course, seeing Lissa in such a skimpy outfit didn't do a thing to help his condition.

If only I could slip off and take care of myself a few times this wouldn't be so bad, he thought while bowing low and getting his "mistress" settled into the low, padded lounger beside Lady Sha'rak's.

But of course that was impossible. Every time his hands got anywhere near his naked shaft, he received a sharp shock. Only to his fingertips, though—his cock was completely unaffected by the shocks. Meaning that while his fingers stung, his shaft never went down. It was beginning to drive him crazy—he only hoped that Lissa remembered to ask for the remote that went with the touch-me-not manacles at the end of the night. If he had to go to bed like this, he couldn't be responsible for the consequences.

To take his mind off his throbbing member, Saber studied their surroundings as he prepared to serve Lissa her supper.

The relaxation grotto looked like a cave, just as Lady Sha'rak had promised. It had stone walls and a high stone ceiling with cool blue-green recessed lights that gave it a mysterious but relaxing atmosphere. Soothing music was being piped in from somewhere and there were several round pools set around the perimeter of the large room that added the soft sound of water, which echoed in the cavernous space. One of the pools was filled with bubbling pale green liquid that released an invigorating herbal smell. Another had calm, dark blue waves lapping against its smooth stone perimeter. A third seemed to be filled with some kind of pink foam that emitted a slightly floral scent.

The padded loungers were right in the center of the space between the pools and surrounded by flowering plants. A low buffet table had been set up beside them, which meant Saber didn't have to reach far to find choice tidbits and fruits to feed his lady. He tried to sniff everything before he offered it to her, wanting to make sure it would be to her liking. As with the breakfast that morning, it was much simpler fare than the formal dinner that had been served the night before. Lissa seemed to find almost all of it pleasing.

Saber was hungry himself but not starving. Before leaving, Llewelyn had shown him where a stash of protein bars for busy slaves were kept. Saber had eaten several and was glad he had — dinner looked like it was going to be a long, drawn-out affair.

Eyeing Lissa's luscious, exposed flesh, he just hoped he could get through it without bursting out of his too-tight slave trousers.

* * * * *

Dinner seemed to go on forever. Lissa enjoyed the food, which was mostly fresh fruit and a few little creamy pastries, but she wished she and Saber could get back to their room. In fact, now that they had searched the ambassador's private library and ascertained that the missing scrolls weren't among her collection, Lissa wished they could leave for good. But Lady Sha'rak was their ticket to the sensation party as well as the other collectors on the list, so they had to stay.

Lissa just hoped their hostess wouldn't make her put Saber through any more torturous or humiliating scenarios. Her "slave" was on his very best behavior tonight—he had kissed Lissa's foot when they came into the grotto and was keeping his eyes modestly downcast as he fed her—so she didn't see how Lady Sha'rak could justify any more of her "training". But she was beginning to see that the Yonnite ambassador did pretty much anything she wanted. Also, she seemed to really *like* the sight of Saber put into an uncomfortable or compromising position.

Lissa couldn't understand such an attitude—did Lady Sha'rak really hate males that much? Or was she taking out her frustration at her hidden submissive tendencies on someone else's slave because she couldn't take it out on her own? Or—

Lady Sha'rak sighed contentedly, breaking into Lissa's thoughts. "Ah, this is lovely, isn't it?" She stretched luxuriously, allowing her relaxation robes to fall open, showing her breasts and a clean-shaven pussy mound.

"Yes, lovely." Lissa looked away and tried, unobtrusively, to be certain the thin panels of her own gown were covering her adequately. It was something she'd been doing all night and not always successfully. The silky peach panels didn't want to stay in place—in fact, they seemed almost made to slip open at inopportune times and flash anyone who happened to be looking. Meaning Saber, of course. Every time her gown slipped open, she felt his eyes drinking her in and though his face displayed no emotion, she could swear that the bulge in his trousers got bigger at such times.

Lady Sha'rak waved her body-slave's hand away. "No more, Llewelyn, I don't want to be too full to enjoy my massage."

"Massage?" Lissa asked, taking the last bit of fruit Saber was offering.

"Why yes, you didn't imagine I'd invite you to my relaxation grotto without planning any kind of *relaxation*, did you?" Lady Sha'rak's blue eyes twinkled. "That would just be silly, now wouldn't it?"

"I suppose so." Lissa cleared her throat. "But, well, who's going to be giving the massages?"

"Llewelyn, of course. He's trained in all kinds of erotic massage techniques and I don't mind sharing him, just this once."

Lissa put a hand to her throat, feeling suddenly ill. The idea of a strange male touching her, rubbing her all over, made her skin crawl. She couldn't let Llewelyn touch her like that—she just *couldn't.*

Saber made a soft but menacing sound and Lissa turned to see him glowering at Lady Sha'rak's body-slave. Clearly the idea of letting another male touch her also bothered him. Or maybe "bothered" wasn't a strong enough word. His hazel eyes were blazing and a low growl was rising in his muscular chest.

"I thank you for your kind offer, Lady Sha'rak," she said quickly. "But it just so happens that my Saber is also well trained in all kinds of massage."

Lady Sha'rak shrugged. "Oh, very well. If you're certain he can do as good a job as Llewelyn."

"*Quite* certain," Lissa assured her quickly. She was relieved to hear the low growl coming from Saber subsiding but her relief was short lived when she considered what she had just done. She'd just agreed to let Saber touch her all over her body. *Well, maybe it won't be that bad,* she told herself uneasily. *Maybe he'll just give me a back massage or –*

"Come on," Lady Sha'rak said, sounding excited. "We can't get massaged until you've experienced the pools."

"The pools?" Lissa looked around. "Um, all right – which one?"

"*All* of them, of course! Come on, take off your robes and let's go."

There was almost nothing Lissa wanted to do less than get completely naked in front of Saber – not to mention Lady Sha'rak and Llewelyn. But there didn't seem to be anything else she could do. Taking a deep breath, she slipped off the loose relaxation robes and followed Lady Sha'rak to the steaming green pool.

"Heat first, then cold, then warmth," Lady Sha'rak lectured as she slipped carefully into the pale green depths. "Do you know how to swim, my dear?"

"A little," Lissa said. Her breath hissed between her teeth as she slid into the overheated water. "My, this is *hot.*"

"Don't worry – we'll only be in the first pool a moment. The water here is infused with *trantha* extract – it opens the pores and cleanses the skin of impurities."

"It's very nice." Lissa found that she was nearly panting with heat as she stood on her tiptoes, swaying in the bubbling green water. She was glad she'd worn her hair up that evening, she didn't want it drenched in the herbal smelling *trantha* extract.

Just when she was feeling like she was getting seriously overheated, Lady Sha'rak cried out, "Switch! Into pool number two, my dear!"

Lissa followed her out of the first pool and directly into the second, which was filled with some kind of pink foam.

Extremely *cold* pink foam.

"Oh!" Lissa gasped as she floundered through the super-cold fluff. "What...what is this?"

"*Barrian* bubble snow, of course. Isn't it lovely?" Lady Sha'rak ducked her head under the surface for a moment and came up laughing. She blew a large puff of the pink foam at Lissa playfully. "It shocks the system and closes the pores. Do you feel ready to get out yet?"

"Y-yes, p-p-please." Lissa's teeth were chattering.

"Come on, then." Lady Sha'rak climbed out of pool number two and headed straight for the third one with its lapping, dark blue waves.

After being alternately boiled and frozen, Lissa was understandably reluctant to go into the third pool. She wanted to at least ask what kind of substance she was going to be getting into but the ambassador didn't give her any time. She slid directly into the dark blue liquid leaving Lissa no choice but to follow.

To her surprise and considerable relief, the substance in the third pool was neither boiling hot nor freezing cold. Instead, it was blessedly and comfortingly warm and soothing. It had a silky, slightly viscous texture that seemed to coat her skin without clinging to it and a light, sweet fragrance that reminded her of exotic blossoms.

"Ah, truly the best is saved for last," Lady Sha'rak murmured, floating lazily beside her. "Go ahead and let your hair down, Lady R'awr. This is *musqueet* oil. It has a lovely conditioning effect without actually getting you wet."

"Really?" Lissa looked down at herself doubtfully but what Lady Sha'rak said seemed to be true. Though the viscous liquid surrounded her and held her up like a gentle hand, it did not make her wet. It did, however, leave a light, golden sheen on her skin and, as she rubbed her arm with her fingertips, she realized her skin had never felt so soft. "This is wonderful," she said, taking down her hair and letting it fan around her shoulders. "I've never felt anything like it."

"That's because there aren't many *musqueets* left." Lady Sha'rak did a lazy sidestroke, dived under and came back up with the air of a confident swimmer. "They're terribly endangered, you know—it cost me a fortune in bribes to get enough of them to fill this pool."

"Um...we're swimming in some kind of *animal* secretion?" Lissa felt a little ill. "I thought this was another plant extract."

"Oh no, my dear—no plant can equal musqueet oil. They make it to keep their coats from getting waterlogged when they swim, you know. They live on a planet that's entirely ocean so you can see why it keeps you dry while conditioning you at the same time."

"Yes, I see."

"We had to milk their hides for ages to get enough oil. I put Llewelyn in charge of the operation—he's very good at practical things, you know. Much more than merely ornamental as so many body-slaves are." She shot her slave a lazy smile, which Llewelyn returned, and then looked back at Lissa. "I can't help noticing that your slave seems to be more than ornamental as well. He appears to serve as your protector and guide as much as your bed toy."

Lissa sensed a trap. "Yes, I rely on him a great deal," she said, trying to sound off-hand. "But in the end, you know, he's just a slave. As you said when we first met, all males must be kept in check and subjugated."

"Did I say that?" Lady Sha'rak sighed. "I suppose I must have, or something of that nature. Well." She pushed her blue-streaked hair back from her forehead. "Speaking of keeping them in check, let's go get those massages now." She snapped her fingers. "Llewelyn. My towel."

Llewelyn came at once. When she climbed out of the pool, he draped a pale pink towel as large as a sheet around her shoulders. He then proceeded to pat her gently all over, obviously taking care not to remove too much of the *musqueet* oil. Lady Sha'rak's bare skin still had a faint golden shimmer when he was done.

"You look lovely, my lady," he murmured to her and Lady Sha'rak gave him a lazy smile.

"Why thank you, Llewelyn. Come, take me to the table and show me your hands haven't forgotten their skill."

"They haven't, my lady. And I have some special warming oil to use on you tonight. On your more..." He paused meaningfully. "Your more *delicate* areas."

"Oh, you *naughty* male." Lady Sha'rak giggled and slapped at him playfully. Then she looked down at Lissa, who was still waist deep in the dark blue pool. "Come on, my dear—hurry up. You have no idea how relaxing a massage can be after one has bathed in *musqueet* oil—you're in for a treat."

"I'm sure I am." Biting her lip, Lissa motioned for Saber. "The towel, please."

She'd been keeping her back to him as much as possible while she and Lady Sha'rak bathed in the various pools. But now she had no choice but to face him as she stepped naked out of the pool and held out her arms to be dried. Still, she found she couldn't quite meet his eyes as he knelt at her feet and blotted her gently with the soft, fluffy towel. Instead, she looked away, biting her lip and feeling more exposed than she ever had in her life.

"You're beautiful, *amalla,*" Saber murmured in her ear as he finally stood. "Lift your chin—don't be ashamed."

"I can't help it," she whispered in a voice so low she was sure only he could hear it. "I'm not...not used to you seeing me like this. Not used to *anyone* seeing me like this. And now this massage..."

"Relax." He brushed his knuckles gently over her flushed cheek. "I swear I'll be gentle."

"Lady R'awr, *do* hurry," Lady Sha'rak called from across the room. "We really can't get started until you come over."

"Oh yes! I'm so sorry." Lissa hurried over and saw that the padded loungers they had been lying on during dinner had now been converted into massage tables. They were raised to waist height and the Yonnite ambassador was already lying nude on her stomach on one of them.

"Have your slave assist you up," she directed Lissa. "And do hurry—we must begin before all the benefits of the *musqueet* oil are gone."

"Of course," Lissa said as Saber lifted her gently and placed her on her table. "But you don't have to wait for me to get started."

"Of course I do." Lady Sha'rak sounded slightly cross. "Because I want your slave to watch Llewelyn and copy every move he makes *exactly*. Now don't say a word," she continued when Lissa opened her mouth to protest. "I know you say your male has training in massage but *no one* is as good at it as my Llewelyn. I actually had him sent away for a month to learn from the *bishwa* Monks on Clarity. I felt lost without him, of course, but the very first time he touched me after he came back I knew it was worth every lonely night I spent."

"That sounds like very specialized training indeed," Lissa said faintly. "Um, very well. I'll be sure Saber copies Llewelyn's every move."

"See that he does," Lady Sha'rak commanded. "And I'll have Llewelyn keep an eye on him to be certain he's doing it right."

Inwardly, Lissa groaned. Oh Goddess, what were they going to do now? She'd been telling herself that she and Saber could get away with just a back massage. Now, he was going to have to copy Llewelyn's every move. And something told Lissa that the special training Lady Sha'rak had sent her body-slave to learn consisted of techniques far more *advanced* than anything she had mentally prepared herself for.

Still, at least she was lying on her stomach with nothing exposed but the sides of her breasts. She closed her eyes and buried her head in her arms, keeping her legs firmly closed, and tried not to tense up. *It's going to be okay,* she told herself over and over. *Somehow we'll get through this. Somehow...*

And then Saber's strong, warm hands were on her shoulders, forcing every other thought out of her mind.

At first Lissa was so nervous she could barely breathe, let alone relax. But soon Saber started kneading the tension that seemed to have gathered in her neck and shoulders away. He had a firm, steady stroke that soothed her mind and eased her body. And, most important, he wasn't touching her anywhere that would make her uncomfortable.

Before she knew it, her body was turning to butter under his touch. Goddess, she hadn't been lying when she told Lady Sha'rak he had special training—he really *was* good at this! So good she could almost forget she was naked and in the position of letting him touch her in a very forbidden way.

But it's not like he's touching anything but my shoulders and back and neck, she told herself with a sigh of relaxation. *It's not like he's touching my —*

"Lower now," she heard Llewelyn say. "Watch what I do and follow along."

Lissa's heart jumped into her mouth as she felt Saber's large hands slowly move down over her lower back and bare buttocks. He continued on, however, passing over her ass to caress her thighs and calves with long, slow, strokes.

It's all right, she told herself when he began to press his thumbs firmly into the arch of her right foot. *It's just a foot massage, that's all.*

She relaxed again as Saber continued on her other foot and didn't even flinch when he began kneading her calves. When he got back to her thighs, however, she had to admit that things were getting intimate again. And then Llewelyn said something that made her heart begin to pound.

"This technique is called 'sliding from behind into the gates of pleasure.' It's very advanced."

"I see." Saber's large hands were resting lightly on Lissa's bare buttocks, as though waiting for instruction. "How is it done?"

"First, have your lady spread her legs," Llewelyn instructed.

Lissa heard a soft moan from Lady Sha'rak's direction and deduced that the Yonnite ambassador had already spread her own legs. But when Saber slid his hands up her thighs and applied gentle pressure, she tensed up and squeezed herself shut.

If she opened her legs for him, if she spread her thighs, he would have a clear view of her swollen pussy. Lissa was almost used to showing him her breasts—although she never would have believed it possible. But the idea of him looking directly at her inner core and knowing exactly how excited she was becoming by this slow, tender massage was too much to bear.

"Come on—what's taking so long?" Llewelyn sounded impatient. "My lady's waiting."

"Just trying to get the technique exactly right," Saber said. Then he murmured, in a voice so low it was clearly for her ears alone, "Lissa."

"I…I can't," she whispered back, tilting her head back toward him and away from Lady Sha'rak and Llewelyn. "I just can't, Saber."

"You *have* to," he returned softly. "Please, *amalla*, you know I would never hurt you…"

Lissa *did* know that. *It's true,* she thought. *No matter what happens, I'm completely and utterly safe in Saber's hands.* It might be embarrassing to let him see her so vulnerable and open, but it wasn't dangerous. He would kill or die to protect her and he would never, never take advantage if he could help it.

Knowing that, she finally understood that she had to let him in.

With a low sigh of surrender, Lissa relaxed, allowing Saber to part her legs and open her thighs wide. A cool breeze brushed over her exposed pussy and Saber offered a soft murmur of wonder when she finally gave in.

"Beautiful," he murmured reverently. "So damn beautiful."

"Finally," Llewelyn said, sounding sarcastic. "Anyone would think you'd never serviced your lady's pussy before. Now watch me and do as I do—place your thumbs just so."

Lissa bit back a gasp when she felt Saber's thumbs land firmly on her swollen outer pussy lips.

"Now rub," Llewelyn continued, ignoring the low groan coming from Lady Sha'rak. "A long, slow, circular motion. The idea is to stimulate the clitoris without actually touching it. Bring it to full engorgement—give her pleasure without completion."

Lissa couldn't stifle a moan when Saber's thumbs began a slow, deep massage of her outer pussy lips. She could feel them pushing inward, nudging hard against the small, sensitive bundle of nerves at her center. And though part of her wanted to close her legs and hide her head in shame, another, deeper part reveled in the delicious pleasure she felt just by letting him touch her.

"So good," she heard Lady Sha'rak murmur and she couldn't have agreed more. The intimate touch in such a sensitive, forbidden area was making her more excited than she could ever remember being in her life. She kept having a feeling like something was building within her—some peak of pleasure that wanted badly to happen. A peak she was sure she could reach if only Saber would keep touching her, if only he would never stop...

"She should be getting wet now, if you're doing it right," she heard Llewelyn tell Saber. "Her pussy doesn't need to be completely soaked—you're not fucking her, after all. Not *now* anyway. But it should be slippery enough to take two of your fingers. Test her out if you're not sure."

Lissa's heart jumped into her mouth. Kindred females had no hymens to form a barrier between themselves and any kind of invader but she still had never had anything inside her before. To her relief, Saber simply said, "She's ready."

"Good. If you're sure, flip her over. Time for a deeper massage."

Deeper? she thought but Saber was already turning her over on her back and smoothing his hands down over her inner thighs.

"It's all right," he murmured, still stroking her gently. "Honestly, it's going to be all right."

Lissa tried to still her pounding heart. "I know," she whispered back. "I just...it feels so strange."

"I did when you touched me too." Saber looked into her eyes. "But just at first. Then I felt only pleasure. Let me give you pleasure too, Lissa. Let me touch you, *please*."

Lissa took a deep breath. "All right," she whispered. "Do...whatever you have to." And closing her eyes, she let her thighs fall open, giving him complete access to her unprotected pussy.

Llewelyn was already talking again when she finally relaxed. "Stroke the inner thighs first and take your time about getting to her sex," he instructed.

"All right," Lissa heard Saber say. Then his large, warm hands were carefully kneading the tender flesh of her inner thighs almost, but not quite touching her core.

"When you feel all her tension relax," Llewelyn continued, "You can turn your attention to the inner, more delicate areas." He murmured to Lady Sha'rak, "This is the warming oil I told you about, my lady. It comes from the Vendon sector and it's said to increase sensitivity greatly."

"That's lovely, Llewelyn," Lady Sha'rak murmured. "Please go on and be sure to give Lady R'awr's slave some oil to use as well."

"Of course, my lady." Llewelyn turned his attention back to Saber. "Watch how I do it. Just a few drops at the apex of her slit. Then spread her outer lips and let it trickle down, making sure it coats the clit."

He must have suited actions to words because Lissa heard another groan from Lady Sha'rak's direction and deduced that

Llewelyn was using the warming oil on her. She was tempted to open her eyes, but there were some things she just didn't want to see. And she felt less embarrassed if she didn't have to watch Saber work on her.

"Get ready," she heard Saber murmur and then she felt some warm, slippery droplets pattering softly down on her vulnerable mound.

When he spread her open fully, she almost gasped but somehow she managed to bite her lip and stifle the sound. It wouldn't do to let Lady Sha'rak know that this was the first time she and Saber had ever done anything like this. But when the warming oil slid slowly into her open pussy and coated the sensitive pearl of her clit, she couldn't help moaning aloud.

"Lovely, isn't it?" Lady Sha'rak said from the other table. "Llewelyn, I don't know how you managed to get this oil but I promise you'll be rewarded for your diligence and thoughtfulness later."

"That's very kind of you, my lady," her body-slave purred. "But the only reward I seek is your pleasure. Are you ready for me to continue the massage?"

"Yes, please, Llewelyn—don't stop!"

"I wouldn't dream of it, my lady." Llewelyn turned to Saber again. "This next part is the most delicate. You will be massaging the oil into your lady's inner cunt and the utmost care must be taken. Use the pad of your right thumb and slide it gently—*very* gently—around her clit in a slow circle. Do you understand?"

"Of course," Saber said.

But though Lissa's entire body had gone tense as a wire, waiting for his touch, he still didn't do as Llewelyn had commanded. At last she opened her eyes and looked up at him.

"Saber?" she asked uncertainly. "Are you...is everything all right?"

"Everything's fine," he assured her softly. "But I'd like you to look at me while I do this. I need to see your eyes to make sure I'm not hurting you."

"Oh..." Lissa whispered. Up until now she'd been able to bear the slow intensity of the massage and manage her embarrassment by closing her eyes, thus isolating herself in her own little world of darkness. Now Saber was asking her to give that up — to look at him as he touched her intimately, perhaps even penetrated her. Could she stand it?

"Saber..." she began.

"Please," he murmured, a troubled look on his face. "Please, *amalla*, I don't want to hurt you."

"All...all right," Lissa murmured at last. "I'll watch." When he still didn't move she added, "Touch me, Saber. It's all right. I...I trust you."

A look of relief and tenderness came over his face. "Thank you. That means a lot to me."

Then he spread her open and placed the broad pad of his thumb directly over her throbbing clit.

Lissa gasped and nearly jumped off the table at the direct contact. She'd never had anyone touch her like this. In fact, she had never even touched *herself* like this. She'd been too ashamed to when she lived on their home planet and afterward, when she was living on First World in the temple, self-pleasure had been frowned upon and outright forbidden by Minverna.

"Are you all right?" Saber asked, looking at her anxiously.

She nodded. "It's just...intense."

"If she can't bear direct contact, slide gently around her clit in a circular motion," Llewelyn said from his place by Lady Sha'rak. "Remember, you must treat your lady as gently as though she were a virgin. Pretend this is the first time she's ever allowed a male to touch her and you are privileged to be that male."

"I think I can manage that." Saber gave her a little half smile, which Lissa tried to return. She couldn't help feeling nervous, though. She could feel her insides starting to tense up again...

And then Saber began circling her clit slowly and carefully, almost but never quite touching her very center.

"*Oh,*" Lissa whispered in surprise. This slow, indirect contact was better, *much* better than a direct touch. She could feel warm currents of pleasure pulling at her as Saber continued the slow caress. Her nipples had hardened into tight little buds at the tips of her breasts and her back was arching, seemingly of its own volition. She could feel a warm, sexual flush creeping up between her breasts and her breath was beginning to come in short little pants.

"Feels good?" Saber murmured, holding her eyes with his own. "Do you like it, my lady?"

"Yes, oh *yes,*" Lissa gasped, arching her back some more. She knew she ought to be lying still so he could work on her but somehow her body wouldn't obey. It seemed like every inch of her was crying out for more, begging Saber to take her to the edge of a precipice she hadn't even known existed until now and push her off.

"Very good," she heard Llewelyn murmur. "You're getting it— it's clear from the way she's responding. Now it's time for the inner massage."

Lissa felt a jolt of uncertainty. *Inner massage?* But Saber held her gaze meaningfully with his as he continued the slow, sweet torture of her clit.

"It's all right, *amalla,*" he murmured. "You know I'll be gentle."

"I…I know." Taking a deep breath, Lissa forced herself to relax again. Whatever happened, they were in this together. Saber wouldn't hurt her or let anyone else hurt her. She was safe with him and knowing that made it easier to open herself to him, to give in and let him do whatever was necessary.

"If your lady is ready," Llewelyn was saying, "Using your other hand, slide your first two fingers deep into her pussy while you *continue* to massage her clit with your thumb."

Lissa felt two blunt fingertips pressing gently against her virgin entrance and she couldn't help closing her eyes, retreating to the safety of the darkness behind her eyelids. But then Saber spoke.

"Look at me," he murmured in a soft, commanding voice. "Stay with me, Lissa. I need you to let me know what you're feeling."

Reluctantly, she opened her eyes again.

"Good." Leaning down, Saber gave the inside of her thigh a warm, gentle kiss. "Slowly, my lady," he said. "I'll enter you slowly, I swear."

"Yes…please," Lissa whispered. And then she felt his two long, strong fingers slipping past her entrance and into her tight virgin channel.

She could barely stifle a gasp at first but when she forced herself to relax she found that it didn't actually hurt at all. In fact, it felt…good. Good to be so filled, good to be penetrated by the male she cared for so very much. It was deliciously, almost dangerously intimate and intense. Looking into Saber's eyes as he pushed deeper into her body, until the tips of his long fingers stroked the back wall of her channel, she thought she had never felt closer to him.

"You're so beautiful, *amalla*," he whispered as he pressed deep inside her. "So beautiful when you let me in."

"Saber..." she couldn't help shifting her hips and the resulting feeling of his fingers moving inside her made her moan. "Saber, please, I need...I don't know what I need."

"I do," he murmured and began to pump his fingers gently in and out of her tight channel. At the same time, he continued the relentless massage of her clit until Lissa thought she was going to go crazy.

She had the feeling of something building in her again. The sensation of climbing higher and higher to reach some elusive peak. The pleasure wound tight inside her, pushing her to the limit but it was a limit she couldn't...quite...seem to...reach.

Then Llewelyn spoke again. "Crook your fingers upward and rub *hard*. Give it everything you've got—make your lady *come*." As he spoke, Lady Sha'rak gave a gasping cry and moaned his name loudly.

Lissa wanted to look and see exactly what was happening but just at that moment, Saber followed the directions he'd been given. Crooking his fingers upward, he rubbed against a spot inside her Lissa hadn't even known was there. A bolt of pleasure shot through her body and she gasped, her hips pumping involuntarily. Then the broad pad of his thumb slid directly over her throbbing clit and a second, even more intense pleasure overtook her.

"Oh! Oh, Goddess! Oh, Saber, *please!*" She clenched her hands into fists, back arching, hips thrusting. It was as though she had finally reached the peak and jumped off, only to learn that she could somehow fly. The pleasure he gave her sent her shooting upward like an arrow from a bow, like a bird set free to soar for the first time in its life.

"It's all right, Lissa," she heard Saber murmuring. "It's all right, *amalla.* Just let it happen—let yourself come."

Coming, I'm coming, she thought deliriously. *Oh Goddess, please, I can't get enough of this pleasure but it's so intense I don't think I can stand much more... So good...so good...*

It was the most intense feeling Lissa had ever had in her life and it triggered something inside her she couldn't understand or deny. As the pleasure finally ebbed, she felt tears stinging her eyes and a sob rising in her throat.

Emotions she had long held in check bombarded her—her forbidden love for Saber rushed over her like a wave. He had touched her so tenderly, given her such pleasure and yet he was the one man she could never have. She ached inside with needing him but it was an ache that could never be healed, a hunger that could never be satiated.

I have to stop feeling this way. After this is all over we'll go our separate ways. Never see each other again. Never...

But the thought of losing him forever was too much to bear. Lissa threw an arm over her eyes, trying unsuccessfully to keep back her tears, trying to hide her shame.

"Lissa? Are you all right? Did I hurt you?" Saber sounded almost panicked.

Somehow she managed to shake her head. "N-no," she whispered. "Just...it was so...so...I've never felt anything like it before."

"It's the massage technique—I told you it was special," she heard Lady Sha'rak say. "Saber, take her to your rooms and hold her. She'll be all right in a little while."

Lissa heard him murmur assent and then he was lifting her and cuddling her close to his broad chest as he carried her away. She buried her face against his chest, breathing in the warm, comforting scent of his skin and tried not to sob.

She had never felt more desolate in her life.

Chapter Fourteen

Saber sat on the bed and held Lissa close, his heart aching for what he had just done. *I shouldn't have touched her like that. I should have found another way, made some excuse. Now she'll hate me forever. She'll —*

"I'm fine now," Lissa surprised him by saying.

"What?" He looked at her uncertainly. "What are you talking about? You can't be. You were just—"

"I was just a little upset." She swiped at her eyes and tried to smile at him. "The pleasure was...very intense. It seemed to...to break something inside me somehow. But I'm all right now, honestly," she continued.

"I don't believe you are." Saber frowned at her sternly. "You're still upset and I don't blame you for it."

"Do you mean upset with *you?*" Lissa struggled to sit up and he helped her, even though letting her out of his arms was the last thing he wanted to do.

"Yes, of course." Saber looked at her, trying to catch her eyes with his. "For touching you the way I did. For...for penetrating you. Lissa, I shouldn't have—"

"Don't be silly." She was blushing and looking away, either unwilling or unable to meet his eyes. "You...you did what you had to do. Just as I did when I had to touch you earlier."

"Lissa, look at me," he insisted. When she still wouldn't, he caught her chin gently with one hand and turned her to face him.

"Look at me," he repeated. "I'm so sorry. I never meant to hurt you."

"You didn't," she whispered. Her jade green eyes filled again and she blinked rapidly, trying to force back the tears. "I've just never...Saber, I've never felt anything so intense. I didn't even know such a feeling was *possible.*"

"So you've never had an orgasm before?" He looked at her uncertainly. "Never touched yourself and made yourself come?"

"How could I?" She looked down and the tears caught in her long lashes sparkled like jewels in the dim light. "I couldn't when I lived under your roof for fear of being caught and it was forbidden at the temple."

"So that was your first orgasm." Saber began to understand. "No wonder it caught you by surprise."

"I'm sorry I got so emotional." She gave a soft, trembling sigh. "It just...seemed to bring all these things to the surface. Things I've been trying not to think about."

Saber didn't need to ask what she meant. "I think about those things too," he murmured, stroking her cheek. "All the time."

"You do?" She looked at him uncertainly and he nodded.

"Yes, of course. I haven't *stopped* thinking about them since the day..."

"The day what?" She frowned at him uncertainly.

Saber looked away. "The day you Renounced me."

It was the first time he'd mentioned the oath she had taken to never have him since she had spoken the words, so long ago on their home planet. Up until then the pain had been too great to even speak of, but after the intense scene between them at the grotto, he couldn't help himself. He had to know.

"Lissa," he said. "Tell me—did you mean it when you Renounced me?"

"I didn't want to." Lissa's eyes overflowed again and she gave a little sob. "Please believe me, Saber. I never...never wanted to say those words to you. To take that oath."

"I know." He pulled her into his arms again. "I know you didn't, *amalla.*"

It had been the worst day of his life when she had taken the formal oath that she would never be his. It had been heard and witnessed only by Saber and his mother, who had discovered their secret love and taken steps to put an end to it.

Afterward, he had always secretly feared that Lissa had meant the words she had said, had doubted that she still felt for him as he felt for her. Now, holding her in his arms, he finally knew what his heart had told him all along—that the oath was all his mother's doing and none of Lissa's.

The knowledge changed nothing—they still couldn't be together. But it lightened his heart and made him feel better. *She still feels for me,* he thought, stroking his fingers through her long, silky hair. *She still wants me as I want her*

Suddenly the emotions he'd kept so rigidly in check came to the surface and he could deny them no longer. Cupping Lissa's face in his hands, he brought her close and kissed her lush mouth as he had so often longed to do.

At first Lissa seemed frozen in place but then she kissed him back so hungrily it took Saber's breath away. Goddess but her lips were sweet! He'd always known it would be wonderful between them but finally kissing her for the first time was everything he'd dreamed of and more. He pressed closer, tangling his fingers in her hair and deepening the kiss. Lissa gave as good as she got, wrapping her arms around his neck and tilting her head to give him better access to her mouth.

They fell back on the bed and suddenly she was beneath him. And naked—still so naked, which was something he had almost forgotten in his concern for her. She felt so soft in his arms, so giving, so open. Saber longed to fill her and not just with his fingers this time. He wanted to taste her, to put his tongue deep in her sweet, wet pussy and make her come again and again. And after that he wanted to spread her legs and fill her with his cock. Wanted to give her the Deep Touch, to Touch her mind as he was caressing her body, to take her completely and hold her within him as he thrust within her until they were one—mind, body, and soul.

He spread her legs and pressed the hard bulge of his cock against her wet, open pussy. Lissa moaned and bucked up against him. Even through the tight slave pants he could feel her heat and smell the warm, feminine scent of her desire. Goddess, they both needed this so badly, needed to be together, to be one. He just wanted to touch her everywhere, to caress every part of her body at once...

Without thinking, Saber used his Touch sense on her, sending his *whisper-fingers* to card through her hair as he stroked her breasts and his *whisper-lips* to caress the tender mound of her pussy as he kissed and licked the vulnerable curve of her neck.

Lissa suddenly froze underneath him. "Saber, what are you doing?" she whispered. "What are *we* doing? What's wrong with us?"

"There's nothing wrong," he protested, his body throbbing with need. "We're showing each other how we feel, giving each other what we need at last."

"No...no!" She pushed against his chest. "We *can't*."

Saber reluctantly rolled off her and Lissa sat up and wrapped her arms around her knees, hiding herself from him.

"We can't," she whispered again. "Don't you remember—we said that even if we lived together we'd never do *that*. You told me you'd be content without it."

"And I would be—if it wasn't possible." He sighed in frustration and ran a hand through his hair. "That was back when we thought the kinship compounds would keep us apart—remember?"

"Yes, but you were...just now you were going to give me the Deep Touch." Lissa squeezed herself tighter, her eyes troubled. "We can't do that, Saber. We're of the same clan."

"I know it. Damn it, I know that." He pressed the heel of his hand to his forehead and took a deep breath. "I guess I just...forgot it for a moment."

"I almost did too," Lissa admitted in a low, trembling voice. "But we can't do that. We can't afford to let ourselves forget—even for a minute. We're playing a part here—putting on roles that aren't real. When this is all over we'll—"

"What?" he said, more harshly than he intended to. "Go our separate ways? Never see each other again?"

"Y-yes." Her eyes were filling again but she dashed the tears away angrily. "I don't want to but we can't help it. We...we can't do anything else. You know what would happen if you took me home as your mate—our people would revolt against you and revile me as an incestuous whore." She shook her head. "I'm sorry, Saber, but that's no way to live. We can't...we just *can't*."

"I know." He took a deep breath, trying to get control. "I'm sorry. I didn't mean to shout at you."

"You didn't—not really. You were just upset. I was too." Lissa sighed and gave him a troubled look. "If only we were from different clans."

"Well, we're not." With a quick movement, Saber got up. "Excuse me, I'm going to get ready for bed."

"Saber..." She put out a hand to him, her eyes still troubled but he only shook his head.

"We have a long day tomorrow, it's better if we get some sleep. So please...put some clothes on and let's go to bed."

Lissa looked down at herself and her face flushed dark red. "Of course," she mumbled. "I'm so sorry."

"Don't be," Saber said shortly. "You're beautiful like that. I just can't..." He shook his head. "It's too hard to see you when I know I can't have you."

Then he turned and left, shutting himself into the bathroom and trying not to remember the hurt look on her face.

* * * * *

The virginal white gown she'd worn the night before had been taken away to be washed by Lady Sha'rak's cleaning staff. Lissa rummaged through her cube looking for another non-revealing nightdress to wear but to her consternation, she couldn't find a thing. Well, nothing *modest*, anyway. She finally slipped into a sheer pale green dress that barely came down past her behind and was practically see-through.

It doesn't matter, she told herself, as she prepared to get into bed. *I'll be under the covers and it will be dark. He'll never see me.*

Just then she heard a *thump* and a loud curse from the bathroom.

She was out of bed in a second flat. "Oh my Goddess, Saber, are you all right? Did you hurt yourself?"

"I'm fine." But his deep voice sounded strained, as though he was in some kind of pain.

"You don't sound fine—you sound hurt," she called anxiously.

"It's nothing. Just these damn...*ouch!*"

This was too much. Without waiting to consider if she ought to do it, Lissa pushed her way into the bathroom.

Saber stood in the middle of the large space with his tight black pants halfway unzipped and a look of frustration and pain on his face.

"Saber?" She approached him cautiously. "What's going on? Can I help you?"

He sighed. "Forgive me for all the noise. It's these damn manacles. I had a hard time with them before but they seemed to have gotten worse. The minute I get my hands anywhere near my zipper, I get a shock."

"The manacles!" Lissa put a hand to her mouth. "I can't believe I forgot to ask Lady Sha'rak for the remote to remove them! Saber, I'm *so* sorry."

"It's all right," he said dryly. "You were a little distracted, remember?"

"Of course." Remembering that she'd been distracted by the feeling of him massaging her naked body and giving her the first orgasm she'd ever had, she couldn't help blushing. But modesty wasn't going to help her now. Quickly, she dropped to her knees in front of Saber and reached for his zipper.

"Hey! What do you think you're doing?" He took a big step back, his lower back hitting the large marble basin in the middle of the room.

"Helping you." Lissa frowned up at him. "If you can't get your pants off by yourself, you need help. What's the problem?"

"There is no problem—nothing I can't handle myself, anyway."

Lissa burst out laughing. "But that's exactly what you *can't* do— handle yourself," she pointed out. The whole situation was so ridiculous, she felt lighter than she had all evening.

"Well…" One corner of his mouth twitched. "It's not funny, you know."

"I know," Lissa agreed, smiling back. "Come on, Saber, don't be silly. It's not like I haven't seen you before. Haven't, you know, *touched* you." She could feel her cheeks getting hot again but she was determined not to back down.

Grudgingly, Saber nodded. "All right. Just be very, *very* careful of the zipper. That's a delicate area down there."

"Of course. I'll be every bit as careful with your delicate areas as you were with mine." The minute the words were out, she wished she could call them back. What had gotten into her, reminding him of all the forbidden things they'd been doing? But she couldn't help herself—she felt like this mission was changing her. Maybe not for the better, but there was no helping that now.

Gently, very gently, she tugged at the zipper. She could see almost at once what the problem was—Saber was achingly hard, his shaft throbbing for release behind the too-tight trousers. The cruel silver teeth of the zipper were pressing hard into his flesh in what had to be an extremely painful way. If she wasn't careful, some of the vulnerable skin was going to get caught as she pulled it down.

"Saber," she said looking up at him. "I'm sorry but I'm afraid I'm going to have to, um, put my hand…I'm going to have to hold your um, you back, as I pull down the zipper or—"

"I understand." His jaw was clenched. "Do what you have to do."

"All right." Still feeling awkward, Lissa slipped her hand into his half open trousers and cupped the warm, smooth shaft just as she had earlier that day during the "training" exercises Lady Sha'rak had put them through. Only this time it was just her and Saber with no one else criticizing or directing. Despite her rapidly beating heart, Lissa found she was considerably calmer under the circumstances.

It took some time and some careful maneuvering, but at last she had the zipper all the way down and Saber was free. But though his trousers were open, Lissa somehow found herself reluctant to stop holding his shaft. He felt so silky and hot in her hand and his scent was spicy and undeniably male. It made her feel almost dizzy with desire. Without thinking about it, she leaned a little closer and wrapped her fingers more firmly around his heated flesh.

"Um…Lissa?" Saber's deep voice was hoarse and uncertain.

"Hmm?" She was still on her knees before him, studying the way her fingers wouldn't quite wrap all the way around his cock. He was so big she wondered how he could ever use it to give anyone the Deep Touch. Unbidden, an image rose in her mind of herself pinned beneath Saber, her legs spread wide with the head of his cock sliding slowly inside her as he Touched her gently with his *whisper-fingers*.

The mental image should have horrified her—instead she felt warm and tingly all over. Her nipples were suddenly tight and her pussy throbbed. Goddess, what was wrong with her? Was his scent affecting her? Or was she just getting tired of being timid all the time?

Lately, even though Saber was supposed to be the "slave" in this situation, Lissa felt like she'd been taking orders from everyone. She wore the ridiculous dresses Kat had packed for her, let Lady Sha'rak boss her around, and even allowed herself to be touched and massaged in intimate, forbidden ways for the sake of their mission. Somewhere deep inside her, something seemed to be saying, *Enough!*

Suddenly it was like a switch flipped inside her. *I'm tired of being afraid all the time, tired of apologizing for everything I do...for everything I want to do. We're in a difficult situation here and I shouldn't have to be sorry for doing what needs to be done.*

"Lissa," Saber said, breaking into her thoughts. "I...uh...you can let go now."

"I guess I should, shouldn't I?" She stroked him slowly up and down, just as Lady Sha'rak had taught her. "But as it happens, I'm not going to."

"What?" Saber clearly couldn't believe his ears.

"I said, *I'm not going to,*" Lissa repeated clearly.

"But you said we couldn't," he reminded her. "That we can't—"

"We won't," Lissa said firmly. "But this is different. Look at you, Saber—you must be in pain from being so, um, so hard for so long. Well, *aren't* you?" she added when he didn't respond.

He frowned. "It's... nothing I can't stand."

"But why should you *have* to stand it when I can help you? Just like you helped me." Daring greatly, she leaned forward and let the warm shaft brush against her cheek.

Saber gave a hoarse groan and looked at her as though she'd lost her mind. "Lissa, just stop, please."

"No." She rose to her feet, still holding him in her hand and continued to stroke. "I want to help you, Saber, and I refuse to stop until...until you're not hurting anymore."

He shook his head. "Lissa, honestly, you don't have to—"

She lifted her chin and stared him in the eyes. "But I *want* to. And I'm your mistress so you'll do as I say."

Saber's eyes widened and a surprised smile quirked the corner of his mouth. "Yes, my lady," he murmured at last. "What would you have me do?"

Lissa felt a thrill of triumph followed closely by a surge of uncertainty. But she was damned if she'd lose the upper hand so soon after she'd gained it.

"Get to the bed," she ordered in the bossiest voice she could manage. "Lie down on your back and put your arms over your head. Uh, but first take your trousers off."

Saber peeled off the slave trousers, being careful not to touch himself, and threw them to one side. Then he stood up completely naked and spread his arms. "You're sure about this?"

Lissa's pulse jumped when she looked at his large, muscular body. He was so much bigger than her, he towered over her and she had never seen him nude before. The sight was mouthwatering and more than a little imposing, but she struggled to keep her face impassive.

"I'm absolutely sure. Now go get on the bed."

Saber did as he was told, climbing into the massive bed and lying down in the very center of it. He raised his arms over his head and gripped the bottom edge of the elaborately carved headboard. Then he looked at Lissa.

"Now what, Mistress?"

"Spread your legs," Lissa commanded, still trying to sound demanding. "I need...need room to work on you."

"Yes, my lady." He complied, spreading muscular legs to leave himself completely vulnerable to her, just as she had been to him earlier. Lissa felt a surprising surge of excitement. She liked the idea of *Saber* being submissive this time, of him lying there, waiting for her to touch him, to give him pleasure.

What are you doing? whispered a little voice in her head. *You just finished telling Saber that you shouldn't touch each other this way.*

Yes, but he's in pain and he can't help himself, she argued back. There were some lines she couldn't cross—taking the Deep Touch from Saber was one of them. But surely no one could condemn her for easing his pain when he was unable to ease himself. When you put it that way, she sounded almost virtuous—like someone on a mission of mercy. Besides, she found that she *liked* being in charge. It was liberating to do what she wanted to do instead of what she thought she *ought* to do. *I'll just ease his torment and then we'll go back to not touching unless we have to,* she promised herself.

Feeling justified, Lissa climbed onto the bed and settled herself between Saber's thighs. She took his thick shaft in one hand at once and then looked lower to study the heavy, round balls that hung within a little sack just beneath it. Something told her they were delicate—even more so than his shaft—so when she cupped them, she was careful not to be rough.

A low groan was drawn from Saber's throat. "Gods...Lissa," he gasped as she continued to fondle and stroke him. "So good...feels so *good*."

"Call me *Mistress*," Lissa commanded, feeling a new surge of confidence. She was doing it—she was giving Saber pleasure just as he had pleasured her earlier. It was a heady, addictive feeling—the knowledge that she had such a big, strong, muscular man completely at her mercy, cupped literally in the palm of her hand.

"Yes, Mistress," he murmured, his eyes fixed on hers.

Lissa stroked him again, causing him to gasp and pump his hips. For a moment she could almost imagine what Lady Sha'rak felt when she "punished" Llewelyn. But no, Lissa told herself. She would never treat Saber the way Lady Sha'rak treated her body-slave. She would use her newfound power only to pleasure him, never to hurt.

What are you talking about? demanded the little voice in her head. *This is a one-time thing – it's not like you're going to make a habit of it.*

Except she might have to—at least in public. It was time she stopped shrinking away from the things she and Saber had to do in order to make their roles more believable and started embracing them. She should enjoy this time while it lasted. Because after they'd found the scrolls and gone home...but Lissa didn't want to let her mind go there.

Instead, she concentrated on caressing Saber's shaft, using long, slow strokes from root to tip until he was groaning softly and pumping his hips in time to the rhythm she set.

"Lissa," he whispered. "Mistress, Gods that's *good*."

"And does it ease your pain?" Lissa asked softly.

"It will in a minute if you're not careful." Suddenly he half sat up and reached for her wrist, stopping the motion of her hand. "Lissa, do you know what's going to happen when you, uh, when you fully ease my pain?"

"You'll have an orgasm. Like you gave me."

"Well, yes..." Saber looked uncomfortable. "But I'm afraid a male orgasm isn't as, uh, neatly contained as a female one. Things are liable to get... messy."

"I know the facts of life, Saber," Lissa said impatiently. "Just because I've never, um, acted them out doesn't mean I don't know how a male and female come together."

"All right. Sorry, Mistress." He held up his hands and lay back on the bed. "Go on then. I just didn't want you to be surprised."

Or frightened, Lissa thought. *He thinks I'm scared of him. Of his body. Because he's different...male.*

In fact, nothing could be farther from the truth. Lissa wasn't frightened of their differences—she was excited by them. From the first minute Lady Sha'rak had forced her to take Saber's shaft in her hand, she'd been curious about the male body—about *his* body. She wanted to know him, to explore all of him from the top of his head to the bottom of his feet. But she especially wanted explore his "delicate areas".

Daring greatly, she let the fingers that had been tickling the tender sack between his legs drift lower. Saber gasped and looked at her uncertainly when she stroked one finger down the short dip between the bottom of the sack and his nether entrance.

"Lissa?" He looked at her in wonder. "What...what are you doing?"

"Touching you. Exploring you." Experimentally, she pressed just the tip of her finger to his tight entrance. "Does that feel good?"

"Incredibly good," he admitted in a low voice. "But it's not...I didn't think you'd want to, you know, touch me there."

"I want to touch you everywhere," Lissa told him honestly. "I know I shouldn't but I do."

"I want you to as well." His voice was tight and strained. "I felt the same way when I was touching you earlier."

"You were so gentle with me," Lissa stroked his cock again and pressed gently with her fingertip until he groaned and writhed.

"Lissa…Goddess!" he moaned.

"Mistress," she reminded him primly.

A small droplet of pearly white liquid had appeared on the tip of his cock and Lissa wondered how it would taste. Somewhere inside her the shocked and frightened priestess she had been on First World protested that such a thought wasn't modest or right but Lissa pushed it away. It seemed the farther she went down this road, the easier it was to ignore the scared little girl she used to be and embrace the woman she wanted to become.

Leaning down, she lapped gently, bathing the head of his cock with her tongue and savoring his rich, salty flavor.

The extra stimulation of her tongue when she was already pumping his shaft and pressing lightly at his nether entrance appeared to be too much for Saber.

"Lissa," he gasped, going rigid. "Get back. I'm going to —"

Before he could finish his words, a warm, wet jet of translucent white spurted from the head of his cock and covered her fingers. Lissa was surprised, but only at first.

He's coming, she thought with a surge of triumph. *I'm making him come — giving him pleasure just like he gave me!*

Feeling empowered, she continued to stroke, holding his throbbing cock in her hand until he finally stopped spurting.

Finally Saber lay gasping on the bed, his arms still raised over his head and a look of wonderment in his eyes.

"I don't understand," he said at last, when he could talk again. "You were so upset earlier when we were just kissing and now...this. What's gotten into you all of a sudden?"

"I don't know." She shook her head. "I guess I'm just tired of being afraid and feeling guilty all the time. And when I saw how much pain you were in, I just...I realized we don't have the luxury of burying ourselves in shame and recrimination. Not if we're going to do what we came here to do."

"I hadn't thought of it like that," Saber admitted. "I guess...I've been feeling pretty guilty myself."

"Well, I'm tired of that." Lissa tossed her hair out of her face. "From now on, let's forget about being from the same clan. We'll do what we have to do and not feel guilty for any of it. Do you think we could do that?"

"We could try." Saber sounded doubtful. "I guess. As long as we don't..."

"No, we won't go that far," Lissa promised, her heart pounding. She looked down at her hand, still covered in the evidence of his pleasure. If any of this got into her, if she would have let Saber give her the Deep Touch and pump the white, creamy cum into her pussy instead of her hand...but no, she wouldn't let her mind go there.

"So we'll just do what we need to in order to play our parts?" Saber said.

Lissa nodded firmly. "Of course."

"What about..." He cleared his throat. "Forgive me, but I can't help remembering the way I'm supposed to acknowledge you when we go to a formal party like the sensation party we're going to tomorrow night."

"You mean when you...when you have to kiss my panties?" Lissa's breath was coming short again and she could feel Saber's cock, which had grown almost soft, getting hard in her hand again.

"Yes, Mistress." Saber's eyes were steady but his deep voice was hoarse. "And remember what Lady Sha'rak said about split panties and that I should..." He cleared his throat. "Should use my tongue on you to show extra respect..."

"Oh." Lissa bit her lip—she hadn't considered this. Yet, it still fell under the heading of things they had to do in order to complete their mission. "Do you want..." She looked at Saber uncertainly. "Would it bother you to...to have to do that?"

"Would it bother me to taste your sweet, wet pussy? Of course not!" His hazel eyes were suddenly half-lidded with lust. "It's my greatest desire."

"It is?" Lissa felt hot all over. Was this really what Saber fantasized about when he thought of her?

"Mmm-hmm." His voice dropped until it was nothing but a soft, sexual growl and she felt a hint of his *whisper-fingers* brush against her cheek.

"I...I don't know if we should do that, if we should go quite that far," she whispered. She wanted to look away from him but his hazel eyes were drowning deep—holding her gaze, making her feel like she couldn't contain herself much longer. "I mean I don't think—" she began again, stumbling over the words.

"Lissa..." he murmured, still holding her eyes with his. "*Amalla...*"

Suddenly the tension between them was too much for Lissa. If she didn't leave the room at once they were going to start kissing again. And this time, Saber had no trousers on to separate them. The nighty she was wearing wouldn't help either—it was too flimsy and see-through to form any kind of a barrier. If she kissed Saber, if she went to his arms and let him pin her to the bed again, there would be no stopping this time. She would spread her legs and let him give her the Deep Touch, whether it was right or wrong.

"I...excuse me," she mumbled. "I...I need to clean up."

She jumped off the bed and raced to the bathroom, her heart beating as she considered what she had just done. And more importantly, what she had *agreed* to do in the near future.

Chapter Fifteen

Draven was sleeping when L snuck into his room.

She didn't even know why she bothered. They had said their goodbyes the night before after supper. To her surprise, Draven had been a perfect gentleman throughout the entire meal. He'd been charming and witty and even made her laugh once or twice — which she almost never did. Her life so far hadn't been very conducive to levity.

And yet, throughout the entire meal, his silver eyes remained blank — devoid of that certain something she couldn't quite name but which seemed vital to existence. A human element, she supposed she would call it if she'd ever been anywhere near Earth. Which she hadn't, no matter what her memories might suggest.

Yes, Draven was definitely lacking something but she felt drawn to him anyway. It was almost as though he had a void inside him, a hole that no one and nothing could fill. L knew that feeling of emptiness well. She lived with it every day. And so, though she reminded herself that the Hoard Master was a murdering bastard who would kill her in a moment if he felt like it, she couldn't help coming to see him once more before she left his twisted realm.

L stood just inside the doorway, still wearing the guise of one of his imps, and watched intently. Trying to understand him. Trying to see what was missing. She'd sent his other attendants away and they were alone in the vast bedroom, which was filled with the treasure of the thousand worlds his forces had despoiled. *Empty conquests,* she thought, watching as he twisted restlessly between his silken sheets.

For the Hoard Master did not rest easy. He groaned, his face tight with some unspoken agony, then put out a hand as though to ward something off—or warn someone. As L watched, his groans became words.

"No," he gasped. "No, I will not accept defeat. I will vanquish you even if it means—" The rest of the sentence trailed off into indistinct mumbling but L found herself fascinated all the same. Unaware that she was doing so, she drifted closer to the vast bed until she was standing right beside it, watching Draven much more closely than she had ever intended to.

His face contorted in pain and to L's surprise she saw something glimmering on the tips of the Hoard Master's inky black lashes. Were those...could they be...*tears?* Surely not—Draven would be the first to claim he had no tears to shed for anyone and yet...

Hardly knowing what she was doing, she reached out a hand to him. It was almost as though she was drawn to touch him, to touch the first evidence she had seen of genuine emotion welling up from within. Her hand changed from an imp's claw to its natural form and she brushed one slender finger against his cheek so lightly it wouldn't have awakened even the most savage beast.

But Draven was more than a beast. In an instant his eyes flew open and one strong, long-fingered hand was wrapped in a crushing grip around her wrist.

L gasped and barely had the presence of mind to change her hand back to the imp's claw before he spoke.

"What in the seven hells," he rasped, "do you think you're doing *touching* me?"

"Forgive me, Master," L begged, doing her best to imitate an imp's frightened squeak. "There was a bug—it was trying to land on your face. Your cheek. I think…think it wanted to drink your tears," she added, almost in a whisper.

"Tears?" Draven let her go and put his own fingertips to his face. They came away wet and he looked at them in bemusement, then sighed. "Damn."

"Master…" L knew she was taking a chance but she couldn't help herself. "Forgive my impertinence but if your dreams were bad perhaps…perhaps you'd like to speak of them?"

"What good would talking do?" Draven sat on the edge of the bed and put his head in his hands. "And why would I talk to the likes of you anyway?" But the words lacked fire and the set of his broad shoulders was dejected, defeated. L's fingers itched to stroke his bare, muscular back but she restrained herself.

"It's true, Master. I'm nothing—nobody. You might as well talk to the wall," she said, still in the imp's high voice. "But the wall won't listen as I will," she added softly. "Or bear witness to your sorrow…whatever it is."

"Well, aren't you perceptive for an imp?" Draven lifted his head and gave her a penetrating stare. "*Very* perceptive indeed."

"Master is too kind," L mumbled, doing her best to look unobtrusive. Damn it, she'd pushed things too far. He was going to guess it was her and the Goddess alone knew what kind of vengeance he would take on her for seeing him in his moment of weakness.

"Where is the shadow caster?" Draven asked, standing and taking a step toward her. "Is she here?"

"Her ship has left the planet, Master," L answered, praying he wouldn't think to check if it was so. "She left word that she would wear your listening device once she boarded the Mother Ship and not before."

"I expected nothing less. She's a secretive one, that L." Sighing, he sank back down on the bed again and looked down at the floor.

Inwardly, L breathed a sigh of relief. She'd managed to get away with her little deception. Now she had nothing to do but excuse herself quietly and get to her ship, which Draven had modified with his new wormhole technology. A quick skip through space and she would be in deep orbit around Earth — the home world she dreamed of every night and had never yet seen with her own eyes.

She was turning to leave when Draven spoke again, catching her by surprise.

"It was the final battle with the Golgoth — Eater of Worlds, Extinguisher of Stars. A being so vast that his evil could have filled the universe if it had been left unchecked. But my maker and Mistress, the Goddess of All Life, refused to let the Golgoth go unchallenged."

Slowly, L turned back.

Draven was still staring at the floor, his head bowed, his broad shoulders slumped. He spoke in a voice so weary it tore at her heart — what little heart she had to tear. L didn't dare to say anything, for fear he would stop talking. After a moment, Draven continued.

"She made me as the pinnacle of her creation — a son to ease her loneliness and a captain to lead her armies. And so when the Golgoth came, threatening to devour and despoil all she held dear, I led the forces of light...." He looked up briefly at L. "I led them straight into its gaping maw. And there I lost them."

"Master?" L whispered, uncertain of what he wanted her to say.

"I lost them," Draven repeated, looking back down at his hands. "There was no way to avoid it. The Golgoth opened a portal into the pit—a wormhole that led to the seventh of the seven hells." He sighed. "We swear by them constantly but few know that they are actually real. And the seventh is the deepest and blackest of them all."

He ran a hand through his hair. "One by one I watched them try to breach the Golgoth's defenses and bridge the gap—one by one they failed and fell into eternal torment. Gods!" His hands squeezed into fists and the muscular shoulders knotted with tension. "I don't *want* to remember this," he hissed, his face contorting with emotion. "Don't want to see it all again. I've kept it buried for years—*centuries*. If it wasn't for the damn *skrillix* venom..."

"What happened?" L asked, unable to help herself.

"What?" He looked up and she saw tears glimmering in his eyes again. "What do you mean?"

"To the Golgoth, Master. How did you defeat it?"

Draven's silver eyes went flat. "What makes you think I did?"

"But, well...you must have. Or else we wouldn't be standing here, would we?" L asked haltingly. "How else could you—?"

"I absorbed it," Draven growled. "With evil so vast, there was no other way to contain it. No way to completely eradicate it." He looked at her, his face cold. "Imagine, if you will, my dear imp, feeling the crushing weight of a thousand billion abominations filling you at once. Murders, lies, tortures and cruelties, the suffering of innocents, the mad laughter of the wicked, the cries of the damned. It was like drowning in poison, like breathing in pus."

"But you did it anyway." L, who was used to looking out only for herself, could scarcely comprehend it. Why would he do such a thing? Why would he sacrifice himself to the evil for anyone, even the Goddess mother he claimed to have loved?

"I had to. As I said, there was no other way," Draven said soberly. Then his face changed, his silver eyes going hard and a cruel smile curving his perfectly shaped lips. "I had to give up my soul to do it, of course—there's no room for a conscience when you're pure evil inside. But I've found the sacrifice is a small one to make. Being soulless allows me to have so much more *fun* than I ever did before."

"Fun?" L whispered.

"Exactly—like the fun I'm going to have with the Goddess's favorite pets—those damn Kindred. Once the shadow caster plants my little device in their sacred grove, of course." He gave L a piercing look. "So she'd better get started, don't you think?"

"I…I'm sure she already has," L said, edging toward the door.

"I certainly *hope* so," Draven drawled. "I hope she doesn't think that just because I enjoy her company and agreed to help her in her quest to get revenge, I would be anything less than *brutal* if she failed me." He gave L a charming smile that never quite reached his blank, silver eyes. "I am, after all, nothing more than a soulless murdering bastard. And what's more, I *enjoy* being a soulless, murdering bastard. You could call it my favorite hobby."

"Yes, Master." L's throat had suddenly gone dry. Though she was a stone cold killer herself, she didn't actually *enjoy* what she did—it was just a job. The gleeful, half-mad look in the silver disks of Draven's eyes said he took great pleasure in the torture and pain of others. That he would take pleasure in torturing *her* if she wasn't very damn careful. "I, um…" L cleared her throat. "I need to fetch—
"

"Go." He waved her toward the door with a last piercing look. "And do *not* fail me."

L left at a run and didn't stop until she reached her ship.

But as she melted into a more comfortable form and set coordinates for Earth, she couldn't help wondering why Draven had told her what he did. It was clear to her now he hadn't been fooled in the least by her form. All along he had known it was her and not some imp he was talking to. So why had he told her his story?

And what the hell was she supposed to think of him now?

* * * * *

Draven tried to go back to bed but there was no more sleep for him that night, no matter how soft his pillows or how silky his sheets. No matter how he tossed and turned, he couldn't find a comfortable position. And every time he closed his eyes, the same question kept recurring.

Why did I tell her? Why?

It was pointless to think about it, of course. The shadow caster was long gone—presumably to fulfill their mission of mutual vengeance on those arrogant Kindred bastards. The thought of what would happen once his device went off was almost enough to bring a smile to Draven's lips—almost.

But then the past came raging in again. The memories he hadn't thought of in years, the feelings he'd tried to suffocate for centuries, flooded him like a tidal wave.

The light in the Golgoth's eyes fading as I took its essence into myself, the feeling of pure evil filling me, overtaking me. The loss of my soul, the look on the Goddess's face when I renounced my place at her side...

"Stop!" he roared aloud. Putting his hands to the sides of his head, he squeezed as though he could halt the endless flow of painful memories by physical pressure alone. "Stop, I can't *stand* it anymore!"

"Master?" An imp—a real one this time—came rushing into the room, its face gray with worry. "Is there a problem?" it asked, its voice trembling with fear.

"It's nothing." Draven squeezed harder, willing the painful thoughts away. "Nothing, leave me."

"But I thought...is there something, anything I can do to ease you?"

Slowly, Draven looked up, a cruel light kindled in his blank silver eyes.

"As a matter of fact, there *is* something you can do." Leaning forward he frowned at the imp. "Take the dagger from my dresser—that one there with the jeweled handle."

"This one?" The imp grasped the lovely but lethal instrument carefully. It was a trinket Draven had picked up on yet another world the Hoard had despoiled. He forgot which one now—they all ran together after a while.

"Yes, that one." Draven nodded. "Have you got a good grip on it?"

"Yes, Master." The imp's claw tightened around the jeweled grip.

"Good." Draven leaned forward, his eyes narrowing. "Now kill yourself. *Slowly.*"

And as the imp made the first cut, he smiled.

Chapter Sixteen

"Oh dear, look at the time! We've scarcely got two hours before the party," Lady Sha'rak fluttered nervously as her slaves cleared the table. "Aren't you excited, my dear?" she asked Lissa. "It's your first sensation party!"

"Of course I'm excited." Lissa tried to look happy but the truth was, she was mostly worried. The surge of confidence she'd had the night before when she told Saber they should stop feeling guilty for their illicit actions was hard to maintain. The voice of her conscience kept trying to whisper that she was doing the wrong thing, going too far. Lissa tried hard to cut it off but she was finding that years of guilty thoughts weren't easy to just ignore.

She wondered how Saber felt. He was sitting quietly behind her, waiting to serve her more food if she asked for it but Lissa was far too worried to be hungry. At least he was no longer wearing the touch-me-not manacles. Lissa had gotten the remote from Lady Sha'rak first thing that morning and removed them. So she wouldn't have to "help" him through any more painful situations.

Thinking of that made her remember his low, hoarse cries as she had stroked him to completion the night before. Goddess, that had been so sexy! Not to mention the surge of power she'd felt from being in charge while he lay there helpless, letting her do anything she liked. Just the memory of his eyes as he came, the way his whole body had trembled beneath her touch, so big and muscular and naked, so completely under her control, made her feel hot and wet between her legs. Gods...she shifted uncomfortably. *I really shouldn't be feeling this way toward Saber. Shouldn't be thinking of him like this...*

"Well you don't *look* very excited," Lady Sha'rak interrupted her guilty thoughts with a frown.

"I...I suppose I'm just nervous," Lissa said, truthfully enough. "As you've said, we don't have Dream Gas where I come from. I'm not sure exactly...what sensation play is going to be like."

"Is that all?" Lady Sha'rak made a shooing motion with one hand. "That's nothing to be worried about, my dear! Listen, I promise I'll speak to Lady Hake'bean and have her find you a particularly *exciting* document for your first play."

"Will she be using the documents in her collection?" Lissa asked hopefully. "Do you think she might have one from the era I was interested in?"

"From the Hoard Wars? Oh yes, certainly," Lady Sha'rak said dismissively. "Lady Hake'bean is always most generous with her documents. The entire collection should be on display tonight."

Lissa risked exchanging a glance with Saber. If the stolen scrolls were at Lady Hake'bean's, they ought to be able to find them.

And the sooner we find them, the sooner we can get back home. Get back to normal. Lissa knew she ought to be happy about the idea but somehow she wasn't. She wondered how Saber felt. Would he be glad to leave this world behind and go back to his own life...or sorry to lose her?

"It all sounds so exciting," she said, smiling brightly at the ambassador. "I guess I'd better go get ready."

"Not so fast, my dear." Lady Sha'rak reached across the table to put a hand on her arm. "I have a little surprise for you." She snapped her fingers. "Llewelyn, bring it out."

Lady Sha'rak's body-slave came around the table at once and presented Lissa with a large black box.

"Oh my!" Lissa looked at it uncertainly but the ambassador was practically dancing with glee.

"Go on—open it!" she commanded.

Lissa flipped off the lid and found a gown that seemed to be entirely made of delicate lace. It was jade green—the exact shade of her eyes and the streaks in her hair, and it looked no more substantial than a cobweb.

"Oh my goodness," Lissa breathed. "It...it's beautiful. And so *thin*. And, er, see-through."

"That's what I was shopping for yesterday," Lady Sha'rak explained. "It's a sensation gown—made especially to give easy access during the party."

Lissa began to get a really bad feeling in the pit of her stomach. What *exactly* were they going to be doing that night? "Um, easy access?" she asked, wishing her voice wouldn't come out sounding so squeaky.

"Of course—for the sensor pads. They help with the Dream Gas conduction. Oh, and I got you some special panties to go with it—look under the gown and see."

Feeling more nervous all the time, Lissa dug around under the silky pile of lace and pulled out a pair of jade green panties trimmed in black lace. As she had feared, they were split in the middle. *But at least they have little strings there,* she thought, looking more closely. *So you can tie them closed.*

"Those little laces are drawstrings," Lady Sha'rak explained, watching as she examined the panties. "You pull them tight and tie them off at the sides, which forms a sort of diamond shaped window right in the middle to frame your slit."

Lissa felt her stomach sink down to her shoes. "You…you mean the strings are to hold the panties *open?*" she asked faintly.

"Well of course! How else could you give access for the sensor pads? And speaking of that…" Lady Sha'rak leaned forward confidentially. "Now don't take this the wrong way, my dear, but I couldn't help noticing the other night that you're not shaved."

"I'm not…oh!" Lissa crossed her legs involuntarily when she realized what the other woman was referring to. "It's not…not required where I come from," she said faintly.

"Well, it is here," Lady Sha'rak said firmly. "You simply *cannot* go out without a clean shaven pussy. Don't worry though, I'll have Llewelyn bring an intimate area razor to your suite and teach your slave how to use it. He can have you smooth and sleek in an instant."

"I'm sure he can," Lissa whispered.

"Good, then let's get ready. Lady Hake'bean doesn't like to be kept waiting and she lives in a building all the way across town."

"All right." Numbly, Lissa handed the box containing the slinky lace dress and barely there panties to Saber and got to her feet. Goddess, she was really going to do this. She was going to shave her private areas and wear a completely indecent dress out in public in order to do the Goddess-knew-what with some kind of sensor pads applied to her most delicate parts and—

"Oh, and one more thing," Lady Sha'rak said, breaking into her thoughts. "Don't bother with wearing the elixirs on your nipples tonight—they interfere with the pads."

"They do?" Lissa frowned. "But I thought you said I always had to wear them in order to have a way to punish my slave."

"Yes, well, any slave who acts up tonight will get the rod—and in a very public way," Lady Sha'rak said grimly. Then she smiled. "All right?"

"All right." Lissa nodded doubtfully. Not for the first time she wished she could ask what her hostess was talking about. What exactly was "the rod" and how was it administered? She shot another uneasy look at Saber. Whatever it was, she didn't want to find out the hard way tonight. They were going to have to be *extra* careful not to offend anyone at the sensation party.

Saber returned her look and gave her a brief nod. Clearly he was thinking the same thing she was.

"Well then." Lady Sha'rak clapped her hands. "Let's go get ready, shall we?"

* * * * *

"Lissa, are you all right in there?" Saber didn't bother knocking. He put his head in the bathroom door and looked.

Lissa was standing in front of the viewer with the ultra-sharp intimate area razor in her hand and biting her lip. She was wearing a robe which was open to expose her pussy but when she saw Saber looking, she quickly closed it, a blush staining her cheeks.

"Oh, Saber! What are you doing?"

"Checking on you. From what Llewelyn showed me, it should only take a few minutes to use that thing." He nodded at the razor in her hand. "But you've been in here over half an hour. Did you manage to, um..." He cleared his throat. "Get the job done?"

"No." Lissa looked down at the razor, which was a thin, pink laser beam about an inch long, pulsing between two slender silver posts. It had a five inch silver handle that hummed faintly as she gripped it but Saber couldn't help noticing she was keeping the laser end as far from herself as possible. "This thing just looks so ...so *lethal*. Honestly, I'm afraid to get it near such a, um, delicate area," she admitted in a low voice.

"Then let me." Coming forward, he knelt at her feet and held out a hand for the razor. "Here."

"Oh, I don't know..."

"I saw all of you last night. I massaged you, remember?" Saber reminded her gently. "It won't hurt to let me shave you now. Besides, *I'm* the one Llewelyn showed how to use the razor because I'm *supposed* to do this. I'm your slave."

"You're not really, though." Reluctantly, she handed him the razor. "Aren't you getting tired of serving me like this all the time?"

"Never." Slowly, so as not to startle her, he opened her robe again. Gods, she was a beautiful sight, her soft little mound so bare and exposed for him. He longed to spread her legs and part her pussy lips with his tongue, to lick her until she moaned his name and pulled his hair, begging for more. Somehow, he restrained himself. "I'd serve you forever if I could," he murmured, looking up at her.

"Oh, Saber..." Lightly, she brushed her fingers through his hair. "It's sweet of you to say but I know this isn't natural for you—for either one of us, really. I mean, you're not really submissive and I'm *certainly* not very dominant."

"You were last night," Saber said softly.

"I...I guess I was, wasn't I?" Lissa's cheeks got even redder. "I...I don't know what came over me."

"I don't either, but I liked it—a lot." Saber tested the razor on his arm, making sure it was the right intensity to cut hair but not skin and then looked up at her again. "Spread your legs, *amalla*," he murmured.

Lissa bit her lip and complied, watching as he carefully applied the razor. "You liked it? Really?" she asked, as the soft mound of curls at the apex of her sex gradually disappeared, vaporized painlessly by the pink line of light.

"More than I thought I would." Saber finished the delicate operation and looked up at her. "When we agreed to come here, I thought I would find it difficult—submitting, I mean. But all the things I've been doing—feeding you, caring for you, massaging you—are the same steps any Kindred warrior takes during his Claiming period when he's trying to win a bride. So..." He shrugged. "It doesn't feel unnatural or wrong."

"Most warriors aren't ordered to lie in the middle of the bed and let their prospective bride, um, touch them, though," Lissa pointed out in a low voice.

"No." Saber switched off the razor, closed her robe, and stood. "But I don't think most of them would have a problem with it. I *know* who I am, Lissa." He stroked her hot cheek lightly with his knuckles. "Submitting to you a little doesn't make me less of a male. I'm happy to spend all day on my knees before you, as long as I get to spend time with you."

"Saber, please..." For a moment she looked like she might cry. "Please don't."

He sighed. "All right, I'm sorry. I just want you to know I don't mind serving you...Mistress."

She sniffed and gave him a trembling smile. "Well, you'd better help your *Mistress* into her dress before Lady Sha'rak starts shouting at us for being late."

"Of course. Because as we know, Lady Hake'bean does *not* like to be kept waiting." Saber grinned and Lissa slapped playfully at his arm.

"No, she doesn't. So hurry up, slave."

Saber pretended to cower. "I will, Mistress. Please don't use the rod on me. Whatever that is."

Lissa looked troubled. "I don't want to find out. I don't think it's anything pleasant." She sighed. "I don't even know what this whole sensation play thing is—I mean, what am I getting into?"

"Whatever it is, I'll be right there by your side to help you through it." Impulsively, Saber pulled her close and kissed her forehead, just as he used to when they were younger.

At first Lissa stiffened but then she melted against him, her arms going around his waist as she pressed her face to his chest. "Oh…" she sighed and Saber could feel the tension leaving her slender frame as she simply clung to him.

He buried his face in her hair, loving the brush of the silky strands against his skin and her delicious, delicate scent. Gods, she felt so right in his arms, like such a perfect fit. It was so easy to forget at times like these when they were laughing together and relying on each other that their relationship was forbidden.

It shouldn't be, he thought with a surge of anger. *The values of our people are old—outdated. Even the other Kindred think so. There is no blood relation between us. If Lissa and I had been born into any other branch of the Kindred, no one would have thought twice about us mating.*

But they *hadn't* been born to any other branch. In the eyes of their people, what they were doing was wrong—unnatural.

*I don't care if it's wrong—it feels good. Feels **right**,* Saber thought rebelliously.

He kissed Lissa's forehead again and the words *I love you* trembled on his lips. But he couldn't say them. Couldn't let his true emotions be known when they would ultimately have to part.

This is all we have, Saber told himself. *This time here together. And then she'll be gone…forever.*

His throat felt tight at the thought. *Oh amalla, I would give anything to stay with you. To not be parted after this is over. I would give up my life – give up the future that has been so carefully planned for me. I would smash it all to pieces for the privilege of holding you every day like this. Of never letting you go.*

But even if he was willing to give up his future, Saber knew it wasn't fair to ask Lissa to give up hers. She was the high priestess of First World now – a position that didn't allow the one who held it to have a mate. He couldn't ask Lissa to abandon everything she'd worked for and come live with him in infamy and shame.

All he could do was hold her close and savor the time they had left.

Chapter Seventeen

L took her ship into stealth mode the moment the wormhole coughed her up on the far side of the small red planet called Mars. She was careful to keep wide of the Mother Ship as she approached Earth and felt a moment of gratitude for the rare alien tech that allowed her to breach the blue planet's atmosphere without alerting either the humans or Kindred of her presence. It had cost her a ridiculous amount of credit but she considered it well worth the expense.

All but invisible both to the naked eye and any kind of radar, she set her small ship down neatly in the shadow of what her memory assured her was the Human/Kindred Relations building in downtown Tampa. Then she simply walked through the open doors and looked around.

It didn't take long to find what she was looking for. On the front counter she spotted a clipboard that appeared to be a kind of roster—a list of names of Kindred and their brides who were visiting Earth. All L had to do was pick a bride to impersonate, kill the hapless girl, and accompany her Kindred warrior (or warriors) back to the Mother Ship. Quick, simple, and easy.

And oh look, here came the perfect target now.

"All I'm saying is let *me* do the talking." The words were spoken by a voluptuous redhead L's memory told her was named Kat. She was talking to a Kindred warrior with black hair and eyes and a scowl on his face. On her other side, another warrior walked, this one with lighter hair and eyes—obviously the two of them were brothers. *Deep and Lock,* supplied her memory.

Most of the time L found it very inconvenient to have memories of people and things she'd never actually seen stuck inside her head. It was painful to have thoughts of someone her memory told her was a friend and then realize that she'd never actually met them. *Those are **her** memories,* she would remind herself. *Not mine. Never mine.*

But for once, the intrusive memories actually come in handy. And L liked the idea of a target that was also a friend of her original. It would be so much more painful when she revealed the truth and they realized that dear sweet Kat was dead.

She waited until the trio had passed through the front doors of the HKR building and then followed as unobtrusively as possible.

This was going to be fun.

Chapter Eighteen

A piercing, musical shriek and a rush of pale blue-white light met them at the high, double doors of Lady Hake'bean's residence.

Lissa winced away but Lady Sha'rak gave her a little nudge in the small of her back.

"Go on, my dear. The music and light work with the gas to heighten sensations."

"Of course." Lissa stepped over the threshold, bringing Saber with her since she was holding his leash. She still hated the fact that he had to wear such a degrading thing. But, as he pointed out, it was better than one of the awful pain collars Lady Pope'nose favored for her slaves.

The leash didn't seem to bother Saber in the least. He came when she tugged at it and the minute they stepped inside, he bent to kiss her foot. Then he followed her quietly, keeping his eyes down and generally doing his best to look like the most docile and trustworthy of slaves.

It troubled Lissa to see him looking so subjugated until she happened to catch his eye. He winked at her and one corner of his mouth quirked up in a small smile. *We're in this together,* his expression seemed to say. *We're just playing parts – it's all right.*

Feeling better, Lissa winked back and then looked around. It was a very crowded party and they seemed to be in some kind of receiving line. At the front on a raised platform, a slave in shiny golden trousers was calling out the names of each attending lady as she and her slave or slaves drew near. There appeared to be something else going on as well but they were at the very back of the line and Lissa couldn't quite make it out so she examined the rest of the scenery instead.

After her eyes got used to the brilliant light, Lissa realized that Lady Hake'bean's home was huge. Lady Sha'rak had explained on the way over that she owned the top two floors of a very distinguished building. Apparently she'd had the layers between the floors knocked out to make cathedral-high ceilings and windows that looked to be thirty feet tall from sash to crown. Long swatches of silky material in all colors of the rainbow trailed from the massively high ceiling, dividing up the vast front room into different areas. It was like an elaborate maze and Lissa kept seeing people slip mysteriously in and out of the silken panels.

One good thing she noticed was that she wasn't the only one wearing a bizarrely revealing dress. She'd barely been able to force herself to leave Lady Sha'rak's house in the thin jade green dress that hugged the sides of her breasts and her hips while leaving her nipples and crotch completely bare. The idea of going out in public with her private areas on display was almost more than she could stand. But as she looked around, she saw that everyone had on the same kind of dress.

Bare breasts and shaved mounds were visible everywhere, peeking boldly through lace, silk, and satin. Lissa couldn't help noticing, however, that the guests who had already been through the receiving line and were milling around the vast space had strange black dots covering their nipples and crotches. Were those the sensation pads Lady Sha'rak had been talking about? Whatever they were, she hoped the adhesive they used to put them on wasn't too sticky. She wasn't anxious to try yanking what amounted to tape off her most sensitive areas at the end of the night.

Suddenly a strong floral odor assaulted her nose and a high, reedy voice said, "A drink, my lady?"

Lissa turned to see a strange creature that looked like a blob of bright pink jelly with a face staring at her. It was seated inside the chest cavity of a bulky black mechanoid with bright red lights for eyes. The blob peered out at her from between metal bars that kept it confined inside its automated prison.

"Excuse me?" Lissa said blankly. It was such an odd looking creature she couldn't help staring although she was sure it was probably very rude to do so.

"A drink, my lady. Would you care for a drink?" The jelly thing waved one limp looking tentacle and the mechanoid's arm came forward, offering a tray filled with small square glasses of pale brown liquid.

"Oh." Lissa reached for one of the glasses. "Well—"

"I wouldn't, my dear," Lady Sha'rak said in her ear. "It's *Lushian* ale. You won't like the side effects."

"Side effects?" Lissa drew back her hands.

"Makes you grow extra appendages," Lady Sha'rak said. "You know—hands, arms, legs…breasts. Some say it adds to the overall sensation play experience but I've never thought so. And sometimes it takes *days* for the effects to fade—it's never fun waking up with an extra nipple in the middle of your forehead. Or an extra vagina where your navel ought to be."

"I guess not!" Lissa took a step back and shook her head at the blob thing. "No thank you!"

"Suit yourself, my lady." It did something with its tentacles that caused its robotic casing to bow and then clanked slowly off to offer the strange liquor to someone else.

"What *was* that thing?" Lissa asked, watching it go. She noticed that as it left the strong floral scent she'd smelled went with it. It was a relief as the cloying aroma had been giving her a headache.

"Oh, just a *nenarch*. I guess you don't have them on Zetta?"

Lissa shook her head. "What kind of creature are they?"

"Well, they're sentient, obviously, but they really can't move very much—those jelly legs of theirs are nearly useless. I'm afraid our mining here on Yonnie Six disrupted a great deal of their homeland. So some of the more liberal-minded ladies have been employing them as mobile air-fresheners and butlers."

"Air fresheners?" Lissa frowned. "I thought that strong smell was coming from the drink it was offering me."

"Oh no, my dear. Every *nenarch* has a different smell. It's a defense mechanism you know, to ward off predators. But they can turn it on at will—it's very useful for keeping the air fresh in such a large crowd."

Lissa wanted to say she thought the *nenarch* stunk, but it didn't seem polite. So she only nodded and said, "I see."

"You don't yet but you will. Once you start into a sensation scenario you'll find the scent much more enticing. Speaking of which—oh look who it is!"

Lissa turned to see a petite girl of about her own age or a little younger approaching them. She had pink, green, and blue streaks in her ebony hair and was wearing very high heels and what looked like an extremely form fitting pink body suit. When she got a little closer, however, Lissa saw that it wasn't a suit at all but some kind of paint. It covered her nude body without leaving anything to the imagination, but she seemed supremely confident as she swaggered up to them.

The girl was leading a slave on a leash behind her—a male so massive he made even Saber, who was well over six foot six, look small. Lissa looked up at him in awe—he was even bigger than the half-breed warrior, Merrick, who up until that point, was the biggest male she'd ever seen. As if to make him even more imposing, the slave's face was covered by a snarling animal mask with glaring green eyes and lips pulled back to show a slavering red tongue and sharp silver teeth.

Altogether, it was the most bizarre combination Lissa could imagine. She wondered who in the world the outlandish woman and her mountain of a slave could be.

"Lady R'awr, meet our hostess for the evening, Lady Hake'bean," Lady Sha'rak said, smiling broadly. "Snyra," she added, turning to the pink painted girl. "It's so nice to see you again—the party seems to be going *splendidly.*"

"Yes, it is, isn't it?" The girl smiled in a self-satisfied way Lissa disliked at once. "It ought to be—I don't like to tell you how much credit it cost to bring in the amount of Dream Gas needed to get this many guests sensitized."

"I'm sure." Lady Sha'rak gave her a respectful look and murmured to Lissa, "Lady Hake'bean just recently came into her fortune after the unfortunate death of her mother in a star ship accident."

"Oh, I'm so sorry for your loss," Lissa said at once.

"Don't be," Lady Hake'bean said dismissively. "Mother was *such* a bore—we never did get along. And now I can spend my credit however I like." She waved at the party. "As you can see."

"Lady R'awr here is visiting from Zetta Prime," Lady Sha'rak said, nodding at Lissa. "She's never been to a sensation party before."

"Well then, you're in for a treat." Lady Hake'bean grinned at Lissa. "The first time you try Dream Gas is always the best."

"I can't wait," Lissa said politely. "You seem to have so much going on here."

"Yes, there are stations for every genre you can imagine. I've hauled out all of Mother's old collection from historical drama, to biographies, to zeno-porn—any scenario you can think of, I have a document for it. Ask any of the *nenarches* wandering around and they'll tell you which station is which." She nudged Lady Sha'rak. "Of course the porn station is the busiest."

"I guess so!" Lady Sha'rak giggled. "I know it's the one *I'm* looking forward to. But Lady R'awr here is most interested in history."

"Specifically the Hoard Wars that occurred on First World about a thousand years ago?" Lissa asked hopefully.

"Oh yes, I think we have something along those lines," Lady Hake'bean said vaguely. "You can ask one of the *nenarches* to direct you." She sighed and put a hand to her forehead. "I'm sorry I'm not more help but Mother had *so many* documents. Still, if we have Hoard War papers anywhere they would be in the historical drama section."

Lissa felt a surge of hope. "I'll be certain to check."

"Do that, just be sure you don't get so into your sensi-play you miss the punishment show." Lady Hake'bean yanked on her massive slave's collar, bringing the huge male closer so that he was towering over her. "Beast and I will be putting it on in an hour or so."

"Oh, all this and a punishment show too?" Lady Sha'rak looked even more excited. "But you're putting it on yourself? Couldn't you find someone else?"

"Well, normally I could count on Lady Pope'nose—she *loves* to punish slaves. But since she's put all of hers into pain collars, she hardly bothers with the rod anymore."

"Mm-hmm, she was saying something like that to me the other day when she came for dinner." Lady Sha'rak nodded. "I saw the new collar in action. It's a bit *extreme* if you ask me."

"And not nearly as much *fun* as a traditional punishment." Lady Hake'bean leaned closer. "Keep it to yourself, but I have a new rod I'll be showing off tonight. Do you want to see it?"

"Oh yes!" Lady Sha'rak clapped her hands. "*Do* show us."

"Beast, hand it over," Lady Hake'bean held out her hand and her huge slave put a strange purple device in her palm. "It's designed for maximum pleasure," she said. "Mine, of course—not Beast's."

Lissa leaned forward almost as eagerly as Lady Sha'rak—finally she was going to see what "the rod" was all about. But the thing Lady Hake'bean was holding in her hands didn't look like any kind of punishment device Lissa had ever seen. It was a little longer than her forearm and appeared to be made of some kind of clear purple rubber. There was a wide oval separating the two halves of the device with one half being much longer, thicker, and knobbier than the other. Each end had a round, flaring knob at the top that reminded her of something, although she couldn't think what. A number of black leather straps hung from it, making Lissa think it was supposed to be worn in some way—but how?

"The smaller end is for me, of course," Lady Hake'bean was saying as she displayed the device. "It fits inside but there are straps for extra stability. There's a vibe right here..." She touched the wide oval that separated the two arms. "For stimulation."

"Oh, of course," Lady Sha'rak echoed, nodding. "But the way it fits — you don't mind the penetration?"

"Mind it? I *love* it." Lady Hake'bean's eyes gleamed. "With every thrust I get double stimulation. Mind you, *Beast* here doesn't like it much." She slapped the massive slave on his muscular arm and a low growling came from inside the animal-faced mask.

"Oh, no?" Lady Sha'rak looked disconcerted. "He doesn't like being dominated?"

"He wasn't born into any of the slave training houses here — he's actually a convict from the Berrack mines on Primus Three," Lady Hake'bean explained. "I saw him the last time I went with Mother to inspect our holdings there. I wanted to get him right away but Mother wouldn't let me." She made a face. "She said it was too *dangerous*, taking a slave from one of those primitive male-dominated societies where the males do the penetrating and never take the rod themselves. Not to mention the fact that Beast here was sent to the mines for multiple murders. He's a *bad boy*, aren't you, my pet?" she cooed at her body-slave.

"Oh my." Lady Sha'rak put a hand to her chest and moved ever so slightly farther away from the huge slave. "Multiple murders? That's...interesting."

"Yes, I thought so too." Lady Hake'bean preened, apparently oblivious to her guest's discomfort. "I sent for him as soon as Mother died and I've been training him ever since. He was a virgin before I got him — never took the rod in his life. But we changed that, didn't we, Beast?" She slapped her slave on the rear this time and the low growl coming from inside the mask rose to a snarl of pure rage.

"Oh dear!" This time Lady Sha'rak took a full step back. Lissa was about to get back from the dangerous slave as well, when Saber suddenly stepped up and put himself between them.

"What's the meaning of this?" Lady Hake'bean looked half angry, half amused. "Lady R'awr, Why is your slave interrupting our conversation?"

"I think he's protecting me." Lissa looked out from behind Saber's muscular shoulder. "Your body-slave is very...er, intimidating."

Lady Hake'bean laughed. "Oh, come now! You're not really *frightened* of him, are you?"

"Well, he *is* rather massive," Lady Sha'rak said carefully. "And you don't appear to have any kind of pain collar or control device on him."

"Don't need one." Lady Hake'bean made a dismissive gesture. "He's chemically castrated. I don't even need to put touch-me-not manacles on him—the only way he can orgasm is when I'm giving him the rod. Prostate stimulation, you know," she said to Lady Sha'rak who nodded doubtfully.

"Of course."

"He pretends not to like it but he comes like an animal every time. Especially when I use this on him." Lady Hake'bean stroked the purple device meaningfully before handing it back to her slave. "Keep that for me, Beast. You'll be enjoying it soon enough."

The snarl of rage rose to a howl of fury and Lissa gripped Saber's arm tightly. His body was trembling and she felt rather than heard the low growl he was emitting. Did he really feel that Lady Hake'bean's slave was a threat? It certainly looked to Lissa like he was—he seemed about to break whatever control Lady Hake'bean had over him and go completely crazy. But instead of running amuck, the massive body-slave simply took the device and stowed it carefully in a pack he was carrying.

"See?" Lady Hake'bean laughed again. "His mind is free but his body is completely under my control." She stroked the muscular arm that was trembling with rage. "This is going to be our first public performance, isn't it, Beast?" she purred, looking at him with obvious lust. "I can't *wait* to make you come in front of all these people."

This time the only response from the snarling animal mask was an ominous silence. For some reason the lack of sound made Lissa even more nervous than the growling, snarling, and howling had.

Apparently Lady Sha'rak felt the same. "Oh, will you look at that," she exclaimed a little too brightly. "We're next to be announced."

"You'd better go then," Lady Hake'bean said. "Have fun at the various stations and be sure you sample documents from every genre." She held out a hand to Lissa. "I'll find you later and make sure you get what you need."

"Oh, thank you!" Lissa started to step out from behind Saber to take Lady Hake'bean's hand, but Saber wouldn't allow it. Putting out an arm he pushed her gently but firmly behind him, keeping himself between her and their hostess's menacing slave.

Lady Hake'bean frowned. "You really should punish that sort of behavior, Lady R'awr—an overprotective slave can become dangerously dominant if you don't watch out. They begin to think they're in charge and then you have to watch your back every minute."

"I see." Lissa nodded. "I…"I'll keep that in mind."

"Let me know if you're interested in chemical castration," Lady Hake'bean said, as she turned away. "I keep the necessary compounds with me at all times. Well—when I'm wearing something to keep them *in.*" She laughed and indicated her nude, pink-painted form as though it was a wonderful joke.

Lissa and Lady Sha'rak laughed too but Lissa got the distinct impression that the ambassador was glad when their hostess moved away.

"Really, she's gone too far this time," the ambassador murmured as they moved up in the line. "Taking a murderous convict who's never been properly trained as a body-slave? It's dangerous!"

"I think so too," Lissa whispered.

"Yes, but you shouldn't show it—or let your slave show it for you," Lady Sha'rak said reprovingly. "He really ought to be punished for such behavior. I'd insist on it if I didn't think it would ruin Lady Hake'bean's punishment performance later."

"I'll speak to him," Lissa promised, her heart in her mouth. "I swear it won't happen again."

"See that it doesn't." Lady Sha'rak gave Saber a reproving look before she and Llewelyn moved up to the bottom steps of the platform.

"You have to be more careful," Lissa muttered to Saber under her breath. "You almost got into trouble just now."

"I was keeping you safe." His voice still sounded husky with protective fury, and she could see the tension running through the muscles of his bare chest. "That female is crazy if she thinks she'll get away with punishing her slave like that in public. He'll kill her for it—didn't you hear the rage in his voice?"

"Of *course* I did but she said he was safe." Lissa didn't sound very convincing, even to herself. "Look, the point is I don't want to have to "punish" you tonight with that rod thing, however it works."

"Didn't you get it?" Saber sounded surprised. He shook his head. "Sometimes I forget how innocent you are. You put it—"

"Oh my Goddess," Lissa interrupted in a horrified whisper. "Look at that."

At the front of the line Lady Sha'rak had climbed the platform and was being announced.

"The Cultural Ambassador of Yonnie Six, Lady Manda Sha'rak," the slave in shiny gold pants was proclaiming. But that wasn't what bothered Lissa. As they watched, Lady Sha'rak spread her legs and leaned back against a wide supportive post that appeared to be placed there for that purpose. The position showed her pussy, framed in crimson lace panties, to everyone watching in the crowded room. Without hesitation, Llewelyn dropped to his knees before her and began laving her exposed pussy with his tongue, taking long, slow licks and clearly savoring his mistress's juices.

Lady Sha'rak gasped and closed her eyes in obvious pleasure. Running her fingers over her body-slave's bald head, she urged him on, thrusting her hips toward him as he licked deeper and deeper.

At last she trembled and let out a loud moan, which was followed by a lot of polite clapping from the onlookers. Then, looking satisfied, she straightened her dress, lifted Llewelyn to his feet, and turned to Lissa.

"Your turn, my dear. *Do* be sure you put on a good show." Then she sauntered off with Llewelyn trailing behind her, licking his lips.

"Oh my Goddess," Lissa whispered again, feeling her blood turn to ice. She had promised to stop feeling guilty about whatever they had to do to make this mission a success but this...this was going too far—especially in a public, crowded place.

"Don't worry," Saber murmured in her ear, as her heart began to gallop in her chest. "I'll just kiss you—no licking, all right?"

Lissa nodded numbly. "All right, yes," she whispered back. "Kissing...that should...that should be all right."

"Of course." He nodded.

And then the slave in gold trousers was saying, "Lady Lissa R'awr of Zetta Prime, guest of Ambassador Sha'rak."

"That's us—let's go," Saber whispered, nudging her gently toward the platform.

On wobbly legs, Lissa climbed the steps leading up to the small stage and made her way to the post. There was a slight ledge where she could rest her bottom, which was a good thing—without the added support she might have collapsed. Her nipples had hardened into tight little points of fear and her legs felt shaky.

Lissa had never liked being the center of attention and when she looked down and saw a crowd of strange faces staring at her, waiting, she honestly wanted to die. She already felt horribly exposed in the revealing lace dress. How could she spread her legs and let these people stare at her while Saber kissed her naked sex? How could she put on an obscene show like some kind of stripper or sex worker? She was a priestess, not a prostitute! Stage fright gripped her throat with an icy hand and she began to panic.

Oh Goddess, she thought, her hands cold and her knees shaking with fright. *Oh Goddess, please, I can't do this. I can't! I **can't.***

"Mistress." Suddenly Saber was on his knees before her. He caught her trembling hands in his and looked earnestly up into her eyes. "Mistress," he said again in a low, firm voice. "You can do this. We'll do it together. It's going to be all right."

"Yes…yes, all right." Lissa did her best to calm her racing heart. She squeezed his hands tightly and took a deep breath. "Yes," she whispered again.

"Good." Saber turned her hands over and kissed her palms gently. "Don't look at any of them—just look at me. Can you do that for me, Lissa?"

"Yes," she whispered again.

"Good. Now open for me, *amalla*. Open and let me in."

"*Moch Daer*," she whispered, feeling herself melt inside. Saber was right—they would get through this together. She would ignore the curious crowd and concentrate only on him. Keeping her eyes on his face, she leaned back against the post, feeling the cool marble chill her skin through the thin lace of her dress.

"That's right, Mistress," he murmured, stroking her legs. "Now open for me."

Spreading her thighs, which she had been keeping tightly closed up until now, was the hardest thing Lissa had ever done. Only seeing Saber kneeling patiently before her, waiting, made her able to do it.

With her pussy shaved bare, she felt more exposed, more vulnerable than she ever had in her life. And it didn't help that the position she was in was causing her outer lips to open, revealing the deep pink of her inner folds. Even the pink pearl of her clit was exposed. Lissa felt like it was throbbing with embarrassment in time to her heart.

"Oh, *amalla*…" Saber took in a deep breath and let out a soft, deep growl of approval and lust. "So beautiful," he murmured, leaning closer, his warm breath blowing across her thighs. "So Goddess damned beautiful…"

"Saber?" she whispered uncertainly but he was already leaning forward to kiss her.

Lissa watched, mesmerized, as he placed a soft, open-mouthed kiss at the top of her slit. His breath on her skin had gone from warm to hot and she felt a sudden shiver run down her spine. Surely she couldn't be turned on by this—not when they were putting on a show for so many people. But when she looked down, all she saw was Saber—the male she had loved for time out of mind—kissing her softly and reverently. Treating her as though she was a rare vase that might shatter if he was too rough.

"Saber," she murmured again as he moved lower and pressed his lips to her flesh again. This time his kiss landed directly between her spread pussy lips.

Lissa gasped and gave a little moan when she felt him kiss her there, his lips moving as slowly and gently as though he were kissing her mouth. Involuntarily, her finger slipped into his hair and tightened, urging him on.

Saber acted on her wordless encouragement eagerly. Pressing forward, he spread her pussy wider with his thumbs and deepened the kiss. Lissa moaned again as she felt gentle suction around her swollen clit. Oh Goddess, he was sucking her there, taking the most sensitive part of her between his lips, kissing her in the most intimate way possible...

But he's still just kissing me, she insisted to herself. *It's still just a kiss...right?*

Her fingers tightened in his hair again and then she felt the hot slide of his tongue against her heated flesh. A low growl of lust came from him, sending a tingle through her entire body as he licked her again, first tracing the sensitive bundle of nerves at her core with the tip of his tongue, then lapping deeper, tasting her with abandon.

Goddess, he's not just kissing – he's tasting me. And everyone is watching and I'm going to…going to… Oh Goddess, if he doesn't stop I'm going to come. Right here in front of everyone!

This last, mortifying thought and the sound of the crowd clapping for them, finally gave her the strength to push him away.

"Enough, Saber," she panted, though she had never felt so unsatisfied in her life. "Enough now – stop!"

"Forgive me, my lady." He sat back at last, his lips shiny with her juices, his hazel eyes drowning deep with lust. "I…lost myself in the pleasure of kissing you," he murmured.

"It's all right," Lissa said, though she felt like she might never be all right again. Every nerve felt exposed and she felt so swollen and hot between her legs she couldn't move without wincing. "Let's just…there are other people waiting to be announced. Let's just go."

"Of course." He took her hand and helped her gently off the stage.

Lissa stumbled twice and would have fallen if he hadn't been there to catch her. Goddess, what was wrong with her? Why was she so unsteady on her feet? It was almost as though her body was protesting the fact that she hadn't let Saber make her come.

But I couldn't, she thought, feeling dazed. *I just couldn't – not in front of everyone!*

What if everyone else was gone and it was just you and Saber? asked the critical little voice in her head. *Wouldn't have been so quick to stop him then, would you?*

Lissa was about to tell that stupid little voice to shut up when an unfamiliar slave with blue hair came up to them.

"Well, well—that was quite a show the two of you put on. Very tender." He smiled mockingly. "I don't think I've ever seen such devotion between a slave and his lady."

Lissa felt her cheeks going red with embarrassment but she reminded herself that *she* was the one in control here. She was a grand lady—as far as anyone knew, anyway—and this person was only a slave.

"Who are you and what do you want?" She demanded haughtily, crossing her arms over her chest.

The slave raised his eyebrows, which were also royal blue. "Touchy, aren't we? Well, my Lady R'awr, *I* am Greggor, Lady Hake'bean's personal director of festivities. She sent me over to see personally that you had a good time. Said something about it being your first sensation party?"

"Oh, yes—yes, it is." Lissa nodded quickly. "And we're very interested in trying some documents from the historical drama section of your lady's collection."

"Yes, yes," Greggor drawled. "She said something about the Hoard Wars?"

"Exactly!" Lissa could barely contain her excitement. "Can you direct us there or take us to them?"

"Well, I'm not taking you *anywhere* before you put these on." Greggor whipped out a piece of clear plastic film that had several black dots in various sizes. "Here."

Before she could stop him, he had peeled off two of the sticky black dots and pasted them directly over her nipples. He was reaching to place a larger, oval-shaped dot over her exposed sex when Saber caught him by the wrist.

"No one touches my lady there but *me*," he growled, giving the other slave a hard look.

"Very well, put it on if you like." Greggor dropped the black oval into his hand and stepped back, rubbing his wrist. "I don't even like females, you know. That's why Lady Hake'bean made me her party planner—I'm *hopeless* at servicing a mistress. Now, when it comes to other males, especially big, strapping, sexy ones..."

He trailed off, giving Saber a significant glance, but Lissa could tell her kinsman was oblivious. All his concentration was focused on his current task of kneeling before her and carefully applying the sticky black oval to her pussy. It just covered her slit and most of her outer pussy lips.

Between this and the nipple dots, I feel more dressed than I have all night, she thought ruefully as he finally stood and put himself between her and Lady Hake'bean's slave.

"Well, if you're quite finished, here are some sensor pads for you," Greggor said. "I don't suppose you'd like *me* to apply them?" He winked flirtatiously at Saber. "I have a *very* steady hand."

Saber frowned and held out his hand silently.

"Fine, *be* that way," Greggor pouted and placed the clear plastic sheet with its remaining dots in his palm. "Paste two on your nipples, wrap one around your cock and you might want one for your anus as well—if you're planning on doing the zeno-porn station."

"Uh, no—no porn," Lissa said quickly. "We're only interested in historical drama."

"So *boring.*" Greggor made a face. "Why don't you let me set you up with a little role-play porn? That's *very* popular tonight."

"Thank you but no. Just the Hoard Wars—those are the only documents we want to see," Lissa said firmly.

"*Fine.*" Greggor sighed dramatically, as though having to escort such boring people was a terrible burden. "Come with me and try not to breathe in too much Dream Gas until we get to the right section. You want your synapses to be fresh for your first sensi-play."

* * * * *

They followed Lady Hake'bean's slave through the milling crowds of party guests and Saber made sure to keep an eye out for anyone else who might pose a threat to Lissa. He didn't like the look of half the slaves here tonight but maybe he was just on edge after watching their foolish hostess and the massive convict she'd taken as a personal body-slave.

"You're a jumpy fellow." Greggor gave him a significant look as they threaded their way through the swirling strips of colored silk and the other half-naked partygoers. "Looking out for your mistress, are you?"

"I do my best," Saber said shortly and then added, "You should do the same."

Greggor widened his eyes dramatically. "You think my lady is in danger?"

"I know she is. We saw the convict she's taken from the mines and now uses as her slave."

"Oh, the Beast?" Greggor gave a delighted shiver. "Yes, he *is* a brute. My lady's mother tried to warn her when she was alive but little Miss Snyra always *was* headstrong. She loves a challenge."

"That male is no challenge—he's her death waiting to happen," Saber said darkly. "I don't think your mistress fully understands the way a male who isn't born into subjugation feels about being dominated and used the way she plans to use him."

"And *you* do?" Greggor raised an eyebrow at him. "Are you telling me you weren't born into one of the slave training houses?"

"We're not from here, we're from Zetta Prime," Lissa put in, joining the conversation. "I didn't get Saber from any, uh, house."

Greggor's eyes widened. "You were born free and taken, as the Beast was?"

Saber shifted uncomfortably. "Something like that."

"And you serve her anyway? You don't mind being dominated? You don't mind taking the rod?" Lady Hake'bean's servant persisted.

"I serve my mistress out of love." Saber frowned at the other male. "Anything she finds it necessary to do to me, I accept for the same reason."

"My, my…" Greggor shook his head. "You really *are* devoted. I've never seen such love for a mistress before."

"Look to your own mistress," Saber retorted. "See if you can't stop the exhibition she's going to put on tonight. The Beast will never forgive her if she uses him so publicly—he'll feel it as an insult to his masculinity—an unforgivable degradation to his very being as a male."

"Oh, there's no stopping Lady Hake'bean when she decides to do something," Greggor said dismissively. "In fact, she said I was to escort you personally to the show—apparently you and your mistress get a front row seat. Oh, look, here we are." He stopped short in front of an area cordoned off by long swatches of silky purple fabric hanging from the high ceilings. "Historical drama. There doesn't appear to be anyone here though. I wonder *why*."

"That's all right," Lissa said eagerly. "We don't mind being the only ones. Saber and I will just look through the documents—"

"Ah-ah-ah." Greggor blocked her way, wagging a finger in her face. "I was told to give you the perfect sensi-play experience and that's *exactly* what I'm going to do. Come this way."

Saber felt a surge of irritation. If it wasn't for the officious slave, he and Lissa might have searched the documents, found the missing scrolls, and been out of the party and off Yonnie Six before anyone was the wiser. Instead, they were saddled with what was surely the most annoying male on the entire planet. With a sigh, he followed Greggor and Lissa into the historical drama area, which was just a makeshift room formed by the hanging purple curtains and filled with stacks of scrolls and books.

"Ugh, there's barely room to move in here." Greggor made a face. "The old mistress was a little too fond of historicals from all different cultures. My mistress has been hoping to sell some of them off to pay for expenses."

"Really?" Lissa sounded doubtful. "I was given to understand that serious collectors rarely parted with the documents in their collections." Which was why they had decided *not* to pose as merchants who wished to buy antiquities in the first place.

"Well, this is a special case." Greggor winked. "Just between us, what with importing and training murderous convicts, commissioning new rods molded especially for her from the most cutting edge artists, and throwing massive sensation parties every other weekend, she's running through her credit like it was water. So if you find something you like, I don't think any reasonable offer will be refused."

Saber and Lissa exchanged a glance. Even better! They could buy the scrolls and not have to worry about getting caught as they left the planet. Eagerly, Saber dug into a bunch of documents that were heaped haphazardly in a pile by the nearest curtain. On the other side of the room, Lissa did the same.

"Well, don't mind me," Greggor said sulkily as they searched. "I'll just be over here, bored out of my skull while you—"

"Look, here it is! I've found it!" Lissa's voice was high and excited.

Saber rushed over to her and examined the ancient scroll she held reverently in her hands. The document was so old it would have been crumbling to pieces if someone hadn't thoughtfully laminated the entire thing in thin sheets of pale blue plastic.

"Listen," Lissa said, unrolling it carefully. "It talks about the Hoard—about how the Councilor and his mate had to decide what to do. And—"

"Found one you like, did you? Good." Greggor whisked the document out of her hand and rolled it up neatly.

"Hey!" Saber reached for the scroll. "Give that back!"

"I don't think so." Greggor put the precious document behind his back. "How can you use it for sensi-play if I don't put it in the dream projector?"

"We don't *want* to do sensi-play," Lissa objected. "We just want the scroll, honestly."

But Greggor was already feeding the end of the long scroll into a flat black device with a blinking red light, which rested in one corner of the room. Saber hadn't seen it earlier, possibly because it was obscured by another pile of documents.

"Get ready," he said. "I'm turning on the gas. In a moment the projector will put you in the document."

"What are you talking abou—?" Saber began but his words ended in a cough. The flat black machine was spewing out a thick white fog. It had a complex, sickly sweet odor that reminded Saber of the scent that had come up from the trench they had ridden over in order to get to Opulex in the first place.

"Is that the Dream Gas?" he heard Lissa say. "I don't like it—it makes me feel funny."

Saber was beginning to feel strange as well. His entire body suddenly felt light—as though he might float away with the least breeze. And as he looked at Lissa, she began to change. She grew several inches taller to start and then her pale blonde hair turned a warm golden brown while the jade streaks in it became a brilliant, emerald green. Her thin lace dress melted into a more modest white gown and her belly grew beneath it as though she had suddenly somehow become pregnant.

"Lissa!" he tried to say but the name that came out of his mouth was, "Zali."

"Kall," the strange new Lissa responded, looking at him in confusion.

Looking down at himself, Saber realized that he had changed too and not just his clothing. He had suddenly and inexplicably sprouted a vast pair of shimmering, iridescent wings.

"What in the seven hells?" he tried to exclaim. But instead he heard himself saying, "Zali, my love. I must go. You know there is no other way."

"But our baby..." Tears glimmered in Lissa/Zali's eyes and she stroked her rounded stomach tenderly. "He'll never know his father if you go."

"Zali, he'll never know either of us. We must send him away— you know this has to be—we have seen it in the Eye of Foreknowlege."

Saber was speaking his lines more easily now and though it was a strange situation, he almost felt like he was getting used to it. Clearly the dream projector took whatever document they picked and turned it into a narrative—a kind of story that the Dream Gas allowed them to participate in. No wonder the porn stations Greggor had tried to steer them to were so popular! With the use of the projector and the sweet smelling Dream Gas, one could become literally *anyone* they wanted to be doing *anything* they wanted with no consequences. Why, he and Lissa...

We could make love, he thought, his mind opening fully to the forbidden possibility. *Without actually touching. Without breaking any taboos.* But he rejected the idea almost immediately.

If they used the Dream Gas to consummate their love it wouldn't be real. Also, he would never be able to give her the Deep Touch unless he was actually physically touching her at the same time he used his Touch sense. And *that* was what Saber wanted more than anything else in the universe—the chance to take her and bond her to him forever. Any substitute, no matter how sweet, would be a pale shadow of what could be if they allowed themselves to come together.

Before he could think any more about his forbidden desires, the scene moved on and he found he was holding a sobbing Lissa/Zali against his side.

"I don't want you to go," she was crying. "It's suicide! I know in my heart if you board a ship for Hrakaz we'll never see each other again."

Saber felt his chest grow tight. The scene they were playing might be over a thousand years old but the dilemma their characters were experiencing ran strangely parallel to his own situation with Lissa.

"I love you," he whispered, wrapping her in his shimmering wings, trying to take away the hurt and pain he felt coursing through her. "I will always love you, my darling. Even unto death and beyond."

"Kall..." Lissa/Zali sobbed against him. "I know we knew this day would come but I didn't expect it to be so soon. Didn't expect to have to lose you like this. I thought...I always thought that in the end we'd be together." She buried her face in his shoulder. "I can stand to die. I can even stand to send our son away and never seen him again. But I can't *bear* the idea of being separated from you."

"It may be our fate to lose each other in this life," Saber replied, stroking her hair. "But I swear to you, my *Lyzel*, I will find you in the next one and we will never be parted again." Gently but firmly he extricated himself from her embrace. "I must go now—you know I must."

"I know." She stepped back, her eyes overflowing with tears. "I love you so much, Kall. I'm so proud of what you're doing. Of what you're giving up." She reached out and stroked the shining edge of one of his wings.

Saber shook his head. "The loss of my wings is nothing compared to the loss of you, Zali."

"Don't." She shook her head. "Please, don't. I can't bear it."

"Goodbye." Saber felt a lump in his throat. This was the final moment between them—the character he was playing wouldn't be able to help his wife through her delivery. He was never going to see his unborn son or hold him in his arms. He was leaving the woman he loved more than his own life and he would never see her again. Gods, this was *terrible*. So sad he wanted to sob but he knew he couldn't—he had to be strong. Had to do this awful thing no matter how painful it was because there was no other way.

But what awful thing is he going to do? Saber wondered, as he stepped away from Lissa's character. *How is he going to stop the Hoard? It's obvious he intends to board a ship to Hrakaz but what is he going to do once he gets there? There must be more to this scroll. It can't be ending here — can it?*

As though in answer to his unspoken questions, the scene changed again and he found himself sitting on the bridge of a primitive looking space ship. He was lifting off the planet's surface and there was a terrible, burning pain in his shoulders for some reason. Looking from side to side, he saw why—his wings were burning away to ash, their vast, iridescent feathers crisping and curling as though they had been touched by some unseen fire.

Saber curled his hands into fists and gritted his teeth against the pain. "Goddess," he prayed aloud. "Forgive me for abandoning your planet. But if this is the only way, then I must take it. If the only way to defeat the Hoard is to—"

Suddenly the scene around him faded and Saber found himself back in the little room made of purple fabric. He was standing opposite Lissa, who was looking around in confusion.

"What happened?" he demanded, turning to Greggor who was watching with a bored look on his face. "Why did it stop? We were just getting to the really important part!"

"Sorry. That was the end of the scroll." Greggor held up the ancient document.

"Oh, no!" Lissa snatched the scroll from him and examined it closely, as though she could make the missing part appear by will alone. "What happened to the rest of the story?"

"Hmm..." Greggor looked over her shoulder. "See this little annotation here?" He pointed at some printing so fine it could scarcely be read. "Says here that part two was sold."

"Sold? To who?" Saber growled.

"Hmm...looks like...Lady P." Greggor looked up. "Probably Lady Pope'nose. She also collects antiquities and historical documents." He looked at Lissa. "Do you know her?"

"We've met her all right." Saber sighed and ran a hand through his hair.

"That must be the recent acquisition she was talking about," Lissa murmured.

"Come to think of it, she *did* recently make some purchases from my mistress—very discreetly, of course. Selling off documents is a bit akin to selling off your children—at least to most of the older collectors." Greggor sniffed. "I mean it can be done but you don't want to *advertise* it or anything. But if she—"

Just then a loud *gooooonnnnng* echoed through the air. It was a sound so loud Lissa put her hands over her ears and the fabric panels that made up their "room" vibrated.

"What was that?" Saber demanded, when the note finally faded away.

"*That* was my mistress letting everyone know the show is about to begin." Greggor grabbed him and Lissa both by the arm and dragged them out of the historical drama area. "Come on, we don't want to be late."

Saber gave one last look at the purple drapes that marked the historical documents room and promised himself they would get the second scroll from Lady Pope'nose. Although how they were going to get the important document away from such a horrible woman he had absolutely no idea.

Chapter Nineteen

"...and that's the whole truth, Grandma. I'm with both of them because I love them both and they love me." Kat took a deep breath and squeezed her men's hands. Lock was standing by her right side and Deep was standing by her left. Both of them squeezed back and she felt a surge of protection and support coming through their bond.

"I love you," she sent to both of them. *"No matter what she says, I promise that won't change."*

"We love you too, little Kat," Deep rumbled in her mind.

"My lady, nothing could change our love for you," Lock assured her quietly but firmly.

"Well!" Grandma stood suddenly and for a moment Kat was afraid she was going to storm out of the comfortably decorated living room with its neat but slightly faded floral print furniture.

Instead, she came up to Kat and hugged her tight.

"Grandma?" Kat was so surprised she didn't know what to do. "I...uh..."

"I'm so glad." Her grandmother's voice was muffled against her shoulder. "I'm just so glad you finally found the right one for you, Kat." She pulled back and looked at Kat with a smile. "Or I guess, the right *ones*."

"You *do* realize I'm marrying both of them, right?" Kat looked at her closely, wanting to make sure what she was saying was sinking in. "I mean, as in a triple wedding?"

"A wedding I'll be proud to attend," her grandmother promised, her faded blue eyes shining.

Kat shook her head. "I don't understand. I mean, I've been worried about telling you this for *months*. I put off the ceremony because I was so afraid you wouldn't attend."

"Katrina Melissa O'Connor!" Her grandmother looked scandalized—which was exactly how Kat had imagined her looking when she broke the news. "How could you even *think* such a thing?" she demanded.

"Well...because of the way you raised me." Kat gave her a bewildered look. "I mean, you have to admit, Grandma, you were pretty strict."

"Because I didn't want to lose you." Her grandmother patted her cheek. "And more importantly, I didn't want you to lose *yourself*, honey. But now look at you..." She stepped back, smiling. "You have a whole new life you love up in that big ship and you've got two handsome men hanging all over you, looking to make an honest woman of you. I couldn't be prouder."

"Mrs. O'Connor, we vow to love Kat forever," Lock said earnestly.

"And protect her with our lives," Deep growled.

Kat's grandmother nodded and smiled. "I can tell how much you two love my little girl. It's been written all over your faces from the minute the three of you came in the door." She looked at Kat. "So when is the wedding? And when can I expect grandbabies?"

"Wow!" Kat started laughing in relief but then her laughter turned into a sob. "Oh, Grandma!" she exclaimed. Rushing forward, she hugged her grandmother hard. "I was so afraid," she whispered through her tears. "I never wanted to disappoint you. Thank you for understanding."

"Of *course* I understand." Her grandmother stroked her hair soothingly. "Having two husbands isn't, well, it's not the *usual* thing. And I'm sure some of the ladies in my sewing circle are going to have something to say about it but, well, I don't care." She pulled back and Kat saw that there were tears in her eyes as well. "As long as you're happy, honey, *I don't care.*" Then she gestured to Deep and Lock. "Get in here, you two. You're part of the family now."

Both men came forward and soon Kat found herself enveloped in a group hug that warmed her heart. For so many long months she had been putting this moment off—the moment when she would reveal the truth to her grandmother. And now it turned out that she needn't have worried at all.

"I should have given you more credit, Grandma," she whispered. "You always were the coolest grandmother in town."

"Well, thank you, honey. That means a lot to me." Grandma patted her back.

When the hug finally broke apart, Kat had to wipe her eyes. "Will you excuse me?" She smiled at her men. "I think I need to go check my makeup and blow my nose."

"Use the upstairs bathroom, honey," Grandma said, smiling. "The downstairs one is a mess right now—I just did a load of laundry."

"Oh, right." Kat knew what that meant. Her grandmother insisted on washing all her pantyhose and fine washables by hand and hanging them to dry over the shower curtain. It had driven Kat crazy when she was a teenager but now she thought it was funny—just one of Grandma's loveable little quirks. "I'll just be a minute," she said and with a last smile at her grandmother and her men, she ran up the steps to the second story with a lighter heart than she'd had in weeks.

The upstairs bathroom was done in pink and purple tile that Kat had helped pick out when she was nine and had just moved into the house. Grandma had pretty much given her free rein in the redecoration, trying to cheer her up after her parents split and it really showed—both here and in her childhood bedroom.

Kat smiled as she looked at the tile. She had told her grandma that she could redo the bathroom again if she wanted to—after all, the bright pink and purple motif wasn't exactly something anyone but a nine year old girl would like. Her grandma stubbornly refused, however, saying she loved it—although she *had* finally replaced the prancing unicorn wallpaper with a coat of plain cream paint.

Looking at it, Kat realized afresh how much her grandmother loved her. *I'm so lucky,* she thought, looking at her tear-streaked face in the bathroom mirror. *I should have given Grandma more credit. She —*

Her thoughts were abruptly cut off when a face appeared behind her in the silver surface of the mirror. A familiar face.

"Lauren?" Kat whirled around, frowning. "Are you all right? What are you doing here in my Grandma's house?"

"I watched the scene downstairs," Lauren said but her voice sounded strange—colder somehow. "Very touching, Kat."

"Yes, my Grandma is cool with me being with Twin Kindred. Such a relief." Kat shook her head. "But... you never did say how you got here?"

"I followed you. But I'll be leaving alone." Lauren held something up and Kat was shocked to see a silver syringe with a three inch long needle in her hand. A droplet of poison green liquid quivered on its tip, shining like a distant star in the dim overhead light.

"Lauren, doll, you're not making a lot of sense." Kat began to back away. "Is everything all right?"

"It will be. Very soon." And then Lauren's features began to run, shifting and flowing like hot wax, changing her into someone else—changing her into *Kat*.

"Oh my God," Kat whispered in breathless horror. What the hell was going on? The thing that had been Lauren now looked exactly like *her*. It was like staring into a mirror, right down to her mussed auburn hair and the mascara smudges beneath her blue eyes.

"What do you think?" A perfect replica of Kat's own mouth twitched up, giving her a sarcastic little smile. "Will it fool Deep and Lock? Will it fool sweet old *Grandma*?"

Kat opened her mouth to scream and the needle plunged down, stabbing her in the neck. A burning river of fire suddenly filled her veins and her legs gave way. *I have to warn them somehow—have to warn Grandma,* she thought frantically. But her mouth wouldn't work and her vocal cords were paralyzed. She tried to shout a warning through her link to Deep and Lock but even that part of her seemed to be frozen.

Please, God, she thought as the stranger who wore her face caught her and lowered her gently to the cool tile floor. *Please don't let her hurt—*

And then everything went black.

Chapter Twenty

"Here we are. Best seat in the house. Be sure you wave when Lady Hake'bean shows up—she told me she'll be looking for you and she'll be *very* offended if she doesn't see you," Greggor lectured as he ushered them through the crowd. They ended up in the front row of plush pink seats, which had been set up around the platform where they had been announced previously. A large area inside it had been screened off with panels of shimmering golden fabric, creating a mysterious barrier between the audience and whatever was set up on stage. Greggor got Lissa settled, winked and said, "Enjoy the show," before bustling away.

Lissa couldn't help glancing at Saber, who was sitting beside and slightly behind her on a plain wooden stool—the seating provided for slaves. She wondered if he was thinking about what had happened earlier between them on that very stage. If he was, his face didn't betray it.

But the illicit kiss he'd placed between her thighs wasn't the only thing Lissa was thinking about. She still had a lump in her throat from the emotional scene they had acted out earlier. It wasn't just the words she had said as they acted their parts either—Lissa had actually *felt* the emotions of her character. The despair at watching him leave, the utter desolation of losing the man she loved and knowing she would never see him again.

The way I'm never going to see Saber again after this is over, Lissa thought. She wrapped her arms around herself and squeezed, trying to push the awful thought away. But this time she couldn't do it. *If only we could be together. If only we could forget about what our people say and do what we want...* But that would mean asking Saber to give up his future position as the Over Chief of the Sun Clan and the Touch Kindred. Lissa *couldn't* do that—it wasn't fair. Wasn't right to ask him to sacrifice his entire life to be with her. *I'll just have to learn to deal with it,* she told herself unhappily. *Just have to —*

"Esteemed Ladies of Opulex," Greggor suddenly boomed from the platform. "I hope you've all been enjoying yourselves tonight."

"Immensely!" someone shouted with a slightly tipsy giggle.

And someone else added, "Nobody throws a party like Snyra!"

"Good, good, I'm glad to hear it." Greggor flashed the crowd a blinding grin. "But the Dream Gas and sensi-play aside, we have another entertainment planned for you tonight. A rare sight—my Mistress, Lady Hake'bean, will be subduing and punishing her new slave for your pleasure. Ladies of Opulex, from the Berrack mines on Primus Three where he was confined for multiple murder, I give you...*The Beast!*"

With a flourish, he ripped down the shimmering golden curtain that hid the stage from view. There was a collective gasp when the Beast, still wearing his snarling animal mask, was revealed. Except for the mask he was nude and it looked as though someone had taken great pains to oil every inch of his massive body.

To Lissa, it looked like every muscle in his huge frame was tensed and trembling with rage. When the curtain came down, he threw back his head and howled—a sound of such pure, unadulterated rage that her blood turned to ice water in her veins. An uneasy murmur ran through the assembled crowd.

The lady sitting beside Lissa shivered and whispered, "Look at that brute! He's not even wearing restraints, let alone a pain collar. How can she control him?"

"I think she said something about chemicals that keep him in check," Lissa whispered back but she couldn't help feeling uneasy herself. Was it her imagination or did the Beast seem more mobile than he had earlier when they had met Lady Hake'bean? He was shrugging his shoulders and moving his head from side to side like a man trying to rid himself of invisible chains. Did he have more freedom of movement than he had before?

"I don't like this." Saber was suddenly between her and the stage. He crouched low and glared at the masked figure, obviously ready for action. "I think we should leave."

"We can't," Lissa objected. "You heard what Greggor said — Lady Hake'bean will be offended!"

"I don't give a damn about that," he growled. "This isn't safe. It's—"

Just then there was a theatrical puff of smoke and Snyra Hake'bean appeared almost directly in front of them. The crowd *ooed* and *ahhed* as she bowed and preened, obviously loving the attention. When she saw Lissa in the front row, she blew her a kiss and waved.

Uncertainly, Lissa waved back. But when her eyes dropped from Lady Hake'bean's face, she saw something truly disconcerting.

Their hostess was still covered in bright pink body paint and wearing ridiculously high heels that caused her to strut when she walked, but now she had added an accessory to her "outfit." At first Lissa wasn't sure of what she was seeing, but when Lady Hake'bean turned to the side, it was clear that the purple rubber rod their hostess had shown them earlier was sticking out from between her thighs. *Half* of it was, anyway. The other half…

Oh my Goddess, it's inside her! And the black straps around her hips are holding it in place!

Lissa's eyes grew wide as the implications hit her. Saber had accused her of being too innocent to understand earlier and she supposed that was true. Everything Lady Hake'bean and Lady Sha'rak had been discussing in their previous conversation had gone right over her head but now it all came back to her.

"It fits inside."

"You don't mind the penetration?"

"Mind it? I love it!"

"Oh my Goddess," she whispered as she watched Lady Hake'bean thrust her pelvis in the air, causing the thick, knobbled end of the rod she wore to dance and jiggle in the blue-white light. Earlier she had thought that it reminded her of something and now she realized what. With its thick shaft and the flared knob at the end, the rod closely resembled a male member—a *huge* one.

"Is...is she going to do to him what I think she's going to do?" Lissa asked in a low voice.

Saber gave her a sober look. "I'm afraid so."

"So *that's* what they mean by giving a slave the rod." Lissa shook her head. "I never...I guess I couldn't even imagine..."

"Of course you couldn't," he muttered. "It's not something that would ever occur to someone like you, *amalla.*"

"But I don't—"

"Observe," Lady Hake'bean cried, walking around the stage, the purple rod swaying jauntily from between her thighs. "I have here my latest acquisition, a new slave I'm still breaking in. Up until now I've been taking it easy on him—giving him the smallest possible rod to get him used to taking his punishment." She held one finger in the air, as though illustrating the size she was talking about, and the crowd responded with uneasy laughter.

"Tonight, however," Lady Hake'bean continued. "I'm going to up the ante." She cupped the purple rod between her legs and stroked it provocatively. "Tonight my Beast will be filled to the core—dominated by his mistress completely, in a way he has never felt before."

The Beast threw back his head and howled again, his huge body positively quaking with rage. The ladies in the crowd exchanged disturbed glances and some in the front row began to scoot back but Lady Hake'bean only laughed.

"Beast!" she commanded, turning to her huge slave. "Assume the position."

Every line of the massive body seemed to scream protest but as they watched, the Beast turned and got onto his hands and knees, presenting his bare, muscular ass to the crowd.

"Very good," Lady Hake'bean proclaimed. "And now, prepare to take your punishment."

She produced a small tube and proceeded to squirt something from it onto her fingers. Walking up to the still-trembling Beast, she thrust her hands between his legs. With one hand she stroked the truly massive shaft that hung down between his thighs and with the other she pressed her fingers deep into his nether entrance.

"What...what is she doing?" Lissa had never witnessed anything like this before—had never *wanted* to witness anything like it. Her mind was still struggling to process exactly what it was Lady Hake'bean intended to do to her slave.

"She's preparing him," Saber murmured back. There was a grim look on his face as he contemplated the scene before them. "Getting him ready to take her rod."

"I can see *that*," Lissa whispered back. "I mean, it's obvious she's using some kind of...of lubricant. But why is she touching him at the same time?" She watched in fascination as Lady Hake'bean stroked her slave's thick shaft, bringing him erect even as she probed and stretched his entrance.

"To force pleasure from him." Saber shook his head. "She's forcing him to respond to her even though you can tell he doesn't want to."

The growling and snarling from behind the mask was getting more and more intense and menacing but Lady Hake'bean paid no attention. At last, when the Beast's cock was fully erect, she slapped his ass and laughed.

"Stop complaining, lover. You know you want it. You love every minute of it—just look how hard you are!" She gave his shaft a last, long stroke, then stepped back and lined up the head of the purple rod with his newly opened nether entrance.

"Goddess, I can't watch," Lissa murmured, horrified. And yet she couldn't seem to look away as the thick purple shaft breached the Beast's opening and slowly began to fill him.

Saber, still crouched between her and the stage, was tense and silent as they both watched the massive slave being filled.

"That's right, my Beast. *Take* it. Take it *all*." Lady Hake'bean was panting hard and Lissa remembered what she had told them about the vibe located in the rod, at just the right place to stimulate her clit. From the way she was grinding her hips, pressing the rod deeper and still deeper into her slave, she must be enjoying its effects right now.

"That's right, I'm in you now—can you feel me?" she crooned to her slave. "In you so deep, fucking that sweet ass and loving every minute of it. You love it too, don't you? Don't you, lover? Tell me all about it."

The Beast howled and trembled, his massive body shaking beneath his petite mistress's onslaught. He looked to Lissa like a statue that was coming to life, like a man fighting to be free once and for all of the chains that bound him. She watched numbly, still struggling to take in the awful sight that seemed to go on and on without end.

Pulling back, Lady Hake'bean withdrew the rod until only the flaring crown remained inside the howling Beast and then rammed it back in again with a grunt. At the same time, she reached around him and began to stroke his cock again, which was rigidly hard.

Lissa couldn't understand his erection. "How can he be like that—be hard for her if he hates it so much?" she asked Saber in a whisper.

"He can't help it. She's stimulating a part inside him—a part that makes it impossible not to respond." Saber looked sick. "Poor bastard. I don't care how many people he murdered, no one deserves this."

"She...she's raping him." Lissa felt sick herself as the scene finally hit home. "Right out in public—in front of everyone. This is awful! He must be in so much pain!"

Saber shook his head. "It's not just the pain. Think of the abject humiliation—his pride will *never* recover. She might as well cut off his balls and feed them to him right now."

As he spoke, Lady Hake'bean gave a mighty thrust and stroked her slave hard at the same time. The Beast roared and trembled as his cock began to spurt hot cum into his mistress's hand.

"That's right, Beast," she crooned, still pumping him. "Come for me. Come and let me know how much you love it when I take you. When I punish your sweet ass."

Pity and horror surged up inside Lissa, making her want to cry or be sick. "We can't just sit here," she whispered to Saber. "We have to say something—*do* something!"

"Do what?" he asked grimly. "It's over now."

Lady Hake'bean's orgasmic gasps of triumph, mingling with her slaves enraged roars seemed to prove his point.

"Still," Lissa insisted. "We have to—"

And then everything happened at once.

With another earsplitting bellow, the Beast gave a convulsive movement and suddenly rose, shaking off his mistress like a massive animal shaking off a tiny, annoying fly.

Lady Hake'bean stumbled backward, almost falling off the stage. It would have been better for her if she had.

The Beast turned on her, ripping off his mask to reveal a face straight out of a nightmare. Tiny red eyes gleamed with a murderous light from under thick, shaggy black brows and two short, sharp horns grew from his temples. His mouth, when he opened it, yawned like a cavern, revealing row after row of jagged white teeth all as long as Lissa's forefinger and razor sharp.

Goddess, she thought numbly, watching as the Beast roared. *I've seen a mouth like that before—where...?* Suddenly it came to her. She had been watching a nature documentary about creatures from Earth with Kat and one of them had been called a shark. *That* was what the Beast's gaping maw looked like—only worse. *Much* worse.

But though the ladies in the crowd were beginning to panic and the Beast was lumbering toward her, Lady Hake'bean clearly wasn't ready to run. She had scrambled to her feet and stood facing the raging monster, her feet planted apart and a look of irritation on her face.

"Beast, heel!" she shouted, putting a hand on her hip and pointing a finger at him. "Get down right now and—"

The Beast leaned over and bit off the finger she was pointing at him. Then he spat it to one side and reached for her, his gigantic hands hooked into claws.

Lady Hake'bean looked numbly at the bloody stump where her finger had been. "No," she gasped and Lissa saw the horror finally dawning in her eyes. At last she was realizing the danger she was in—but it was too late. "No," she said again. "No, you can't. I bought you. I *own* you. I—"

The Beast cut her off. "You...fucking...*bitch!*" His voice was like thunder and Lissa felt frozen to her seat as she watched him grab the petite Lady Hake'bean and shake her until her multicolored hair whipped around her face. "You want to fuck the Beast?" he snarled, his eyes narrowed with hate. "Fine, my lady, but you'll pay the fucking *price.*"

With a savage growl, he sank three rows of knife-like teeth into her shoulder and ripped off her arm like it was a chicken wing. Lady Hake'bean screamed, the stump at her shoulder spouting crimson jets into the air. The Beast laughed—a bone chilling sound that made Lissa's stomach feel like it was filled with ice. He shook his former mistress one last time, then tossed her bleeding body to one side, as though she was nothing more than a broken doll.

"Oh my Goddess," screamed the woman beside Lissa, startling her from the trance-like state she had somehow fallen into. "He killed her! She's dead—Lady Hake'bean is *dead!*"

Her piercing shriek seemed to draw the Beast's attention. His tiny red eyes tracked downward and settled on Lissa.

"Fucking bitches—all of you!" he roared. Mouth stained with blood, he jumped from the stage, the impact shaking the floor when he landed with a dull *thud*. He reached for Lissa with arms that seemed miles long.

"Lissa, *run!*" Saber was suddenly between them, rising from the protective crouch he'd assumed to ram full-speed into the charging Beast.

"Saber!" Lissa's paralysis broke and she jumped to her feet, intending on saving the man she loved.

"Go—get to safety!" Saber commanded, still grappling with the enormous foe. The Beast was a full head taller than him and much more massive but he seemed to be holding his own, until the other male lowered his head to bite again.

"No, I won't leave you!" Looking for a weapon, Lissa grabbed one of the plush pink chairs by the back. It was a substantial piece of furniture but fear for Saber gripped her and it felt almost light in her hands. Running around behind them, she swung the chair with all her might, slamming the solid wooden legs hard against the Beast's skull.

She'd been hoping to knock him out but the Beast was little more than momentarily stunned. He shook his head and turned, his eyes fastening on her face again.

"What's wrong, little mistress?" His thick voice gurgled in his throat, as though he'd been gargling with blood. "You want your turn? You want to be next in line to fuck the Beast?"

Pushing Saber away, he lumbered toward her, his jaws gaping wide to expose three slavering rows of bloody dagger-like teeth.

Lissa screamed and stumbled backward. She still had the chair in her hands—indeed, her fingers had tightened on the plush pink back and refused to let go. Lifting it with arms that suddenly felt like lead, she poked it at the Beast, trying to keep it between them, trying to warn him off.

"No," she gasped. "No, please..."

Suddenly Saber was there again. He jumped the Beast from behind and locked one muscular arm around the convict's thick neck. "Run, Lissa!" he panted, squeezing tight. "Run, *now!*"

This time Lissa tried to obey orders but somehow she couldn't. Her body refused to listen to her and her fingers still wouldn't unclench themselves from the back of the plush chair. The Beast charged toward her with Saber clinging to his back. As she stumbled backward his arms reached for her, his hands hooked into claws. Lissa felt a terrified shriek rising in her throat...

And then the narrow red eyes rolled up in the Beast's head and the vast form slowly crumpled to the ground before her.

Saber rode the other male down to the floor, keeping an arm locked around the Beast's thick throat. He stayed there for a full minute after they landed and then, when it was clear the Beast was truly unconscious, he took the huge block-like head in both hands.

Lissa felt sick. "Saber?" she whispered. "Saber, what—?"

Saber ignored her and looked at the enormous head between his hands. "I'm sorry, Brother," Lissa heard him mutter to the bloody face. "I don't blame you for what you did. But it's better this way. They'll only torture you more if I let you live."

He gave a sharp, sideways twist and there was a sickening crunching sound. When Saber released it, the Beast's head flopped to one side, his thick neck bent at an unnatural angle.

"Oh!" Lissa sobbed, half hysterical with horror and sorrow. "Oh no...oh my Goddess..."

"I'm sorry, Lissa." Saber left the gigantic body and came to her, putting an arm around her shoulders. "I'm sorry but I had to do it. He's better off dead than living like this—being taken for sport in front of a crowd of gawkers. That's no way for any male to live. Better to die free than exist in such vile bondage."

"I know...I guess you're right." Lissa hid her face in his chest, not wanting to see the blood and carnage left behind. "But oh, Saber...that was *awful.*"

"It was," he said grimly. "All of it. But it's over now, *amalla.* And I swear if I can help it you'll never have to see anything so ugly ever again."

Lissa closed her eyes but all she could see was the savage display the Beast had put on when he broke his chemical bonds — all she could hear was his enraged roars as his mistress thrust into him again and again — stripping away his dignity and pride, taking him as no one — male or female — should be taken by another.

A cold chill came over her when she remembered Lady Sha'rak telling her she should give Saber the rod, to keep him in line, to punish him. *Never,* she vowed to herself as she hugged him tight. *I'd never do that to him! No matter what they say or do to us while we're here, nothing could make me hurt the man I love like that. Nothing!*

* * * * *

Saber couldn't stay still on the ride home. He felt restless, filled with adrenaline, his muscles twitching with tension and his mind replaying the violence over and over until it was nothing but a meaningless wash of gore. But one thing kept repeating in his mind again and again, an endless loop he couldn't turn off.

I almost lost her. If I'd been a fraction of a second too slow the Beast would have gotten her — he would have killed her as he did his mistress. Oh Goddess, amalla, no...no, no, no...

Lady Sha'rak and Llewelyn were both subdued and there was no conversation at all, which suited him well. He felt words brewing inside him, emotions building that he had vowed to hide and never act on. But now he couldn't help himself — it was all he could do to keep his feelings in check until they reached Lady Sha'rak's residence and went to their suite.

The minute the heavy door was shut behind them and he was sure they were alone, Saber could hold the words in no longer.

"Lissa," he said, taking her hands. "I'm sorry, but I have to say this. I love you."

"Saber?" She looked at him uncertainly, her eyes widening. Plainly he had caught her off guard but Saber couldn't stop.

"I love you," he repeated. "With my whole heart — with everything that's in me. I love you and I can't stand the thought of losing you, of being parted forever."

"I love you too," Lissa whispered.

"I know you vowed never to have me and I don't blame you for taking that vow," he continued on, determined to get the words out before his courage failed. "But I can't stand this anymore. I..." Then her words sank in and he stared at her, wide-eyed. *"What* did you say?"

"I said I love you too!" Lissa's voice trembled and her eyes filled with tears but she blinked them away. "Goddess, Saber, I know it's wrong but I still love you so much. I...I never really stopped."

"Really?" He looked at her uncertainly, his heart filling with hope.

"It's true." She wiped her eyes and nodded, a miserable but determined look on her face. "I can't deny it anymore," she said in a low voice. "Not to you and not to myself either. I know we can never be together but I can't pretend not to feel what I feel."

"Oh Lissa...*amalla*..." Saber cupped her cheek and looked into her eyes. "Why can't we be together?"

"Be-because." She sniffed and swiped at her eyes again. "You know why, Saber. The Clan would hate me—they would never accept me as your mate. And I can't ask you to give up your future just to be with me."

"I thought the same thing about you," he said softly. "I thought I couldn't ask you to give up being the High Priestess to be my bride. But *amalla...*" He stroked her cheek gently, looking into her eyes. "I can't think like that anymore. After what almost happened tonight I realize I can't live without you—can't bear to lose you. I know it's selfish to ask it, but will you give up your life on First World to bond with me?"

"I want to—I'd give up *anything* if we could be together," she whispered. "But Saber, are you sure? Your father and mother, the clans—"

"Can all go straight to the seven hells for all I care," he answered roughly, pulling her close. "I don't care about any of that, *amalla*. Not as long as I can be with you. Not as long as I never have to let you go."

Lissa looked up at him, her eyelashes still sparkling with tears. "You don't," she whispered, reaching up to caress his neck with her small, soft hand. "If you're really sure, Saber."

"I've never been more sure of anything in my life." Pulling her into his lap, he kissed her long and hard. And for the first time, he felt her kiss back with absolutely no resistance or reluctance at all. She tasted so sweet, felt so yielding in his arms that he wanted to take her then and there. To make her his forever so that they could never be parted again.

"Saber," she whispered against his lips and then he pressed deeper, demanding entrance to her mouth. She opened for him gladly, stroking his tongue with hers and inviting him in.

"No guilt," he told her, when they finally broke apart, panting. "No shame anymore. We're going to forget here and now about being from the same clan. We're going to leave our people's antiquated customs behind us and never think of them again. You're not my sister or my kinswoman, Lissa—you're my *bride*. And I intend to claim you that way with no hesitation and no apologies."

"You mean…" She bit her lip. "You want to give me the Deep Touch?"

"That's *exactly* what I mean," Saber told her in a soft growl. "Gods, I love you, *amalla*. Need to show you how much. Need to make you mine."

"I want you to show me too. To…to give me the Deep Touch." A hot blush stained Lissa's cheeks but she lifted her chin and continued. "But *after* we're mated, all right, Saber? I want…I want us to have a joining ceremony first. I know you've been waiting a long time but can we do that? Can you wait just a little while longer? I want to be joined in the sight of the Goddess before we take the final step."

Saber felt his insides clench. He sighed and forced the need inside him, the urge to take her and make her his, to subside. Slowly, he nodded. "Of course. Anything you want—as long as you promise you'll be mine as soon as we get back to the Mother Ship."

"The minute we walk in the door we'll head straight for the sacred grove and find a priestess," Lissa promised. "I won't even wait for Kat to plan our ceremony. We can celebrate afterward."

"That's good." Saber kissed her deeply again and looked into her eyes. "Because I can't wait to take you, *amalla*. Can't wait to make you mine—completely mine."

"I can't wait either." She gave him a smile so filled with hope and need it nearly broke his heart. "Kiss me again—I love to feel your mouth on my lips."

"Your lips aren't the only place I like to kiss you, you know," he murmured, stroking her face.

Her cheeks went pink and she looked down, as though she couldn't bear to meet his eyes. "Are you talking about earlier tonight? When you...kissed me on the stage when we were announced at the party?"

"You know I am," Saber growled softly. "I've been wanting to kiss you there for a long time, you know and I didn't get to spend nearly as much time as I wanted to doing it."

"Oh..." Lissa bit her lip. "Maybe...maybe you could practice for next time?" she said hesitantly. "I mean, in case we get invited to any more formal parties."

Saber gave her a hungry grin. "You know, that's not a bad idea. Do you want me to show you how I'm going to do it? How I'm going to show my love and devotion to you when they announce your name?"

Lissa licked her lips, looking both nervous and excited. "Please...please do," she whispered.

"Fine. Here—stand against the bed." Rising, he pushed her gently into position against the side of the high bed. Both of them had removed the black sensory patches earlier and she was still wearing the jade lace dress and the split panties that framed her shaved pussy perfectly. It made Saber's cock achingly hard just to see her but he forced himself to be careful as he arranged her pose.

"Oh, you want me to stand?" She sounded surprised.

"We have to practice, right?" Saber cocked an eyebrow at her. "Pretend that's the post." He deepened his voice. "Announcing

Lady R'awr." Then he dropped to his knees before her and smiled at her, "Are you ready?"

Lissa blushed and giggled nervously. "Don't be silly, Saber, get up. You don't have to be down there."

"Of course I do—you're my mistress." Putting his hands on her hips, he leaned forward and kissed her gently on the thigh.

The laughter left Lissa'a face. "After what we saw tonight, I don't think I *want* to be the mistress anymore. That...that was awful."

"It was," Saber agreed calmly. "But it doesn't have to be that way between us."

"It won't be—never—I swear," Lissa promised fervently. "I would never...never do that to you. No matter what!"

"I know you wouldn't, *amalla*." He kissed her thigh again. "I think we're getting off the point, though."

"The point is I don't want you on your knees to me—not anymore." Lissa frowned and tried to make him rise but Saber stayed stubbornly where he was.

"No," he said gently. "The point is, I don't *mind* being on my knees to you. Not if it means I get to do this." Leaning forward, he placed a soft, open-mouthed kiss at the top of her mound, just as he had earlier that night.

Lissa gasped and jumped a little. "Saber!"

"It's true," he assured her. He took a moment to admire her pussy, framed in the lacy split panties, and then kissed her again. This time he allowed his tongue to slip out and trace her slit, a gentle, hot caress that made her moan softly. He looked up at her. "Should I continue, Mistress? I don't think I've paid you nearly enough respect yet. I need to try harder."

"Yes," Lissa whispered. "I...I think maybe you should."

"Good." Saber framed her hips with his big hands. "Then spread yourself for me, *amalla*. Spread yourself and let me taste you."

With a low, needful moan, she complied, parting her thighs much more readily than she had earlier and treating him to the sight of her swollen outer lips spreading open to reveal her pink inner cunt.

"Gods, you're beautiful." Saber had to take a long moment to appreciate the sight of her. Her swollen folds reminded him of an exotic flower and her clit was a little pink pearl, just waiting to be stroked and tasted. She had a warm, feminine fragrance that drove him crazy with wanting her, making him eager to bury his face between her thighs to lap and suck and taste until she was moaning his name and scratching his shoulders.

Somehow Saber held himself back. Lissa was still incredibly innocent and inexperienced—he didn't want to frighten her by being too aggressive. Leaning forward, he nuzzled his cheek against her spread mound, both marking her with his scent and bathing himself in hers.

Lissa gave a little cry as he rubbed his scratchy cheeks against her tender inner thighs. Saber felt her getting hotter and wetter as he drew out the exquisite torture, kissing and nuzzling all around her pussy, but never quite giving her exactly what she needed. He longed to taste her honey, to press his face between her legs and thrust his tongue deep in her cunt but once more he held himself back.

"My lady," he murmured, looking up at her. "If I might be permitted to kiss you *inside...*"

"Yes, all right..." Lissa spread her legs more, making herself totally vulnerable to him.

"Good," Saber purred roughly. "That's good, Mistress." Placing his thumbs on her outer lips, he spread her even wider, revealing all her secret treasures, opening her to his gaze.

Lissa moaned breathlessly as he bent to place a gentle kiss on her clit and then he felt her soft little fingers carding through his hair, urging him on.

It was all the encouragement Saber needed. Pressing forward, he sucked the throbbing pink pearl of her clit into his mouth and laved it eagerly with his tongue. Her rich, salty/sweet taste exploded across his tongue, making his cock throb with need. Lissa gasped and pressed forward, offering herself even more and another surge of lust shot through him.

"Gods, *amalla,*" he growled hungrily. Gripping one of her legs, he lifted it, spreading her to the limit. He placed her thigh on his bare shoulder, wrapped his arm around her leg to hold her open, and lashed her tender folds with his tongue, tasting her, making her his.

"Saber!" Her voice was a wail and her fingers tightened in his hair, letting him know how he was affecting her. He felt her slender frame tremble in his arms and then she was pressing her hips up to him in mute supplication, offering her slick, wet flesh, her pussy flowing with honey as she begged for more, begged him to never stop.

It was more than Saber could stand. He had to have her—had to be inside her even if it wasn't with his shaft. He already had Lissa off balance; it was a simple matter to push her back onto the bed, putting her in a much better position to be penetrated.

She went willingly enough when she realized what he wanted, her thighs drifting open naturally as though it was right to offer herself so intimately to him. A tight fist of need clenched in his chest as he realized she would offer herself the same way if they were making love, if he was giving her the Deep Touch. Gods, how he wanted to take her that way. But not yet...not quite yet.

"Saber," she cried breathlessly, thrusting her hips upward, her pussy seeking his tongue. "Saber please, don't...don't stop..."

A mad lust came over Saber. His cock was so hard inside the tight leather slave trousers he could have fucked a hole through a brick wall. Gods, he loved her! Loved everything about her. Her scent and her delicious salty/sweet flavor, the soft, helpless sounds she made when he pleasured and licked her, the way she moved her hips, thrusting up to him, seeking his tongue, the way her small fingers tangled in his hair...they all urged him on. But most of all he loved the wet pink folds that parted so willingly for his tongue and the slippery, sweet honey that welled up from inside her little cunt as he tortured her with his mouth.

With a low roar, he gripped her ass in both hands and pulled her up to his mouth. Then he thrust his tongue inside her, fucking her pussy in the only way he could—doing his damndest to fill her even if it wasn't with his cock.

Lissa wailed and the fingers in his hair clenched hard. "Saber! Oh Goddess...Saber...oh, *Saber*..."

His name was like a prayer on her lips and it only made him hotter. Gods, she sounded so *close* and he wanted to make her come with all that was in him. Wanted to feel her pussy spasm around his tongue, wanted to taste the fresh wetness of her orgasm as she gave herself up entirely to the pleasure he gave her.

"*Saber!*" she gasped breathlessly. "*Moch Daer!* Please, I'm so close…so *close.*"

He looked up briefly and growled, "Then come for me. *Now.*" Then he sucked her clit between his lips again and plunged two thick fingers deep into her wet, open pussy, pumping as hard as he could.

Lissa cried out and nearly bucked off the bed. At the same time he felt her inner walls clench around him and knew she was coming, coming so hard and just for *him*. All for *him*.

He lashed her clit furiously with his tongue and continued to thrust, tasting fresh wetness as her pussy milked his fingers. And then his need was too great.

With his free hand, he reached down and popped open the black trousers. Grasping his shaft he pumped himself once, twice, three times, and came in a hot rush as Lissa pressed her open pussy to his mouth and cried his name, coming harder than she ever had before.

When she finally stopped gasping and moaning, he climbed onto the bed with her and held her tight, never wanting to let her go. Lissa buried her face in his neck and pressed herself against him, trembling with the aftershocks of orgasm.

Finally, when she could speak again she looked at him and whispered, "Are you sure, *Moch Daer?* Are you really sure this is what you want? That *I'm* what you want?"

"*Amalla…*" He stroked her hair away from her face and looked into her eyes. "I've never been more sure of anything."

She looked troubled. "But I'm just an orphan, an outcast with no family or status. Are you sure you want to give up everything for me? Your parents…the clans…"

Saber put a finger to her lips to silence her. "I love you," he told her fiercely. "I love you and want to spend the rest of my life with you. Nothing and no one can change my mind about that. Do you understand?"

She searched his eyes with her gaze for a long moment then, finally, she nodded. "Yes," she whispered and snuggled against him. "Yes, *Moch Daer*. I do."

"Good." Saber kissed her forehead. "Then go to sleep. Tomorrow we'll worry about getting the second scroll from Lady Pope'nose. And then we'll go home and start our life together—as a warrior and his bride."

Lissa yawned and smiled happily. "I want that, too. Will we live on the Mother Ship with Kat and the others?"

Saber thought of the reaction the other Kindred had to having a Touch Kindred in their midst. But surely if he was mated and bonded to a female, they wouldn't feel so threatened. If they could let a Scourge live among them, he was certain they could learn to tolerate him.

"Certainly," he told Lissa. "If you want to."

"I do." She yawned again. "Oh, I'm so *tired*. What is it about this whole thing—about having an orgasm—that makes you want to go to sleep?"

"It's because you're so happy and relaxed afterward that you don't care about anything." Saber yawned himself and smiled back at her. "It's been a long night—let's get some rest."

She murmured something in reply but he didn't quite hear it. As they fell asleep in each other's arms, he vowed again silently that he would keep her close. Now that they were finally together, nothing and no one would ever be able to tear them apart again.

Chapter Twenty-one

"Are you sure you're all right, Kat?" Deep, the male with the black eyes and hair frowned at her as he piloted the small shuttle toward the Mother Ship. "You've been pretty damn quiet since we left your grandmother's house."

"Deep is right," Lock, the light twin put in. "You seem different—subdued."

L shook her head and smiled in what she hoped was a reassuring way. "I'm fine, boys, really—don't worry about me. I'm just, you know…processing."

The words sounded strange to her, but the memories from her original assured her they were something that Kat would say. Then again, it was those same memories which had kept her from pushing the plunger all the way down and injecting the full dose of sleep venom into the real Kat's neck.

She had tried to do it—the other girl was helpless on the floor and it would have been the easiest thing in the world to simply deliver the killing dose. But her memories kept whispering that Kat was a friend—someone who had reached out a helping hand when she was scared and alone. Someone sweet and kind who put others before herself—who had been kind to her out when she had no one else to turn to.

It didn't seem to matter that L wasn't really the person Kat had helped. The memories and impulses from her original were too deeply ingrained in her to break. In the end, though her finger lingered long over the syringe's plunger, she simply wasn't able to make herself inject the last half of the venom.

Which means instead of dying neatly and conveniently, Kat is going to wake up with nothing worse than a bad headache and come looking for her men in a few hours, L thought grimly. *Possibly even sooner.*

For the thousandth time she cursed herself for a fool—why had she let weakness and sentimentality keep her from finishing the job? She never had before. Yex claimed she was the most ruthless shadow caster he had ever trained but he would be ashamed if he could see her now.

Never mind, L told herself, watching in the viewscreen as the curving side of the vast Mother Ship appeared. *It won't take long to find the center of the ship and plant Draven's device. And when it blows, it won't matter if one extra human is alive or dead.*

She still had no idea what the tiny silver chip she carried was going to do but she had visions of some kind of mass destruction. Maybe it would release a poisonous gas that killed the Kindred as they stood. Or even better, some kind of virus that would slowly but surely infect everyone aboard, starting with those in the sacred grove and working its way outward.

L intended to be long gone by the time whatever it was reached the outer edges of the ship, of course. She would steal one of the shuttles—maybe even the one they were riding in now—and fly back to Earth where she would pick up her own ship. Then she could go back to her life, feeling vindicated because revenge was hers at last.

She should have felt a surge of triumph at the thought. Instead she only felt vaguely uneasy and the image of Kat, lying cold and silent on the bathroom floor, kept flashing before her eyes. *Stop it,* she told herself angrily. *Whatever is making you soft, making you weak, get over it! Remember why you're here. They left you there, light years from home. Left you to be used and abused in a life of sexual servitude and pain. They deserve to die and all their friends can die with them!*

"Well, here we are. Home, sweet home." Deep guided the small craft into the docking bay of the Mother Ship and set it down neatly, at the end of a long line of similar craft.

"Great!' L jumped up almost before the shuttle touched down. "I'm *so* glad to be back."

"Really?" Lock frowned at her. "I mean, it's good to be home but weren't you happy to visit with your grandmother? I always got the impression you missed her and wished we could see her more often."

"Yes, it's wonderful the way she accepted us, isn't it?" Deep raised an eyebrow at her.

"It's amazing." L forced a smile. "In fact, I'm going to go tell the girls all about it right now." She was almost out the door when Deep caught her by the arm.

"Wait a minute," he rumbled. "You can't just leave us like this. We should celebrate." He pulled her closer and buried his face in her hair. "If you know what I mean…"

L went rigid in his arms. "Later," she said, trying to push him away. "We can celebrate later."

"What's your hurry?" Deep pulled back from her, a frown on his face. "Did you use some kind of scent spray back at your grandmother's house? You smell…different."

L's heart started hammering in her chest. Her scent was what had given her away the first time, when she'd been sent to exchange places with her original. She couldn't let herself be caught out again! "Um…" she said frantically. "Yes—a scent spray. I mean, a perfume. I used some new perfume. Sorry if you don't like it."

"It smells familiar—almost like something Lauren wears," Lock said, coming up behind her.

L's heart really began to pound. They were smelling her original's scent! She had to get out of here—had to leave *now* before they found out her secret.

"Lauren loaned it to me," she improvised rapidly. "Look, boys, I *really* have to go now. But I'll see you back at the suite later—okay?"

Deep was still frowning but at least he had released his hold on her. "Sure, all right. But don't be too late."

"It's my turn to cook dinner and I'm planning something special," Lock added. "to celebrate."

"Yummy, I can't wait," L gabbled, slipping out from between them and almost running through the shuttle door. "I'll see you later."

"Goodbye, little Kat."

"Goodbye, my lady."

The masculine voices faded behind her as she walked briskly down the long row of parked shuttles and headed for the exit.

It wasn't until she finally made her escape from the echoing docking bay and lost herself in the hustle and bustle of the busy ship that she allowed herself to breathe a sigh of relief. They really weren't following her—she had pulled off the deception and was now inside the Mother Ship with no one the wiser.

Once she was certain she was alone, she ducked behind a support pillar and shifted quickly to another form. Then, remembering her promise to Draven, she turned on the small listening/recording device he'd given her and affixed the sparkling crystal stud to her earlobe. Let him watch as she wreaked his destruction on the hapless, unsuspecting Kindred—L didn't mind that. But when she went to seek her own personal vengeance she intended to shut the device back off. There were some things that ought to be kept private.

She plunged back into the fast moving crowd and headed for the center of the ship.

It was time to get to the sacred grove.

* * * * *

"Did Kat seem like she was acting funny to you?" Deep asked his twin as they left the shuttle.

"A little." Lock frowned. "And I can't say I care for that new perfume she was wearing. She doesn't smell like herself at all."

Deep laughed. "I have to agree but *you* can be the one to tell her that, Brother. I'm not touching it with a ten mile pole."

"A ten *foot* pole," Lock corrected absently. "The Earth saying is, 'I'm not touching that with a ten foot pole.' A mile is a considerably larger unit of measurement."

Deep shrugged. "Either way, I'm not touching it. I—"

"Hello? Hello? Is this thing on? Can anyone hear me?"

Deep jumped as the strange voice invaded his head. "What in the seven hells?" he growled. Who would dare bespeak him in such a familiar fashion? It went past rude and straight into downright insulting.

"Who is this?" he thought back fiercely. *"And what do you want?"*

"Deep, honey, is that you? I'm so sorry, I barely know how to work this thinky-think contraption. Kat was trying to show me but I still don't have the hang of it."

"Grandma?" he said aloud, raising his eyebrows. "That's all right, the think-me does take some getting used to. But...may I ask why you're bespeaking me?"

"I'm calling to tell you that you might be in danger, honey. Something isn't right."

"What?" Deep looked at Lock who was frowning and making 'what the hell is going on?' gestures in the air. "What are you talking about?"

"What I'm talking about is that whoever you got up there with you, it's not Kat." Grandma's mental voice sounded grim.

"What? How can that be?" Deep demanded. "If we don't have Kat, who do we have? And where's the real Kat? Where is our bride?"

"Don't get upset, the real Kat is here with me. I found her upstairs babbling about a syringe full of green poison. She was trying to crawl down the stairs to warn me — would've fallen if I hadn't chosen that exact moment to go to the bathroom."

"Goddess!" Deep ran a hand through his hair in agitation. "Are you certain she's all right?"

"I called 911 and they sent out a crew to check her. She's already doing better than when I found her but we're on the way to the hospital anyway. Kat wouldn't relax until I called you. She would have done it herself but she's got an awful headache — says she can't stand to concentrate hard enough to use this thinky-thought thing yet."

"Of course, I understand." Deep nodded although he knew she couldn't see him. "We'll be back to check on her as soon as we find out what's going on."

"Just you be careful!" Grandma warned. *"Kat says this person or thing, whatever it is, attacked her. Says it looked just like **her** — like Kat, I mean."*

Deep felt a cold finger of dread skate down his spine. "So we have to assume that she — or it — could look like Kat or possibly anyone else."

"Exactly. So be careful! And Kat says to tell you she loves you – both of you."

"We love her too. We'll be back with her as soon as we can. Bespeak me again if anything changes," Deep said.

"I will. Oh, we're at Tampa General now. Have to go."

The connection was severed abruptly, leaving him with an ache right behind his eyes. But Deep wasn't worried about his headache. He looked at Lock. "How much of that did you get?"

"Only a little—something to do with Kat. Is she all right?"

"She's going to be fine," Deep said, hoping it was true. "But she's not here—she's still back on Earth with her grandmother."

Lock's face went pale. "Then who or what have we just brought aboard the Mother Ship?"

Deep shook his head. "I don't know. But we've got to find her and stop her before it's too late!"

* * * * *

It was already too late.

L had finished hiding the small silver device in the branches of one of the holy green and purple trees and was already leaving the sacred grove when she heard the alert sounding. A picture of Kat flashed on the massive viewscreen, which was normally camouflaged by the clouds in the "sky" of the park-like area that surrounded the grove. A stern, disembodied voice asked that all Kindred and their brides be on the lookout for her.

L, of course, had long since assumed another form. She walked quietly out of the area and boarded a tram that would take her back to the outermost edge of the ship. She intended to be right by an exit before she detonated the device. Then she would wait. If the effects were lethal, she would leave, knowing her revenge was assured. But if they turned out to be less than completely deadly, she had decided to stay aboard and take matters into her own hands. There was no chance she'd ever get aboard the Kindred Mother Ship again—she had to see this to the end while she could.

After reaching the edge of the ship, L found a small corridor behind the docking bay that appeared to be deserted. Taking a deep breath, she pulled out the detonator and pressed the button.

Then she waited.

Chapter Twenty-two

"Are you almost ready, my dear? Lady Pope'nose doesn't like to be kept waiting, you know." Lady Sha'rak's voice drilled through the thick door of Lissa's bedroom as though it wasn't there.

"In a moment. I'm just waiting for my slave to come back from running his errand," Lissa called back, trying to make her voice light and easy. "He should be back any moment."

"Well, he'd *better* be." Lady Sha'rak sounded peevish. "Lady Pope'nose—"

"Doesn't like to be kept waiting. Yes, I know."

Lady Sha'rak made a dissatisfied *hmmph*. "Fine. Just let me know the moment he arrives."

"I will, I promise," Lissa called back.

She waited until click-clacking of Lady Sha'rak's high heeled shoes faded down the corridor and then began pacing again, which was what she'd been doing from the minute Saber left their suite.

The morning had started well enough with Lady Sha'rak informing Lissa at first meal that she was to be the primary guest for a small get-together at Lady Pope'nose's dwelling. Apparently she was being honored for owning the slave who had saved the entire assemblage the night before from the rampaging Beast.

Lissa had wanted to point out that it was *Saber* who should be honored, but of course she couldn't. And Saber didn't mind—he was just happy that they were getting into Lady Pope'nose's house without any trouble. In fact, both of them were happier now—Lissa had never felt so free and so light since she'd admitted her feelings for Saber and he had reciprocated them. She had slept in his arms all night without a shred of guilt and woke feeling wonderful.

She *had* been feeling wonderful, anyway, until the little white stone in the delicate silver wire bracelet Kat had given her turned brilliant, blood red.

It had caught Lissa by surprise, mainly because she had never really expected it to happen. She had stared at it in consternation through the rest of the meal, wondering what awful thing was happening back at the Mother Ship.

Saber had noticed the stone changing color too. The moment they were alone, he had suggested that he "run an errand" for Lissa, going back to their ship to find something she had forgotten. There he would be able to access the viewscreen and find out what was happening so many light years away.

He had gone right after first meal, expecting to be back soon but now it was almost time for the dinner party. Lissa paced nervously, chewing on a thumbnail. What was taking him so long? And what was going on? What—?

Just at that moment, Saber let himself quietly into the room.

"Saber!" Lissa pounced on him and hugged him. "I was so worried! What happened?"

He frowned. "It took me more time than I'd thought to work my way back to the ship. As for the Mother Ship, to be honest, I'm not exactly sure what's happened there. There was some interference from the Earth's sun and the transmission had to be brief."

"Well, who did you talk to?" Lissa asked. "Was it Sylvan?"

"Actually it was Sophia." Saber looked puzzled. "She didn't seem like herself *at all.*"

Lissa bit her lip. "Something awful must have happened. What did she say?"

"First, they're under some kind of attack by the Hoard. Sophia didn't give me specifics but it sounds like the whole Mother Ship is in chaos."

"Oh no!" Lissa put a hand to her chest. "Are they all right? Has anyone...died?"

"She didn't tell me. She *did*, however, ask if we had the lost scrolls yet." Saber shook his head. "I had to tell her no but that we were hoping to get them tonight. She said the sooner we got them the better—the Council wants to bring the war to Hrakaz, the Hoard's home world. To do that, they need to know how they were defeated before. Counselor Rast is standing by too, in case they decide to launch the attack from First World."

"Goddess!" Lissa started pacing again. "We *have* to get them tonight! We can't wait a single minute longer."

"Don't worry," Saber said soothingly. When she ignored him and kept pacing, he stood in her path to make her stop. "Lissa," he said gently, taking her by the shoulders. "I mean it—*don't worry*. We'll find the other scroll at Lady Pope'nose's and get it tonight—I'm sure of it."

"But how?" Lissa demanded. "How will we search her house without her knowing?"

"I've already thought of a way—we're going to split up. Just before dinner I'll do something to annoy you and you'll ask Lady Pope'nose if you can borrow one of her slaves to feed you and send me away. *Supposedly* I'll go back to the ship while you and the other ladies eat. But actually—"

"You'll be searching her private library. Of course!" Lissa threw her arms around his neck and stretched up onto her tiptoes to kiss him. "Saber, you're a genius."

"I know." He smiled modestly. "And the minute we get out of Lady Pope'nose's, we'll make an excuse and head for our ship. We'll be out of here and back to the Mother Ship before the night is out."

Lissa felt some of her excitement leak away. "So we can find out what it is the Hoard has done to them. Oh Goddess…"

"Whatever it is, they're strong enough to get through it," Saber said comfortingly. He kissed her on the forehead. "We all are."

Lissa tried to feel more hopeful. "I know. You're right."

"The main thing is that we *have* to get that second scroll." A look of fierce determination crossed Saber's face. "And we *will*. No matter what it takes."

"Of course we will. And then you and I will start our life together and never look back." Lissa tried to smile as she said it but somehow her mouth wouldn't bend that way. She couldn't shake the feeling that things weren't going to go quite as smoothly as she and Saber could wish.

The sense of uneasy foreboding shadowed her heart as she and Saber finished getting ready. It hung over her head like a dark cloud as they rode with Lady Sha'rak and Llewelyn over to Lady Pope'nose's home, a building on the far side of Opulex where the sadistic mistress owned a floor and a half.

Lissa tried to shake off her unease and think about her future with Saber. She had so much to be happy about—no matter what else happened, she was going to spend the rest of her life with the man she loved. But the ominous apprehension just wouldn't go and with it came a multitude of questions. What had the Hoard done to the people she loved? Would they be the same or had something happened that would alter them permanently?

The questions bothered her until she walked across the richly carpeted threshold of Lady Pope'nose's dwelling and Lissa realized she needed to concentrate on playing her part. Taking a deep breath, she lifted her chin and decided to push everything else out of her mind.

One of the strong smelling *nenarches*, encased in a silver metallic mechanoid, met them at the door. It escorted them down a long hallway, hung with expensive looking 3D art and into a receiving room decorated in pink and pale green stripes. There, Lady Pope'nose was sitting on a faintly vibrating scrolled leather couch. She was sipping something that smelled even stronger and more unpleasant than the *nenarch* from a cup with a thin, elaborately scrolled golden handle.

"The ladies R'awr and Sha'rak," the *nenarch* said. It waited a moment for Llewelyn and Saber to bend and kiss their respective mistress's feet before waving a limp jelly tentacle and causing its mechanoid casing to clank out of the room.

"Oh my dear Lady R'awr!" Lady Pope'nose put down her drink and came forward to greet Lissa with a smile on her thin lips which *almost* reached her eyes. "I hope you don't mind that it's just the three of us for dinner. After the heroics of last night I'm afraid I wanted to keep you all to myself."

"That's fine." Lissa smiled back, trying to sound natural. "And last night was nothing, really—just Saber showing his training."

"Well, all I can say is if he's half as well trained in the bedroom as he is when he's fighting then he's a real treasure." Lady Pope'nose leaned forward as though to speak confidentially. "Speaking of that, would you care to sell him?"

"What? No!" Lissa exclaimed before she thought about it. "That is, I mean, uh, you wouldn't want him."

"Wouldn't want him?" Lady Pope'nose laughed. "I doubt that could be true. Why, put a pain collar on him and he'd be my dream male."

Lady Sha'rak laughed. "Oh, naughty! You're so *bad*, my dear, Nola."

"I know." Lady Pope'nose smirked and said to Lissa. "Just *think* about it, my dear. I like to collect valuable things and your slave proved his worth last night."

"Yes, well, if only he'd stop proving his more *irritating* qualities, I'd be happy," Lissa grumbled. "Maybe he's not yet recovered from the fight but he's just been so—"

Just at that moment, Saber stepped on the trailing back of her gown, exactly as they had planned. Lissa lurched forward and the elaborate bustle at the back of her dress ripped.

"Saber!" she stormed, rounding on him. "What's *wrong* with you today?"

Saber hung his head. "Forgive me, my lady. My clumsiness is inexcusable."

"You're absolutely right—it is." Lissa turned to their hostess. "My dear Lady Pope'nose, do you think you could possibly loan me one of your body-slaves for dinner tonight. I think I'd better send Saber here back to the hovercoach."

Lady Pope'nose's eyes gleamed. "Certainly I can loan you a slave but why not just borrow a pain collar instead? I always keep extra—they're so *useful*."

Lissa recoiled inwardly at the suggestion but she had expected nothing less from the bloodthirsty Lady Pope'nose. Somehow she managed to keep her disgust from showing on her face—she hoped, anyway.

"I thank you for your kind offer, Lady Pope'nose," she said, smiling. "But I simply can't risk doing anything to my slave that might compromise his reflexes or damage his nervous system. He is my only source of protection on the trip back to Zetta Prime and as a well-traveled woman of the universe, I'm sure you know what an awful threat space pirates are these days."

"Oh well, yes, that's true," Lady Pope'nose conceded with poor grace. She brightened. "But you *could* just give him the rod." She licked her thin lips. "We have a private area for such punishments if you're a little *shy* about punishing in public."

This time Lissa had to work even harder to keep her face blank. "I would but I'm just *famished* right now and I'm sure you and Lady Sha'rak are too. I wouldn't want to keep anyone from dinner just to punish a slave."

Lady Pope'nose sighed. "Very well, you can borrow my Jakely for the banquet. I've been trying to train him for dinner service anyway."

"Thank you—you're much too kind." Lissa smiled sweetly and then turned back to Saber. "Get back to the coach," she said sharply, snapping her fingers as though he was a pet who had been bad. "And no dinner for you tonight—think about *that* and try to be more careful where you step next time."

"Yes, Mistress." He bowed submissively and kissed her foot in what Lissa hoped was a suitably humble way. Humble enough, anyway, to appease the other two ladies. Lady Pope'nose and Lady Sha'rak both always seemed to be overeager to punish their slaves, or see someone else's slaves punished.

"Rise," she told Saber after she thought he had lingered long enough. "And go."

"Yes, Mistress." He rose and disappeared silently into the gloom of the hallway from which they had come.

"Well." Lissa turned back to the other two ladies with a bright smile. "I'm so sorry about all that unpleasantness. Lady Pope'nose—what amazing thing have you planned for dinner, if you don't mind me asking? Lady Sha'rak here has told me what a gourmet you are."

* * * * *

Saber walked quietly along the hallway, eyes scanning from side to side as he searched for the library. He hoped that was the place Lady Pope'nose was keeping her collection—it would make the most sense. Unless she kept it locked away in a vault somewhere with a three foot thick metal door. In which case, they were well and truly out of luck.

But if that's the case, if she's got it locked up somewhere, we'll just have to find another way, Saber thought grimly. *One way or another, we're not leaving without that scroll.*

It took a long while to explore the maze-like dwelling and he was beginning to get worried when, down a smaller marble hallway that branched away from the first, he found what he was looking for. A vast door with an ornate golden latch and a scrolling golden plaque that read *Library* in discreet lower case script was suddenly before him.

Saber was sure that the door would be locked or at the very least there would be a slave posted to guard the collection inside. But to his surprise, the latch opened easily and when he slipped inside the room, it was completely empty. Empty of people, that was—it was filled to overflowing with the triangular books and data disks the Yonnites used.

And standing in the middle of the room, displayed in a clear case, were a number of ancient looking documents. Saber approached cautiously, looking around to see if there were any listening or recording devices. He saw nothing obvious but he was still careful to make no sound as he walked.

On top of the case was a silver and crystal stand — something one would use to display only the finest and rarest of acquisitions. And on the stand was something that looked familiar.

Saber's eyes widened when he saw the blue laminated scroll that exactly matched the one they'd been using the night before for sensi-play. *That's it! I know it is!*

He strode forward and reached out a hand for it…but then drew back. *I don't like this — it's too easy. The door unlocked, the library full of precious documents unguarded. And the exact document we want laid out on a silver and crystal tray. What the hell is going on here?*

"Go on, take it. It won't bite."

The voice from behind him startled Saber so much he jumped. Turning he saw Llewelyn leaning against the doorframe of the massive door, grinning at him sardonically.

"What are you doing here?" Saber demanded.

"I could ask the same thing. Or rather, my lady could. But I think we both already know that, don't we?" Llewelyn nodded his bald head at the missing scroll. "Go on, take it. That's why you came here, isn't it?"

"I don't know what you're talking about. I was just looking for the bathroom." Saber drew back his hand and started to move away from the case.

"I don't think so." Llewelyn raised his hand and pointed a blaster at Saber's face. "Take it now — go on, pick up the scroll."

"What?" Saber frowned at him. "Why are you so eager for me to pick it up?"

"Because." The other slave gave him a nasty grin. "You have to be caught in the act." He gestured with the blaster. "Go on now, pick it up. If you don't I'll blow a hole in your worthless hide. Who will protect your sweet little mistress then?"

* * * * *

"So Lady Hake'bean is expected to make a complete recovery but I can't help thinking she'll never be quite the same." Lady Sha'rak shook her head sadly and allowed the slave, which Lady Pope'nose had loaned her, to feed her another morsel of food. She had sent Llewelyn away on some kind of errand.

"But how is that possible? Her arm..." Lissa swallowed, her throat suddenly dry. "It was ripped completely off and...and mangled."

"Oh, they can clone those parts." Lady Pope'nose waved airily. "Although getting an exact match can be somewhat problematic. It's lucky you and your body-slave were quick thinking enough to stop the brute before his rampage spread any further."

Lady Sha'rak shivered. "Such a dreadful business! I *knew* that animal was dangerous."

Lissa couldn't be silent. "He was dangerous because Lady Hake'bean *made* him dangerous," she said in a low voice.

"I beg your pardon?" Lady Pope'nose gave her an incredulous look. "What exactly are you implying, my dear Lady R'awr?"

"I'm just saying that she shouldn't have done...*that* to him, especially not in front of everyone." Lissa lifted her chin. "It enraged him, which put everyone in the room in danger."

"Oh *I* see what's going on here." Lady Pope'nose raised an eyebrow at her. "You're one of those people who doesn't believe in giving her slave the rod, aren't you? *That's* why you refused my offer of a private punishment area when your slave misbehaved."

Lissa felt sick. Lady Pope'nose had already tortured two of her slaves since dinner had begun—activating their pain collars for no other reason than she didn't like the looks on their faces. It turned Lissa's stomach so that she could barely choke down the morsels of food her own dinner-slave, Jakely, was offering.

"I would *never* treat Saber that way," she said, unable to hold her true feelings in anymore. "Never!"

Lady Sha'rak sighed. "I can't say that I'm surprised—you're awfully soft on your body-slave. But I *am* disappointed."

"What—disappointed that I refuse to hurt the man I...I mean, disappointed that I refuse to hurt my slave?" Lissa demanded. She knew she ought to hold her tongue—there was no point in antagonizing their hostess. But she also knew that as soon as Saber found the lost scroll, they were going to leave and never return to this horrible world where slavery and rape and cruelty were the norm and she couldn't help wanting to have a final say.

"It's wrong," she continued, looking Lady Pope'nose in her pale, beady eyes. "Wrong to treat another being that way."

Lady Pope'nose raised one perfectly shaped eyebrow and looked down her long, boney nose. "So now I'm some sort of monster because I know how to punish my slaves correctly? Manda," she said, turning to Lady Sha'rak. "What kind of person is this that you've brought to my house? Some kind of…of…*abolitionist?*"

"Certainly not!" Lady Sha'rak sputtered. "She's just…Lissa is just overly fond of her slave. In fact, I think she's in love with him—it's clouded her judgment considerably."

"I see. Of course." Lady Pope'nose nodded thoughtfully. "For a moment there she almost sounded like someone from one of those benighted planets where males are dominant."

"You know, there *are* societies where males and females are equal," Lissa said, lifting her chin.

"Oh, *those*…" Lady Sha'rak dismissed them with a wave of her hand. "Completely ridiculous as we all well know. Males are incapable of making their own decisions—they make a complete muddle of things if they don't have a female to watch out for them."

"Saber is more than competent to run his own life." Lissa was deep in the heat of the argument now, forgetting that she ought to back off and play her part. "He's one of the most intelligent, capable people I know and it doesn't matter that he's male."

"Oh my." Lady Pope'nose gave her an amused glance. "You really *are* in love with your slave, aren't you, my dear? Is that why you've never punished him properly? You're afraid you'll lose his affection if you give him the rod?"

"I don't give him the rod because I'm not a *rapist*," Lissa said hotly.

"Lady R'awr!" Lady Sha'rak said sharply. "That kind of language is unforgivable! Apologize to our hostess at once!"

"No, no, Manda. Let her have her say." Lady Pope'nose still looked more amused than offended. "She's in love, as you said earlier. And I suppose your slave, Saber, loves you back?" she asked Lissa sweetly.

"He does." Lissa knew she was going too far but it was too late to back out now.

"Of *course* he does." Lady Pope'nose gave a very unpleasant, cawing laugh. "But let me ask you this, my dear — how long do you think that love would last if you punished him as you should? Would he still be so devoted if you gave him the rod? Or would all those pretty little feelings pop like bubbles in the sunlight the minute you truly dominated him and put him in his place as you ought to do?"

"Your question doesn't have an answer," Lissa said, glaring at the other woman. "Because I would never, *ever* hurt the male I love that way. I would never betray his trust and violate his body just to make myself feel important."

Finally her words seemed to have struck a nerve. Lady Pope'nose's thin face darkened and she glared back at Lissa. "Really, that is most — "

Suddenly a blaring siren filled the air and the overhead glows began flashing alarmingly.

"Oh!" Lissa gasped, half rising from the table. "What is it? What's happening?"

"A robbery!" Lady Pope'nose jumped to her feet. "Someone's been into my collection!"

"Oh dear! We must leave at once!" Lady Sha'rak exclaimed, scrambling up from her reclined position. She grabbed for Lissa's arm but there was no way Lissa was going anywhere without Saber.

"No!" She tore her arm from Lady Sha'rak's grasp, ripping the elaborate lace sleeve of her dress as she did. Then she ran after Lady Pope'nose, praying to the Goddess that Saber was all right.

Chapter Twenty-three

The minute Saber's fingertips brushed the missing scroll, an alarm started blaring, lights flashed, and solid plasti-steel bars grew up from the floor around him, forming an instant cage.

"Very nice." Llewelyn laughed and finally lowered the blaster, tucking it into the small of his back. "As I said—caught in the act."

His words were followed by the shrill sound of feminine voices and the *tap-tap-tapping* of high heeled shoes running down the marble hallway. Saber gritted his teeth. Damn it! *Now* what were they going to do?

"What's going on in here? What happened?" Lady Pope'nose arrived first, closely followed by Lissa and Lady Sha'rak.

"It's just what it looks like, I'm afraid, my lady." Llewelyn bowed regretfully. "I walked in here and found him going straight for your collection."

"I knew it!" Lady Sha'rak burst out. "I *knew* it."

"What Llewelyn says is untrue," Saber growled. "He held a blaster on me and forced me to touch the document and trigger this trap."

"Silence, slave!" Lady Pope'nose barked. She turned to Lady Sha'rak. "What do you know about this? Come, Manda, you must know *something* or you wouldn't have sent your slave to follow Lady R'awr's."

Lady Sha'rak looked uncomfortable. "Well, it's nothing I *knew* exactly—more like just a suspicion." She shook her head. "A suspicion that has sadly, now been confirmed." She turned to Lissa.

"You're not from Zetta Prime at all, are you? And Saber isn't even your slave. You tricked me into taking you in so you could worm your way into my home and the homes of my friends and steal their documents!"

"A document thief? You brought a document thief into *my* home?" Lady Pope'nose demanded. "Manda Sha'rak, how *dare* you?"

"I had to know," Lady Sha'rak protested. "And your protection system is the best in the city, Nola. I knew he could never get away with anything—not the way you've got this place wired." She turned to Lissa. "I'm right, aren't I? Don't try to deny it. I had Llewelyn do some checking into your background so I know it's true."

"Is that right?" Lissa stormed, crossing her arms over her chest. "Well, *we* did some checking into *your* background too. We found your stash of male-dom porn, *my lady*."

Lady Sha'rak went pale. "Why you...how...how dare you tell such lies?"

"It's not a lie and you know it, Manda." Lady Pope'nose sounded almost bored. "Don't look so shocked," she continued when Lady Sha'rak gaped at her. "Everyone who's anyone in this city knows you let your slave mount you."

"I...you..." Lady Sha'rak looked like she didn't know whether to be outraged or burst into tears.

"Oh stop." Lady Pope'nose frowned. "We don't have time to discuss your perversions, Manda—we need to get back to the matter at hand." She turned to Lissa. "Which is deciding what to do to these *thieves*." She turned to one of her slaves, who had followed them down the hallway. "Gorum, hold her. I want to make sure she doesn't go anywhere until we get to the bottom of this."

The huge slave grabbed Lissa's arms and pinned them behind her back.

At the sight of another male touching his female, Saber felt the protective rage rise inside him. "Let her go! Don't touch her!" he shouted through the bars of the cage.

"Silence, slave," Lady Pope'nose snapped. "Little Miss R'awr isn't going anywhere until we get some answers."

"Wait, please," Lissa pleaded. "You don't understand."

"Then *make* us understand," Lady Sha'rak snarled at her. "Please explain why you came here pretending to be a friend and abused my hospitality!"

Lissa shot a pleading look at Saber but he only shook his head. Anything he said would be automatically discounted because he was male. She would have to give their explanation and hope for the best.

"All right," Lissa said at last. "All right, it's true—I'm not from Zetta Prime. But I'm not a document thief either. I'm only here to find some missing scrolls that were stolen and sold from my planet."

"And your planet is…?" Lady Pope'nose prodded.

Lissa sighed. "First World. I came from First World."

"The Kindred home world!" Lady Pope'nose's boney nose winkled in disgust. "That benighted race filled with males who dominate their females?"

"They don't dominate us," Lissa protested. "We're equal!"

"Equal? Is that right?" Lady Pope'nose said coldly. "Answer me this then, Lady R'awr—if that is even your name. Who gets penetrated during sex?"

Lissa's cheeks were bright pink but she answered anyway. "The female does. But that doesn't make us inferior to our males. It's just...the way things are. The natural order of things."

"*The natural order of things?* For the male to be dominant?" Lady Pope'nose shook her head. "This is unbelievable."

"Why is it so unbelievable?" Lissa asked. "You just now said yourself that everyone knows Lady Sha'rak and Llewelyn practice the exact same acts you claim to find disgusting in my people."

"Now see here," Lady Sha'rak began but Lady Pope'nose spoke over her.

"It's *one* thing for Manda to indulge herself in a little kinky sex with a well-controlled and properly dominated slave from time to time," she said. "And *quite* another to engage in such acts on a daily basis with a free male who has never known proper submission in his life. Males are beasts, as everyone knows. If you allow them too much leeway you wind up with an arm ripped off."

"As Lady Hake'bean learned to her sorrow," Lady Sha'rak put in.

"The Beast wouldn't have ripped Lady Hake'bean's arm off if she hadn't been *raping* him in the middle of a crowded party!" Lissa exclaimed.

"How dare you?" Lady Pope'nose narrowed her eyes. "I should have you executed this moment for daring to utter such disgusting heresy under my roof."

Saber's hands clenched into fists around the bars. "Don't touch her. So help me Goddess, if you do—"

"Well, well—look at that." Lady Pope'nose strolled over to the cage, taking care to stand just out of his reach. "Manda, dear, I do believe he *does* love her—maybe even as much as she loves him. And they think of themselves as *equals*. How very singular."

"Indeed." Lady Sha'rak, who seemed to have recovered some of her dignity, came to stand beside her friend. "A most disgusting and unnatural relationship."

"But interesting." Lady Pope'nose held up one long finger. "You have to give them that, Manda."

"Look, we're sorry we deceived you," Lissa said. "But please, just let us go. Sell us the scroll my people need and you'll never see us again, I swear."

"*Sell* one of my documents?" Lady Pope'nose sounded aghast.

"Why not?" Lissa asked. "I know it's not usually done but Lady Hake'bean sold it to you."

"Snyra Hake'bean is an ignorant child who is selling off her mother's valuable collection as fast as she can to feed her ridiculously indulgent lifestyle. I am *not* Snyra Hake'bean!" Lady Pope'nose exclaimed.

"Forgive me, I didn't mean to offend you." Lissa took a deep breath. "Please try to understand—my people are under attack. We *need* this scroll—not for any kind of sensi-play or collectable value but because it may be the key to keeping us from being destroyed by the Hoard."

"The Hoard?" Lady Sha'rak frowned. "I thought they were killed off a thousand years ago—by the Kindred."

"They were driven underground but they're back now and more of a threat than ever," Saber growled.

"And why should I care what kind of threat your people are under?" Lady Pope'nose snapped.

"You ought to care because the Hoard won't just stop with us." Lissa leaned forward, as far as the brawny arms of the slave that was holding her would allow. "They could come for you next! Our Council has reason to believe that the Hoard has worm hole generating abilities now. They may be light years away but they can be on your doorstep tomorrow if my people can't hold them back."

"Lissa speaks the truth," Saber said, adding his voice to hers. "If you've really read any of these old documents you've been collecting you'd know that once the Hoard lands they strip a planet bare — why do you think they're called The Darkness which Eats the Stars?"

"Your scare tactics won't work on me," Lady Pope'nose sneered.

"Well then, let me offer you something besides fear," Lissa said, sounding desperate. "Look at the mirror-mere dagger I carry on my belt. It's solid and genuine and worth more than your entire collection put together. You can have it—just trade me the document I need, then Saber and I will be on our way."

"Absolutely not! The dagger is mine!" Lady Sha'rak snapped, jumping into the conversation.

"What?" Lissa looked at her blankly. "It's not yours—I brought it with me."

"Under the hospitality laws of Opulex I have the right to ask for any one item from you as a hostess gift." Lady Sha'rak eyed the dagger greedily. "And I've had my eye on that from the moment I first saw you, my dear."

"No *wonder* you were so eager to have us stay with you," Saber growled. "And you pretended you thought Lissa was a distant relation."

"Well, the two of *you* pretended to be persons of quality from Zetta Prime," Lady Sha'rak shot back. "After all the time and trouble I've spent on you, I *deserve* that dagger. I *earned* it."

"Manda, do stop yammering—you can have the dagger," Lady Pope'nose said, sounding irritated.

"What?" Lady Sha'rak looked at her uncertainly.

"I said, you can *have* the dagger," Lady Pope'nose repeated. "I want something else." Her pale eyes gleamed as she looked between the bars of the cage, eyeing Saber as though he was a prime cut of meat. "I want the slave."

"No! Absolutely not!" Somehow Lissa tore free of the burly slave who was holding her and ran to stand in front of Saber. She put herself between him and Lady Pope'nose and glared fiercely at the other woman. "You can't have him!"

Saber felt sick but he had sworn to see this mission through to the end.

"Lissa," he said softly, reaching through the bars to stroke her hair.

"No!" She shook off his touch and turned to face him. "Forgive me, Saber, but I can't—I just *can't* let her have you. Not even to save everyone we know and love. I'm sorry."

"Ah, true love..." Lady Pope'nose laughed nastily. "Very well, my dear—it's too much trouble to break a free-born slave anyway. They're always so *exhausting*."

"Then...you'll take the dagger after all?" Lissa asked uncertainly.

"No, of course not. The dagger goes to Manda." Lady Pope'nose gave them an evil grin. "What I want is something completely different."

"Well...what?" Lissa asked, looking worried.

Lady Pope'nose's eyes gleamed. "Why, I simply want to see your male's domination at your hands. I want to watch as you punish him properly for the first time."

Lissa went positively pale and Saber felt his heart clench in his chest.

"You mean...?"

"Yes." Lady Pope'nose nodded. "I want to watch you give him the rod."

* * * * *

"I can't do this. I can't do this to him." Lissa paced back and forth in the private punishment area, which was actually a small, plush bedroom stocked with every conceivable sexual torture and punishment device imaginable. Paddles hung from pegs on the walls, whips and riding crops decorated the dresser. Gags and restraints of every kind spilled out of drawers.

And then there were the rods. Lady Pope'nose had already spent a good half hour with her picking out just the right one and they were still looking.

"You *must* do it," she said coldly, giving Lissa a disdainful look. "Those are the terms of our agreement. You will dominate your lover—that is, fuck him to completion while Lady Sha'rak and I watch from another room on the viewing device above the bed. Then and *only* then will I give you the scroll you so *desperately* need and let you be on your way. And remember," She held up the rod she apparently wanted Lissa to use. "You must make him submit *completely*—and by that, I mean I want to see him come."

"How can I possibly promise that?" Lissa looked at the selection of harnesses in dismay. "I can't *make* him—"

"Oh, yes you can!" Lady Pope'nose gestured with the thick black rod with a bulbous end and flipped on a small switch at its base. "Prostate stimulation," she explained while Lissa stared at the massive, vibrating monstrosity in horror. "This one has a vibe implanted that will hit him at just the right angle. He'll come harder than he ever has in his life. And if that doesn't do the trick, there's always *manual* stimulation."

"I don't care what our agreement says, I'm not using *that* on him." Lissa crossed her arms over her chest. "It's too big! Saber's never done anything like this before any more than I have—I don't want to hurt him."

"Very well." Lady Pope'nose made an irritated gesture. "I do have a smaller one. And after all, pain isn't the object of this little exercise—pleasure is."

"I don't understand." Lissa shook her head. "I mean, I know why you want to make me dominate him. But why do you want me to make him...to make him come?"

Lady Pope'nose's pale eyes gleamed. "Why because, my dear. In my experience—and believe me, I have had *plenty* in my day—nothing strips a male of his dignity like forcing his pleasure." She leaned closer to Lissa. "You think he loves you with all his heart? Wait until you take his male pride and shred it to bits by forcing him to come for you. We'll see how well your precious *equality* works when he's the one being penetrated instead of the other way around."

"Stop it!" Lissa almost shouted. She put a hand over her eyes and had to breathe deeply before she could go on. "Just don't...don't say things like that. Saber loves me and he always will, no matter what you make us do to each other."

"Very well. Think whatever you like." Lady Pope'nose smiled coolly. "Now then, I believe we were looking for a smaller rod? I do have one whose size you might prefer but it's the same kind Lady Hake'bean was wearing the other night."

"The same kind? You mean..."

"Yes." Lady Pope'nose pulled out a much smaller rod—a slender silver, double ended one. She raised an eyebrow at Lissa. "I hope you're a fan of deep penetration, my dear."

"Oh my," Lissa whispered faintly.

"This end fits inside you." Lady Pope'nose gestured to one end of the rod. "Every time you thrust into your slave—excuse me, your *lover* — you'll receive an answering thrust as well—most pleasurable. *And* it has a vibe for both of you—why, you might even come at the same time."

"I don't want to...to come while I do this to him!" Lissa exclaimed. "That would be sick! Like I was *enjoying* his humiliation."

"So you prefer the other rod?" Lady Pope'nose held up the massive black shaft again and wiggled it tauntingly. "It won't give *you* nearly as much stimulation—although I'm afraid it might give your poor Saber rather a *lot*."

"No." Lissa swallowed hard. She couldn't use that huge thing on Saber. It would have to be the silver rod. "No, I guess...guess I'll take the other one," she said at last.

"A wise choice." Lady Pope'nose looked at the slender silver rod thoughtfully. "You know, I actually bought this one for when I was rewarding my slaves instead of punishing them. But as none of them ever seems to deserve a reward, I've never had a chance to use it." She smiled cruelly at Lissa. "I hope you enjoy taking it on its maiden voyage."

"You know I won't." Lissa felt like her heart was made of lead. "Why are you doing this?" she asked. "We've never done anything to you. Saber probably saved your life last night when he killed the Beast before he could go after anyone else. Please..." She put all the pleading she could into her voice. "Please, just let us read through the scroll. You don't even have to give it to us—just let us make a copy and take it home."

"I think not, my dear." Lady Pope'nose looked down her boney nose at Lissa. "I *might* have considered such a scenario had you not been so high and mighty at dinner. But after hearing you rant and rave about how you would never 'rape' the man you love, I can hardly give up the chance of seeing you do exactly that, now can I?"

"I was wrong," Lissa said humbly. "Wrong to speak to you in such a disrespectful manner. If you would only—"

"Yes, you were. Very wrong indeed," Lady Pope'nose said briskly. "And now you're going to pay the price. Later on, when this is all over and your precious lover can't even look you in the eye because his pride is broken at your feet, just remember, my dear, *you* brought this pain and humiliation down on yourself."

Lissa's throat was tight with tears. "Please," she choked out. "Please, don't make me do this."

"Oh, I'm not *making* you do anything. If you like, you and that Saber creature of yours can leave right now." Lady Pope'nose gave her an evil smile. "Of course you'll be going *without* the document you so desperately need but that's neither here nor there to me." She held out the silver rod to Lissa. "Now do you want to take this and should I have your lover shown into the room? Or do you wish to leave?"

With a shaking hand, Lissa took the rod. "Send him in," she whispered and then sank down on the bed, her legs too weak to stand.

"Very well," Lady Pope'nose sneered. "And a final word of advice, my dear—don't forget to use plenty of lubricant. You'll find it on the bedside table. Males almost always need it—especially when they're *virgins.* Which your dear Saber won't be for long."

And with a very unpleasant laugh, she left, closing the door behind her.

Oh Goddess, please…what am I going to do? I can't do this to Saber – I can't! Lissa thought helplessly. But if she didn't, the entire Kindred race might die. They might be dying even now as she sat here on the bed, racked with indecision and guilt. She could either debase the man she loved, probably ruining their relationship forever…or stand idly by doing nothing during the genocide of her people. It was a horrible choice…

"It's no choice at all." Saber's deep voice in her ear made Lissa jerk her head up.

"I…" She licked her lips, which were suddenly much too dry. "Did I say that aloud?"

"Enough for me to understand what you're thinking." Saber sat down beside her and put an arm around her shoulders. "Lissa, we're going to have to do this. You know it's true."

"I don't know any such thing." Lissa pushed his arm away and stood up on shaky legs. "I can't do this to you, Saber. I can't."

"Listen to me." He rose and put his hands on her shoulders. "It's going to be all right."

"No, it won't!" she said wildly. "I can't treat you like Lady Hake'bean treated the Beast."

"That was different," Saber objected. "She was humiliating him in front of an audience."

"*We* have an audience." Lissa pointed to the small black dot above their heads – the viewing device. "Lady Pope'nose and Lady Sha'rak are going to be watching our every move."

"Then we'll put on a show," Saber said calmly. "We'll do anything necessary to appease them and get the scroll."

"You don't understand," Lissa whispered. "She said...she wants me to make...to make you come. With...with the rod. Just the way Lady Hake'bean forced the Beast to come." She shivered, remembering the disgust and pity in Saber's eyes as they had watched the awful show the night before. He had spoken of how the Beast's pride would never recover—how would his own pride handle the same treatment? Lissa didn't want to find out.

Saber took a deep breath. "Well...then I guess I'll come. Come on, *amalla*..." He stroked her cheek, which was wet with tears. "Why are we making such a big deal out of this?"

"How can you ask me that?" Lissa whispered, looking up at him. "You *know* why."

"Think of it this way—what if the situation was reversed? What if Lady Pope'nose demanded that *I* penetrate *you?* What if she wanted to watch while I gave you the Deep Touch—what would you do then?"

"I'd open myself to you, of course," Lissa said, swiping at her eyes. "I wouldn't like it that we had an audience but as long as it was *you* who was giving me the Deep Touch, I'd be all right."

Saber smiled gently. "That's exactly how *I* feel right now. As long as you're going to be the one doing it to me, I'm all right with being..." He cleared his throat. "With being penetrated."

"I don't see how you can be," Lissa whispered in a trembling voice. "No matter what you say, I don't see how you can really be all right with me...with me *raping* you." The word wanted to stick in her throat but she forced it out anyway.

"Lissa, no." Saber shook his head and brushed a strand of hair out of her eyes. "It's not going to be rape," he told her firmly. "Because we won't *let* it be."

"But then what—?"

"It's going to be about submission." Saber took a deep breath. "My submission to you, *amalla*."

"But this is different from kissing my foot or helping me dress or feeding me during mealtimes," Lissa protested. "I'll be invading you...forcing you..."

"You can't force the willing." He drew her close and kissed her gently on the forehead. "It's all right, Lissa. Everything is going to be all right."

"Yes, yes, everything is going to be just wonderful," Lady Pope'nose's nasal voice came from a speaker high in the corner of the ceiling. "If the two of you will ever just *get on* with it. You'd better get started directly or I'm going to withdraw my offer and kick you out of my home with nothing!"

The speaker crackled and then everything was silent again. Lissa looked at Saber. Though her heart was aching, she knew that she really had no choice.

"All right," she whispered. "Let's do it."

Chapter Twenty-four

Saber felt strangely calm about what was about to happen, maybe because it didn't seem real. Was he really going to open himself this way, to allow his body to be penetrated, to be fucked in a way he had never even considered before?

It seemed he was.

It'll be all right, he told himself over and over even as he told Lissa the same thing. *We love each other. We can get through this—we have to if we're ever going to get that damn scroll.* And Saber was determined they would get it—no matter what it took.

Lissa was obliviously having a much harder time with what they were about to do than he was. Though he tried to reassure her, she still obviously felt awful about it. Not to mention the fact that she was scared to death. And when she showed him the rod she was supposed to use on him, Saber understood why.

"Damn it, what in the seven hells is this?" he demanded, looking at the slender silver rod. He could feel some of his passiveness melting as he considered its shape.

"I'm sorry," Lissa whispered. "I...I picked the smallest one she had. I thought..."

"But this goes *inside* you," Saber protested, gesturing with the rod. "Inside both of us, I mean."

Lissa bit her lip. "I know. I didn't want to use one like that. I've never...you know I've never had anything inside me. Except for when you massaged me and...and tasted me." She blushed bright pink when she said it and Saber felt his heart clench.

"I know, *amalla*," he murmured, brushing her hot cheek with his knuckles. "That's what upsets me. I know you're a virgin and, well, *I* wanted to be the first one inside you. I wanted to break you in gently. Now…"

Lissa made a sound that was half laugh, half sob. "I guess we'll both be losing our virginity tonight."

"It's not the way I thought it would happen," Saber admitted. "But it does seem that way." He sighed. "You're sure this is the best, uh, tool for the job?"

"The other ones she showed me were so much bigger." Lissa's eyes widened. "Almost as big as…as you are."

Saber frowned and shifted uncomfortably. He was all right with this, he told himself—honestly, he was—but he *damn* sure didn't want anything near as big as his own shaft penetrating him. "Well…" He sighed. "I guess we'll have to stick to this one then."

"I guess so." Lissa took the silver rod from him and looked at it doubtfully. "I guess…I guess I'd better put it on. Or, uh, in…"

She was wearing another Yonnite dress—a black and white one this time, which opened just above the navel to reveal her crotch. Wispy little black and white panties of the same pattern were also visible when she spread her legs. Lissa pulled them to one side and began to fumble with the silver rod but Saber could see at once there was a problem.

"Wait a minute." He took the rod from her gently and looked into her eyes. "Are you even wet enough to take that?"

"I…I don't know." Lissa bit her lip. "I think…I guess I just wanted to get it over with."

"I do too," Saber admitted. "And I'm sure once we get down to the, uh, actual act, it will go pretty fast. But I don't want you hurting yourself just because you're upset."

"All right." She took a deep breath. "I'm just so...so nervous."

"Don't be." Saber cupped her cheek. "It's not going to be a big deal—we won't *let* it be a big deal. Once we get you comfortable wearing the rod you'll put it in me, thrust a couple of times, I'll finish and that will be it. All right?"

"I guess..." She still looked troubled.

"Just relax," he said softly. "And let me get you ready. Here— lay back on the bed with your legs hanging down."

Lissa did as he ordered and Saber sat on the floor between her legs. "Now," he murmured, "Let's get you out of these panties."

She let him take them off, then spread her legs and said in a trembling voice, "All right...put it in."

"Not yet." Saber cupped her bare sex in his hand, feeling her heat and the way she shivered under his touch. "Not yet, *amalla*. I told you, I have to get you ready. Have to get you wet and hot enough to take this."

He brushed the head of the silver rod against her inner thigh and Lissa jumped and moaned.

"Saber...*please*. What are you going to do?"

"Well, first of all, I'm going to get you good and wet." Leaning down, he nuzzled her with his lips, kissing her pussy softly but thoroughly until he felt her start to move against his mouth.

"Oh, Saber," she moaned softly. "I can't help it...when you kiss me like that..."

"I'm glad you like it." He kissed her again, this time spreading her outer lips with his thumbs and sucking her clit as well. "Because I *love* it."

"You do?" She looked down at him uncertainly.

"Hell, yes," Saber assured her. "Your scent is so sweet and warm and you taste so good...salty and hot. Not to mention the sounds you make when I taste you." Keeping her pussy spread open, he kissed her again, loving the breathless little cry she gave in return. Goddess, he could do this all night. But a slight noise from the speaker in the corner reminded him he didn't *have* all night. He needed to get Lissa used to the rod, used to the idea of having it inside her so they could get this done.

Who's going to get **you** *used to having it inside* **you?** demanded a sarcastic little voice in his head but Saber did his best to ignore it. *This is no big deal,* he insisted to himself. *It will probably take no time at all to finish up and get out of here. We'll get the scroll and leave this benighted planet and never think about what had to be done to get it again.* Then he turned his attention to the matter at hand.

"Okay now, Lissa," he murmured, finding the switch that turned the vibe on her side of the rod on. "I'm going to use this on you just a little to get you used to it."

"All...all right," she whispered. "I guess that's okay."

"Good. Just a little at first," Saber promised. He touched the vibrating head of the rod to her open pussy and Lissa nearly jumped off the bed.

"Oh! That felt really...really good." She looked down at Saber, breathing hard. "Is that normal?"

He smiled. "I think so. I take it this is the first time you've used one of these?"

"Of course." Lissa looked scandalized. "I'm a priestess—remember?"

She looked more like a sexual goddess to Saber. He loved the picture she made, all spread out on the bed, her pink pussy wet and swollen from the teasing of his tongue and the vibrating rod. She looked incredibly hot...and also much more relaxed, which was good. She needed to be open and calm in order to do this. So did he, for that matter. It was a good thing he felt perfectly fine with this whole thing or he'd be really upset right now. And he really did, he told himself firmly. He felt good—everything was going to be fine, honestly. *Who are you trying to convince?* the sarcastic little voice murmured. Saber pushed it away.

"Again," he said. This time he touched the vibrating rod to her pussy and held it there, right against the side of her little pink clit.

"Oh! Oh, Saber!" Lissa was twitching her hips from side to side, making it hard for him to stay in place and her breasts were heaving. "Oh Goddess!" she moaned. "Oh please!"

Just as it looked like she was going to come, Saber withdrew the rod and placed it at the entrance to her pussy instead.

"Inside you now, *amalla*," he murmured. "Nice and slow."

Gently he slipped the flared silver head past the entrance of her pussy and then he pressed up and in, slowly sliding the long shaft to the very end. There was a bump in the middle of the rod, between the two halves, and he could feel it vibrating against his fingers as he slipped the silver shaft all the way into her. *Another vibe. Probably to stimulate her clit while she fucks me,* he thought, feeling weirdly calm about the idea.

Lissa was still moaning softly but she showed no discomfort when the silver rod reached the end of her channel. Instead she looked down at Saber, as he secured the black straps around her thighs.

"I...Saber?" she asked softly and he looked up.

"Yes, *amalla*?"

"It still feels really good. I...I don't know how to feel about that."

"About what?"

Lissa shifted, as though getting the rod settled more comfortably inside herself. "About, you know, feeling good while I...while I take you."

"I'd much rather you had pleasure than pain," Saber told her truthfully. "It's all right if you feel good, you know that. Now come on..." He patted the side of the bed. "Stand up and walk around. Get used to it."

Lissa did as he said, looking unsure of herself at first. "It keeps shifting around inside me," she said at last, moving her hips experimentally. "It feels...strange but good."

"Good to be filled?" Saber murmured, wondering if he would feel the same way. *Of course not,* he told himself uneasily. *Just because that bitch Lady Pope'nose is making me do this doesn't mean she can make me enjoy it. This is going to be a strictly in and out, one time only event and it probably won't even last two minutes. Afterward we'll forget about it and get back to our lives.*

"Just...good." Lissa looked at him uncertainly. "Um...how do I look?"

Actually, she looked damn hot, although he found it hard to admit. Not just because she was beautiful — which she certainly was. But the sight of that slender silver rod rising from between her thighs seemed to do something to his insides. Saber had no idea what it was until he looked down at himself and realized he had an erection. Damn it, this couldn't be turning him on, could it?

It's just because she looks so hot in that Yonnite dress that shows everything, he tried to tell himself but he wasn't completely sure that was true.

"You look beautiful,' he said, answering her question and trying to quell his own internal worries at the same time. "Uh, but it might be easier to do this without the dress."

"Good point." Lissa slipped off the bulky black and white dress, which left her wearing nothing but the rod. To Saber's dismay, the sight of her completely naked and about to fuck him made his cock even harder. Goddess, they needed to get this done before he lost himself entirely in this weird scenario.

"I...I think we'd better get going," he said quietly.

"All right." Lissa still looked uncertain. "Saber, please...I'm still not sure I can do this."

"Yes, you can. You *have* to." Saber took both her hands in his and kissed them gently. Then he took a deep breath and murmured, "Mistress, I submit."

"Saber?"

She made his name a question but he only stroked her cheek and kissed her. Then he walked to the end of the bed, slipped out of the tight slave trousers, and lay down across it. Burying his head in his arms, he spread his thighs and repeated, "Mistress, I submit. Take me."

* * * * *

A part of Lissa melted when she heard those words in his deep, soft voice. Goddess, he really was going to let her do this. He really was going to open himself for her penetration and give himself to her the way Lissa had always fantasized giving herself to him. She couldn't help admiring the sleek, muscular lines of his body as he lay open for her and she felt a surge of adrenaline — it was the same way she had felt the first time she jerked him off. When she'd ordered him to lie on the bed with his arms above his head and let her touch him and make him come.

What's wrong with you? You're not supposed to be enjoying this, Lissa chided herself guiltily. But there was part of her—a part buried so deep it felt like a stranger inside her—that loved the feeling of dominance, the rush of power she got from having such a strong, fearless warrior make himself vulnerable to her.

She started to go over to the bed and then remembered Lady Pope'nose's advice about lubrication. Saber had made sure she was wet enough to take the rod inside herself—she could do no less for him.

The silver rod bounced as she walked, shifting inside her in a way that was both hot and a little frightening. Lissa had never had anything bigger than Saber's fingers inside her before and though the silver rod wasn't much wider, it still filled her in a much more substantial way. It made her wonder what having his shaft inside her would feel like.

Just the thought of that made her blush although she supposed her embarrassed reaction was silly. After all, just look what they were about to do!

But it's not going to be a big deal, she told herself firmly. *Lady Pope'nose is so full of herself she thinks she can ruin our love. Well, she can't. Like Saber says, it will be short and over before we know it. There's no reason that him submitting to me this way has to change us. And it's not really even submission – it's just an act.*

She found the small tube of lubricant where Lady Pope'nose had said it would be and brought it over to the end of the bed where Saber was still lying on his stomach, waiting for her. He was quiet but she could see the tension in his big body—his muscles were knotted and tight and his jaw was clenched. He jumped when

Lissa touched him on the small of his back and then laughed nervously.

"Sorry. Guess I'm a little jumpy."

"Saber," she began. "Are you sure—?"

"Yes." He shifted on the bed, as though trying to get more comfortable. "We have to. Just...be careful. I've never had, uh, anything up there before."

"I know you haven't. You know I'll treat you gently." It felt odd to be the strong one, to be the one reassuring Saber instead of the other way around. And yet, somehow it felt *right* too.

I could do this, Lissa found herself thinking. *I could be a mistress like Lady Sha'rak and all the rest of the females who live here. Not all the time, maybe, but in the bedroom. I could be kind and gentle and calm, just the way Saber is with me.*

Gently she stroked his back and the rounded curves of his ass, admiring his big, muscular form and soothing him as she might a wild animal she wanted to tame.

"It's all right, *Moch Daer,*" she murmured as she stroked him. "I promise it's going to be all right."

Saber gave another half strangled laugh. "I thought that was my line."

"It is—most of the time," Lissa said lightly. "But this time it's mine." She stroked his lower back and let her fingers trail lightly between his spread cheeks. "I'm going to use some lubrication on you now to...to get you ready. Is that all right?"

"Yeah." His jaw clenched again. "Go ahead—do it."

"All right." Lissa squirted a generous amount of the slippery clear jelly onto her fingers and stroked between his cheeks again.

She let one fingertip slip down and trace his nether entrance, just as she had the night she was playing "mistress" with him.

Saber jumped and gave a muffled curse.

Lissa pulled back at once. "I'm sorry—did I hurt you?"

"No. It's just...cold." He turned his head to look at her. "Go ahead and, uh, stick it in now, okay?"

"I need to get you ready first!" Lissa objected. "I need to open you up—stretch you a little bit." She circled his tight rosebud again. "I promise I'll be gentle," she murmured. "Just try to relax."

"I'm trying." He took a deep breath and seemed to force himself to go limp against the pillows. "All right, go ahead."

Lissa stroked his entrance again, this time inserting the tip of her finger. Saber shifted but didn't say anything, which made her brave enough to go further. Slowly, she slid the rest of her finger into him, watching to make sure he wasn't in any pain.

"Is this all right?" she murmured and he nodded and gave a muffled assent.

"Good." She spent some time sliding her finger gently in and out and then decided it was time to add another. Saber made no protest, though his face was closed and his eyes were tightly shut.

"Relax," Lissa murmured, scissoring her fingers gently to stretch him. "Relax, *Moch Daer.*"

"Trying...to." His deep voice was hoarse but he didn't seem to be in any pain. To the contrary, when she looked between his legs, Lissa could see that his heavy shaft was erect and brushing against the mattress.

She didn't know what she had expected to find when she penetrated him but Saber was tight and hot inside—it was like stroking warm, wet satin. And once she was sure he wasn't in pain, she rather liked the way he jumped and quivered when she explored him. There was one spot especially…when she pressed her fingertips against it, he moaned and rubbed his rigid shaft against the comforter. *Prostate stimulation,* whispered Lady Pope'nose's voice in her brain. Was this the area she was talking about?

"Lissa…" Saber's voice brought her back from her speculation. "No more stretching, okay?" He sounded shaky. "I think I'm as ready as I'll ever be. Just…put it in."

"You're sure?" Lissa removed her fingers slowly and replaced them with the bulbous head of the silver rod.

A shiver went through Saber's entire body and his jaw clenched again. "Yes," he muttered, his deep voice hoarse. "Yes, just…just do it. Just fill me."

"All right. I'll go slowly," Lissa promised. "Tell me to stop if it hurts." She added some more lubrication and pressed inward, watching as the silver rod penetrated him.

Saber's back arched and he gave a low groan as she took him. He seemed to be fighting to keep still, his hands clenched in the comforter and his eyes tightly closed. Lissa was anxious that she might be hurting him but he didn't say anything, just lowered his head and lifted his hips, as though offering himself for the final penetration.

He wants to get it over with, that's all, Lissa told herself uneasily. But part of her—that buried mistress part—liked the way it looked. Liked the way he gave himself to her, submitting to her penetration even though it must seem strange and unnatural to him.

"It's all right," she whispered as she pressed into him. "It's all right, Saber. I'm almost there."

At last she was all the way in, the end of the silver rod flush with his buttocks. Lissa was pressing hard against him and she could feel the rod shift inside her as she did so. Her position also rubbed the vibrating knob in the middle of the rod against her clit, making her bite her lip and moan. Goddess, that felt *good*.

A sudden rush of guilt swamped her. She shouldn't be enjoying this! After all, Saber certainly wasn't—or was he? A quick peek between his legs revealed that his cock was harder than Lissa had ever seen it. Not only that but it was dripping a river of pre-cum. He'd seemed so certain that this act between them would be meaningless and quickly over. Could it be that it was affecting him more than he'd anticipated?

"Saber?" she asked uncertainly. "Are you all right? Does it hurt?"

"No..." He shifted his hips experimentally, causing a small part of the silver rod to slip out and then press in deep again. This time Lissa joined him in moaning—the small motion had thrust the rod into her pussy, pressing the flared head against the end of her channel and making the vibrating bump between them kiss her clit.

"Saber?" she managed to ask. "Goddess, that's amazing. How...how does it feel for you?"

He muttered something she didn't catch and she had to ask him to repeat it.

"Good." He spoke through gritted teeth and his fingers clenched harder in the coverlet. "Damn it, I said it feels *good*."

"Then should I...?" Lissa moved experimentally, withdrawing a little and then pressing back in until they both gasped. Goddess, she knew she shouldn't be enjoying this but there was no denying that between the rod filling her pussy and the vibe buzzing against her clit, the sensations were intense.

"Yes." Saber's voice was choked and a shiver ran through his big body as he spoke. "Yes, Goddess damn it, do it. Get it over with and *fuck me.*"

Lissa's hips were already working, moving almost as though her body had a mind of its own. She braced herself on her knees and gripped his thighs, sliding the silver rod in and out of her lover in short, hard thrusts. Saber had shifted to his hands and knees as well but his head was lowered, his strong features closed as he submitted to her fucking.

His cock was still standing at attention, the heavy shaft swaying with each thrust of the rod inside him but he showed no signs of coming yet. *"There's always manual stimulation"* Lady Pope'nose's words rang in Lissa's memory. Should she stroke his cock while she did this? Probably so — if she wanted to make him come she would have to.

Bracing herself with one hand on his hip, she reached between his legs and captured him, cupping the hot velvet shaft firmly and circling it with her fingers.

"Lissa...*Gods!*" Saber gasped and pumped hard into her hand. He was breathing harder now, almost panting, his muscular chest expanding like a bellows with each breath.

Lissa stroked him, taking care not to lose her rhythm as she continued to fuck. The buzzing of the vibe was beginning to get to her. With every thrust it rubbed against her clit just the right way as the rod bumped the end of her channel. The pleasure was beginning to build and she felt that part of her, the mistress part, beginning to come out into the open, just as it had the night she had first made Saber come.

"Is this all right?" she murmured in a low voice, stroking and thrusting at the same time. "Is this how you like to be touched? How you need to be fucked?"

"Gods!" Saber appeared to be losing himself as well. His shaft was throbbing in her hand and his hips were bucking back to meet hers, matching her rhythm as he gave himself to the pleasure she was giving him.

"Is it?" Lissa insisted, with a particularly deep thrust. Forgotten was the fact that they had been forced into this act, forgotten were all her fears that it would change things between them. All she could feel was the push and thrust of the silver rod inside her, all she could hear were the low groans of pleasure being ripped from her lover's throat as she thrust into him, harder and harder.

But still he didn't come.

Lissa was close herself. She could feel her orgasm building and she knew she didn't want to come alone. She needed Saber to come with her, needed to give him the same pleasure she was experiencing at the same time. Suddenly she remembered that certain spot inside him that had made him jump and gasp when she pressed it with her fingers. Maybe if she got just a little higher on her knees and angled the rod a certain way...

"Oh! *Gods*, Lissa!" Saber's deep shout vibrated through her entire body and his big form clenched like a fist.

She was worried at once. "Did I hurt you?"

"No." He shook his head, his eyes still tightly closed. "No, do it...do it again. And this time don't stop."

Lissa took a firmer grip on his cock and thrust at an angle again. And again and again as Saber groaned beneath her and thrust back. Broken words fell from his lips and every muscle in his big body was tight.

"Lissa...*amalla*. There...right there. Gods, please...please...yes. Take me harder. *Fuck me!*"

Lissa felt a surge of power mixed with a rush of tenderness. To think that Saber would open himself to her, would allow himself to be so vulnerable made her love him all the more.

As her sense of power grew, so did her own pleasure. She gave a final strangled moan and pumped hard into him, feeling the silver rod penetrate both of them to the core. At the same time the buzzing vibe pressed hard against the tender button of her clit, sending her into the stratosphere as the most intense orgasm she'd had so far rocked her to her foundations.

Saber was apparently finding release as well. He moaned her name and she could feel his thick shaft spasming in her hand. Spurt after spurt of hot seed wet her fingers with his release as he came over and over. The mutual pleasure seemed to tie them together, creating a special space occupied only by them. Lissa had never felt so close to him.

We made love, she thought, wonderingly. *It wasn't what I thought it would be like my first time but that was making love, all the same.* The only way it could have been better would be if Saber had given her the Deep Touch. But then, he was going to do that as soon as they got back to the Mother Ship so she didn't have long to wait.

At last Saber groaned and collapsed, his big body utterly limp and spent. Lissa draped herself against his back and kissed him between the shoulder blades.

"I love you," she whispered, stroking his heaving side with one hand. "Goddess, Saber, I love you so much. That was...amazing. The way you gave yourself to me..."

He twitched under her and muttered something.

"What?" Lissa leaned forward to hear.

"Out of me." His deep voice sounded tired and not very happy. "Get it out of me, *now*."

"Sorry! I didn't realize..." Lissa sat up and quickly slid the vibrating rod out, then turned it off. "Better?" she asked timidly.

"Yes..." He rolled on his side and took a deep breath. "Much."

"Did...did I hurt you?" Lissa wanted to touch him. Wanted to run her fingers through his hair, which was damp with sweat, but somehow she didn't dare.

"No." He grimaced and sat up. Moving to the side of the bed, he put his head in his hands a moment and breathed deeply, his sides heaving. "No I'm...fine."

"You don't seem fine," Lissa objected.

But he only shook his head and repeated, "I'm fine." He cast a quick look in her direction and his eyes hardened. "Get that damn thing off, will you? We need to get out of here."

"Oh. Of course." Lissa fumbled for the straps and winced as the silver rod slid out of her pussy. She felt empty inside now and not just for the lack of the rod. "Saber..." she began. "About what just happened..."

Saber's broad shoulders hunched. "It's over," he said flatly. "Let's just...not mention it again, all right?"

Lissa felt a rush of panic. Goddess, it was happening. Just as Lady Pope'nose had predicted—Saber was withdrawing from her. Now that she had taken him, he hated her.

"Saber," she whispered brokenly. "I...I'm so sorry. I didn't mean—"

"Nothing to be sorry about." But he didn't meet her eyes. Instead, he fumbled for his black trousers and pulled them on as though he couldn't wait to cover himself.

Lissa put her clothing back on too, slipping into the discarded panties and rumpled black and white dress as though in a dream. It was true—she had ruined their relationship. Maybe she had hurt him somehow. Or maybe it was as Lady Pope'nose had said— forcing a man's pleasure stripped him of his dignity. Either way, Saber hated her now and she didn't blame him one bit.

"Well now." The door opened and Lady Pope'nose came in. In one hand was the blue laminated scroll. She came to a stop in front of the bed where Saber was still sitting, putting on his boots. "That was quite a show you put on," she purred, holding out the scroll. "More than worth the price of this old document, I do believe."

"Shut up." Saber snatched the scroll from her hands and stood up, towering over her. "You got what you wanted. Now we're going."

"I think we *all* got what we wanted, if what I saw was any indication." Lady Pope'nose gave him a nasty grin. "And how did you enjoy being dominated, my dear? Did it fulfill a need, deep down in your soul that you didn't even know you had? Does it make you want to bend over and beg your sweet mistress to fuck your ass over and over again?"

"Leave him alone!" Lissa pushed her way between them and faced Lady Pope'nose with her hands on her hips. "Haven't you done enough damage?"

"I think it was *you* who did the damage, my dear." Lady Pope'nose smirked. "Excellent technique, by the way—for a novice you did extremely well. In fact, I don't believe I've ever seen a slave so thoroughly dominated and *fucked* in all my years."

"*Gods.*" Saber pushed past her and headed for the door.

Lissa spared one last glare at Lady Pope'nose. "You're a horrible person," she said, trying to keep the tears of rage and sorrow that rose in her eyes from falling. "I hope you end up just like Lady Hake'bean. That would be exactly what you deserve."

Then she followed Saber down the long hallway. He was striding fast, however, and she didn't catch up with him until he was already over the threshold and out into the dark, steamy night.

"Saber wait, please." She grabbed him by the arm and tried to get him to face her. "Please," she pleaded when he wouldn't turn. "Don't listen to her. You know what a horrible person she is."

He shook his head. "I'm sorry, Lissa, but I can't talk about this right now. I just...I just want to forget it. All right?"

Lissa felt the tears that had been threatening earlier overflow her eyes and wet her cheeks in a hot flood. "I'm so sorry," she whispered again. "Oh Saber, I'm so sorry. Do...do you hate me now?"

"No." He looked away, the side of his jaw clenching. "I hate myself." Then he sighed. "Come on—we need to get this scroll back to the Mother Ship. Let's go."

Chapter Twenty-five

It hadn't been at all like Saber had expected.

Before they got started he had been telling himself over and over that everything was fine — that it would be over and done with quickly. That he could give his body without letting his emotions become involved.

Well, he'd been wrong. Abysmally, shamefully, humiliatingly wrong.

He'd been so sure he could remain impassive, just lie there and take it, then forget about it afterward. But he hadn't counted on the pleasure. The incredible, scarily intense, mind-meltingly hot pleasure of being taken, of being penetrated by the woman he loved.

Over and over he heard his own voice, begging hoarsely for Lissa to take him harder, to fill him, to *fuck* him. Goddess, what was *wrong* with him?

What must she think of me now? He gave her a sidelong glance as he started the ship's engines. There had been complete silence between them all the way from Lady Pope'nose's home to the docking yards. Lissa sat beside him in the passenger's chair, staring out the window, pale and withdrawn.

She probably hates me. She's probably lost all respect for me. Exactly the way he had lost all respect for himself. Saber closed his eyes briefly, wishing he could just block the whole past hour and a half out of his mind. Better yet, he wished he could go back in time and not have taken this mission at all.

He'd been so certain when this all began that it wouldn't change him, that he could handle any form of submission. He'd been fine with playing the part of her slave, fine with serving her on bended knee—hell, he'd even enjoyed it! He liked catering to Lissa, being her protector and slave. He'd even enjoyed it when she played "mistress" with him and jerked him off. But none of that had been so invasive. So…private.

Saber had spent years reining himself in, keeping his emotions in check. Letting Lissa fuck him had stripped away a protective shield around his male psyche he hadn't even known he had—a shield he certainly hadn't been ready to lose. Being penetrated had made him feel so helpless…so vulnerable. The silver rod pressing inside him had rendered him powerless in a way no enemy in battle ever had.

And he'd enjoyed it. He'd enjoyed it *way* too much.

I gave it up like a bitch in heat, he thought morosely, punching buttons far harder than he needed to. *Lissa must think I'm not fit to be her mate, her protector.* Not when he couldn't even protect himself from the insidious pleasure of being taken. Not when he opened himself and begged for more so desperately.

Saber could still feel the warm slippery lube between his thighs as well as a slight tingling—the aftermath of being fucked, he supposed. But the slight stretching pain that was even now fading was nothing to the pain in his heart. A pain he was certain would never fade.

The humiliating thoughts and memories went round and round in his head in a loop he felt powerless to shut off or stop. So he was immensely relieved when the viewscreen flickered to life and he saw Sophia's image.

"You're coming home?" As it had the night before, her voice sounded different to Saber. Slightly deeper and more authoritative somehow.

"Yes." He cleared his throat. "We, uh, got the scroll. We're on the way."

"Good." Sophia blew out a breath and ran a hand through her hair. "Something has to be done—things are insane here on the Mother Ship."

"What happened?" Lissa asked anxiously, entering the conversation. "What's going on? Is everyone all right?"

"Everyone is most certainly *not* all right." Sophia sighed. "But no one is dead, if that's what you're asking. Though I fear that my brother will soon wish he was dead."

"Your brother?" Saber frowned. "I didn't know you had a brother, Sophia."

"Sophia doesn't but *I* do. I just..." She shook her head. "I can't explain now. You'll find out soon enough when you get back here. I'm having them open the fold now—come home."

The words were like a shot to Saber's heart. Home. Yes, he and Lissa *had* agreed to make the Mother Ship their home. But now...

Now we'll probably go our separate ways, just like we were going to before. I never penetrated her with my cock so she's technically still a virgin—she can go back to being the High Priestess. And I'll go back to rule the Touch Clans just like Father wants me to.

The knowledge was like a stone in his heart. Despite everything, he still loved Lissa but after the way he'd acted, he didn't see how she could love him back. Didn't see how she could respect him anymore. He'd heard the pity in her voice all too plainly when she said she was sorry for what they had done. She shouldn't have to be with a male she pitied—it wasn't fair to ask that of her. Wasn't fair to ask her to stay with a male who had no pride left and no hope of ever regaining it.

"We're coming," he told Sophia. "I see the fold, we'll be entering it in just a minute."

"I'll have someone meet you and try to explain." Sophia seemed to hear something in the background. She frowned. "I have to go— they need me in the med center."

"The med center?" Lissa frowned as Sophia's image abruptly winked out and the blackness of space replaced it. "Since when does Sophia work at the med center? I thought she taught art to the little ones. And what was all that about her brother?"

Saber shook his head. "Something strange is definitely going on." He sighed. "I guess we'll find out what it is when we get there."

"Saber, wait." Lissa put a hand on his knee. The soft touch made him jump as though he'd been burned and she pulled back immediately. "I'm sorry. I just...before we go back I wanted to talk."

Saber looked straight ahead. *She's going to tell me now. Say that she can't be with me anymore. That we need to go our separate ways.* He didn't feel able to hear that right now, even though he knew it was coming.

"There's nothing to talk about," he said gruffly, still not looking at her.

"Yes, there is," Lissa insisted. "Saber, everything was fine between us until—"

"Until you fucked me?" he growled. "Yes, it was, wasn't it? And now everything is different—changed."

"I didn't want it to change." Lissa sounded like she was trying to hold back tears. "I didn't mean for it to change."

Saber blew out a breath. "I didn't either. But it did. Lissa..." He finally turned to look at her. "I think it's better if we just forget about it. Maybe if we forget about *everything*."

"*Everything?*" she repeated, her eyes getting wide. "You mean just...go our separate ways?"

"Isn't that what you wanted? What we were always going to do once this mission was complete?" he asked harshly.

"Well, yes but...but that was before," she whispered.

"A lot of things were before." Saber felt horrible — like the worst person in the world. But he didn't want to drag this out. "Let's just move on, all right?"

"What if...what if I don't want to move on?"

"You have to." His throat felt tight. "Listen to me, Lissa — you're beautiful. You'll find a male who will love and appreciate you. One you can care for." *One you can respect,* he thought but didn't say.

"Saber...I...I..." But she couldn't say anymore — tears choked her.

For Saber, there was nothing more to say. "We're coming to the fold," he said, staring straight ahead again. "Make sure your belt is fastened securely. It may be a bumpy ride."

Chapter Twenty-six

Baird had woken the morning before feeling strangely tired and heavy. He lay in bed, trying to understand what was wrong—had he eaten too much pizza the night before? It was his favorite Earth dish and since Olivia didn't have to watch her weight during her pregnancy, they had it at least once a week. But the heaviness didn't seem to center in his stomach exactly, it was lower—a feeling of fullness in his pelvis that wouldn't go away. What could it be?

He reached down to touch his belly, expecting to find washboard abs—he took care to keep in shape because Olivia loved his stomach muscles for some reason. Instead, he felt a swelling—a *huge* swelling. Gods, what was wrong with him? Had he somehow grown a tumor overnight? He needed to get to the med center right away!

"Olivia?" he said but his voice came out strange—high and feminine. He cleared his throat and tried again. "Olivia?"

"Huh?" She didn't sound like herself at all—her voice was deep and harsh. Baird turned his head to look at her—was she getting a cold?

The light was still dim and his wife was just a bump under the covers. A very *large* bump. Did she have some pillows stuffed down there? Now that she was in her last quadmester and ready to give birth at any day, she claimed the only way she could lay on her side was with lots of extra support. But it would take six or seven pillows to make that much of a lump under the bedspread.

"Olivia?" he said again in his strange, high voice. And then someone kicked him.

From the inside.

* * * * *

Liv was woken by high piercing screams of pure terror.

"What? What is it?" She sat up at once, barely registering how easy it was. For the past few months as her belly grew bigger and bigger she had started needing assistance to get up from anywhere. But this time she popped right up with the frightened screams still echoing in her ears.

"Olivia, is that you? Are you in there?" The voice was high and feminine but also familiar.

"In where? What are you talking about?" Her voice sounded terrible—so hoarse and deep. Was she getting a cold? That was all she needed just when the baby was about to arrive.

"In there," the person beside her in bed said. "In my body."

"What? What are you talking about, 'your body'?"

Liv looked down at herself. Even in the dim lighting it occurred to her that something was wrong. Then she realized what it was— her stomach was completely flat.

"Oh my God!" She began feeling her abdomen frantically. "The baby? Where's the baby?"

"It's in me! I can feel it kicking—*ow!*"

Liv looked at the ceiling and bellowed, "Lights, bright!"

The resulting brilliance nearly blinded her but when her eyes finally adjusted she looked at the person who was sharing the bed with her and saw...herself.

"Who...who are you?" she demanded, staring at the doppelganger.

"It's me—Baird," the person who looked exactly like her said. "And you're me—just look at yourself, *Lilenta.*"

The use of his pet nickname for her finally convinced Liv that it really was her husband in her body. But then if he was in her, where was she?

She was almost afraid to look down at herself in the bright light but she had no choice. Reluctantly she pushed back the covers and looked down the length of her tall, muscular body. Broad shoulders, washboard abs, and...

"Oh my God," she said aloud. "I've got a cock. And it's *hard.*" She looked up at Baird. "I'm *you.*"

"And I'm you," he whispered and burst into tears.

"Oh no—no, don't do that! It's all right...everything will be all right," Liv tried to comfort him by clumsily putting one long, muscular arm around his slender shoulders. It felt weird to touch herself from the outside but no matter what was going on, she couldn't stand to see her mate so upset.

"I...I'm sorry," Baird gasped at last. "I don't know what's wrong with me. I can't...can't seem to stop crying."

"It's the hormones," Liv said, realizing it was true. "You're super pregnant, which makes you super emotional."

"But I don't understand—how did this happen? Is it some kind of bad dream?"

"If it is, we're both having it." Liv hopped out of bed. "Come on, let's see if we can get some help. Maybe Sylvan will know what's going on. Uh...this isn't some kind of a weird Kindred thing, is it?"

"Of course not!" Baird was trying to get out of bed too but in the extremely pregnant body he couldn't manage it. "Uh—help me out, *Lilenta.* I can barely move!"

"Here you go." Liv came around the side of the bed and pulled him to his feet. "Wow, it feels great to be able to move again. I can even touch my toes—watch." She bent down quickly and rose with no problems. Her new body was big and a bit ungainly and so tall she felt like she was looking down from the top of a step ladder, but just being able to move with ease felt wonderful.

"Good for you, touching your toes. I can't even *see* mine." Baird grumbled. He put a hand to the small of his back. "Goddess, this is *terrible.* Everything aches and I have the worst indigestion—how do you stand it?"

"It's not easy," Liv admitted. "In fact, I've been pretty much miserable all the time for the past month." She sighed. "I don't know what's going on but I kind of hate to trade you back."

"You—*ow!* He kicked me *again.*" Baird pressed a hand to his rounded belly.

"Yup, he's an active little guy," Liv admitted. "Kicks all the time."

"All the time?" Baird winced. "Really?"

"I'm afraid so." She sighed. "Look, we need to get to the med center and get this taken care of. Come on." She took a few steps and stopped. "Uh…"

"What is it?" Baird came waddling over, one hand pressed to the small of his back and the other cupping his belly.

"Your, uh, equipment." Liv looked down uncertainly at the bulge tenting the front of her sleep pants. "It's still hard. How do I make it go down?"

Baird sighed. "You probably just need to piss. If that doesn't work, try jerking off."

"Really? That's what you're doing every morning in the bathroom? I thought you were just taking an extra-long shower."

"Well, I didn't want to bother you, *Lilenta*. As you say, you've been so miserable this past month." He looked sheepish and Liv couldn't help thinking it was strange and surreal to see his facial expressions being made by her own face.

"Yes, well..." She sighed. "Okay. Let me go in the bathroom and see what I can do."

"Not until I get in there." Baird winced. "My bladder is bursting! It feels like he's resting right on it."

"That's because he's head down now — he's ready to come out any day," Liv reminded him.

Baird went suddenly pale. "Gods, you're right! This baby could come at *any minute*." He began waddling as fast as he could toward the bedroom door.

"Hey, where are you going?" Liv demanded. "The bathroom's *that* way."

"Forget the bathroom." Baird was already panting with exertion but he showed no signs of stopping. "We have to see Sylvan and get ourselves switched back *now*."

* * * * *

"But there's no switching back — at least, we haven't found a way yet," Olivia, who met Saber and Lissa at the docking bay, explained. Of course, she was wearing Baird's body but Lissa had gotten to know her well enough to recognize her speech patterns. Also, she *moved* like a woman. It was strange to see the massive warrior's body walk with a sway in the hips and even stranger to watch as Olivia forgot her hair was short and tried to sweep it back over one shoulder.

"No wonder you're worried," she said. "This must be so frightening for you."

"It takes some getting used to," Olivia admitted, in her deep, growling voice.

"Liv—there you are." Sylvan—or rather Sophia in Sylvan's body—came mincing up to stand by her sister's side. "Baird said you were here explaining everything to Lissa and Saber."

Lissa couldn't help staring again—it was so strange to watch the blond Kindred doctor's face making his mate's facial expressions.

"They just got in, as you can see." Olivia gestured at the two of them. "What's up? What does Baird need now?"

"He says to find out if anyone is going down to Earth so they can bring him back a gallon of Ben and Jerry's Brownie Batter ice cream—not the yogurt kind, the *real* ice cream."

"Got it," Olivia muttered. "The real stuff. But it only comes in pints—not gallons."

"He knows that." Sophia nodded. "He says he wants at least eight of them—a gallon."

"God," Olivia shook her head. "All right, tell him I'm on it. Anything he wants, he gets. After all, he *is* twelve months pregnant." She looked over her sister's broad shoulder. "Oh, and speaking of pregnant, here's your better half."

"Sylvan!" Sophia turned and Lissa watched as the Earth girl's mate—who was, of course, wearing her body—came striding across the docking bay. Once again, it was strange to watch him walk. The small feminine body moved with masculine purpose and for some reason, he wasn't wearing any shoes.

"Sophia, sweetheart." Sylvan reached up to give her an awkward embrace. Sophia tried to hug him back but it looked to Lissa like she wasn't quite sure what to do with her long, muscular arms.

"I thought you were in the med lab," Sophia said, looking down at her husband. "Is something wrong?"

"I had something important to tell you but now I can't remember what it was." Sylvan looked irritated. "Damn it, I can't *think* in this body."

"It's the pregnancy hormones," Olivia said. "Did you know that you lose ten IQ points with every baby you have?"

"Yes, the pregnancy hormones!" Sylvan exclaimed. He looked up at his wife. "I felt them."

"What? You felt what?" Sophia frowned.

"The babies—I felt them move for the first time." Sylvan stroked the softly rounded curve of his abdomen.

"You did? Oh my God!" Sophia dropped to her knees and pressed her cheek to his belly. "When? Where?"

"Just a few minutes ago, on my way up here."

Sophia looked up at him, her face a mixture of joy and disappointment. "That's wonderful, honey. But, well....*I* wanted to be the one to feel them kick the first time."

"Don't worry about that," Olivia said dryly as Sophia finally got to her feet. "You'll get kicked *plenty* once we get switched back into our right bodies. Just ask Baird."

Saber cleared his throat. "So has *everyone* aboard the ship been affected?"

"Almost everyone," Sylvan said, still stroking his belly. "The mated Beast Kindred and Blood Kindred have all swapped bodies with their brides. The unmated males seem to have swapped with whoever they were closest to at the time that whatever is causing this phenomenon first happened." He frowned. "I'm afraid there have been some savage conflicts in the unmated males area because of it."

"Apparently the guys don't want anybody else, er..." Olivia cleared her throat. "Handling their equipment, if you know what I mean."

"Of course." Lissa nodded. "That, uh, makes sense, I guess."

"Pretty much the only unaffected ones are Lauren and Xairn," Sophia said. "Sylvan thinks that's because Xairn is Scourge, not Kindred."

"What about Merrick and Elise?" Olivia asked. "I thought you said they might have been unaffected because Merrick is a hybrid."

Sylvan shook his head. "I checked on them earlier—they've swapped all right. They've just decided to stay in their suite and try to ride things out until we can set this right. Speaking of that..." He turned to Saber. "You said you got the scroll?"

"Here it is." Saber handed it over without meeting the other male's eyes. "I hope it helps," he muttered.

"So do we." Sophia put a hand on his arm. "Thank you so much for getting it. You two are heroes."

"Thank you," Lissa whispered through numb lips. Saber said nothing—he only stared at Sophia's large hand on his arm until she murmured,

"Sorry," and withdrew.

Lissa didn't want to cry so she tried to turn back to the conversation at hand. "You said how this, er, swapping has affected everyone else. But what about the Twin Kindred?"

"Oh, we're affected all right." Suddenly Deep and Lock, Kat's mates, came around the corner to stand with them.

Sylvan frowned. "What is this—some kind of docking bay meeting? What are you two doing here?"

"We're here to meet our lady Kat," Deep said courteously. "She's being flown up from Earth on a shuttle—which is probably that one landing now." He pointed at a small silver shuttle touching down in the landing area. "We put off bringing her back for as long as we could so as not to confuse and frighten her but…"

"But she's going to find out somehow. And the longer we keep her in the dark, the angrier she's going to be," Lock, the light twin finished. He frowned at Sylvan. "Hey, Brother, you mind me asking why in the seven hells you're running around barefoot?"

Sylvan looked down at his bare feet and grimaced. "I had on some of Sophia's shoes—you know the kind with heels? But they felt *horrible*. My arches were killing me—I had to take them off."

"Wait a minute." Sophia rounded on him, putting a ham-sized fist to her narrow hip. "Were you wearing the red ones with the little tiny bows?"

"Well…yes." Sylvan looked uncomfortable.

"Honey! Those are my favorite pair of Jimmy Choos!" Sophia's blond brows drew low and her deep voice boomed. "Where did you leave them? Those were *expensive*."

"I don't know—all right?" Sylvan burst out. "I can't remember. Just like I can't remember what I came down here to tell you in the first place. This ridiculous body—"

"Is carrying your twin babies, which is why it's so forgetful." Sophia had a dangerous glint in her ice blue eyes. "And if you *ever* want to touch it again once you get out of it, you'd better watch what you say, Mister!"

"I'm sorry!" Sylvan looked like he might cry.

"Stop it, Sophie! Apologize *now*," Olivia demanded, grabbing her sister by the arm. "You can't yell at Sylvan like that—he's *pregnant*."

Lock shook his head. "Wow and I thought *we* had it bad. At least we still have the right equipment—even if it is someone else's."

"Don't be insensitive," Deep chided his brother. "Sylvan and Sophia are going through a lot right now. They don't need you gloating and making things worse."

"Who's gloating?" Lock demanded. "You think I *like* this? Even if we *are* twins, it's still weird."

Lissa frowned as she tried to follow this exchange. Clearly something had happened to the two of them since she had last seen them. Deep, the dark twin had always been more argumentative and cantankerous while Lock was the soul of courtesy.

"So did the two of you...?" She frowned at them and made a back and forth motion with one hand.

"Yup." Lock sighed. "It's a real pain."

"The only pain I feel is the damage you're doing to my reputation," Deep who was apparently Lock snarled at his brother. "Everyone thinks I'm an insensitive bastard now because of you."

"So?" Lock who must be Deep smiled lazily. "What's the big deal about that?"

"Hello, boys, what did I miss?" Kat came striding up, a frown on her face. "And why the hell didn't the two of you visit me in the hospital? Some fiancés you are. I had to make all kinds of excuses to my grandma about why you couldn't come."

"Forgive us, my lady." The dark twin went to one knee before her and kissed her hand gallantly. "It was inexcusable for us to not visit you. But your grandmother assured us you were safe. And well, things aboard the Mother Ship…"

"Are all fucked up at the moment," the light twin finished for his brother with a frown. He came forward too and gave Kat a hug. "Welcome home, little Kat."

"Wait a minute, wait a minute…" Kat pulled out of the embrace, frowning at her males. "What's going on here? Why are you two talking like that? It's like invasion of the body snatchers around here or something."

"Actually, that's not far off," Olivia said. Rapidly, she recounted what had happened to everyone aboard the Mother Ship while Kat gaped at her.

Finally she shook her head and looked back at her males. "So you're Deep?" she asked, pointing at the light twin. "And you're Lock?" pointing at the dark twin.

They nodded in unison.

"But we don't have it nearly as bad as everyone else," Lock who was actually Deep put in. "Sylvan and Baird are pregnant and Baird could go into labor at any time."

"Not to worry though, my lady," Deep who was Lock said soothingly. "Saber and Lissa have returned with the missing scroll. Since we're almost certain this is a Hoard attack, we're hopeful that the scroll will contain information about how to best the Hoard Master and switch things back to normal."

"Got the scrolls, did you?" Lock who was Deep smirked annoyingly at Saber. "Interesting. And what *exactly* did you have to do to get them?"

"You son of a bitch," Saber growled. Stepping forward he punched Lock in the jaw, causing the light twin to stagger backward. Then he elbowed his way through the little crowd and stormed off, away from the docking bay.

"Saber? Saber, wait!" Lissa tried to run after him but he was walking fast, his broad shoulders set in lines of angry tension. And though she was sure he heard her call his name, he never even turned around once. After a moment she gave up and slowly made her way back to the little group in the docking bay.

"Look what you did," Deep who was Lock was complaining as he examined his brother's jaw. "That's going to leave a mark. Can't you stop being an arrogant bastard at least while you're in my body?"

"Sorry." His brother winced and rubbed his jaw. "Damn, those Touch Kindred pack a punch! All I did was ask what he had to do to get the scroll."

"He did much more than should ever have been required of him. Of either one of us." Lissa's voice trembled. "It...I think it broke something in him. I know it broke something in me," she added as the tears stung her lids.

"Oh, Lissa, hon..." Kat put an arm around her shoulders and shot Lock who was Deep a dirty look. "It's all right," she said. "Everything is going to be all right, doll."

"I'm sorry," Lissa whispered in a choked voice. "I...I don't have any right to be upset. Not with everything all of you are going through." She sniffed and swiped at her eyes. "Did...does anyone know what caused this body swapping in the first place?"

"We think it has something to do with the imposter we accidentally brought up from Earth," Deep who was Lock said. "It impersonated my lady Kat and fooled us into bringing it aboard.

We've searched the entire ship but we can't find it—probably because it can change forms at will."

Sylvan snapped his fingers. *"That's* what I was coming to say. I've been doing some research and the only kind of creature I've read about who can mutate their body to assume other forms is a shadow caster—they come from the splicing district on *O'ah.*"

"Wait a minute—isn't that where Lauren and Xairn went to get their DNA altered?" Olivia asked.

Sylvan nodded. "Yes, it is." He shook his head. "The strange thing is, that shadow casters are usually clones. Because only a clone has the necessary genetic elasticity to mutate their shape at will."

Sophia frowned. "But Kat hasn't been cloned, have you, Kat woman?"

Kat shook her head slowly but Lissa noticed that her face had gone suddenly pale. "I wasn't but Lauren *was.* And that thing...before it took my face and looked like me, it looked like her first." She looked at Sylvan. "It looked *just like Lauren.*"

Sylvan's delicate features grew grim. "When was the last time anyone spoke to Lauren and Xairn? They may be in grave danger."

Chapter Twenty-seven

L knocked at the door and then slid away quickly, assuming another form. There was a pause and then she watched from the corridor as the door slid open and her original looked out.

Her original who had been completely unaffected by the device Draven had hired L to plant on the Mother Ship. Everyone else on the damn ship was in an uproar—but not L's original or her man. As far as L could tell, the two people she hated most in the universe were doing just fine. They had each other and they were perfectly happy and unaffected by Draven's grand revenge scheme.

It made L so angry she had taken out the crystal surveillance device he had given her to wear and ground it to shards beneath her heel. She was certain that had pissed the Hoard Master off but she really didn't care—she had no intention of ever returning to his horrible planet. Instead, she was going to stay here and take her revenge into her own hands.

To that end, she'd been watching her original, tracking her every movement for the past few days, observing everything she did, listening in on every conversation. She'd had several good opportunities to kill her already but for some reason she hadn't taken them.

L wasn't sure what kept her from completing her revenge. Maybe it was the memories or maybe the same emotional weakness that had been growing inside her since she had spared Kat's life instead of killing her. She hated her original with every fiber of her being—she was sure she did. And yet...and yet somehow she just couldn't bring herself to do the final deed.

The weakness ends now, L told herself firmly. *This is it. They're looking for me everywhere – I can't hang around here forever. I have to do what I came to do and get out.*

L watched as her original looked up and down the seemingly empty corridor.

"Hello? Is anyone there?" Lauren looked perplexed.

L allowed herself a small smile, although it didn't really show in the form she had taken. She was disguised as part of the curving silver wall. Taking an inorganic form was difficult and exhausting but it was only for a moment. As soon as her original turned her head to look down the hallway, she melted into a more familiar form and stepped forward.

"Oh, Olivia!" Lauren put a hand to her chest. "What are you doing here? You scared me to death! Or...er..." she frowned. "Is that you or Baird? Sorry, it's just...everything is so confusing now."

"It's me," L said in a perfect imitation of the blonde Earth girl's voice. "I just came to tell you we found a way to switch everyone back. Ugh..." She put a hand to her back and stroked her fully rounded abdomen. "Can I come in and sit down? Ever since I switched bodies back with Baird I feel more pregnant than ever."

"Of course you can." Lauren patted her own belly, which was also curving, though not nearly as much. "I know the feeling—I get more preggy every day."

"Thanks." L waddled past her into the spacious living area. "Oh..." she sighed as she sank down into one of the plush couches. "That's better. Where's Xairn?"

Lauren shut the door. "He's out running an errand. I wanted to go with him but he asked me to stay put—they still haven't caught that weird whatever it was impersonating Kat, you know?"

"Yes." L stood and began to shift, her features flowing and changing as she assumed her original form—the one that was identical to the female across from her. "I know."

✳ ✳ ✳ ✳ ✳

Lauren felt like her heart had just frozen in her chest. The face staring back at her was her own, down to the last detail. She knew at once who it was—her clone. The one they had left behind in the splicing district of *O'ah*.

"Oh," she whispered, putting a hand to her chest. "It's *you*."

"Yes, it's me." The clone stepped forward, a cold light gleaming in the amber eyes identical to Laruen's. "The one you left behind, hundreds of light years from the planet my memories told me was home. The one you left to be sold into the skin trade, to satisfy the animalistic lusts of any male with enough credit to buy me. The one *he* found unacceptable—defective. Disgusting. All because I wasn't really *you*."

All Lauren's instincts told her she should run but emotion kept her rooted to the spot. Ever since she and Xairn had fled the splicing district of *O'ah*, she had feared, in the back of her mind that this day would come.

At first she'd been angry and scared that the clone of her had been made at all. But later she'd begun thinking of it from the clone's perspective—after all, it wasn't *her* fault she'd been made. And if she really did have all Lauren's memories, if she actually thought she *was* Lauren, how horrible must it have been to be left behind, to see their ship blast off and leave her stranded on an alien world so far from home. To know she could never, ever get back...

"Oh," she whispered, coming forward. "I'm so sorry. So, *so* sorry."

"What?" The clone had raising some kind of a weapon—to Lauren it looked like a syringe filled with green goo—but she stopped in mid-motion and frowned at Lauren instead. "What did you say?"

"We never should have left you there," Lauren whispered, holding out a hand to the other girl. "You must hate me so much."

"I do." The clone lifted her chin but some of the fire had gone out of her eyes. "I've been planning how to kill you ever since you left me."

The threat was frightening, of course but Lauren thought she heard something else in it as well. A plea for recognition, perhaps. The cry of anger and pain from a lost, frightened child who has been shut out in the cold night.

"I'm so sorry," she said again, holding out both hands this time and taking another step forward. "We left you in that horrible place with no one to trust, no one to care for you. No way to get home." She shook her head. "I don't have any excuses to give you except that I was scared half out of my mind. The idea of being replaced, of Xairn abandoning me for someone who looked just like me—who practically *was* me—was so frightening I couldn't face it. I had to run away."

"That was exactly how I felt. I wanted to run away too." The other girl's voice wobbled, just a bit. "But there was nowhere to go." She swiped at her eyes angrily. "I remembered growing up in California, remembered Mom. My childhood there, the first boy I ever kissed. High school. College. Opening a bakery. Being taken up to the Scourge father ship and held. Falling in love with Xairn…but none of those were my memories. They were *yours*."

"They're yours too," Lauren whispered. "You're part of me, don't you see? You're like the sister I never had."

"Stop it!" the clone barked angrily. "Stop pretending to care!"

"You know I'm not pretending," Lauren said softly. "You know because you have my thoughts and feelings and memories. You know because you *are* me."

"Not anymore." The clone crossed her arms protectively over her chest. "I took another path. I toughened up—did what I had to survive."

"And I don't blame you for that," Lauren said. "But deep down under all that, you're still me. Still the same basic person. So you know when I say I care, that I'm sorry, I mean it with all my heart."

"I'm a trained assassin! A shadow caster," the clone protested, taking a step backward. "I could kill you in the blink of an eye."

"You could," Lauren admitted. "You still can if you want, but that won't heal your heart or stop the pain. Only love can do that."

"What are you talking about?" the other Lauren scoffed. "Are you saying you love me?"

"I don't know because I don't really know you. But I could," Lauren said softly. "Mom could too."

"She wouldn't want me!" the clone protested. "You're just saying anything you can to save your life."

"That's not true and you know it." Lauren took another step toward the retreating clone. "Did you know that I had a twin sister but she died when I was born?"

"That's not true—that's nowhere in my memories."

"That's because Mom only told me recently, when I found out I was pregnant," Lauren said quietly. "She kept it from me for all these years because she didn't want to hurt me." She sighed. "Growing up, I always felt like a part of me was missing. I wanted a sister so badly—I used to ask Mom for one constantly when I was little. I only stopped when I realized how sad it made her."

"Oh…" The soft exclamation sounded broken somehow and Lauren sensed she was getting through to the other girl.

"So I finally get a chance to have a sister and what do I do? I abandon her." She shook her head. "Truly, I don't deserve another chance. But I wish you'd stay—stay and give me a chance to love you the way you ought to be loved. Like the sister I've been looking for all my life." She held her arms open. "Please?"

The other girl hesitated. Lauren could tell she wanted to come in for a hug but she was still wary, still scared.

"You wouldn't be so quick to say you could care for me if you knew what I've done," the clone whispered. "I've killed so many people."

Lauren regarded her steadily. "I'll tell you exactly what I've told Xairn—you did what you had to do to survive in a tough situation. I don't judge you for that."

"But your friends— I'm the one who set off the device that swapped their bodies and minds."

This gave Lauren pause. "Well," she said at last. "Can you swap them back?"

"I don't know." The clone shook her head. "I shouldn't even be telling you this. Draven paid me to do the job. I did it but it didn't affect you and Xairn. And that made me so *angry* – you're the ones I wanted revenge on in the first place."

"And do you still?" Lauren asked, her heart beating hard. Had she gotten through to her clone? Or would this conversation end with her death?

"I...I don't know." A troubled look passed over the familiar face. "I want to believe what you say. And my memories of wanting a sister and feeling I was missing something are the same as yours. But..." She shook her head. "I just don't know if I can trust you."

"Do you trust yourself?" Lauren asked softly.

Slowly, the other girl nodded.

"Then you know you can trust me too. Don't you see? You're not really my clone—you're my twin. We're sisters. Now come here and give me a hug."

She held out her arms demandingly and this time the other girl came to her without protest. Lauren folded her in her arms and held her tight, so many emotions rushing through her she couldn't help but cry.

"My sister," she whispered into the other girl's ear as tears stung her eyes. "You're my sister."

The clone hugged her tentatively at first but then her grip became tighter and she began to cry too.

"I've been so afraid for so long. Alone for so long. I hated you so much but now...now I just want to come home."

"You're home," Lauren assured her. "You're finally home."

Just then the door to her suite burst open, allowing a crowd of people armed with blasters and led by Xairn to charge in.

"She's strangling her!" someone shouted. "That clone-thing is strangling Lauren! Shoot! Shoot!"

"No, wait!" Lauren pushed her clone behind her protectively. "Get back—she's with me."

"But which one of them is which?" Kat, who was at the front of the charge, demanded. "How can we be sure the real Lauren isn't being held hostage here?"

"I can tell them apart—I have before," Xairn growled. Stepping forward, he inhaled deeply, his red-on-black eyes narrowing as he analyzed their scents. "Lauren," he said at last, frowning at her. "Why are you protecting this imposter?"

"She's not an imposter." Lauren lifted her chin. "She's the sister I always wanted but never had. And you'd damn well better treat her that way—anyone who doesn't will have to answer to *me*."

"Lauren, honey, think what you're saying," Kat said gently. "This, er, *person* attacked me and sneaked aboard the ship. We're pretty certain she's the reason everyone has swapped bodies like some kind of a B grade horror movie."

"I am," the clone said unexpectedly. She stepped out from behind Lauren. "I admit what I did but I'm willing to help fix it. And as for you, Kat," she continued. "I'm very sorry for assaulting you. But you should know that I could have killed you instead—I intended to, actually. But my memories—Lauren's memories—stopped me." She held out a hand. "Can you forgive me?"

"Well..." Kat looked at her uncertainly. "I have to be honest, doll, I'm a little creeped out right now. But if you can switch my men back to their regular bodies, I think I can see my way clear to giving you a pass this time." She cleared her throat. "As long as you promise never to come near me with a shot full of green goop again." She nodded at the syringe the clone was still holding.

"Oh!" the clone dropped the syringe and took a step back from it. "I'm sorry—I didn't realize I was still holding it."

Lock, who was actually Deep, had come in with Kat. He reached down and snatched up the syringe. "So that's it? We just forgive her and pretend she's part of the family?"

"I'm *not* pretending." Lauren narrowed her eyes at him. "Have you ever heard the tale of the prodigal son in the Bible?" She put an arm around her clone's shoulders. "Well, she's like that. She..." Abruptly she stopped and looked at the other girl. "I'm sorry, I don't know your name. Do you go by Lauren too?"

The clone shook her head shyly. "No, that name belongs to you. I just call myself L."

"L." Lauren smiled. "I like that."

Sylvan, who was still in Sophia's body, came forward and addressed them both. "You realize she'll probably have to go before the Kindred Council?"

Lauren bit her lip. "I hadn't thought about that. I don't want anything bad to happen to L."

Sylvan shook his head. "It probably won't—if she can fix what she's done. No deaths have resulted from L's mischief, which is very lucky for her." He looked at L. "Can you fix it?"

"Yes." L lifted her chin and nodded toward the door. "All of you come with me right now—we're going to take care of this."

"Wait for me!" Lauren grabbed her hand and smiled at L's surprised look. "I've waited years to have a sister and I let you go once. I'm not letting go again."

The tentative smile that L returned warmed her heart. "Okay," she said softly and squeezed Lauren's hand. "Let's go."

Chapter Twenty-eight

"So they're going to change us back?" Baird couldn't keep the hopeful sound out of his voice as he struggled to sit up in bed.

"That's what they say." Olivia sighed and then smiled at him and pressed his hand. "I'm glad. I didn't want to miss giving birth to our son. Even if it probably is going to hurt like hell."

Sophia, who was still in Sylvan's body, nudged her in the ribs. "Don't talk like that. At least not until after everyone is switched back."

"Right. Sorry." Olivia nodded. "Sylvan's at the scene, right? Are they doing it yet?"

Sophia closed her eyes for a moment, concentrating on the mental link she had with her husband. "Sylvan says they're in the sacred grove and Lauren's clone is showing them the device. She's going to try and switch it off—everybody get ready!"

Baird and Olivia held hands tightly.

"Ready!" they said in unison.

"Okay." Sophia got a look of anticipation on her face. "She's switching it off...now."

Everyone waited tensely, expecting to be catapulted into their respective bodies but nothing happened. Then Baird let out a horrible groan.

"Honey, are you okay?" Olivia opened her eyes and looked anxiously at her husband, who was still stuck in her body. "Did whatever they did to the device hurt you?"

"I...I don't think so." He groaned again. "I just had the worst pain—a massive cramp, like someone stabbing me in the back."

"Oh God." Olivia looked up at her sister. "Get Sylvan here quick. I think he's in labor!"

* * * * *

Sylvan stepped out of the bedroom and swiped at his forehead with the back of one arm in a most unladylike way. "He's all right for now. I've given him something to delay the labor but it won't last for long."

"What are we going to do?" Olivia was practically wringing her hands with worry. "I feel awful! I was so glad to have some time off from being pregnant but I never meant for it to go this far. I never meant for him to actually *have the baby!*"

"I know you didn't, mate of my kin." Sylvan squeezed her arm reassuringly.

"It's not your fault," Sophia chimed in, putting an arm around her sister.

"I know it's not but it *feels* like it is. I was so tired of feeling miserable all the time."

"Of course you were," her twin murmured. "I'm sure we'll *all* feel that way in our last quadmester. The human body isn't really *meant* to spend a whole entire year being pregnant."

"Sophia is right." Sylvan nodded. "But don't let guilt overcome you yet, Olivia. There is still a chance that we might get the two of you switched back in time for you to give birth. We just need to study the scrolls from First World and see what they say about how to defeat the Hoard Master."

"I'll tell you what they say," a new voice said from the doorway. They all looked up in surprise as Lissa came in, a copy of the ancient scrolls dangling limply from one hand.

"Lissa, honey, are you all right?" Sophia asked carefully.

"Sorry for coming in unannounced." Lissa's eyes were red, as though she'd been crying. "But since everyone has been busy with everything else, I decided to study the scrolls myself."

"And what did you find?" Sylvan asked, coming over to her.

"That everything we did to get this…this *stupid thing* was all for nothing." Lissa's hand tightened on the paper, crumpling it. "It says here that no one—male or female—born of woman can kill the Hoard Master."

"No," Olivia whispered. "No, that can't be true."

"I'm afraid so," Lissa said. "The only way Counselor Kall overcame him a thousand years ago was by making the ultimate sacrifice—he left First World and in so doing, he lost his wings. Without them, he had no advantage in the fight with Draven and no way to heal himself. And so he lost his life."

"Are you saying that someone has to *die* in order to kill the Hoard Master and swap us all back?" Sophia demanded.

Slowly, Lissa nodded. "And so I'd like…I'd like to volunteer myself."

"*What?*" Olivia and Sophia said at the same time.

"You can't be serious." Sylvan looked at her blankly.

"Oh, yes, I am." Lissa lifted her chin. "Just wire me with some kind of explosive and send me to him. The minute we come in contact, you can press the button and blow both of us up."

"We could never do that, Lissa," Sophia said, looking shocked.

"And besides, Merrick already tried to blow him up once," Olivia pointed out. "It didn't work."

"It *will* work," Lissa insisted. "I tell you, I've been studying this scroll for hours—a sacrifice is the only way to best the Hoard Master."

"If a sacrifice is needed, I'll be the one to make it."

They all looked up as L, followed by Lauren, Xairn and Kat, came into the room.

"What did you say?" Olivia asked, frowning.

"You heard me. I brought this mess on you all," L said, crossing her arms over her breasts. "And I vowed to fix it. So if anyone has to make a sacrifice, it will be me."

"But...but I just found you again." Lauren looked stricken.

"I know." L squeezed her hand. "And I'm sorry, my sister. But I have to fix the damage I did. Besides..." She smiled. "No one else is as qualified as me to do this. I've already gotten onto Hrakaz undetected once and I can take any form I need to in order to get to him."

"But L—" Lauren began.

"No, I've decided." L frowned. "I was afraid switching off the device might not work. Draven told me when he gave it to me that it was tied to his will—he's the engine behind it. Stop the engine and you stop the effect."

"So you're going to kill him?" Sylvan asked.

"If there's no other way," L said grimly.

"Kat, is Lauren's clone in here with you?" Deep who was actually Lock suddenly appeared in the doorway of the now crowded living area.

"She's here—where have *you* been?" Kat asked, turning around.

"Fielding a call from First World. Nadiah is on the viewscreen in the viewing room. She says she needs to talk to L."

"What? But how does she even *know* about L?" Lauren demanded. "We just found out about her ourselves and Nadiah is light years away!"

Lock shrugged. "She says she has a message from the Goddess. Something she needs to tell L before she goes to Hrakaz."

"So she not only knows about L, she knows she's going to try and stop the Hoard Master too." Sophia shook her head in wonder. "That's amazing."

"That's the Goddess," Sylvan said reverently. "Go L—don't keep her waiting."

"I'll go with her," Lauren said but Lock shook his head. "Nadiah says only L is to go."

L frowned. "Did she say what she wanted to talk to me about?" she asked.

Lock shook his head. "No, only that she needed to speak to you. Come on—let's not keep her waiting."

Chapter Twenty-nine

L followed Kat's man to a room dominated by a viewscreen that took up one whole wall. On the screen, looking regal, was a slender woman with pale blonde hair and blue-green eyes. Beside her stood an imposing man with a huge pair of feathery, iridescent wings.

"You must be L, Lauren's sister," the woman smiled at her. "I'm Nadiah and I'm happy to meet you."

L was surprised. How could this woman, whom she had never seen before, know that was how Lauren thought of her? How could she know it was how L thought of herself, after finally making contact with her original?

"I am," she said carefully. "Well, actually, I'm her clone."

Nadiah shook her head. "Sister is the word I was given by the Goddess. She wants to speak to you, you know. Before you leave for Hrakaz."

"I don't mean any disrespect but I don't really believe in any—"

That was as far as L got before Nadiah's eyes, whites and all, turned a solid emerald green and her voice took on a deep and powerful resonance L could feel all the way down in her bones. Goosebumps rippled down her arms and her doubt disappeared in an instant—she knew instinctively that she was in the presence of the supernatural. The very air around her seemed to crackle as the Goddess spoke.

"My daughter, it does not matter if you believe in me for I believe in *you*. I foresaw your coming thousands of years ago. Why do you think I spoke the prophecy over Draven's birth into this universe that no one—male or female—born of woman should be able to best him? I knew that you would come—you who have neither mother nor father—to save him from himself."

"I don't know if I was going to *save* him, exactly," L said, frowning. "Actually, I'm pretty sure I'll have to kill him."

A look of pain passed over the Goddess's delicate features. "If he dies now, in his current soulless state, he will be cast into the seventh hell—the pit from which there is no escape. Not even I can draw him from such depths—his damnation will be final and eternal." She drew in a deep breath and the emerald green eyes shone with unshed tears. "My prodigal son. How I would mourn his loss."

L felt a twinge of sorrow for the Goddess's pain. The prodigal son—wasn't that what Lauren had compared her to? A child who had gone far astray but who still wanted to return home?

"I'm sorry," she said, crossing her arms over her chest. "But I'm not sure what else I can do."

"There is a way, my daughter, if you are brave."

L lifted her chin. "I'm not afraid of anything."

"Good." A smile curved the Goddess's lips. "Then listen well— the loss of his soul is what turned Draven into the creature he is today. I had hoped that during his enforced convalescence over these last thousand years it might have regenerated."

"It may have—a little," L said cautiously. "He, uh, shared some things with me that were surprisingly personal. And even though he sent me to sabotage the Kindred, he didn't want to kill them—he just wanted to do some mischief." She shrugged. "Although I admit, switching everyone into different bodies is more than just mischievous. It's painful and I'm sorry for it."

"You shall undo all the sorrow that has been done by your hand," the Goddess said. "What you tell me of Draven cheers me greatly but I fear we don't have time for his soul to regenerate further. His next attack on my other children may be more savage and they are in chaos now, unable to defend themselves."

"The body swapping *has* caused a lot of confusion," L admitted ruefully. "But what can I do to stop Draven short of killing him?"

"As I said before, it is his lack of more than a shred of a soul that makes him as he is. If you are willing to share *your* soul with him, his conscience and innate goodness would return—as well as his other angelic attributes."

"Share my soul?" L objected. "But...I'm a clone. I don't have a soul to share."

"Yes, you do, my daughter." The Goddess smiled at her. "You have the soul of Lauren's twin—the one who died when her mother gave birth to her. Why do you think you felt so drawn to her? Why could you not kill her? Why were you unable to resist her love when she offered it to you?"

"Her...her twin?" L shook her head in wonderment. "Then...I really *am* her sister?"

"Search your heart, L," the Goddess said gently. "You know it to be true. Her soul cried out to yours and yours answered it. That is why you felt so instantly at home in her arms. That is why you are willing now to risk your life to save those she loves." She leaned forward. "But I believe you feel such an affinity for Draven too, do you not?"

L thought of her pity for the Hoard Master when he cried out in his sleep, of her horror at hearing his sad tale and her wonder that he would reveal it to her at all.

"I do," she admitted. "But Goddess, he's utterly ruthless. And I don't have any idea how to go about sharing my soul."

"I will not lie, it is dangerous in the extreme. And failure could result in your death."

"Just tell me," L said. "I told you I'm not afraid."

The Goddess smiled. "Your courage does you credit, daughter. Very well, I will tell you. Listen carefully…"

She outlined her plan while L listened, taking mental notes. As the Goddess said, it was extremely dangerous—an all or nothing shot. To an outsider it would look like suicide. But when she thought of the tears in Draven's blank silver eyes and the pain in his voice, she knew she had to try it. She just hoped she would survive but if she didn't…

"I'll do my best," she told the Goddess. "But you're right—it's really risky. What if I fail?"

The Goddess looked sad. "If you fail, Counselor Rast will repeat his father's sacrifice. He will likely not survive and all of First World will be in mourning, especially this little one I am speaking through now. But he should be able to put Draven out of action for at least another thousand years."

L drew herself up. "That's not going to be necessary. I *refuse* to fail."

"I'm so proud of you, my daughter." The Goddess smiled gently. "I thank you for your courage. And I swear to you now that even if you are not able to bring Draven back to himself, you will not die in vain. You and your twin, Lauren *will* be united after death. That I promise you."

"Thank you." L felt a lump in her throat. "I…I'd like that. I'd like a chance to get to know my sister."

"And you will," the Goddess said gently. "In the fullness of time. Now go and take my blessings with you."

"Thank you, Goddess." L bowed her head respectfully and left the viewing room.

She wanted a chance to say goodbye so she decided to try and find her sister. But when she looked up, Lauren was already coming down the hallway toward her.

* * * * *

The minute Lauren looked in her sister's eyes, she knew.

"You're going, aren't you?" she asked, gripping L's hand and squeezing it tightly. "You really are going."

"I have to, Lauren. I'm the only one who can." L squeezed back. "I'm so sorry. I know we haven't had much time together."

"Much time!" Lauren exclaimed. "We haven't even had a whole hour alone. I feel like we've got a lifetime of catching up to do and now you're leaving again, possibly never...never to return." She could barely get the words out; they stuck in her throat and made her want to cry.

"I'll be all right," L assured her earnestly. "This kind of thing is my bread and butter — I've had the best training in the universe."

"I don't want you to go," Lauren whispered. "I mean, I understand why you have to. But I can't help it. I feel like we were meant to be together."

"That's because we were." L smiled at her sadly. "The Goddess told me there was a reason for our instant connection."

"There is? What?" Lauren looked at her anxiously but L only shook her head.

"I'll tell you when I get back — I promise."

"But—" Lauren began but just then Olivia came jogging up to them, still wearing her mate's body.

"Hi guys, I don't mean to butt in here but we kind of need to know what L is going to do. Because, well…" Her face twisted. "Baird has gone into labor again and this time Sylvan says he can't stop it."

"I'm leaving right now," L assured her. "I was just saying goodbye to my sister." She pressed Lauren's hand again. "I have to go, you know I do."

"I know." Lauren pulled her into a tight hug. "Just be careful. And come back to me—we have a lot of talking to do. And I still have to introduce you to Mom."

"I want to meet her with all my heart—especially since the memories I have of her tell me what a wonderful mother she was." L sounded wistful. "I always wanted a real mother."

"She's going to love you," Lauren assured her. She sighed. "Well I guess…guess you should go. Do you want me to come to the docking bay with you?"

L shook her head. "I can run a lot faster than you—I'm not pregnant. And time is of the essence now." She nodded at Olivia who was still wringing her hands in agitation. Then she looked at Lauren. "Goodbye, sister."

"Goodbye, sister," Lauren echoed. "I…I love you."

A warm look came into L's amber eyes. "I love you too. And I promise I'll be back."

With a final wave, she set off at a jog down the corridor. When she passed the curve in the long metal hallway, she disappeared from sight.

Lauren sighed heavily. "There she goes. I basically just met her and yet…I feel like I've known her all my life."

"I'm sorry," Olivia said sadly. "It's not right for us to ask you to risk your sister."

Lauren shook her head. "No, it's fair. You and Sophie and Kat all sent your men to help Xairn when he had to face off against the AllFather. You put your happiness on the line for me—I can do no less for you."

"I just want you to know how grateful I am." Olivia pressed her hand. "And how sorry. But, well, I'd probably better get back to Baird. He's uh, not handling the contractions very well."

Lauren sighed. "I understand—go be with him."

Olivia squeezed her hand one more time and then went jogging down the corridor, in the opposite direction L had taken.

Lauren walked slowly back, her feet dragging and her eyes unseeing as she somehow traversed the long metal hallway. Would she ever see L again? It sounded strange since they had just meet but she truly did feel that she had just sent a beloved sister into the lion's den. *We belong together. She's part of me.* A part she had barely even begun to know before it was ripped away...

"Lauren..."

The deep, familiar voice shook her out of her silent contemplation. Lauren looked up to see Xairn striding along the corridor.

"Olivia said I could find you here. Are you all right?" he asked gently, putting an arm around her. "You're crying."

"Am I?" Lauren put her fingertips to her face and they came away wet. "Oh. I guess I am."

"You cared for her deeply, didn't you?" Xairn asked. "I can see it in your eyes."

"She was like the sister I never had." Lauren took a deep breath and let it out as a sob. "I know...know that doesn't make any sense but it's how I feel."

"It's all right." Xairn pulled her close and stroked her hair gently. "Everything will be all right, my love."

Lauren buried her face in his broad chest and breathed him in, the dark spicy scent that had come to mean safety, security and love. But though Xairn's strong arms around her comforted her as nothing else could, she couldn't stem the rising tide of sorrow or shake the feeling that she would never see L alive again.

Chapter Thirty

"She broke the device! Damn it—how dare she spoil my fun! What's the point of switching them around if I can't see the results?" Draven raged, kicking aside the imp who was timidly offering him wine. "I should have planted a real bomb—one that would blow the entire fucking ship out of the sky! I should—"

"My, my—such language. You kiss your mother with that mouth?"

"What?" Draven turned in surprise just in time to see part of the wall melt into a human shape. It was the shadow caster in her true form—a slender girl with amber eyes and creamy light brown skin. He blinked and she was gone again, perfectly camouflaged somewhere in the room.

"I met her, you know—your mother." Her voice came from somewhere on his left.

"I don't have a mother," she said sharply. "Any more than you do."

"Not true. I met the Goddess and she still cares for you, Draven. In fact, she loves you desperately."

"Why should I care?" he demanded, searching the room with his eyes. Where was she exactly?

"Because she loves you. Loves enough to give you another chance."

"So she sent you? After converting you to "good"? Now why in the seven hells would she bother doing that?" Draven snarled, still looking for her.

"Maybe because she thought I cared for you." The shadow caster's voice was little more than a whisper now. "She thought there was something between us…something that might grow."

Draven was shaken but he tried not to show it.

"And you *believed* her?" he sneered, attempting to sound incredulous.

"I wouldn't be here if I didn't," she murmured, right in his ear this time. "And if I didn't feel the same."

Draven whirled to find her fully visible again and standing right in front of him. In one hand she held a small, silver, deadly looking blade. As he watched, she sliced the skin of her palm, opening a line of crimson in her creamy brown skin.

"What are you—?" he began but the shadow caster disappeared again.

The next moment, Draven felt a sharp pain in his own palm. When he looked down, he saw that she had sliced it open as neatly as she had her own.

"You bitch!" he growled as his wound oozed a dark, blackish-red. His blood wasn't quite the same color as the ichor the imps and trolls had running sluggishly in their veins, but it wasn't far off. He was corrupted through and through, right down to the molecular level.

"I met the Goddess," the shadow caster said. "And she asked me to give you something."

"And what might that be?" Draven demanded, instantly suspicious. The Goddess had promised retribution if he harassed her other children again. Not that he feared her but still, she wasn't known for breaking her word.

Suddenly, the shadow caster appeared right in front of him and clasped his wounded hand with her own. She entwined their fingers, pressing their bleeding palms together.

"A soul," she said.

"A what?" Draven tried to pull free but she clung to his hand tenaciously. "I don't need a soul! And I don't *want* one."

"Nevertheless," the shadow caster murmured. "Here I am." She squeezed his palm and murmured, "Your blood and mine, mingled together."

"Stop it!" Draven ordered but instead of obeying, the shadow caster looked into his eyes.

"Your gaze and mine, fixed to the same point, held to the same purpose," she said, holding his eyes with her own, bewitching amber gaze.

"I said, *stop!*" Draven wanted to look away but there was part of him—a part so small he hadn't even known it existed—that wanted to keep looking into those lovely golden-amber eyes. Somehow he couldn't tear his gaze away.

The shadow caster leaned forward until her lush lips touched his. "Your breath and mine," she whispered against his mouth. "Merged as one." She kissed him gently and to Draven's surprise, he found himself kissing her back.

Her lips were so sweet, so yielding and Draven felt something flowing between them—some connection that nourished his heart. It was like a sudden, drenching rain in an arid desert that hadn't known moisture in over a thousand years. He drank her in, deepening the kiss, never wanting it to end.

When the shadow caster finally pulled away, her eyes were drowning deep. "Draven..." she murmured. "I never told you but my name is L."

"L?" He shook his head. "I still don't understand. Why are you doing this?"

"Because if I can be saved, you can too. But you have to make a choice." Suddenly the knife in her hand disappeared to be replaced by a syringe filled with poisonous green liquid. "Sleep venom," L said, seeing his eyes widen. "A little renders the body unconscious—the entire amount in this syringe will kill."

"You can't hurt me with that." Draven gave her an amused smile, beginning to regain his footing. "I'm immune to every poisonous substance in the universe." He frowned. "Well, except for *skrillix* venom. But that's neither here nor there."

"This isn't for you—it's for me." Before he could stop her, the shadow caster plunged the needle into her own thigh and pressed the plunger down.

"What are you doing?" Draven felt a sharp stab of some emotion he couldn't name—something he hadn't felt for untold thousands of years—somewhere in his midsection. "Are you insane?" he demanded.

"I haven't injected it all." Already her amber eyes were fluttering and her breathing was more labored. "You can save me—if you want to. I've opened a link between us. Pour your will to live into me, merge your spirit with mine—take a part of my soul. It's the only way to heal me." Her eyelids fluttered again. "Or...or finish the injection. Either way, make your choice soon. I think...I think I may have injected a fatal dose after all."

Her amber eyes rolled up in her head and her grip on his hand loosened. Without another word, she collapsed.

"L!" Draven caught her before she hit the floor and cradled her head gently in the crook of one arm. Quickly, he swung her up in his arms and carried her to the bed. Lying her down gently on the black satin coverlet, he assessed her condition.

She was breathing…but just barely. Her narrow chest rose and fell shallowly — so shallowly he could barely see it move. Looking down, he saw the lethal syringe still sticking out of her thigh. There was less than half an inch of the poisonous green sleep venom left.

Draven snatched the needle out and tossed the syringe away in one swift, angry motion. Then he asked himself what in the seven hells he was doing.

She's nothing to me – nothing. I should have injected the rest of the poison and let her go. Why should I care if she lives or dies?

But that deeper part, the part so new and small and yet so strong he couldn't ignore it spoke back. *You care for her. You have from the first. You can't just let her die!*

Draven shook his head. If he did as she said, if he reached through their connection to give her his strength and take part of her soul in return, he would be a different creature. All the guilt for the horrible deeds he had done, all the pain and suffering he had caused, all the shame he had accrued over thousands of years of pillaging other planets would have to be faced. It would be beyond excruciating. The onslaught of emotions would be an exercise in pure, unremitting agony.

No, he thought. *I can't go through that, not even for her. Not even for the first female I've felt anything for in thousands of years. I can't —*

And then L stopped breathing.

* * * * *

L drifted in the blackness. Somewhere far in the distance she could see a familiar pinpoint of light, which she instinctively knew was her former life. She was floating in a featureless black void, tethered to that life by only the thinnest thread. Even as she watched, the speck of white seemed to get farther away.

Inwardly, she mourned for lost opportunities, for the life she had thrown away so recklessly, gambling on a long shot. But she had always known the Goddess's plan was risky. It relied too much on Draven – on the hope that the shred of a soul he had regenerated would be enough to make him care for her. On the supposition that there was some good – however deeply buried – still left inside him.

Shouldn't have done it, she thought as she felt herself being sucked deeper into the void. *He doesn't care enough. Not enough to save me. I've failed...*

The thread that held her to the pinpoint of light finally snapped. So this was the end. She was lost in the blackness with no one to care for her, no one to pull her back. No one –

Suddenly a hand grabbed hers.

"What...?" L looked around uncertainly. What she saw surprised her – the white light of her old life was much closer and Draven was reaching through it, one long, muscular arm strained to the limit as he struggled to hold her.

And it *was* a struggle – the void *wanted* to suck her down and away, back into the blackness. It clung to her, inky black tendrils wrapped around her arms and legs and torso, unwilling to let her go.

"L," Draven grated, still pulling on her hand. "Fight it! Come back to me!"

"I can't." She shook her head weakly. "I can't move. The connection between us...isn't strong enough." She looked at the hand holding hers. Had his grip slipped, just a little? Already the light of her old life was becoming distant again.

"No! I won't let you go, damn it!" Draven gritted his teeth.

"There's only one way to strengthen the connection," L reminded him faintly. "My soul—you need to take half of it."

He swore violently. "That's exactly what I was trying *not* to do."

"You must," L whispered. "Otherwise..." Her hand began to slip out of his, losing the tenuous grip that barely held them together.

"All right, all right—I'll do it." Draven looked grim as he tightened his grip. "But only if you promise to stay with me."

L frowned. "Stay with you where? On Hrakaz?"

"Of course not." He blew out a breath in obvious frustration. "I'll have to spend years—millennia—making up for the sins I've committed and the wrongs I've done. I'll probably be admitted to the Goddess's realm, but only on a provisional basis. It's going to be a long, hard sentence and I refuse to serve it alone. So I'll take half your soul and your deal *only* if you promise to stay by my side and keep me company."

L bit her lip. "But my sister, Lauren...I only just met her..."

Draven frowned. "I haven't taken half your soul yet, my darling. Which means for all intents and purposes, I'm still a complete bastard. So choose—stay by my side and keep me company for the time it takes to compensate for my sins. Or die now. Hurry up and make your choice."

L's heart squeezed in her chest as though someone had put it in a vice. "Can...can I at least say goodbye to her?" she asked in a choked voice.

Grudgingly, Draven nodded. "I'll grant you that, at least. But then you must come with me and live in the sphere the Goddess occupies, which is as far above the mortal realm as the top of the sky is from the bottom of the ocean. Do you understand?"

"Yes," whispered L. "I understand."

"L..." His harsh voice grew softer. "I'm not just asking this because I want a fellow inmate to serve my sentence with me. You were right about there being something between us. I just want time to explore it. I want time with *you*."

L felt her heart warm. "I want time with you, too," she said, looking into his silver eyes. "And I think my sister will understand." She sighed. "All right, I'll stay with you. Just save me and release your hold on those of the Kindred Mother Ship."

Draven chuckled. "Adding to the bargain? Well, I don't like it. But I'm sure I'll be much more amenable once I have a soul and can feel guilt again." He sighed deeply. "Here goes, my darling. This is going to hurt—for *both* of us."

L gasped in agony as a piercing pain hit her somewhere between her heart and her navel. It was as though she had a box inside her, a chest hiding some precious treasure even she had not known was there. Now someone had gotten into that chest and was prying the lid open, seeking to plunder what was hidden inside.

It's all right, she told herself, trying to breathe through the pain. *You told him to take half. Just relax and let it happen.*

Then there was a tearing pain—by far worse than the feeling of having her secret chest opened. An agony so great L screamed aloud, sure she was dying or being torn in half. *Oh Goddess,* she thought wildly. *It hurts...it hurts so much! I can't* —

And then, just as suddenly as the pain had started, she felt it end.

"There," she heard Draven say. His grip on her hand tightened again and then he was hauling her down, out of the blackness and into the window of light. L marveled at the sudden strength of their connection. He pulled her as easily as though she were a kite he'd been flying on a day that wasn't particularly windy.

She opened her eyes to find herself in her physical body again, being held on the bed in Draven's strong arms. He was looking at her with eyes that were no longer blank silver but a deep, emerald green. *True green,* L thought and wondered where the words had come from.

But even more surprising than his eyes was the vast pair of wings that now sprouted from between his shoulder blades. They reminded L of the wings she had seen on Counselor Rast, but Draven's were even bigger and more sweeping. The air around their iridescent feathers seemed to sparkle with some repressed energy.

"Oh..." she whispered, awe overcoming her. She had Lauren's memories of going to church as a little girl and seeing pictures of angels. That was what Draven looked like now — an angel.

A smile curved his lips. *"Quite a transformation, isn't it?"*

"Yes. Yes it is," L said and then realized something. "You...did you just speak *inside* my head?"

"Yes. And you can speak to me the same way if you want to."

"I can? Oh! I can!" She looked at him in wide-eyed wonder. "How is that even possible?"

"I believe we now have what the Kindred call a 'soul bond'." He looked at her anxiously. "I hope you don't mind."

"No..." L closed her eyes, reaching within herself to where she felt his touch. Having him inside her mind felt both incredibly intimate and incredibly right. It seemed to fill a void inside her — a gap she hadn't even known she possessed. Suddenly it came to her what had happened.

"I'm not lonely, anymore." She opened her eyes and looked up at Draven in wonder. "For as long as I can remember I've felt isolated...alone. I don't feel that way anymore."

"I don't either." He smiled at her and stroked her hair. "Neither of us will ever be lonely again. Don't you see, L? I've been waiting for you for thousands of years, waiting for you to set me free. And now you have—I thank you for that."

"You're welcome," she whispered, reaching up to touch his face. It was amazing what the new eyes did for him. Before he had been devilishly handsome but also frightening, the blank silver gaze lending an air of barely controlled madness to his visage. Now she saw nothing but calmness, sanity and love in his gaze. And one more thing as well...sorrow.

"*Draven?*" she sent, testing out their new connection. "*Are you all right? You look so...sad.*"

"*I am.*" He shook his head. "*I'm sorry, my darling. Now that I have a soul again, I also have a conscience. And I cannot help thinking of the horrible things I've done since I turned my back on the Goddess and left all goodness and decency behind.*"

"*You couldn't help yourself,*" L protested. "*You had to absorb the evil of the...what was that thing again?*"

He smiled and said aloud, "The Golgoth. But I can't blame everything on that. I have to take responsibilities for my actions, and part of that is grieving all the harm I have done."

L sat straight up in his arms as a realization hit her. "Oh my God—speaking of harm, you have to reverse the body swap you put on the Kindred Mother Ship, *now*. Baird was in the middle of having a baby when I left and Olivia was so upset! Not to mention what a mess everyone else was in!"

"Of course!" Draven closed his true green eyes for a moment and frowned. "Done," he said, looking at her. "Will you please give my apologies to everyone aboard when you go back to say goodbye to your sister? I want to apologize in person but somehow I don't think they'd let me on the ship."

"You're probably right," L said dryly. "Yes, I'll try. No one had died from the body swap at least—not when I left anyway."

"That's good." Draven took a deep breath and looked around. "I have a lot of cleaning up to do and I need to start here. Hrakaz is a cesspool of living filth." He sighed. "Do you know it was a pretty little world, full of greenery and clear streams when I first came? I perverted it—corrupted it and filled it with creatures that were abominations. Blasphemous mockeries of the gift of creation my mother, The Goddess, bestowed on me."

"Then you need to start by putting it back the way it was—as much as you can, anyway." L leaned forward and kissed him lightly on the mouth. "You do that while I go say goodbye to Lauren. When I get back…"

"*If* you come back, you mean."

L frowned. "What are you talking about?"

He looked at her sadly. "I have a soul now, L—thanks to you. I'm no longer ruthless or shameless enough to demand that you stay with me for all eternity. We haven't consummated our relationship or completed our bond. If you wish to live with your sister aboard the Mother Ship, I will understand."

"But—"

"In time, as both halves of our souls regenerate, our bond will gradually fade," Draven continued relentlessly. "You can find another male to be mated to—one who hasn't got a past filled with murder and debauchery and violence."

"Listen to me." She put both hands on his cheeks and looked him in the eyes. "I don't care about your past—I have a past too, you know! You think you're the only one who ever shed innocent blood? Hell, I made a *career* out of it. But if the Goddess can forgive me and give me a fresh start, she can give you one too. And I'll be there with you every step of the way."

"All the same." He put his hands over hers. "I want you to take some time—it's going to take me a while to clean up the mess I've made here. So live with your sister on the Mother Ship—give yourself a month. I won't ascend to the Goddess's plane until then—I'll wait until I'm sure. And if you don't come back...well..." He shrugged, his wings rustling. "Then I'll know. And I won't hold it against you."

L sighed. "All right—I'll stay with her a few days. We need some time to catch up anyway. But I said I'd be back and I will."

"I hope so." Draven pulled her close and kissed her gently, starting a fire inside that seemed to sweep through her and make her hot all over. "Be careful," he said, when he pulled away at last. "I'll be here waiting...and hoping."

"I'll be back," L promised. And she meant it—she was ninety-nine percent sure she would.

Chapter Thirty-one

"Push! *Push!*" Liv encouraged her husband, holding his hand tightly as he bore down. His long blonde hair was matted to his face and his silver-gray eyes looked wild as he gasped and tried to obey her command.

"It's coming!" Sylvan, who was still in Sophia's body exclaimed. "I can see him—I can see the head!" He looked up. "Just a little bit more, Baird. Stay with me—just one more big push and—"

Suddenly the room spun around them. Liv found she was no longer leaning over her husband, encouraging him to push. Instead she was lying on the special birthing bed, her legs up in stirrups and a horrible pain inside that felt like it was splitting her in two.

"Ahhh!" she wailed in anguish. And then her body wanted to push—she couldn't help it and couldn't stop it. She pushed with all her might and something popped out of her like a cork from a bottle.

"Oh my God!" Sophie, who was suddenly in her right body, gasped. She was kneeling between Liv's knees and barely managed to catch her squalling, red-faced nephew as he came into the world. "The baby!" She looked up at her sister and Baird who still looked as shocked as she felt. "The baby—I've got the baby!"

"And I *had* the baby," Olivia whispered. "I can't believe it."

"You only had the last minute and a half, *Lilenta,*" Baird disagreed in his deep, rumbling voice. "*I* was the one who went through hours of labor in order to push the little guy out in the first place."

"Let's just call it a team effort." Sophia looked down at the baby in her arms. "Look at all that black hair on his teeny little head!" She smiled at her sister ecstatically. "He's gorgeous but do I, uh, cut the cord now or what?"

"I'll do that." Sylvan came into the room at a run. "Is everything all right? I missed the birth."

"Only by a second or two." Liv laughed in relief. "God, I can't believe we're all finally back in our right bodies!" She watched anxiously as Sylvan took the baby from Sophia. "Is he all right?"

"I think so." Sylvan cut the cord and checked him out thoroughly. The baby objected to this treatment with a howl of indignation, which made Sylvan smile. "There's certainly nothing wrong with his lungs, anyway." He cleaned the infant up and wrapped him in a warm white towel before handing him gently to Olivia. "Here you are, mate of my kin—your first born son. Have you thought of a name?"

"Baird Junior," Liv said at the same time Baird said,

"Daniel."

They both looked at each other, frowning.

"But I thought we said we'd name him after *you*," Olivia said.

"No, we said we'd name him after your father." Baird frowned. "Anyway, *I* should get to pick. I went through days of misery and hours of labor to get him here."

Olivia arched one eyebrow at him. "And you think just because you did a few days in my body you get to have naming rights? What about the *months* of misery I spent carrying him to term?"

"Olivia, Baird..." Sylvan held out his hands for peace. "Why not Daniel Baird?" he said, when he had their attention. "That way you both get what you want."

"Well…" Olivia turned her attention to the red-faced baby who had stopped crying almost as soon as he was placed in her arms. "I guess he *does* look a little like a Danny."

"He's beautiful," Sophia cooed, leaning over to look at her nephew. "Now I can't wait until mine come out. If they're half as cute as little Danny here I'll be over the moon."

"They'll be beautiful, *Talana*," Sylvan assured her, putting an arm around her and squeezing. "Because they're going to look like you."

"And you." She smiled up at him. "We're having twins so we get double the joy — don't forget."

"My darling," Sylvan said solemnly. "I honestly don't mind if you have a dozen, as long as *I* don't have to give birth to them." He shook his head. "If I'm never pregnant again it will be too soon. I'm so glad to be me again — I can finally *think*."

"Oh?" There was a dangerous glint in Sophia's green eyes. "And what exactly are you *thinking* right now, dear husband?"

"I'm thinking…" Sylvan took a deep breath. "I'm thinking what a beautiful, brave female you are and how lucky I am to have you as the mother of my children."

"All right then." Sophia nodded. "Just keep thinking that way."

"Nice save, Brother," Baird murmured, coming up to clap Sylvan on the back.

Sylvan grinned at him. "It's the truth, you know. Spending time in my mate's body has given me a whole new perspective."

"Don't talk to me about perspective." Baird shivered. "I've had as much of that as I can stand."

"I hear you, Brother," Sylvan agreed wholeheartedly. Then he looked at Sophia. "Guess what, *Talana?* I finally remember where I put your chewy shoes."

She frowned. "My *what?*"

"You know…" Sylvan frowned. "The ones with the heels and the little red bows? I remember where I kicked them off at."

"Oh, my Jimmy Choos!" Sophia laughed. "That's great, honey, but those heels are really too high. I won't want to wear them again until after the babies are born."

"That's good." Sylvan sighed. "It'll give me time to get you a new pair."

"What? But I thought you said you remembered where you put them!"

"I do." Sylvan looked sheepish. "I got so mad at how much they hurt my feet I pushed them down the incinerator chute."

"You *what?*" Sophia demanded. "I…you…"

Before she could get any further, Baird started laughing. Olivia joined him and soon even Sophia had to laugh too.

"All right," she said at last, giving her husband a hug. "I'll forgive you this time, Sylvan. But don't *ever* borrow my shoes again."

"*Talana,*" he said seriously. "I think I can safely promise you I never, *ever* will."

* * * * *

"Oh, it's you! You're back!" Lauren slid the door to her suite all the way open and embraced her sister excitedly. "I was so afraid you wouldn't make it," she whispered, hugging the other girl to her tightly. "I thought I'd never see you again."

"I promised I'd come back," L reminded her, smiling. "Are you going to leave me standing out here in the hallway?"

"Of course not. Come in, come in!" Lauren ushered her into the suite where Xairn was standing there, smiling at his new sister-in-law uncertainly.

"Um..." He cleared his throat. "I guess we've never really be introduced."

"You mean since the time you sniffed me out on *O'ah*? Or the dreams I sent?" L held out a hand.

"Well...yes." Xairn took her hand and shook it hesitantly.

"I'm sorry about those, by the way," L said shortly. "I'm sorry for a lot of things."

"We have all done things we regret," he said gravely. "I accept your apology."

"Good!" Lauren exclaimed. "So there won't be any awkwardness between us. Because I want you to stay here, all right?" She smiled at L. "At least for a while until you get your own suite. And tomorrow we're going to go down to Earth to meet Mom."

L bit her lip. "I can't wait. But...are you sure she'll want to meet me?"

"I explained everything to her — well, mostly. All except the big secret you said you'd reveal when you got back. You know, the reason we had such an instant connection?" Lauren raised her eyebrows, obviously waiting for an answer.

"Oh, that." L smiled. "Well, you see..."

She told her sister about having the soul of her twin, the soul of the baby who had been lost at Lauren's birth. What she *didn't* tell was the fact that she'd given half of that soul to Draven. Or that she had promised to go back to him and complete their bond.

It can wait, she told herself, even as Lauren gushed over their shared relationship and the fact that she had even better news to tell their mother. *It can wait until later. She's so happy now, I don't want to spoil things for her...*

Chapter Thirty-two

"What's this I hear about you being suicidal, doll?" Kat put an arm around Lissa's shoulders and led her gently away from the other girls who were cooing over Olivia's new baby. They were in Lauren's suite—well, Lauren's and L's, who had quickly become a part of their little circle in the weeks since she had returned.

"What?" Lissa looked at Kat, frowning. "I...I'm not suicidal. Who told you that?"

"Sylvan did when he said you offered to strap a bomb to yourself and press the trigger once you got within exploding distance of Draven." Kat frowned and steered her into the food prep area. "Come on in here. I can always say I'm testing the new cupcakes Lauren made for me to taste so I could choose what I want for my wedding cake."

Lauren looked blankly at the luscious rows of frosted mini-cakes that were Lauren's specialty. There appeared to be every flavor imaginable and she was sure they were all delicious, but she had no urge to try any of them.

"Well?" Kat said, nudging her with an elbow.

"I..." Lissa cleared her throat. "I just wanted to do my part."

"By blowing yourself up?" Kat said gently. "There has to be more to that story than just a rampaging case of Kindred patriotism. So come on, hon—spill it. What happened between you and Saber that made you want to bite the big one?"

"I...I don't want to bite anything." Lissa gave a little sob. "I just want Saber not to hate me anymore."

"Who says he hates you?" Kat asked, frowning.

"He does." Lissa sobbed again. "Or well, he said he hated *himself*, anyway."

"What?" Kat shook her head. "What *exactly* did the two of you have to do to get that scroll?"

"I can't tell you." Lissa swiped at her eyes and hung her head. "It's too awful. Too…private."

"What's too private?" Lauren suddenly came bustling into the room. Lissa could tell it was her because she was wearing her hair up while L usually wore hers down.

"Oh good, Lauren—I'm glad you're here." Kat came forward and put a hand on Lauren's arm.

"Why? Because you're hoping to get a jump on everyone else during the taste test of the wedding cake cupcakes?" Lauren shook her head. "Honestly, Kat—you and your sweet tooth. Are you *sure* you're not pregnant?"

"Bite your tongue!" Kat rolled her eyes. "My poor Southern Baptist grandma already has to deal with me marrying two guys instead of one. If she thinks I have a bun in the oven at the same time she'll have a stroke for sure."

"You better hurry and get married then." Lauren smiled at her. "You know there's no birth control in the world that will protect you against Kindred joy juice. And you're getting *twice* as much as the rest of us. It's a wonder you're not knocked up already."

"Speaking of getting knocked up…" Kat looked at Lissa speculatively. "Is that it, hon? Did you two have to do the deed and now you're afraid you're pregnant?"

"Oh, no—nothing like that. Well, not exactly, anyway." Lissa shook her head miserably. "I'm sorry, Kat. You're a good friend but well, I just can't tell you what happened."

Kat frowned. "Is it because of those stupid clan laws your people have? Are you still feeling like Saber is your brother?"

"No, it's not that either." Lissa frowned. "I wouldn't have thought it was possible but, well, I actually got over that idea while we were on Yonnie Six." She cleared her throat embarrassedly. "I, um, really had no choice. Neither of us did."

"I see..." Kat nodded. "So if you and Saber got over the whole silly taboo thing and were happily playing your parts, something else must have happened."

Lauren gave her a long look. "Let me take a guess: you and Saber did something kinky—something *really* kinky—and it was too much for him to handle. Am I right?"

Lissa looked at her in amazement. "How...how did you know that?"

"Are you kidding?" Kat laughed. "Little Miss Lauren here is the *queen* of kink. She and her man are all into whips and chains."

Lauren gave a long suffering sigh. "Now, Kat, try to put a rein on your dirty mind for once. You'll have Lissa here thinking I'm completely depraved." She turned to Lissa. "What we're really into is D/s—domination and submission. Basically I, um, *offer* myself to him and he dominates me. It's not nearly as out-there as Kat would have you believe and it can be very pleasurable when it's done right."

Lissa bit her lip and looked at her friends. "But what...what if it's done wrong?"

"Okay, that does it." Kat banged a hand on the countertop. "Now I *really* want to know what happened."

Lissa told as much as she felt comfortable relating, which wasn't very much, at all. She explained how she had played Saber's mistress and how their roles had taken them farther and farther down a dark and twisted path neither would have trod on their own. Then she explained how they had gone one step too far and afterward, Saber had turned cold to her. When she was done, Kat shook her head.

"You talk in circles better than any lawyer I ever met. I *still* don't know exactly what happened to upset Saber so much."

"You don't *have* to know," Lauren pointed out. "All you really need to know is that his masculine pride was hurt." She sighed. "You know, our men are so wonderful I think we forget sometimes that they are, after all, only men. Even if they are from an alien race beyond the stars and all that sci-fi crap, they still have the same basic male insecurities that men from Earth have."

"Lauren's right," Kat said, nodding. "I love Deep and Lock to pieces but sometimes they make me want to pull my hair out." She sighed. "Of course, I can't live without them, which is why I'm finally marrying them. But sometimes, I swear…"

"Having two guys to satisfy instead of just one *would* be a tall order," Lauren agreed. "But listen, sweetie," she said, turning to Lissa. "The answer is simple. If Saber's pride was hurt because he had to submit to you, just turn the tables."

"What?" Lauren frowned. "I don't understand."

"What I mean is, *you* need to submit to *him*," Lauren said earnestly.

"I…but I don't know how," Lissa exclaimed. "I barely knew how to dominate. And just when I thought I was getting the hang of it, well…" She looked down. "That was when Saber got upset and said we should forget anything had ever happened between us."

"Aw, you poor thing!" Kat put an arm around her shoulders and squeezed.

"Don't worry about learning how to submit. It's not that hard—actually, it's really kind of fun." Lauren smiled. "I'll give you some pointers and even loan you an outfit to wear. I guarantee Saber won't be able to resist you once I'm done with you."

"Really?" Lissa looked at her hopefully. "You honestly think it's not too late?"

"He's still here, isn't he?" Kat asked practically. "If he's so anxious to move on why hasn't he left the Mother Ship and gone back to his home planet?"

"That's true, I guess," Lissa said and sighed. "I just hope...I hope I can get through to him. That I can make him see reason."

"You will, doll." Kat squeezed her and gave her a wink. "You two were meant to be together—I could tell it the first minute I laid eyes on you."

"I remember thinking the same thing," Lauren said, smiling. "And if you can get over something as big as that ridiculous taboo your people laid on the two of you, you can get over a little wounded pride."

"I hope so." Lissa sighed. "I really hope so."

"I *know* so," Kat said firmly. "Now come on, let's start bringing out the cupcakes so we can all have a taste. The suspense is *killing* me."

"I just *bet*." Lauren smiled sweetly at her. "Say, Kat, you know how I crave raw meat and Liv craved all those weird combinations of sweet and salty?"

Kat frowned suspiciously. "Yeah? So?"

"So you know what I heard women who are pregnant with Twin Kindred babies crave?" Lauren asked. "*Sweets.* Lots and lots of chocolate and candy and pie and cookies, and *cake.*"

Kat went pale. "You're making that up."

"Uh-uh. I'm not." Lauren laughed. "But you're not worried, are you? I mean, it's not like you're late or anything, right?"

Kat looked almost green. "Actually, I *am* late. Oh my God, Lauren—what if you're right? And you *know* how fast you start showing with twins—just look at Sophia."

Lauren grinned at her. "When did you say you were planning your wedding ceremony for?"

"Yesterday." Kat grabbed a plate of cupcakes. "Come on—we need to pick the cake quick and get everything planned while I can still fit into Grandma's wedding dress."

Lauren laughed and grabbed a tray as well. "It's going to be all right, Kat. We'll get you down the aisle in time."

"We'll have to," Kat said grimly. "Or Grandma will kill me before I get a chance to say 'I do'."

Lissa picked up a platter of cupcakes as well and followed the other two girls as they chatted and laughed. She couldn't help wondering if she would ever *really* feel like part of this group. If she could make things right with Saber it might be possible. She could imagine a life here on the Mother Ship, spending time with Olivia and Sophia, and Kat, and Lauren, and L, and Elise, who was quiet but very kind.

What she *couldn't* imagine was going back to First World alone. Of course, Nadiah was there and she was a dear friend. But Lissa didn't know if she could go back to being a priestess and pretend like nothing had happened. Didn't know if she could forget the past and move on when just being without Saber hurt her so much it was painful to draw breath.

I love him so much, she thought, setting down the plate and watching silently as the other girls all chose cupcakes to taste. *If only I can make him see that before it's too late…*

* * * * *

"I love her *so much*," Saber explained to the mechanoid tending bar at the tiny, off-hours tavern on the far edges of the Mother Ship. "So damn much—but I can't be with her now. Not after…what happened."

"Allow me to express deepest sorrow and commiseration for your troubles," the mechanoid replied in a tinny, robotic voice. It clearly had limited sympathy programming but at least he didn't have to worry about it blabbing his secret shame. Which was the reason this tiny bar had become his favorite spot on the entire Mother Ship recently.

"Another." He slapped a cred chip down on the sticky bar and held up a finger. "Make it a double this time."

The mechanoid gave him an artificial frown. "Your pardon, valued customer, but my programming tells me you have had enough."

"I have *not*." Saber glared at it. "I'm trying to drown my sorrows, damn it!"

"He's right," a voice behind him said. "There's not enough liquor in the world when a male is hurting. Serve him what he wants."

Saber swiveled in his chair to see Merrick, the huge half Blood, half Beast Kindred striding toward him. He was absolutely the largest male Saber had ever seen—well, excluding the Beast who had been Lady Hake'bean's slave on Yonnie Six, that was. Still, Saber couldn't help being in awe of such a large and powerful male.

"Hello, friend." Merrick smiled at him. "You're the Touch Kindred everyone was so pissed about having on board before you got those lost scrolls and became a hero, right?"

"Right." Saber turned back around and slumped in his chair. "Don't remind me."

"Sorry. Didn't know it was a touchy subject." Merrick sat down beside him and thumped the bar with his huge knuckles. "Hey, where's the drink my friend ordered?" he demanded, glaring at the mechanoid.

"Your pardon, sir. But this gentleman is at his limit. I cannot serve him anymore," the mechanical intoned hollowly.

"Fine then." Merrick slapped a cred chip on the bar. "Give me a bottle of fireflower juice and two glasses and make it quick."

"An entire bottle?" The mechanoid looked at him uncertainly. "But I am not programmed to sell an entire bottle at once. Unless the subject is over seven standard feet tall and weighs over three hundred pounds, there is no way he could safely metabolize so much alcohol."

"Take a look at me." Merrick gestured to himself. "I fit the fucking description, right?"

The mechanoid appeared to be scanning him and then doing a series of calculations. "Actually, you do."

"Good. Then serve me one whole bottle of fireflower juice and two glasses. *Now.*"

Saber wasn't sure if mechanoids were able to feel intimidation but this one certainly seemed to. It moved so fast serving the huge hybrid that its mechanical arms were little more than a blur. In short order an entire bottle of the milky white fireflower juice and two shot glasses were sitting in front of Merrick.

"Good." The hybrid nodded in satisfaction. "Now go clean the other end of the bar and don't bother me again unless I ask for more."

"Oh, sir," the mechanoid protested. "After serving you an entire bottle, there is no possibility of me serving you even *more.*"

Merrick glared at it for a long moment. "*What the fuck* did you say to me?"

If a mechanoid could look scared, this one certainly did. "I said...I will be over here cleaning the bar until you wish further libation, valued customer." It eased carefully away and began cleaning the far end of the bar vigorously with a damp cloth.

"That's better." Merrick grinned at Saber and poured them both a drink. "Here you go—to drowning your sorrows."

"To drowning my sorrows." Saber clinked glasses with him—he enjoyed the Earth custom of saluting your drinking companions that he had picked up while staying on the Mother Ship.

Merrick downed his shot of the strong liquor in one gulp and poured himself another. "Although if you don't mind me saying, I don't see what sorrows you have to drown, friend. Since you brought back the scrolls that told how to defeat the enemy, you're accepted and respected here on the ship. You could settle down here if you wanted to—you and that pretty little female who went with you."

Saber frowned and took another sip of his own shot. He could feel the potent fireflower juice working on him and he didn't want to say anything he would regret.

"Actually, that was exactly my plan," he said, after giving it some thought. "But I can't now."

"Why?" Merrick downed another shot and refilled Saber's glass as well. "If you don't mind me asking," he added.

"I don't care." Saber frowned. "I can't always promise to answer but you can ask all you damn well want."

"Okay." Merrick took another drink. "So I'm asking. What's wrong?"

"Why do you care?" Saber countered, taking another drink himself. He knew he should slow down but the fireflower juice was so smooth and mellow on his tongue he couldn't seem to stop drinking it.

Merrick shrugged, his huge shoulders rolling. "I guess because you're an outcast, like me. Not an outcast really but, you know..." He made a vague hand gesture. "Different. Even back when everyone was pissed off we let a Touch Kindred aboard, I wanted to get to know you. Just never got the chance until now."

Saber gave him a look from the corner of his eye. "Must be hard — being the only one of your kind."

"You tell me," Merrick shot back. "I don't know any other Touch Kindred who would have been willing to break his people's taboos to go on a mission to Yonnie Six with the girl he loves."

Saber frowned. "How...how can you tell I love her?"

"It's written all over your face, Brother. Every time you look at her." Merrick clapped him on the back and poured him another drink. "It hurts to see you so fucking miserable. And my Elise says your girl is hurting too. She's moping around all the time, looking like she wants to die. So what is it that has the two of you so upset?"

Saber shook his head. "I...I can't talk about it."

"Sure you can." Merrick poured him another drink. And another and another until Saber felt dizzy.

"I..." He shook his head as Merrick waited. "I can't..." No matter how much he wanted to unburden himself, he couldn't make himself explain the humiliating circumstances behind his split with Lissa.

"Just tell me," the hybrid urged. "What exactly happened there on Strap-on Central that split the two of you up?"

Saber started and nearly fell out of his chair. He looked at Merrick in horror. "You...what did you just say?"

"What, you mean Strap-on Central?" Merrick grinned at him. "That's just what we used to call Yonnie Six. I haven't lived my whole life on the ship, you know. I used to be freelance—did a lot of smuggling. That was our nickname for that crazy planet."

Saber felt sick. "So everyone knows...what goes on there?"

"Oh, I doubt it." Merrick made a dismissive gesture and poured himself another drink. "Kindred steer clear of it. They have the right genetic combination to mate with us but the way they treat their males..." He shook his head. "Not fucking good."

"I agree." Saber sighed and took another drink himself. He tried to remember how many fireflower shots he'd had. Was it three? Five? More? Whatever the number, the alcohol seemed to be lubricating his mind. All the embarrassing, shameful memories he'd been trying to suppress suddenly came back. And then he heard himself say,

"I thought it would be no big deal."

"Uh-huh." Merrick nodded sympathetically and didn't ask *what* wouldn't be a big deal, which encouraged Saber to go on talking.

"It was the only way to get the scroll. And I thought I could handle it. I mean, I'd been acting like Lissa's slave for days. I helped her get dressed, I fed her, I massaged her..." The memory of rubbing her naked body all over until she came for him made Saber hard and he shifted uncomfortably. "Hell, I even got down on my knees and kissed her foot every time we went somewhere new. And I had no problem with it. *None.*"

"Doesn't sound so bad," Merrick said neutrally, pouring him another shot.

"That's the thing—it *wasn't.*" Saber drank the fireflower juice and sighed. "I really enjoyed it because it meant I got to be close to her, to touch her. But I was just playing a part. When we…did what we had to do to get the scroll…"

"It got real?" Merrick suggested.

Saber nodded. "Exactly. I just…I never expected it to feel so…so…damn *good.*" He could feel his face getting red and he took another hurried gulp of fireflower juice to cover his embarrassment.

"So let me get this straight…" Merrick took another drink too. "Lissa fucked you and you liked it and now you don't know who you are or what's wrong with you."

"Exactly!" Saber put his elbows on the bar and cradled his head in his hands. "I…I shamed myself, Brother. You should have heard me—I begged like a bitch in heat while she was…doing it to me."

"So you broke it off because you couldn't stand to look in her eyes knowing that she'd seen you that way—out of control. Needy. Fucking weak. Is that it?" Merrick demanded.

"It is." Saber nodded. "What woman could respect or love a man after seeing him in such a position?"

"Well," Merrick said casually, taking another drink. "I know Elise loves me."

"*What?*" Saber looked at him in disbelief. "You don't mean to say you two…"

"Not exactly." Merrick laughed. "Although I wouldn't be opposed to it—not after what happened during the days we were all body-swapped."

Saber narrowed his eyes. "What *exactly* happened?"

Merrick grinned. "How much do you know about bonding fruit?"

"Um..." Saber frowned. "Isn't that the fruit they give to females mated to Twin Kindred to help them, uh stretch for their mates?"

"Exactly. Or anybody else who needs a little help with our Kindred-sized shafts." Merrick poured more fireflower juice into his shot glass and contemplated it. "Well, you've seen how petite Elise is and how big I am. So she eats the fruit on a regular basis."

"Go on." Saber nodded.

"Thing is..." Merrick drank a shot. "Bonding fruit also has an aphrodisiac quality to it. Which means whenever a female eats it, a few hours later she becomes horny as hell." He looked at Saber. "And guess what Elise had for a midnight snack on the night we all switched bodies?"

"Goddess," Saber murmured. "You mean..."

"Uh-huh." Merrick nodded. "She'd eaten practically a whole bowl full of the damn stuff. I was so horny I was climbing the fucking *walls*. Or at least, the body I was in was horny."

Saber cleared his throat. "So...what did you do?"

"What do you think I did, Brother? I gave it up for her." Merrick got a faraway look in his mismatched eyes. "She must have had me in every possible position. Up against the wall, flat on my back, on my hands and knees..." He laughed. "While the rest of the ship was going crazy, the two of us were fucking like *Blitherian* bunnies. And you know what?"

"No," Saber muttered, still stunned. "What?"

"I loved *every fucking minute of it*." Merrick downed another glass and slapped it onto the bar. "It was the most amazing sexual experience of my entire fucking life and I wouldn't trade it for anything."

"I can't believe it." Saber looked at his massive drinking companion again. "But you're...you're..."

"In love with the female who fucked me. Same as you," Merrick said mildly. "What's the big deal?"

"I..." Saber shook his head, still trying to wrap his mind around the concept of the huge hybrid warrior happily giving himself to his female with no regrets. "I don't know. But how can she respect..."

"Take it from me, showing emotion while you're making love isn't what makes your female lose respect for you," Merrick growled. "What makes her lose respect is when you act like an *asshole* about it afterward because your fucking pride was hurt." He pointed a finger at Saber. "This isn't about her at all—it's about *you*. Get over it and go apologize to her. Tell her you love her and that you want to be with her forever. Don't lose her over one stupid little incident that neither one of you could help."

"You're right," Saber whispered. "Goddess, I wonder if she can ever forgive me."

"The way she looks at you? I think she'll find a way," Merrick said dryly.

Saber nodded at him. "You've opened my eyes. How...how can I ever thank you?"

"Just do right by your female." Merrick shook his head. "There was a time I wanted to give up on Elise too, you know. But Sylvan wouldn't let me—he was a true friend to me that day."

"As you've been a true friend to me today." Saber raised a hand in salute. "Thank you, Merrick. I'm going to do as you suggest and seek out my female." He got out of his chair, staggered and almost fell.

"Whoa, there, Brother." Merrick caught him under the arm and helped him back up. "I'm glad you're going to go find her, but why not wait until tomorrow? You're pretty drunk right now."

"Tomorrow, it is," Saber vowed. And though he was well past his limit, thanks to the fireflower juice, he knew that he meant it. He wasn't going to let his hurt pride stand in the way of having the woman he loved. If the huge, hulking Merrick could give himself to his female and have no shame about it, Saber was certain he could feel the same.

Lissa, he thought, as he walked unsteadily out of the bar. *I love you so much. I just hope I'm not too late to tell you.*

Chapter Thirty-three

Lissa shifted nervously from foot to foot as she tried to work up the courage to knock. People walking by in the corridor looked at her curiously — or so it seemed to her — making her feel even more self-conscious. She wrapped the large overcoat Lauren had loaned her more tightly around her body and hoped no one had caught a glimpse of the more provocative outfit underneath.

Lauren had given her several different outfits to try on — most of them seemed to consist of some kind of black leather with lots of straps and buckles. But they felt uncomfortable and none of them seemed to work. Finally, Lauren shook her head.

"I just don't think you're the bondage slut type, honey. Let's try something else. How about a naughty school girl look?"

"A naughty school girl?" Lissa looked at the short, ruffled skirt and the tight white, transparent blouse uncertainly. "What does that mean?"

"It's a male fantasy," Lauren explained, smiling. "And believe me, the male doesn't have to be from Earth to get it. Xairn loves it and he's Scourge, as you know."

"What do I have to do?" Lissa asked, as she wiggled into the tiny, short skirt and the tight blouse. It seemed to be missing a few buttons because it barely covered the curves of her breasts. But even leaving out from the missing buttons, it almost seemed irrelevant, since her nipples were clearly visible through the mostly translucent fabric. There didn't appear to be any panties to match the short green skirt that barely came down to her upper thighs. There were, however, some innocent looking white thigh-high hose, which almost met the bottom of her skirt. Little black shoes Lauren called "Mary Janes" completed the outfit.

"Just act like you've been bad and you know you deserve a punishment," Lauren instructed. "Tell him you need to be spanked."

"Spanked?" Lissa looked at her in alarm. "Really?"

"Well, if spanking isn't your thing, just tell him you need to be punished. *Sexually*," Lauren emphasized with a grin. "Get down on your knees and nuzzle your face against his shaft. Or climb on the bed on all fours and present yourself to him. Let him know he's in charge."

Lissa bit her lip. "What if...what if he doesn't want me? What if he turns me away?"

"Well, then at least you know you've given it your best shot and you can move on. But look at yourself, honey!" Lauren put an arm around her shoulders and turned her until Lissa was staring at a full length viewer. "You're *gorgeous*," Lauren emphasized softly. "He'd have to be out of his mind to turn you down."

Lauren looked at herself, the tight shirt barely containing her breasts, the tiny skirt threatening to reveal her pussy at any moment and her long blonde hair with its jade streaks falling free around her shoulders. The outfit was almost as revealing as the ones she had worn on Yonnie Six but less elaborate. And somehow, more alluring. Or she thought so, anyway.

"I guess I do look pretty," she admitted at last. "But this...what I'm about to do, is so *forward*. No self-respecting female of my clan would go to a male's domicile and offer herself like this."

"No female would date a male of her own clan either though, would she?" Lauren asked. "If you can get past that, you can deal with being a little bit aggressive. Besides, once you get inside his place, you're going to be the sweetest little sub anybody ever saw. Just call him Master and ask him to punish you—believe me, you'll get results."

Lissa had agreed to the plan and wrapped herself in the large overcoat before venturing over to Saber's suite. And now, here she stood in front of his door, trying to remember what she was supposed to do.

She raised her hand to knock...and put it down again. Goddess, what was she doing here? Was she crazy? Saber didn't want her anymore—why was she throwing herself at him like this? *Just look at you,* whispered a little voice in her head. *Standing here in a public hallway with hardly anything on under that stupid coat. What would the people passing by think if they knew what you were going to do? What would the people back home think? What would —*

Just then the door slid open, revealing Saber. He was dressed in his best uniform—black flight pants and a deep purple shirt buttoned up to his chin. There was a determined look on his face and he was holding a bouquet of sweet smelling, exotic blossoms from Earth in one hand. When he saw Lissa standing there, his look of determination melted into one of surprise.

"Lissa?" he said uncertainly. "Are you all right? Why are you here?"

"Can I come in?" Lissa asked desperately. Standing out in the public corridor wearing next to nothing under the bulky overcoat was frazzling her nerves. "Unless you're going somewhere," she added belatedly, realizing he had been about to step out.

"Oh no. I mean, I was but...I don't really need to now. Please, come in." He ushered her into the suite and shut the door behind her. "Is everything all right?" he asked, putting the bouquet down carefully.

"Of course. It's fine, everything's fine." Lissa drew the coat closer around herself. What was wrong with her? Why couldn't she remember anything Lauren had told her? Why wouldn't her frozen mind thaw and tell her what to do?

"So...you just came by to say hello?" He looked at her quizzically.

"Yes, I... No." Lissa took a deep breath and lifted her chin. *It's now or never,* she told herself sternly. *The worse he can do is say no. You have to at least try!*

"Well then, why...?"

Lissa dropped the coat. "Master," she said in a trembling voice. "I...I've been a very bad girl. And I need...need you to punish me."

* * * * *

Saber looked at her blankly. "What? What are you talking about?" He was trying to keep his eyes on her face but the provocative outfit she was wearing kept drawing his gaze. He'd seen her completely naked and also dressed in the strange, elaborate clothes of the Yonnites, but somehow nothing else had seemed as sexy to him as the flirty little skirt and the see-through blouse she was wearing.

"I...Master, I..." Lissa shook her head, looking defeated. "I can't do this—I don't know *how* to do this."

"What are you trying to do?" Saber murmured, stepping closer to her.

"Seduce you, I guess." She looked up at him, her jade green eyes filled with uncertainty and her cheeks stained red with embarrassment. "But I'm not doing a very good job of it."

"Actually, you're doing an excellent job." Saber brushed his fingertips lightly over her hot cheek and she blushed even harder.

"I am? It...it doesn't feel like it."

"I promise, you are." He gave her a smile. "Please...go on."

"Oh..." Lissa smiled back tentatively. "All right...Master," she said. "As I was saying, I've been bad."

"Oh?" Saber growled softly. "And how bad have you been, Lissa?"

"Very...very bad," she said breathlessly. "And...and I need to ask your forgiveness."

Before Saber could reply, she sank down on her knees in front of him and pressed her soft little cheek right against the crotch of his black flight pants.

"Gods!" Saber muttered hoarsely. He'd been hard before — just seeing her in that little outfit guaranteed that. But now he was rock-solid — his cock throbbing and so rigid he was almost in pain. "Lissa," he said, reaching down to stroke her hair. "You don't have to do this."

"Yes, I do." She looked up at him, her lush pink lips set in a determined line. "You submitted to me on Yonnie Six and now *I* want to submit to *you*."

"Oh, Lissa..." He stroked her hair again, remembering his "submission" to her. He felt a hell of a lot better about it after his talk with Merrick but just the memory of offering himself the way he had, not to mention the intense pleasure that had resulted, still made him both confused and hot.

"I want to give myself to you," she whispered. "That is…if you still want me."

"I never stopped wanting you," Saber assured her, his voice hoarse.

"I never stopped wanting you either. Let me show you how much." With trembling fingers, she unsnapped his pants and pulled down the zipper, letting his cock spring free.

Saber groaned as she took it in her hand and rubbed her cheek against it. Gods, her skin was so soft! Then she pressed her lips to his shaft and he thought he might explode.

Her soft, tentative kisses soon turned to more daring tongue play. Lissa licked him from the base of his shaft up to the head and then down again, only stopping to dart the tip of her little pink tongue playfully into the small opening at its tip.

Saber felt like his nerves were on fire. He knew she'd never done anything like this before but Gods, she was *amazing* at it. Or maybe it was just the fact that the woman he loved so desperately was on her knees to him, pleasuring him. The sight of her kneeling there, doing everything she could to make him feel good was making him so hot he could barely stand it.

"Lissa," he murmured, stroking her hair as she licked and kissed him. "Gods…so *good*…"

"I'm glad you enjoy it, Master." She gave him a shy smile before continuing to lick him. But it wasn't until she actually sucked the broad head of his cock between her lips that Saber knew he had to stop her. As delightful as the oral pleasure was, if he let it go on, he would wind up coming in her mouth.

"Lissa," he murmured, pulling her gently away. "Lissa no, stop."

"Didn't I do it right?" She looked up at him, her eyes filled with hurt. "I tried to, Master. I—"

"You did it perfectly—too perfectly," he said dryly. "I just don't want to lose control and come in your mouth." He stroked her hair away from her face and looked at her meaningfully. "I don't want to do that to you."

"I know something you can do instead." Lissa rose gracefully to her feet and walked over to the couch. Slowly, she lowered herself down until she was on her hands and knees with her lovely, rounded ass in the air. "Please, Master," she murmured, looking at him. "Please, take me."

Saber groaned aloud at the erotic picture she made. Her prone position had caused the little green skirt to rise and he could see that she was wearing no panties under it. He walked over to her, unable to stay away. Her pussy was like a ripe pink flower, the soft outer petals opening to reveal her slick inner folds and he could smell her warm, feminine fragrance. It made his mouth water for the taste of her pussy and he longed to plunge his tongue deep in her tight channel and tonguefuck her until she moaned his name.

"Saber?" she whispered and he realized that her face was white and she was trembling. The signs of her obvious fear and anxiety drove back some of his lust.

"Yes, Lissa?" he asked softly.

"Are..." She swallowed and he heard a click in her throat. "Aren't you going to do it? Aren't you going to take me?"

"Do you *want* me to?" he asked, putting one hand on her exposed ass.

"Oh!" Lissa jumped at his gentle touch. "You know I want you to. I've just never...except for the...the you know...never had anything, um, in me before."

"I know you haven't." Saber stroked the rounded curve of her ass soothingly. "So why are you so determined to have me there now?"

"Because." She gave him a look that was both frightened and resolute. "It's only fair. You gave everything you had to me — I want to do the same for you. You, um…" She looked at him uncertainly. "You don't have to give me the Deep Touch, if you don't want to. You can just…just take me. To…to make things fair."

Saber felt his heart clench in his chest. "Making love shouldn't be about what's fair," he protested. "It should be about giving pleasure, opening yourself to the one you love."

"I thought that too," Lissa whispered. "But…it didn't quite seem to work out that way."

"No," he said. "I guess it didn't." He stroked her ass again, thoughtfully. "So you really want me to take you? To penetrate you and fill up?" he murmured, looking her in the eyes.

Lissa looked more frightened than ever but she nodded anyway. "That's exactly what I want…Master."

Saber had an idea. "All right then," he growled, giving her a stern look. "Put your head down and your ass in the air and spread your legs for me. *Now.*"

For a moment Lissa looked like she was going to object but then she took a deep breath and did as he said.

It made Saber's heart ache to see the look of fear on her face as she tucked her head down and raised her soft, rounded ass higher for him. Clearly she thought he was just going to take her — use her to gratify his lust and then cast her aside. But there was no way he could do that to her — it would ruin her prospects of going back to her life as a priestess for one thing. And for another, he couldn't treat the female he loved like that. Still, she had gone to the trouble of coming to his suite and seducing him—he had to give her something.

"Hold still," he told her sternly. "And don't move while I penetrate you. Do you understand?"

"Yes, Master," she whispered, her voice quivering. "I...I understand. No matter what you do or how deeply you take me, I swear I'll hold still."

* * * * *

Lissa waited, her entire body tight with tension and her hands balled into fists.

Any minute now, she told herself nervously. *He's going to put it in me. His whole long, thick shaft. And I have to hold still and take it, have to open myself for him and take everything he has to give. I swore I would.*

She was already wishing she hadn't given that particular promise. Saber's shaft was huge and she was worried about being able to take all of it inside her. But if she had to—

"Oh!" she gasped as something hot and warm and wet caressed the delicate inner folds of her pussy. She whipped her head around to see that Saber was on his knees behind her. "Saber?" she asked, uncertainly.

"Hold still," he growled softly, nipping gently at her right cheek. "I said I would penetrate you—I didn't say with what."

"But...but I'm supposed to be your slave now," Lissa protested, feeling confused. "It's *my* job to give *you* pleasure—not the other way around."

"Exactly," he murmured, lifting his head to look her in the eye. "And nothing gives me more pleasure than to eat your sweet little cunt. So spread your pussy wide for me and let me in—I want to put my tongue all the way inside you. Want to feel you coming all over my face."

"Oh..." Lissa whispered, feeling a shiver of pure desire run through her. "Is that really what you want, Master?"

"It is," he growled. "So open yourself for me. *Now.*"

With trembling fingers, Lissa reached back and did as he demanded, spreading herself as wide as possible, opening herself completely. She could feel the cool breeze on her unprotected inner pussy, especially against the hot, throbbing button of her clit, but she didn't try to cover herself. If this was how Saber wanted her—completely spread open and vulnerable for him—then this was how he would have her.

Saber wasted no time in taking advantage of her new position. With a low groan, he pressed his mouth to her open pussy and began to suck and lick and kiss until Lissa was gasping with pleasure. He'd never tasted her this way before—from behind. And somehow being put in such a helpless, animalistic position while he licked and tasted her pussy made her hotter than she ever have been in her life.

His quick first onslaught soon changed to something much more deliberate. Clearly he was taking his time, enjoying her pussy to the fullest. Lissa gasped and squirmed, trying to hold still as she had promised she would, trying to give herself completely. The slow, hot slide of his tongue over her clit seemed to go on forever, driving her closer and closer to the edge. Finally, when he pressed deep inside her quivering channel, she knew she was going to come.

"Saber," she moaned as she pressed back against him, shamelessly offering her pussy for his tonguefucking. "Saber, oh Goddess, please...please..."

Saber didn't disappoint her. With a low growl, he went back to lashing her clit with the talented tip of his tongue. At the same time, he thrust two long, thick fingers deep in her cunt and began to rhythmically fingerfuck her, pushing her harder and faster toward the edge than she'd ever been pushed before.

To her mingled shame and pleasure, Lissa found she couldn't keep her promise—she couldn't just hold still and take what he was giving her. Instead she moaned and cried, pressing her hips backward, angling her pelvis to give him better access to her pussy as he licked and sucked and fingerfucked her until she begged for more and moaned his name.

"Saber," she cried as the warm tide of orgasm began to wash over her. "Please don't stop! Please…oh, *please.*"

He lapped and sucked, staying with her until the last trembling aftershocks of the orgasm were over. Then Lissa felt him pull away and she knew what was coming next.

His cock, she thought apprehensively. *He'll put it in me now—of course he will. He made me more than ready to take him and now he'll fill me up, just as I always dreamed of him doing.*

But though she waited, she didn't feel the broad, blunt head of his cock stroking over her tender, sensitized flesh. At last, she turned her head to look at him.

"Saber?" she asked softly. "Don't…don't you want me?"

"I do." He sighed. "I do, *amalla* – but not like this."

It was the first time since their split that he had used the cherished term of endearment and Lissa felt her heart leap in her chest. Still, she tried to push down her sudden joy—maybe he didn't mean anything by it. Maybe he'd just called her that out of habit.

"Then…how?" she asked, sitting up and facing him when he didn't seem inclined to do anything but sit there and look at her.

Saber took her hands in his and looked into her eyes. "I want to take you properly, *amalla,* in the bed. I want you under me, open for me. I want to see the look in your eyes when I thrust my shaft home inside your sweet, wet cunt for the first time. And…I want to do *this.*"

Lissa gasped when she felt his invisible *whisper-fingers* plucking gently at her hardened nipples. At the same time, his *whisper-lips* caressed her cheek in a tender Touch kiss.

"Oh," she whispered, understanding at last. "You…you want to give me the Deep Touch?"

"I do." Saber stroked her cheek with his knuckles. "I don't want to make love to you unless I can do it properly. Unless I can bond you to me for life."

"But…" Lissa shook her head. "I want you to—I do—with all my heart. But I thought you didn't…"

"I was a fool," he said harshly. "I let my pride get in the way of our love and for that I'm so sorry, *amalla.* I was…" He looked down. "I was ashamed of the way I reacted to being taken. I…I didn't expect it to feel so good. So *right.*"

"It felt right to me too," Lissa admitted in a whisper. "But not *just* because I was taking you—it felt right because we were giving each other pleasure. I only wanted to show you how much I love you, Saber. I'm sorry if I went too far."

"None of it was your fault," he murmured. "I was the one who let myself get upset over nothing. I felt like you couldn't respect me—like you'd be afraid I couldn't protect you after you saw me so weak…so needy."

"That's not true!" Lissa protested. "I *never* lost respect for you, Saber. And as for you being weak, that's ridiculous! I know exactly how much strength it took for you to open yourself to me the way you did."

Saber looked down for a moment. "It...wasn't easy," he admitted at last. "And it was confusing as hell. When I saw you wearing that thing—that strap-on rod—it made me..." He looked up at her. "It made me fucking hot, Lissa," he said in a low voice. "And I couldn't figure out why. But I think now it was because it was *you* wearing it—because somewhere inside I knew I'd be giving myself to you and part of me wanted that. Wanted it a hell of a lot."

"It turned me on too," Lissa whispered, biting her lip. "I felt like...like a part of me I had never even known existed was coming out. The mistress part. And I felt so bad afterwards when I knew you were upset because, well...*I enjoyed it.* I enjoyed dominating you." She swallowed hard, her throat making a dry little click. "You'll probably hate me all over again now that you know that."

He shook his head. "Of course I don't hate you, *amalla*. And you're right—it shouldn't matter who takes and who receives—it should just be about giving each other pleasure. And you did—give me pleasure, I mean. Almost more than I could stand. It overwhelmed me—which is why I acted like such an idiotic fool afterward." He cupped her cheek and looked into her eyes. "I love you so much, Lissa. Can you ever forgive me for pushing you away?"

Lissa smiled at him, feeling warm all over. "I'll gladly forgive you if you'll just do one thing for me," she murmured.

"Name it," Saber said earnestly. "Anything I can do to make it up to you, I swear I'll do it. Even if you want to take me again—I'll give myself to you here and now. I just don't want to lose you."

Lissa gave him a little smile. "Well...I may take you up on that sometime in the future. But for now, what I mainly want is for you to return the favor."

Saber frowned. "Meaning?"

"You said when I took you I gave you overwhelming pleasure." Lissa raised an eyebrow at him. "So how about if *you* take *me* this time?"

"Gladly." He swung her up in his arms and lifted her off the couch, making for the rear of the suite. "But properly, just like I said. In the bedroom."

"Of course." Lissa practically purred with pleasure and anticipation as he laid her down in the middle of the large mattress. Swiftly, he stripped off his uniform until he stood before her nude.

Lissa took a minute to drink him in. Though she had seen him naked before, his tall, muscular form still made her mouth water. At the thought that his hard body would soon be covering hers, she felt a delicious shiver of fear mixed with desire. He was so big but she knew he would be gentle with her.

She started to take off her own clothes but Saber stopped her with a raised hand. "Let me."

He crawled on the bed beside her and slowly began unbuttoning her blouse. The buttons, which were already strained to the limit by her full breasts, popped loose easily, baring her naked breasts to his gaze.

"Gods, your breasts are beautiful," Saber murmured hoarsely, tracing a slow, ticklish line around one stiff nipple.

Lissa moaned and bit her lip as his gentle touch set a fire inside her. She only wished he would pay attention to her other nipple as well. But no sooner was the thought in her head, than Saber was gratifying her wish. She felt his *whisper-lips* close around her other peak, lapping and sucking, tugging gently at the stiff little nub until she cried out as sparks of pleasure shot straight from her nipples to her pussy.

Saber watched her writhe under his gentle torture. "Gods, *amalla,* I love to Touch you while I touch you. I can feel your body reacting to me—feel your pussy getting wetter and hotter with every Touch."

"I...I always wished you would Touch me—like this, I mean," she admitted in a breathless voice. "Even back when we thought it was wrong. I wanted...wanted you so much."

"I wanted you too," Saber growled. "From the first minute I saw you. You don't know how many times I've fantasized about this, *amalla.* How many nights I lay awake and imagined exactly how I would take you if I ever got the chance."

"Show me," she whispered, lying back on the pillows and spreading her legs. She didn't know where she got the courage to be so bold but somehow it felt right to open herself to Saber. Almost as though they were meant to be together and now, after years of waiting and sorrow, they would finally become one.

"My pleasure," he murmured, sliding into position between her legs. "Mmm..." He looked down at her. "I was going to take off all your clothes but I think I like the look of you this way better."

Lissa looked down at herself and had to admit she *was* a sight. Here she was, lying on her back with her legs spread, her blouse unbuttoned to show her ripe pink nipples and her little ruffled skirt raised to show her open pussy. She looked ready to be taken—ready to be *fucked.* And that was exactly what she wanted Saber to do.

"Please," she whispered, reaching for him. "Please, *Moch Daer,* I can't wait any more."

"You won't have to." Saber reached between them and Lissa drew in a quick, hissing breath when she felt the blunt probe of his cock sliding over the heated, slippery folds of his pussy. Goddess, this was it—he was finally going to do it! Saber was finally going to slide his thick cock deep inside her and make her his forever.

She felt the head of his cock breach her entrance and then he was sliding slowly forward, pressing just the first inch of his thick shaft into her pussy.

Lissa couldn't help wincing a little. He was so *big*. But she told herself that she wanted this and she could stand it. She could open herself and take all of him, every last inch.

But to her surprise, instead of pressing deeper into her, Saber stopped.

"Saber?" she asked uncertainly. "Is...is everything all right?"

He gave her an anxious look. "That's exactly what I wanted to ask you, *amalla*. Do you feel all right? Does it hurt?"

"It's a little tight," she admitted breathlessly. "But not in a bad way. It's just kind of...stretchy."

"Let me try something." He got a look of concentration on his face and then Lissa gasped as she felt him Touching her again. Suddenly, *whisper-tendrils* were stroking her down below, slipping over her swollen clit and making their way into her pussy, though how they were able to enter with the first thick inch of Saber's shaft blocking the way, she had no idea.

Regardless of how they got there, the *whisper-tendrils* were obviously there for a reason. They teased her clit ceaselessly, causing her pussy to make even more honey, making her slick and wet to ease his entrance. At the same time, she felt them stretching her gently open, widening her channel just for him, to allow his shaft to enter her without causing pain.

"Oh!" she gasped as the tendrils continued to work on her. "Oh, that feels...feels so *good.*"

"I'm glad," Saber murmured. "Are you ready now, *amalla?* Ready to have me all the way inside you?"

"Yes." Lissa reached up and cupped his cheek, looking into his eyes. "Yes, Saber. Put it in me—all of it. *Now.*"

He gave her an amused grin. "Is that an order, Mistress?"

"Yes," Lissa told him, using her best haughty Mistress voice. "It is. And I *insist* on being obeyed."

"My lady's wish is my pleasure," Saber growled softly. Then, with a low groan, he obeyed her order.

Lissa cried out in sudden pleasure as she felt his long, thick shaft slide all the way home inside her. Goddess, he was so much bigger than the rod she'd had on Yonnie Six—bigger than she could have imagined taking if it wasn't for the soothing *whisper-tendrils* that continued to caress and stroke her swollen clit.

She waited for Saber to move inside her, to fuck her. But to her surprise, he held perfectly still.

"Saber?" she asked, looking at him. "I'm all right—it doesn't hurt. You can...you can move if you want to."

"Oh, I want to. But first look down, *amalla,*" he murmured, his deep voice hoarse. "Look down—I want you to see. Want you to watch while I fuck your sweet little pussy and fill you with my cum for the first time."

He raised off her a bit and Lissa looked down to the place where they were joined. Goddess, was that really her? Was it really the shy little priestess from First World lying here wantonly open for the man she loved? Legs spread wide and pussy impaled, stretched to the limit by his thick cock, buried to the root in her no-longer virginal cunt?

"Goddess," she whispered. "That's...it's incredible. To see you in me, I mean."

"I think so too. Now watch," Saber commanded.

Slowly, he withdrew almost all of his cock, sliding his shaft, shiny with her cunt honey, gradually out until only the last thick inch and the broad head remained inside her.

"Oh!" Lissa moaned. "Please, Saber—put it in again. *Please.*"

"I'll be happy to—since you asked so nicely." With another deep groan, he thrust all the way inside her again until Lissa could feel the blunt head of his cock pressing hard against the end of her channel, kissing the mouth of her womb.

Goddess, it felt good. So good she only had one thought.

"More!" she begged shamelessly. "Please, Saber—I want *more.*"

She didn't have to ask him twice. With a deep groan, he withdrew and slid into her again...and again and again, finding a rhythm that pleased them both as he fucked deeply into her pussy.

Lissa wrapped her legs around his narrow waist and gripped his broad shoulders, reveling in the deep thrust and pull of his thick shaft inside her. But she wasn't content to just lie there and take what he was offering. With a soft moan, she began to work her hips, catching his rhythm, thrusting up at the same time he thrust down, trying to make herself even more open, trying to take him even deeper into her pussy.

Sooner than she would have imagined, Lissa felt the stirrings of another orgasm building. The delicious pulsing thrusts of his cock deep inside her would have been enough to make her come but the entire time, Saber never stopped Touching her. As she moaned and writhed under him, bucking her hips up and shamelessly offering herself, Lissa felt his *whisper-tendrils* stroking her clit and his *whisper-lips* sucking and licking the hard buds of her nipples. It seemed to go on and on, without end and she knew that soon she was going to explode.

Saber must have felt through his Touch sense how very close she was because he began to speak.

"That's right, *amalla*," he murmured, stroking deeply into her. "Come for me—want to feel your tight little pussy squeezing my shaft, making me shoot my cum deep inside you."

His hot, dirty words combined with the deep thrusts and the sweet touch of his *whisper-tendrils* finally drove Lissa over the edge.

"*Moch Daer!*" she wailed as a second, much more intense orgasm washed over her. "Oh yes, please...in me! In me so *deep*."

"Yes, Mistress," he growled softly in her ear. And then he pressed hard and deep inside her and Lissa could feel him coming in hard, short spurts that bathed her womb in his hot seed, sealing their bond and making them one forever.

* * * * *

The intense lovemaking seemed to wear Lissa out. Or maybe it was all the stress she'd been under before they even got started. Saber was still amazed at how bold she'd been, coming to his room to seduce him. Of course, he had been on his way to her suite to apologize and try to win her back just when she showed up, so he'd been more than a little nervous himself. Either way, it felt wonderful to just relax and hold each other.

He cradled her in his arms, holding her close even after their bodies had parted, and felt like the luckiest male in the universe. She was so beautiful and delicate and perfect and she was his...finally his. After years of longing for her, years of dreaming of her and waiting for her, he could finally claim her as his bride and never let her go.

"I longed for you too," he heard her say inside his head.

"Oh, amalla…"

At the sound of her mental voice, a joy almost too great to bear pierced his heart. There was no greater proof of a true soul bond between a Kindred and his mate than the mental connection bonded couples shared.

"I love you," she sent, obviously enjoying the new connection as much as he did. *"I never stopped, even when your mother made me swear the oath that I would never have you."*

Suddenly, she sat up. "Oh, the oath!"

"What about it?" Saber yawned contentedly.

"I broke it!" Lissa looked upset. "I swore never to have you but now…now I have."

"Twice as I recall." Saber smirked at her. "The first time being on Yonnie Six—you actually broke the oath there. And in the most literal sense possible." Now that they had consummated their love in a more traditional manner, he found he was regarding the experience with Lissa on "Strap-on Central" in a much more positive light. Far from shaming him, it now seemed ridiculous that he'd ever been so upset about it in the first place. And the pleasure had been mind-blowing.

But Lissa still looked upset. "How can you make jokes about this?" she demanded. "I'm a priestess—or I *was*, anyway. I can't believe I broke such a sacred vow."

"My mother forced you to take that vow—you never would have done it on your own," Saber pointed out. "You could argue that any promise given under duress isn't legally binding." He shrugged. "At least that's what I'm going to say when I inform my parents about why I'm not going home."

"Oh, Saber..." Lissa bit her lip, her lovely jade green eyes troubled. "I feel so bad about that—about you giving up your whole future for me."

"Lissa..." He sat up and took her face in his hands. *"Look at me,"* he sent through their new link. *"You **are** my future. There is no one I would rather be with. And if that means leaving my home world to be with you, I'll gladly do it without a second thought."* He kissed her lightly on the mouth. "So let's stop worrying about it and just enjoy it, all right?" he finished aloud.

"Oh Saber..." Her eyes flooded with tears but he was relieved to see that she was smiling too. "All right," she whispered. "I'll try not to worry. I just feel so bad about disappointing your parents. About taking you away from home—you would have made a wonderful Clan Overlord."

"Father's second in command has a son who can take my place," Saber assured her. "You might remember him—Reddix?"

Lissa frowned. "I do remember him a little—but isn't he the one whose Touch sense is all wrong?"

Saber nodded. "His Touch sense is reversed—he can't Touch anyone else but he can also feel the emotions of others as a physical sensation on his body. It can be something of a burden but he bears it well."

"That must be awful, feeling everyone else's emotions all day." Lissa shivered. "How can he possibly function like that?"

"He takes an herbal extract which helps him block most of it. It won't interfere with his being a good chief." Saber laughed. "Whoever he mates won't be happy though—she'll have to get used to the idea of her male being Touched constantly, by any female who sees him."

"Why?" Lissa asked. "Is he that attractive?"

Saber shrugged. "To females he is. His father was of the Star clan and you know how rare they are—their physical features are said to have an almost bewitching aura."

"I don't remember him being that irresistible," Lissa said. "Of course," she added, snuggling closer to him. "It could just be because I had eyes only for you."

"Possibly." Saber smiled. "Or it could just be because Reddix hadn't reached his maturity before you left. Once he did, his Star clan heritage became a lot more apparent. But he manages—when he goes to places where he isn't known, he wears a cloak with a hood—that minimizes the problem."

"Oh." Lissa nodded. "I see. But if his Touch sense is reversed, what happens when he finds the female he wants to bond with. Will he be able to give her the Deep Touch?"

Saber shook his head soberly. "I don't think so. We only talked about it once when both of us were pretty drunk. He's decided never to take a bride because of it—because he thinks he could never, well, satisfy a female. Not without being able to Touch her. But again, he doesn't need a bride to be a good Over Chief."

"I guess not," Lissa said doubtfully. "Poor Reddix! I had no idea having his Touch sense reversed had resulted in such a tragedy! When I think how awful it would be if you hadn't been able to give me the Deep Touch..." She shook her head.

"But I *was* able to." Saber pulled her closer. "And I'd like to again."

"Mmm..." Lissa was practically purring, her eyes half-lidded in anticipation. "What are you waiting for?"

"I'm not waiting," Saber growled softly. "Get on your hands and knees, *amalla*. I want to take you from behind this time."

She flushed deep red but he could see the pleasure in her face. "Gladly, Master," she murmured. She was just getting into the position he'd requested when a loud pounding on the door made them both jump.

"Oh my Goddess, what in the world?" Lissa gasped.

"Stay here," Saber ordered, pulling on his flight pants as she scrambled to get under the covers. "I'll go see what it is."

He strode out of the bedroom and over to the door of his suite. Outside, he could hear several voices talking.

"It seemed to be coming from in here," the first voice said.

"Who lives in this suite, anyway?" asked a second.

"The Touch Kindred—you know, the one who brought back the lost scrolls?"

"I heard they could touch people with their minds," a third voice chimed in. "But this is ridiculous."

"What's ridiculous?" Saber demanded, opening the door.

Three startled warriors, two Beast Kindred and one Blood Kindred, stood just outside staring at him in surprise.

"Is there a problem?" Saber demanded when none of them seemed willing to speak.

"Excuse me, Brother..." The Blood Kindred cleared his throat and looked somewhat embarrassed. "But are you using some kind of...some kind of air-born aphrodisiac in there?"

"What?" Saber frowned. "What are you talking about?"

"Well, my bride and I have the suite right next to yours." The Blood Kindred held out his hand. "Forgive me for not introducing myself earlier."

"And we're on the other side, two doors down," One of the Beast Kindred said. "Our brides are sisters so we share a double suite."

"It's nice to meet you," Saber said. "But I still don't understand what the problem is."

"Well, it's like this..." The first Beast Kindred looked ashamed but determined. "A little while ago, my bride was struck with some kind of insatiable lust. Hell, I was too."

"We all were," chimed in the second Beast Kindred and the Blood Kindred warrior nodded.

"In fact," he added. "It appears the entire row of suites that are connected to yours experienced the same thing. It was almost as though everyone living in this row had suddenly consumed large quantities of bonding fruit. And we were wondering...we were trying to figure out..."

"We wanted to know if you did it somehow," the first Beast Kindred said bluntly.

"Goddess..." Saber put a hand to his head. "As a matter of fact, my bride and I..." He cleared his throat. "I was, ah, using my Touch sense on her. Which I would never use on anyone else," he added hastily. "But I must admit that those in the immediate vicinity may be, um, affected when we Touch Kindred make love." He frowned. "I don't know why the effect traveled so far, though. Maybe the alloy that makes up the walls of our suites acted as some kind of a conductor."

"I knew it!" the first Beast Kindred exclaimed. "Brother, let me be the first to shake your hand."

"What? Why?" Saber looked at him, bewildered, as the burly warrior pumped his hand.

"Why?" The second Beast Kindred laughed. "My Brother and his bride had been fighting for days. They love each other to distraction but they're both very stubborn people."

"I'm not even sure what the fight was about," the first Beast Kindred admitted sheepishly. "But your little Touch wave was so potent, we both forgot to be angry."

"My female and I were affected similarly," the Blood Kindred put in. "I thought she'd never stop!"

"We just wanted to thank you." The second Beast Kindred shook his head. "Best sex I've had since I bonded my bride to me in the first place." He shook Saber's hand as well. "Welcome, friend. I hope you're planning to stay on board the Mother Ship."

"Well, I *was* thinking about it," Saber confessed.

"Good." The Blood Kindred shook his hand too. "We're glad to have you. And I think if this...*ability* you Touch Kindred have was more widely known and understood, the rest of your people would be welcome here as well." He smiled at Saber, showing his fangs. "Something to think about, Brother."

"Well, we'll let you get back to your bride now." The first Beast Kindred winked at him. "Have fun!"

The three of them left, still laughing and talking among themselves, leaving Saber to stare after them in bemusement. Finally, the echoes of their voices faded and he shut the door and went back to the bedroom.

"What was that all about?" Lissa asked anxiously. "I could only hear part of it—is everything all right?"

"More than all right, apparently." Saber grinned at her. "It seems our neighbors in the suites on either side of us got the uh, full effect of our bonding just now."

"Oh my Goddess!" Lissa's cheeks turned bright pink. "You mean they…"

"Uh-huh." Saber nodded slowly.

"That's…that's *mortifying!*" Lissa gasped, putting a hand to her face. "Goddess, I can't believe this. They must be so upset!"

"Upset?" Saber laughed. "They *loved* it. They came to thank us."

"They did?" Lissa looked at him with wide eyes.

"Uh-huh." Saber shed his pants and climbed into bed beside her, snuggling close under the covers. "So what do you say we give them round two?"

"Oh Saber, we *can't* – it would be like putting on some kind of a…some kind of a sex show!" she protested. But he could already feel her body moving against his, responding to his closeness.

"So we'll put on a show," he murmured, cupping one of her breasts while he Touched the other. "Now be a good girl and obey your master."

"I thought *I* was your *mistress*," she whispered a little breathlessly as she pressed her naked body close to his.

"We can take turns," Saber decided, smiling as he kissed her. "I like it both ways."

"Oh." Her eyes widened as she took in his meaning. "I do too," she confessed.

"Good. Then get back on your hands and knees."

"Yes, Master," she murmured, getting into position again.

Saber got behind her and stroked her softly rounded buttocks, urging her thighs even farther apart. Lissa moaned her submission and opened for him, welcoming his shaft deep into her hot, wet pussy.

Saber slid into her, filling her to the hilt for the second but not the last time that night.

They proceeded to put on a show.

Chapter Thirty-four

"So I understand you and Saber were the cause of a pretty hot time on the sixtieth row of suites the other night," Kat said casually, as she poured Lissa a steaming hot cup of *klava.*

"Oh, Goddess." Lissa put a hand to her face. But though she was embarrassed, she couldn't help the smile that crept across her lips. She and Saber had been at it for hours — pleasuring each other and making love while he Touched her over and over until she was completely exhausted.

"Look at her — she's blushing!" Lauren exclaimed. "If I would have known what a hot time that little outfit I loaned you was going to cause, I would have told you to bring Saber to your suite instead — it's only a few down from mine."

"Oh please," Kat snorted. "Like you *need* a reason to have hot sex with Xairn. If the clothes you loaned Lissa are anything like your other "play outfits" you're probably setting the sheets on fire every night."

"Speaking of hot sex," Lauren said sweetly. "How exactly did that little test you took come out, Kat?"

Kat sighed. "I was afraid you would ask. Actually, I have the results right here." Reaching into her pocket, she drew out two perfectly formed miniature flowers. Both flowers were a deep, brilliant turquoise.

"Oh!" Lissa leaned forward to get a closer look. "That's positive, right?"

"Uh-huh." Kat smiled ruefully. "Little Miss Lauren was right— I've got some buns in my oven just like practically everyone else around here."

Lauren grinned at her. "I'm so excited for you! But…turquoise? I've seen pink for girls and blue for boys and I know white means you're not pregnant. But I've never seen that color flower before. Is it because you're carrying Twin Kindred babies?"

Kat shook her head. "Nope. The color freaked me out at first, too but Deep and Lock assured me that it's perfectly all right. It's a rare but not unheard of variation that happens sometimes with Twin Kindred—it just means the babies will have special abilities."

"Special abilities? Like what?" Lissa asked.

Kat shrugged. "We won't really know until they come out. They might become seeker-finders, like Deep and Lock. Or any number of other possibilities." She grinned. "Whatever they are, if they're anything like their fathers, they're going to be a handful."

"Don't worry, Kat." Elise, who had been in the food prep area quietly fixing herself a cup of tea, came over and rubbed Kat's shoulder. "I'll help you out when the time comes. I'm officially designating myself the babysitter for everyone else since I'm just about the only one left who hasn't boarded "the baby train" as you put it."

"That's sweet, Elise." Kat pressed her hand gratefully. "But you could be pregnant by the time I'm ready to pop. A lot can happen in a year."

Elise shook her head. "I don't think so—I'm just not ready yet. And I have a theory about Kindred babies—they don't come until you're ready for them."

"I don't know about *that*," Kat snorted. "I certainly don't *feel* ready."

"But you are," Elise said quietly. "You've finally told your grandmother about your men and you've got your ceremony all planned out."

"I guess so," Kat said grudgingly. "But I'm *not* ready to get even fatter than I already am!"

"It's only for a year," Lauren said soothingly. "And after that, you'll probably look better than you did before you had the babies. Just look at Olivia—you can't even tell she gave birth!"

All eyes turned in the direction of Olivia and Sophia who were sitting on the couch, cooing over little Daniel. He was an energetic, curious baby with his father's inky black hair. His eyes, however, were his most striking feature. They had been newborn blue at first but had resolved into a curious mixture of Olivia's and Baird's, with alternating rings of gold and silver-gray.

Everyone who saw him exclaimed over the unusual combination, which was beautiful but also a little disconcerting. It gave Daniel a strange, far-seeing look that was odd in such a young baby. In fact, that seemed to be what Olivia and Sophia were talking about now.

"I feel like he's looking right through me," Sophia murmured, stroking the baby's cheek gently to make him coo for her. "I wonder if *my* babies will have combination eyes."

"That would be beautiful—blue and green," Olivia said. "You know he's so good at night? He hardly ever cries. He just looks at me with those eyes and I know what he wants. Is that weird?"

"It's maternal instinct," her twin said comfortingly. "It doesn't make little Danny psychic—it just makes you a good mom."

"I hope you're right." Olivia laughed. "The last thing I need is a baby with super powers running around."

"You mean like the ones *I'm* going to have?" Kat asked, holding up her twin turquoise flowers.

"Oh!" Olivia laughed. "You know what I mean, Kat woman. I wasn't talking about…never mind."

"So how are the wedding plans going?" Sophia asked. "Have you picked out a cake yet?"

"She's going to have four layers," Lauren said, naming them off. "Chocolate with raspberry filling, white chocolate with apricot, Lemon with strawberry—"

"And vanilla with bonding fruit," Kat finished for her and winked. "That should ensure we have a happy honeymoon, don't you think?"

Olivia snorted. "You and every other unsuspecting guest who takes a piece. You'd better keep a good eye on that layer, Kat. It could cause havoc if the wrong person ate some."

Kat waved a hand dismissively. "Don't worry—I'll be sure no unbonded people eat any. It's strictly a married-folks-only layer. We'll even put a sign on it to be sure."

"That sounds like a good idea." Sophia nodded approvingly.

"As long as nothing goes wrong," Elise murmured.

"It won't," Kat protested. "And enough about me." She turned to Lissa. "I want to know about you, doll. Did you and Saber decide to stay aboard the Mother Ship or not?"

"Well…" Lissa hesitated. "I really want to but Nadiah was so upset when I called her that I'm thinking we might go back to First World."

"Aww, and we were just getting to know you!" Elise pressed her hand gently.

Lissa smiled. "We'd still come back and visit you often. And we can't leave right away, anyway."

"Why not?" Lauren asked.

"Because..." Lissa made a face. "We have to wait for the delegation from Tarsia—our home planet. When Saber called to tell his parents that he resigned his place as the Over Chief of all the Clans, they were understandably very upset." She sighed. "When he told them *why*, they grew almost hysterical. His mother did, anyway."

"Oh, no!" Sophia exclaimed. "So what are they going to do?"

"They're sending a delegation headed by the one who would have to take Saber's place—his name is Reddix," Lissa explained. "To try and persuade Saber to change his mind."

"How insulting!" Kat exclaimed. "Don't they know you're already bonded?"

Lissa nodded. "I don't know what they hope to achieve—there is no way of separating us now. But apparently it's a custom when an Over Chief resigns. Anyway, Saber knows the leader of the party—he's one of his closest friends. So he's willing to stay and gratify his parent's wish so he can spend some time with Reddix before we leave for First World."

"More Touch Kindred aboard the ship." Olivia shook her head. "I would say that's going to be a problem but after what happened the other night with you and Saber, the rest of the Kindred will probably throw a party the minute they touch down in the docking bay."

Lissa blushed and smiled. "There's that, too. The metal alloy that makes up the Mother Ship seems to act like some kind of conductor. If we move to First World and live in the holy mountain with Nadiah and Counselor Rast, we don't have to worry about everyone knowing when we...you know."

"Do the nasty?" Kat asked, laughing.

"Exactly." Lissa nodded, blushing even harder.

"I can see how broadcasting your love every single time would get old fast," Elise said thoughtfully. "Some things are meant to be private." She gave Lissa a discreet wink.

Lissa, who knew the story of what had happened between her and Merrick and how Elise's mate had talked Saber around, gave her a grateful smile in return. "Yes," she said. "Some things should remain private."

"Speaking of private, where is L?" Kat asked, looking around. "I could swear she was here just a minute ago." She looked at Lauren. "Is she all right? It's been nearly a month since she came on board to stay but she just doesn't seem to be clicking with us."

"She's so quiet all the time," Sophia said.

Olivia nodded. "I have to say it, Lauren, but she doesn't seem, well...happy here."

Lauren got a troubled look on her face. "She's had a hard life, you know? But she enjoys living on the Mother Ship. And she *loves* my mom. They're always catching up. In fact..." She stood up with a little effort since she was beginning to really show now. "I'll go check my suite and see if she's there. She might be using the Think-me to talk to Mom right now."

"Go ahead." Kat patted her arm. "But be sure you come back soon—it's almost time for dessert."

"What dessert?" Olivia laughed. "We haven't even had *lunch* yet."

Kat got a mulish look on her face. "Listen here, Missy, I spent almost a year waiting on you and getting you every disgusting combination of preggy woman food imaginable. Now that *I'm* the one who's knocked up, if I say it's time for dessert—it's damn well *time for dessert!*"

Olivia and Sophia laughed. "Easy, Kat woman!" Liv said. "If you want to eat your dessert first, who am I to stop you? In fact, if you want to get started right now I still have a pint or two of the Ben and Jerry's Brownie Batter in my freezer. Baird didn't get through it all before my little Danny boy here popped out." She shook her head. "Wow, we're really going to have some weird stories to tell our kids when they grow up, won't we?"

"Better save it for a while," Kat advised tactfully. "No kid wants to know it was actually their father who gave birth to them."

"It wasn't," Olivia exclaimed indignantly. "I was there at the very end."

"Yes, but—"

"Excuse me," Lauren said, laughing. "But I really need to check on L. You guys go right on arguing. If I'm not back in time, Kat can have my dessert."

"I'll take you up on that, you know," Kat promised. "So you'd better come back."

"I will." Lauren gave them a last smile before she swished out the door.

Lissa watched her go and felt a pang as the door shut behind her. Lauren and Kat and all the girls here on the Mother Ship had become such good friends. She missed Nadiah and was grateful her friend wanted her to come back to First World, but she would be sad to part with the Earth girls aboard the Mother Ship.

Well, she comforted herself. *We won't be leaving for a while anyway. We have to stay and meet the delegation from Tarsia so I'll at least get to see Kat's joining ceremony and taste some of her bonding fruit cake.*

And she knew that no matter where she settled, she would have Saber at her side to love and protect her. To dominate her and sometimes, to submit to her as well. It was going to be a long and happy life and she would live it with the man she loved.

* * * * *

Lauren found her sister staring moodily at the viewscreen, which had been set to show the space outside the Mother Ship. They were orbiting the Moon so the Earth was nothing but a blue disk in the sky, but that wasn't what L was looking at. Her amber eyes, identical to Lauren's, were trained on a point far beyond the Earth, studying the vastness of space as though there was something on the other side of it she longed for and could never have.

"Hey..." Lauren came up behind her and put a hand on her sister's arm. "Are you all right?"

"Oh!" L jumped and then smiled at her. "I'm fine. I was just...thinking."

"You miss him, don't you?" Lauren asked quietly.

"I don't...I...How did you know?" L asked at last.

"I knew there had to be a connection between you — otherwise you never could have talked him around to changing everyone back to their right bodies," Lauren said. "He must have cared for you very much to do that."

L looked down at her hands. "He did more than just switch everyone back — he took on the burden of guilt he'd been earning for over a thousand years and all because he loved me." She shook her head. "I know everyone thinks of him as evil but there was a reason he acted the way he did. And, well…I made him a promise. But now…"

Lauren felt a lump in her throat but she refused to let herself cry. "You want to go back to him, don't you?"

L sighed. "Yes. I've tried to fit in here, Lauren and I love your friends but…well, I feel like I belong with him. We…we bonded — well, partially bonded, anyway. Without him I feel like…like part of me is missing."

Lauren took a deep breath. "Then you should go."

L shook her head. "You don't understand, sister. If I go…there's no going back. He — Draven — will have to ascend to the plane the Goddess lives on and he wants to take me with him. So if I go…" She bit her lip. "I'll never see you again."

This time Lauren couldn't hold back the tears. "Oh, L…"

"Don't worry," L said quickly. "I'm not going. It's probably too late anyway. He said he'd wait a month and if I didn't come…"

"No." Lauren shook her head. "No, you should go. It's just…I'll miss you so much."

"I'd miss you too." L looked at her. "But you know, when the Goddess spoke to me, she promised you and I would be reunited after death. So…it's not like I'd *never* see you again."

Lauren managed to laugh through her tears. "Right. So I just have to wait until I kick the bucket to meet up with my sister again?"

"I guess so." L sighed and shook her head. "You're right — it's awful. I'm going to stay here."

Lauren took a deep breath and wiped her eyes. "No you're not. You're going. Come on." She grabbed her sister's arm and started marching her toward the door.

"But...but are you sure?" L asked, turned to face her. "Lauren, are you really *sure?*"

"I'm positive." Lauren pulled her into a tight embrace and hugged her twin fiercely. "I swore to myself I'd never lose you again, L," she murmured into her sister's ear. "But I can't stand in the way of your love. I can't make you miserable just to make myself happy."

"Oh, Lauren..." L hugged her back. "I'm so glad you understand. I was so afraid to tell you...to tell Mom."

"She'll understand," Lauren said firmly. "She knows about giving up everything for love—how do you think she had us?"

"All right." L pulled back and Lauren saw that her eyes were shining with unshed tears. "Like I said, it might be too late though. It's been a month—he may already be gone."

"Any man who wouldn't wait for you is a fool, honey. And I'm not just saying that because you look exactly like me." Lauren gave her a watery smile. "Come on, you're leaving now."

"Thank you," L whispered. "Thank you for this, Lauren. For everything."

"You're welcome." Lauren smiled. "Just promise me that when you're up in heaven with the Goddess, or wherever it is you live, that you'll look down on me sometimes."

"I will," L promised. "And I'll keep a special eye on your little girl." She patted Lauren's rounded tummy gently. "She's going to be amazing, you know—the first mostly Scourge female in generations. I don't know where she'll find a man to keep up with her."

Lauren laughed. "She'll probably need two of them—maybe some Twin Kindred could keep her in line. Who knows?"

"I will," L promised. "And I swear I'll do all I can to keep her from harm's way."

"I'll tell her all about you," Lauren said softly. "And how she has her own special guardian angel looking down, keeping an eye on her."

"You do that." L hugged her once more and then sighed. "I have to go. It may already be too late."

"It won't be." Lauren lifted her chin. "Go on—we've said our goodbyes. Run to the docking bay, I can tell you want to and a pregnant lady is just going to slow you down."

L kissed her cheek. "You're the best sister anyone could ask for," she whispered. "I love you, Lauren. I'll always love you."

And then she was gone.

Chapter Thirty-five

Draven looked around him one last time. Gone was the underground bunker he'd spent so many thousands of years in. Gone also were the soulless trolls and imps he'd brought into being to be his army and sole companions in his exile. He was standing on the surface of Hrakaz.

Once a barren, rocky void teeming with the disgusting imps and trolls, the land was now quiet and empty as far as the eye could see. The streams were finally flowing clean again and here and there he could see greenery sprouting. The tiny planet was coming back to life.

But restoring Hrakaz to its former state was only the start of what he had to do. So many evil deeds had to be made up for, so much retribution had to be paid to the races he had displaced or in some cases, nearly wiped out altogether. It was going to be the work of centuries.

And it looked like he was going to do it alone.

Even now he could feel the Goddess calling him. Wondering why he had not yet ascended to her plane.

"Just a few minutes more, Mother," he sent, flexing his wings, which were tired from so much work. *"I promised her I would wait. I need to make sure she's not coming."*

The feeling of waiting from the Goddess faded somewhat but didn't go away all together. Draven knew his heavenly mother was anxious to welcome him home and he was anxious to see her too.

But he couldn't help hoping against hope that L would come. Wishing to see her one more time. If only...

But no, she probably wasn't coming. He should just go now and get it over with.

With a sigh, he turned his eyes to the light purple sky of Hrakaz...

And saw a single, small craft descending.

* * * * *

She was barely out of the door before Draven caught her up in his arms and swung her around and around until L was dizzy.

"You came! You actually came back!"

"I promised I would, didn't I?" she demanded, laughing.

He set her down but kept his arms and wings wrapped around her, holding her close. "I was afraid you'd change your mind."

"I almost did," L admitted. "It was hard—so hard—to leave my sister. But in the end, she understood why I had to go."

"I'm glad you had time to say goodbye." Draven kissed her softly. "But I'm even happier that you're coming with me."

L looked around. "Are we going now?"

He shrugged. "There's no reason to delay. My work here on Hrakaz is complete. In a few years it should be back almost to the way it was when I found it."

L cleared her throat. "Oh, all right. Well, then I guess...let's go."

Draven frowned. "Are you all right? You seem anxious."

"Well..." L gave him a weak smile. "I'm a little nervous to meet your mother in person. It's not everyone who can say their mother-in-law is a Goddess."

Draven kissed her again. "She's going to love you. In fact, she already does. She loves you for saving me—if it wasn't for you and the half soul you gave me, I'd still be trapped in misery and darkness." He nuzzled her cheek. "I love you so much, L. How can I ever repay you?"

L smiled. "I love you too, baby. And as for repaying me, we can discuss that later. After we meet your mom maybe we can find a little privacy. You know, maybe complete our bond?"

Draven's true green eyes grew dark with lust and he gave her another, much deeper kiss. "It would be my pleasure, darling. Now hold on tight—we're going to ascend."

He took a firmer grip on her and L put her arms around his neck and held on. Draven's great wings beat the air and then they were airborne, flying high over the quiet landscape of Hrakaz.

"This is amazing," she said in his ear. "But are we going to fly to where your mother is? I mean, won't the air get awfully thin if you go too high?"

"Look up," Draven murmured.

L did and gasped when she saw a shimmering, silver portal above them in the sky. "Oh, it's beautiful. Is it some kind of gateway?"

"Exactly." Draven kissed her again as his great wings pumped the air. "And we're going through it…together."

The End

If you've enjoyed this book, please take a moment to leave a review for Exiled on Amazon at

www.amazon.com/dp/B00AB4KSIY

Good reviews help readers decide to try new books. And more readers means I can keep writing for a living and feeding my readers' Kindred cravings. ;)

Now continue the Kindred saga with book 8, Shadowed, Reddix and Nina's story.

Also by Evangeline Anderson

You can find links to all of the following books at my website:
www.EvangelineAnderson.com

Brides of the Kindred series

Claimed (Also available in Audio and Print format)

Hunted   (Also available in Audio format)

Sought   (Also Available in Audio format)

Found

Revealed

Pursued

Exiled

Shadowed

Chained

Divided

Devoured (Also available in Print)

Enhanced

Cursed

Enslaved

Targeted

Forgotten

Switched (coming 2016)

Mastering the Mistress   (Brides of the Kindred Novella)

Born to Darkness series

Crimson Debt (Also available in Audio)

Scarlet Heat   (Also available in Audio)

Ruby Shadows (Also available in Audio)

Cardinal Sins (Coming Soon)

Compendiums

Brides of the Kindred Volume One

  Contains Claimed, Hunted, Sought and Found

Born to Darkness Box Set

  Contains Crimson Debt, Scarlet Heat, and Ruby Shadows

Stand Alone Novels

The Institute: Daddy Issues (coming Feb 14, 2016)

Purity (Now available in Audio)

Stress Relief

The Last Man on Earth

YA Novels

The Academy

About the Author

Evangeline Anderson is the New York Times and USA Today Best Selling Author of the Brides of the Kindred and Born to Darkness series. She is thirty-something and lives in Florida with a husband, a son, and two cats. She had been writing erotic fiction for her own gratification for a number of years before it occurred to her to try and get paid for it. To her delight, she found that it was actually possible to get money for having a dirty mind and she has been writing paranormal and Sci-fi erotica steadily ever since.

You can find her online at her website www.EvangelineAnderson.com

Come visit for some free reads. Or, to be the first to find out about new books, join her newsletter.

Newsletter – www.EvangelineAnderson.com

Website – www.EvangelineAnderson.com

FaceBook – facebook.com/pages/Evangeline-Anderson-Appreciation-Page/170314539700701?ref=hl

Twitter – twitter.com/EvangelineA

Pinterest – pinterest.com/vangiekitty/

Goodreads – goodreads.com/user/show/2227318-evangeline-anderson

Instagram – instagram.com/evangeline_anderson_author/

Audio book newsletter – www.EvangelineAnderson.com

CPSIA information can be obtained
at www.ICGtesting.com
Printed in the USA
LVOW12s1358230917
549812LV00002B/383/P